HEALING HEARTS AT THE
BUMBLEBEE BARN

JESSICA REDLAND

B
Boldwood

First published in Great Britain in 2023 by Boldwood Books Ltd.

Copyright © Jessica Redland, 2023

Cover Design by Debbie Clement Design

Cover Photography: Shutterstock

Every effort has been made to obtain the necessary permissions with reference to copyright material, both illustrative and quoted. We apologise for any omissions in this respect and will be pleased to make the appropriate acknowledgements in any future edition.

A CIP catalogue record for this book is available from the British Library.

Paperback ISBN 978-1-80162-455-8

Large Print ISBN 978-1-80162-454-1

Hardback ISBN 978-1-80162-453-4

Ebook ISBN 978-1-80162-456-5

Kindle ISBN 978-1-80162-457-2

Audio CD ISBN 978-1-80162-448-0

MP3 CD ISBN 978-1-80162-449-7

Digital audio download ISBN 978-1-80162-452-7

Boldwood Books Ltd
23 Bowerdean Street
London SW6 3TN
www.boldwoodbooks.com

To Auntie Mary, with love xx

1

BARNEY

'Barney!'

I was applying toothpaste to my toothbrush when a high-pitched shriek made me drop both items into the sink and race back into the bedroom.

'Olivia? Are you okay?'

'No! Make it stop!' She pulled the duvet over her head with a groan.

The beeps on my mobile phone alarm reached a crescendo as I grabbed it from the bedside drawers, flicking on the lamp at the same time.

'Sorry. I thought I'd switched it off.'

She yanked the duvet back and narrowed her eyes at me. 'Well, you obviously hadn't. It's 5.30, Barney. Who the hell gets up at this time on a Saturday?'

'Erm, me.'

She shoved her long platinum-blonde hair back from her forehead and scowled. 'Why?'

'Because I'm a farmer,' I said, trying to keep the sarcasm at bay, 'and that's what we do.'

'But it's Easter weekend. It's a bank holiday.'

'And I'm not a bank so I'm not on holiday.'

'That's not funny, Barney. *You're* not funny.'

With a disgusted, 'Urgh!' she pulled the duvet back over her head and I sighed inwardly as I lowered myself onto the edge of the bed, a sinking feeling in my stomach in recognition of where this was heading.

'I'll be out for a couple of hours,' I said, gently placing my hand on her rigid back. 'I'll make you some breakfast when I get back.'

No response.

'I'll see you later, yeah?'

Silence.

I flicked the lamp off and returned to the bathroom. Arms braced against the sink, I squinted at my reflection in the mirror and slowly shook my head. I wouldn't see Olivia later. She'd be gone by the time I returned – another relationship over when it had barely begun.

'Probably just as well,' I murmured, retrieving my toothbrush and paste from the sink. Lambing season would start imminently and my already limited social life would take a nosedive. Olivia would never have stuck around through the long hours and sleepless nights, no matter how 'adorable' she imagined it would be to bottle-feed any lambs that couldn't be fed by their mothers. When she'd gushed about that on the night I met her – out for my best mate Joel's birthday last month – I'd known it wouldn't last that long. It never did. Was it time to give up and accept that it was never going to happen for me? That I was destined to run Bumblebee Barn on my own and was never going to have children to pass the farm down to?

Ten minutes later, I pushed open the door to the boot room off the farmhouse kitchen.

'Morning, Bear! Morning, Harley!'

My Border Collie brother and sister team scrambled out of their beds for a scratch behind the ears.

'It's a wet one this morning,' I said, raising the blind on the door and looking out at the rain. It was so heavy, I couldn't even see the other side of the farmyard.

I slipped on my waterproof boilersuit, shoved my feet in my wellies, pulled a fleece-lined beanie hat over my messy dark hair and grabbed the keys for the quad bike before leaving the house, ready to start another busy day on the farm. The sun would rise in about an hour so the sky should already have been lightening, but the steady downpour kept it dark and dismal. Like Olivia's mood.

In the garage – the large barn where I kept the most frequently used vehicles – Bear and Harley jumped onto the seating platform on the back of my red quad bike and we set off into the darkness.

Bumblebee Barn – a large farm on the Yorkshire Wolds – had been in our family for 112 years. It had started as a smallholding run by my great-great-grandfather Dodds on Mum's side of the family and had passed down through the generations. Each new owner had expanded the farm, although Granddad's purchase of neighbouring Whisperwood Farm had made the biggest impact, doubling the size to seventy-six hectares.

The whitewashed T-shaped farmhouse couldn't actually be seen from the road. It was approached by a track flanked by crops and tucked away behind several barns. The boot room and kitchen doors at the back of the house opened onto the farmyard and the front of the house overlooked a large garden with stunning views across the land.

When Granddad retired, Bumblebee Barn should have passed to one of his two children, but Mum, who ran a successful catering and events management business, wasn't interested in farming, and the less said about her younger brother Melvin, the better. It had therefore skipped a generation and I'd become the new owner ten and a half years ago when I turned twenty-one.

An increase in size hadn't been the only major change for Bumblebee Barn. It had started off purely arable, but Whisper-wood Farm had been pastoral with cattle and sheep, so the new larger farm became a mixed one and had stayed that way. I'd sold off the last of the cattle last year, we still had two breeds of sheep, but my legacy was pigs. It had been Joel's suggestion. He was a shift manager at Claybridge Fresh Foods, a local factory special-ising in bacon and pork products. He'd mentioned that the factory was expanding and there was a shortage of local suppliers, so I'd acted quickly and now Bumblebee Barn was one of their main suppliers, bringing in a valuable income stream for me to invest back into the farm, embracing new environmentally friendly thinking.

I'd never taken the farm for granted. I knew how fortunate I was to have a vocation and a home that I loved thanks to the hard work put in across several generations. I hoped it would stay in the family for generations to come but that meant having children of my own, and that wasn't looking hopeful. When it came to farm-ing, I felt like I was winning. When it came to relationships, not so much.

* * *

It had stopped raining when I returned to the farmyard a couple of hours later. Olivia's car was gone. Even though it was expected, my stomach still lurched at the sight of the deserted farmyard.

'Another one bites the dust,' I muttered to Bear and Harley as they jumped down from the quad bike after I parked in the garage and cut the engine.

I crouched down beside Harley and scratched her ears while Bear took a drink from the water trough.

'She lasted six weeks. Bit of a record for me. Can I get a high five?' I held my palm towards Harley and she placed her front paw against it. 'Good girl.'

'Who's hungry?' I asked them. 'Let's grab some breakfast.'

They followed me across the farmyard through the puddles.

'Who thinks she'll have left a note?' I said, opening the boot room door and removing my hat, wellies and boilersuit. 'No, me neither. Text? WhatsApp? What's that, Bear? You think she'll ghost me? I think you could be right.'

I sat down at the kitchen table a little later with a bowl of porridge but had to really force the first spoonful down my throat. The second attempt was no easier. I dropped my spoon into the bowl and pushed it aside, taking a gulp from my milky coffee instead.

It was so quiet in the kitchen – just the occasional sigh from the dogs punctuating the silence. A kitchen like this should be alive with activity and laughter. It was a kitchen for a family. A home for a family.

I ran my hands through my damp hair and sank back in the chair, gazing up at the beams on the ceiling. It wasn't that it was over with Olivia that bothered me. If she hadn't walked out, I'd probably have ended it myself as I knew we didn't have a future together. What bothered me was that I couldn't foresee a future with anyone. Just me, the dogs, the farm and the *everything's fine and I love my life* face I wore every time I saw my family or friends. Why was it so hard to admit the truth?

2

BARNEY

I was at the kitchen sink peeling potatoes late the following morning when I spotted my younger sister Fizz's electric-blue Mini pulling into the farmyard.

The family used to gather together for a roast every Sunday, alternating between the farm, our parents' house and our grandparents' bungalow. Tensions in the family across the past eighteen months had disrupted that and the new 'normal' routine was lunch here on the last Sunday of each month, although a full turnout was rare. I understood why things had to change, but I missed the happy, loud family meals.

Today would be different. I was expecting a full house of my parents, grandparents, Fizz, her girlfriend Phoebe, and Phoebe's adopted ten-year-old daughter, Darcie. I'd been looking forward to it for weeks.

Bear and Harley darted outside to greet Fizz and I smiled as she ran round the yard with them playing chase. Even though she'd passed on the offer to run the farm with me, she was always destined to work with animals and had a full-time role at

Hedgehog Hollow Wildlife Rescue Centre in Huggleswick, about twenty minutes' drive from here.

'Morning!' she called as she pushed the kitchen door open. 'Your sous chef's here. Mmm! That smells awesome. Lamb?'

'It's Easter Sunday so it has to be, with all the trimmings.'

'Aw, Barney, you spoil us.'

I wiped my hands and gave her a hug.

'I see the hair's pink again,' I said when we pulled apart.

She pushed a stray lock behind her ear. 'I always feel more me when it's this colour.'

'Suits you.'

'So where've you hidden her?' she asked, glancing round the kitchen as she washed her hands.

'Who?'

'Olivia. I've been dying to meet her.'

I picked up a potato and tried to sound casual. 'Yeah, well, that's not gonna happen.'

'No!' she cried. 'Don't say it!'

I shrugged. 'She dumped me. Well, she didn't actually tell me I was dumped, but driving off before breakfast yesterday without a word and blocking me on social media sends a clear message.'

'Aw, Barney. I'm sorry. Are you okay?'

'I'm fine,' I lied. 'I've been expecting it since the start. Now stop yakking and peel some carrots.'

Fizz grabbed a peeler, but I knew there was no way she'd manage to peel even one carrot before questioning me further. She excelled herself by only managing two scrapes.

'You were really expecting it from the start?' she asked.

'Yes.'

'Why?'

'Because that's what always happens.'

'That's a bit defeatist.'

'But true.'

She shook her head. 'It doesn't have to be like that. Not if you pick the right person. You know what your problem is?'

'No, but I'm guessing you're about to tell me.'

'You keep choosing the wrong women.'

'How do you know? You've hardly met any of them.'

'But the ones I've met were like carbon copies of each other. You have a type. You go for tall, blonde, stunning, great figure, fake nails, nice clothes... and absolutely no interest in farming.'

I opened my mouth to object, then closed it again. I couldn't argue with that.

'So what if I do have a type? It's not a crime, is it?'

'Absolutely not, but if a relationship's going to last, it's got to be about way more than looks. That's so superficial and I know it's not who you are.'

She picked up her carrot and resumed peeling.

'So what was Olivia's biggest gripe?' she asked. 'Because they've all had one.'

'The early mornings.'

She tutted. 'What have we had so far?' She laid the carrot and peeler down and started counting on her fingers. 'Nat hated the mud, it was the smells for Hope, Jenna didn't like dogs, Maddie was vegan, and Bella was obsessed with health and safety, convinced every building was a death trap and every piece of equipment was about to sever a limb.'

I ran my fingers through my hair and grimaced. 'Not a resoundingly successful track record.'

'Let me ask you a question.' Fizz grabbed my wrist and led me over to the table, sitting down opposite me. 'I want you to be honest with me and with yourself. Do you really, truly want to meet someone special? Because there's nothing wrong with wanting to stay single, you know.'

It was a good question, but I'd known the answer to it for a long time and every short-term failed relationship made my dreams less likely to come true.

'Yes, I *do* want to meet someone. I want to get married and I want to have children. This is a family farm. Always has been. I don't want to let the side down and be the generation where it all stops.'

'Is that really the reason?' she asked gently, fixing her eyes on mine.

I was pretty sure she already knew the real reason. My sister had always been perceptive and, despite being two years younger than me, was wise beyond her years.

'Is it not a good enough one?' I swallowed down the lump that had unexpectedly blocked my throat.

Fizz took my hand across the table and gave me a reassuring smile. 'No. It's a great one. I can imagine you here surrounded by animals and children.'

I used to be able to, but it had faded with each failed relationship to the point where it was merely a distant blur.

'I had an idea a few months back,' Fizz said, releasing my hand. 'It's a bit radical and definitely a long shot, but I'm sure I saw something on the socials earlier this week if you're interested...'

I shrugged, frowning. 'I might be. If I knew what you were talking about.'

'Do you trust me?'

'Always.'

'Good. Then leave it with me to do some investigating and I'll come back to you as soon as I can tell you more. If I'm right and there's a second chance, I think it's worth a try.'

I shrugged, still lost. I did trust her. Radical or not, Fizz would never come up with something that didn't have some mileage.

3

AMBER

After a day of on and off downpours, Easter Sunday dawned with blue skies and bright sunshine. It was still chilly, but I loved weather like this. It made me feel fresh and alive as I travelled from London to Kent to spend the day with my family. It must have been at least four years since the whole family had gathered together at Green Acres and I was so excited about seeing them all. I wished my boyfriend Dan could have come but his family were having a get-together too and we'd decided it was better to spend the day apart than disappoint one family.

As it always did, a feeling of peace and contentment filled me as I pulled onto the gravel driveway outside my parents' Grade II-listed farmhouse set in three acres of land. I'd missed this place. Built in the late nineteenth century, it oozed character, with leaded windows and thick beams on the walls and ceilings.

I hadn't lived at Green Acres for a decade, but I still thought of it as home and wondered if that feeling would ever go away. The one-bedroom flat where I lived at the moment had been bought for practical reasons – new, safe, central – rather than being a decision of the heart. It was ideal as a base when my work took me all over the country and I spent so little time in London, but it wasn't homely. I'd never labelled the house I'd bought with Parker 'home' either, which was weird when we'd chosen it together. Maybe the place that felt like home was less about the building itself and more about the people who lived there.

I parked next to Sophie's car. My sister – aged twenty-three and younger than me by eleven years – hadn't moved out of Green Acres yet. I knew Mum and Dad were dreading the day she did, partly because they'd be left trundling round the enormous five-bedroom house on their own, but mainly because they were worried about Sophie. We all were. It had been five years, but there were still repercussions.

I went straight round the back, knowing everyone would be gathered on the terrace, wrapped in blankets, the spring chill taken off by the patio heaters. We'd always been an outdoorsy family.

My mobile started ringing and I inwardly groaned as my agent Esther's name flashed up on the screen.

'Go away, Esther!' I murmured, declining the call. 'Not today!'

I switched my phone to silent and shoved it in my jeans pocket. I knew exactly what Esther wanted and my answer was still a resounding no. Pestering me on a bank holiday Sunday during my lovely trip to Green Acres was not the way to get me to change my mind, and she knew that, so she had to be desperate. I loved her and would be forever grateful for the many opportunities she'd put my way, especially when I'd been adamant that I'd wanted to progress in my career as a television producer without my parents' help. Using the Crawford name would have opened so many doors but I'd wanted to prove I was good enough on my own merits, so I'd adopted Mum's maiden name, had gone out there as Amber Simpkins, and worked my socks off to get noticed. The gamble had paid off and I was now happy to use my real name, knowing I'd built my reputation on ability rather than connections.

'Here she is!' Dad called, waving at me when I entered the garden.

'Sorry I'm late. Traffic was hideous.'

I kissed Dad on both cheeks, then did the same to my brother Brad – who was two years older than me – and his longstanding girlfriend Tabs. After a quick exchange about journeys and the weather, I headed into the kitchen.

Mum was brushing a marinade onto a tray of kebabs, but there was no sign of Sophie.

'So Dad wasn't kidding about a barbeque instead of a Sunday roast,' I said.

'Amber!' She put the brush down, wiped her hands on a cloth and drew me into a tight hug. 'So glad you could make it and, no, he wasn't kidding. You know your dad and outdoor dining.'

Dad had acquired Mum's passion for cooking and had become such a fan of cooking and eating al fresco that he'd created an outdoor kitchen area with a double barbeque, stone-baked pizza oven, drinks fridge, bar and sink. I'd joined them for Christmas dinner last year and even that had been done on the barbeque. Turkey and pigs in blankets kebabs were a first for me – and absolutely delicious.

'Where's Sophie?' I asked.

'Upstairs. She won't be long. She has some news for us.'

'What sort of news?'

'I've no idea. She wouldn't give any hints.'

'Intriguing.' I glanced towards the door to make sure Sophie wasn't about to walk in on us talking about her. 'How is she?'

Mum lowered her voice and kept her eye on the door. 'Good form at the moment. She's been getting out and about more and has reconnected with some of her old friends, but some days are still a struggle.'

I sighed and nodded. 'That man has so much to answer for.'

'Have you seen him recently?'

'No. He does his thing and I do mine and, thankfully, there's still no crossover. There's no way I could ever work with him again.'

I shuddered at the thought. After what he did, I had no time or respect for Parker Knowles. To think I once loved him.

Feeling my mood sinking, I removed an apron from one of the drawers and pulled it over my head. Focus! 'What can I do to help?'

'You can finish the marinade while I prepare the stuffed peppers and you can tell me all about the wrap party.' She narrowed her eyes at me. 'Unless you pulled an Amber.'

I laughed at the phrase my brother had coined. To 'pull an Amber' was to either avoid a night out or to show your face and slope off to bed early. It was only ever used with affection, and it didn't bother me because it was true. I'd never been one for parties, so the sooner I could leave, pull on my PJs and settle into my bed, the better.

'I might have done,' I said as I stirred the marinade. 'It was a tiring shoot, but you know I'm never rude. I managed a couple of hours then slipped out quietly. I don't know how you lot manage it.'

'I often ask myself that too.'

My whole family worked in television, but I was the only one who worked on the other side of the camera. My passion for the outdoors had helped me develop a career specialising in country-side-based shows. My regular gig over the past five years had been Sunday night staple, *Countryside Calendar*, which carried a strong seasonal focus on the highs and lows of living and working in the countryside. We'd just wrapped the winter season – a bit later than planned thanks to some bad weather delays – while simultaneously starting to film spring.

I loved my role on *Countryside Calendar* so much that, despite long hours, I never really felt like I was working. I'd been blessed with a great director and crew, I'd seen much of the stunning countryside the length and breadth of the UK, and I'd met some fascinating people. I also had the flexibility to create a filming schedule which allowed me to work on other projects between filming, keeping me constantly on the go – exactly how I liked it.

The rest of my family were on-camera, but it had never appealed to me. I was an introvert and preferred the anonymity that being a producer usually afforded me.

My parents, Cole and Jules Crawford, were a power couple. Dad was a multi-BAFTA-winning actor. He had a gift for accents – a talent my sister had inherited – and had proved his versatility across a range of roles. For the past six years, he'd played the eponymous role in the exceptionally successful 1960s-set Sunday night drama, *Darrington Detects*, about a Dorset-based detective turned man of the cloth. I was so proud of him, although I'm not sure I'd ever get used to the 'sexy vicar' tag.

Mum was an exceptional chef and gardener with two long-running shows – *Jules in the Garden* and *Jules in the Kitchen*. She'd been presenting on TV since before I was born and it was spending time with her in the studio during the school holidays that had captured my interest in how shows were made.

My brother Brad's first acting role had been at the age of ten as Charlie Bannister in the UK's most-watched soap opera, *Londoners*. The camera loved him with his dark hair and cornflower-blue eyes, just like Dad's, and he still played Charlie today. Tabs had started on *Londoners* a few years after him and their first on-screen kiss as teenagers had led to their first off-screen one. They'd been together ever since. Neither of them wanted marriage, having seen it as the kiss of death for the relationships of so many of their showbiz pals, and they didn't want children either, but they were completely devoted to each other. Seeing them cosied up together, Sophie often created a heart shape from her fingers and said, 'Aw, relationship goals.'

As for my sister, she'd also had early success with the lead role in a long-running teen/adult crossover drama series called *Mercury's Rising*. For seven years and eight series, she'd played rising performing arts star Mercury Addison and been tipped for great things, but now her CV was full of guest appearances – one-episode parts – in TV dramas and the occasional advert because she lacked the confidence to audition for anything bigger or more regular.

It broke my heart to see because Sophie had been bursting with confidence and enthusiasm until she turned eighteen and took part in *that* show. It was only afterwards that Mum, Dad, Brad and I all admitted to each other that we'd had doubts. If only we'd voiced them at the time, not that Sophie would have listened if we had. Our family philosophy was to encourage and support each other to follow our dreams. Nobody could have predicted that Sophie's dream would have become a nightmare which nearly destroyed her.

'Amber! I didn't realise you'd arrived!' I dropped the brush with a splat onto the kebabs as my little sister launched herself at me. 'I've missed you!'

'I've missed you too, Soph.' At five foot six, she was three inches shorter than me, so my nose brushed the top of her head as I hugged her, breathing in the smell of coconut conditioner. She was dressed casually in jeans and a sloppy sweatshirt. Her auburn hair – a colour all the women in our family shared – was pinned onto the top of her head in the sort of effortlessly messy style I never managed to pull off.

'I hear you have news,' I prompted.

'I do, but all will be revealed over lunch. No clues! Ooh! You'll never guess who I saw the other day...'

As Sophie told me about an old school friend she'd caught up with, it gave me a warm glow to see the old confidence back in her smile and her voice. Whatever her news was, it had definitely had a positive impact on her. There'd been a time when I feared we'd never see the carefree playful Sophie again.

'She *does* seem on good form,' I said to Mum after Sophie went outside to help Dad. 'Has she had some professional help?'

'Not that I'm aware of.'

Sophie had been offered so much support back then and on a frequent basis ever since, but she'd refused to take any of it. She wanted to forget it and move on. Which would have been fine if she'd been able to do that, but we all knew how much of a struggle the last five years had been. Hopefully this big news heralded a breakthrough and this happy, positive Sophie was here to stay.

* * *

Mum and I were about to carry the food out when her mobile phone, lying on the worktop, started ringing. As she reached for it, I spotted the name flashing up on the screen: Esther Pendry-Jones.

'Mum! No!'

But it was too late.

'Esther! It's been too long,' Mum gushed. 'How are you?'

Like a petulant teenager, I released a little whine and grimaced at Mum. She rolled her eyes at me.

'Your first grandchild? Oh, that's wonderful! No, she didn't say, but she's only just got here... Yes, of course you can...'

Mum turned back to me and I made a cutting motion across my throat, but it was ignored.

'I'll just put her on.' Mum thrust her phone into my hand and I forced a smile to hopefully lighten my tone.

'Hi, Esther. Happy Easter!'

'Have you been screening my calls?' she asked in her clipped home counties accent, straight to the point as always.

'Of course not, but lunch is nearly ready so I don't have long to chat.'

'We don't need long. You know why I'm calling.'

'And you know my answer's no.'

'But it's a great opportunity and the pay's amazing.'

'Esther! When have I ever been driven by the money?'

'Fair enough, but there is something about this project that I believe will ignite your passion. It's—'

I'd already heard enough. Nothing she could say was going to convince me, so I might as well save us both the time.

'Sorry, but there is nothing on this planet – make it this universe – that would cause even the teeniest tiniest flicker of passion from me. It's reality TV. You know how much I *hate* reality TV.'

'I know, darling, but this is different. This is set in the countryside. This is about farmers.'

'I'm still not interested.'

'I'll email you the details.'

'And I won't read them.'

'It'll work perfectly round your *Countryside Calendar* commitments. Filming starts in a fortnight in Wales and, wouldn't you know, spring's *Countryside Calendar* is set in Wales. How convenient is that?'

'Very, but it's still a no.'

'You'll get to visit so many wonderful places – Norfolk, Devon, Yorkshire, Northumber—'

'Which I get to do with *Countryside Calendar*,' I interrupted.

'But they've specifically asked for you, Amber, and I might have...'

As she tailed off, my stomach went into spin cycle.

'You've already told them I'll do it, haven't you?' I hissed between gritted teeth.

'The contract's sitting in my inbox ready to send over to you for signing.' She must have realised that she was sounding a little desperate because she cleared her throat and the persuasive business tone was back. 'I don't see why it's such a big issue. The groundwork for most of the episodes has already been done so it's an easy job alongside your existing commitments and the massive bonus is that you'd still be paid as though you'd done everything.'

I shook my head, wondering if she'd even listened to me when I said it wasn't about the money. I was aware that I'd had a comfortable upbringing, but Mum and Dad had worked hard for their success and those values had been instilled in my siblings and me from a young age. I appreciated a good salary, but it wasn't everything to me. I knew how lucky I was to have a job I loved and that gave me way more satisfaction than money ever could. I didn't have an extravagant lifestyle. I still had the same reliable 4x4 I'd had for years and I couldn't remember the last time I'd been on holiday. There was no point spending money on anything for the flat when I was hardly ever there, and my wardrobe was casual and practical. Money was *not* a motivator.

'My lunch is ready,' I said to Esther. 'I need to go.'

'I'm emailing you the contract and the details. Promise me you'll look at them.'

'Okay, I'll look at them, but I won't be signing. Reality television set in the countryside with farmers is *still* reality television and I'm not going there. Bye.'

I disconnected the call and shuddered. It was so uncharacteristic of me to be blunt like that, but she'd left me with little choice. She was a brilliant agent and a friend, but she'd disappointed me with her persistence on this project. How was it suddenly my problem that the producer had been dismissed following allegations of indecent behaviour on his last show? Why was I the one who needed to step into the breach when I had no experience or interest in reality TV? I couldn't care less that it would be an easy gig with the ideal location to fit round my existing commitments. There was a principle at stake here and I'd have expected Esther to have understood that and to never have approached me about it in the first place. She did, after all, know why I hated reality TV. And that wasn't anything to do with being a TV snob or not enjoying it as a viewer. If only...

* * *

'What's Esther done to upset you?' Brad asked when I joined them on the deck. Mum must have mentioned that I hadn't wanted to take the call.

I didn't want to say much when Sophie was listening, so I kept my answer vague.

'There's a project she wants me to do which I don't want to do and she's being more persistent than usual, but I've been firm and that's the end of it.'

Except it wasn't because a copy of the contract attached to one of her incredibly persuasive emails was very likely sitting in my inbox right now. I'd glance at it, but not until I was back at my flat tomorrow. For now, it was valuable family time, and I didn't want any further distractions.

We'd always been a close family and get-togethers were invariably full of laughter. We thrived on playful banter and, this afternoon, it was good to see Sophie dishing it out, winding Brad up that Tabs had given her permission to take their new sports car for a spin. I wouldn't say Sophie was a terrible driver, but she was shockingly bad at judging distances when it came to parking and frequently pranged her car into fences, bollards and a host of other obstacles.

'If I put a dent in it, I can always knock it out with one of Dad's hammers,' Sophie deadpanned. 'Go on, Brad! If you loved me, you'd let me have a go.'

She was such a good actor, playing with every emotion, and she had my brother completely reeled in.

'I do love you, Soph. It's just, erm… you see…'

Tabs snorted with laughter and Brad heaved a sigh of relief. 'You're winding me up?'

'Of course I am!' Sophie declared, her eyes sparkling with mirth. 'But it bodes well for my career that I had you convinced.'

'Lunch is ready,' Mum called from the barbeque.

Brad, Sophie and I raced each other up to the table and squabbled over the 'best seat' – even though there wasn't such a thing – just like we used to do as kids.

'I could have sworn you three were meant to be responsible adults, not toddlers,' Tabs said, laughing as I gave up and left Sophie and Brad to battle over the same seat as though it was the only one left in a game of musical chairs.

'Adulting is seriously overrated,' Sophie said, giving Brad a nudge in the stomach before darting away from him to avoid retaliation. 'Anyway, I'm not that far out of my teens but these two are heading for their forties!'

'Oi!' I cried. 'I've only just turned thirty-four so I'm closer to thirty than forty. Brad, on the other hand—'

'Is still a few weeks from turning thirty-six, thank you very much,' he said. 'Mid-thirties. *Mid*. Nowhere near forty!'

Trays of food were placed on the table and my stomach rumbled appreciatively as we piled our plates high.

'Are you going to share your news?' Mum asked Sophie.

We all looked expectantly towards my sister.

'Okay. Prepare yourself because it's a biggie.' Her eyes shone and there was excitement in her voice. 'You know how I went to London a couple of times last week to audition for guest-star roles? I told a little porky. It was really an audition, then a call-back, for a lead role in *The Book Sleuths* – the next Becca Scarsdale series.'

A collective gasp went round the table. Sophie was right about it being a biggie – her feeling ready to audition for a lead role was huge in itself but this wasn't auditioning just for any series. Becca Scarsdale was a multi-award-winning drama writer with the Midas touch when it came to her scripts and casting.

'And you got the part?' I prompted.

'I wish!'

My confused expression about how upbeat Sophie sounded was mirrored on everyone else's faces.

'The feedback was amazing,' she explained. 'There were four of us called back and it was a close thing between me and one other. Even though it didn't go my way this time, the exciting part is that Becca Scarsdale herself said I had star quality and that I must audition for her next series.'

'Oh, Sophie, that's wonderful,' Mum said, rushing round the table to give her a hug. 'I'm so proud of you for putting yourself out there again. You're really okay about not getting the part?'

'I'm really okay. Honestly, I didn't expect to get an audition, never mind a call-back. It's not like I've done anything major since

Mercury's Rising. It was time to try again and I'm glad I did. Next time. Or the time after.'

Although her voice was light and confident, I was sitting beside her and didn't miss the wringing of her hands under the table. There wasn't a single person here today who'd have underestimated how big a deal it was for Sophie to attend the audition and, despite the positivity about the feedback, we all knew she'd be crushed by getting a no.

'I love Becca Scarsdale dramas,' Tabs said, 'but aren't they usually set up north?'

'Yes.' Sophie picked up her kebab and slowly removed each item with her fork while we waited for her to expand. 'This one's set in York.'

'As in North Yorkshire?' Brad exclaimed.

'Unless there's another York I'm not aware of.'

I glanced round the table and sensed everyone thinking the same thing as me: *thank God she didn't get the part!* Taking on the lead in a major new drama was one thing, but moving five hours away to do it was far too much.

Dad raised his bottle of lager. 'To our amazingly talented Sophie, getting out there and getting fabulous feedback from the one and only Becca Scarsdale.'

We all toasted to her. Although it was a no, it was the biggest cause for celebration we'd had in a long time. It didn't seem that long ago when we feared she'd never act again. We'd even feared she'd never leave the house again.

* * *

'That was a surprise about Sophie,' I said to Mum as we stacked the dishwasher together a little later. 'You had no idea?'

'None at all. I can't help thinking she kept it quiet because of the York thing, thinking we'd have tried to talk her out it.'

I glanced out the window. Sophie had unearthed the old swing ball set and was playing it with Brad.

'What if she had got the part?' I asked.

'I can't bear to think about it. I don't know whether she's strong enough yet to go from guest star to lead role, but to do that and live so far away from home...' Mum ran her fingers through her wavy dark auburn hair and exhaled. 'Does it make me a horrendous mum to say I'm glad she didn't get the part?'

I shook my head. 'It's how I feel and I'm pretty sure it'll be how Dad, Brad and Tabs all feel too.'

'Your dad and I will encourage her to go for bigger London or locally based roles. I know we can't keep her home forever, but she needs baby steps. A lead role in York is like giant leaps and she's not ready for that.'

Mum looked so worried that I wrapped my arms round her. 'It's over now. It was a no. Good plan to keep her focused more locally. I'll encourage her with that too.'

4

BARNEY

As Bear, Harley and I were crossing the farmyard to the house on Monday evening ready for our tea, Fizz drove through the gate and waved at me.

'I could have sworn I only saw you yesterday,' I said when she parked and opened her door.

'Yes, well, I'm gracing you with my presence again because we have important things to do.'

'Like what?'

'Step one in finding your future wife.' She opened the boot and handed me a couple of pizza boxes. 'But we can't do that on an empty stomach.'

Inside, Fizz switched on the oven to warm the pizzas while I removed my boilersuit and fed the dogs.

'Might as well get started while the oven's heating up,' she said, pulling a laptop out of her bag and placing it on the kitchen table.

'You're going to sign me up for online dating,' I said, plonking down beside her.

'Nope. We're going to apply for you to appear on a TV show.'

'You're hilarious.'

'I'm not kidding.'

She opened up her laptop, revealing a promotional page for a new TV show called *Love on the Farm*.

'Reality TV?' I could hear my words dripping with doubt.

'Yes, but different.' She clicked onto another screen. 'Read this. I spotted it on a community Facebook page.'

I scanned down the details.

Are you a Yorkshire-based farmer looking for love? Perhaps we can help you find it! We're seeking farmers of any age, ethnicity or sexual preference to take part in a new television programme. We're passionate about our countryside and the vital role farmers play, but we know that the long hours and (sometimes) remote locations can make meeting the one a challenge. We'll be using personality and values profiling to find some potential matches and the rest is up to you. Your preferences, your farm, your future partner.

'What do you think?' Fizz asked, her eyes shining.

'I'm not sure. It's TV.'

'And...?'

'And I thought finding the right person would be a bit more natural and low-key.'

Fizz crossed her arms and raised her eyebrows at me. 'Like going out on the pull with Joel? How's that working out for you?'

I couldn't help smiling at that. 'Fair point. But you really think reality TV is going to work better?'

'Maybe not, but it's worth a try. They say the definition of insanity is doing the same thing repeatedly and expecting a different result, so I say let's do something different. You don't get much more different than a search for love on national television.'

She sounded so enthusiastic and I couldn't fault her logic, but reality TV?

'I'm not sure. Isn't reality TV for fame-hungry wannabes?'

'Maybe on some shows, but this is different. Read it again. Do you think it sounds like that type of show?'

I scanned down the information once more and shrugged. 'I doubt many of the farmers will be fame-hungry, but I bet the potential partners are.'

'And they'll get weeded out in the vetting process. Come on, Barney. It'll be fun. What's the worst thing that could happen?'

I stared at the blurb, rubbing my hand across the stubble on my chin. Should I? It did sound more genuine than most reality TV shows, and Fizz was right about me not having much success myself.

'If I did apply – and that's a big if – I doubt they'd choose me. I bet they'll get hundreds if not thousands of applicants.'

'Someone has to be picked and you have as good a chance as any. Is that the only thing that's stopping you?'

'No. I hear you that it's something different, but do I really want that type of different?'

'Why don't we fill in the application form and see what happens? If they say no, we've lost nothing. If they say yes, we can debate it then. Nothing ventured, nothing gained.'

My sister could be very persuasive when she believed in something.

'If I say yes, will you stop spouting motivational quotes?'

She squealed and clapped her hands together. 'I'll take that as a yes. It's gonna be awesome.'

I winced as she clicked the 'apply now' button. Awesome? I doubted it, but she looked so happy playing matchmaker that I didn't have the heart to stop her. There was no way I'd get selected, so it was pointless fretting about it. I'd let her have her fun and, when I was rejected, we could consider something less radical.

'I wonder why it's only Yorkshire,' I mused.

'I'm guessing they didn't find anyone suitable in Yorkshire on their original appeal and are trying again. I was going to suggest you apply when I first spotted it, but I faffed and then Granddad had another mini-stroke so it went out my head.' She wiggled her fingers over the keyboard. 'Do you want me to type?'

'Only if you put what I want.'

'As if I'd do anything but that.' Her attempt at looking horrified had us both laughing.

Ninety minutes later, the pizza was long gone, and the application form was complete with several photos of me in 'full farmer mode' attached.

'Are you ready?' Fizz asked, as the curser hovered over the 'send' box.

'No, but do it anyway.'

My stomach lurched as she clicked the button and a thank you message appeared on the screen. It was rare that anything made me nervous, but this had definitely given me butterflies, which was stupid when the chances of the producers picking me were miniscule and, if they did, the chances of them finding my perfect match were even more remote.

Fizz closed her laptop. 'If this doesn't come off, we should get you registered on an app.'

'We'll see.'

'Don't give up, Barney. She's out there somewhere. We just need to look a little harder. We'll find your Phoebe for you.'

Fizz and Phoebe had got together at Christmas the year before last and it was great to see my sister so happy. They'd been friends for a couple of years first and Fizz reckoned it was the friendship that made their relationship so strong, but it wasn't going to happen that way for me. I didn't have any female friends and, for someone who ran their own business with one full-time male employee, a part-time male groom, and a handful of contractors when needed (all male), I doubted finding new female friends would be any easier than finding a relationship.

'I won't hold my breath.'

'Are you okay?' Fizz placed her hand on my arm. 'You seem really down.'

I smiled as brightly as I could. 'I'm fine.'

Her eyes searched mine and she shook her head. 'Not buying it. You're with the queen of facades and keeper of secrets here. Talk to me.'

She could say that again! It had been a longstanding family mystery as to why Mum's younger brother, Melvin, had suddenly emigrated to Arizona to be a ranch-hand instead of taking over Bumblebee Barn from Granddad as planned. It had remained an even greater mystery as to why he'd stayed away for sixteen years but, in November the year before last, our grandparents had announced how excited they were that their son was returning home for Christmas with his wife and two young daughters. The thought of seeing him again had been too much for Fizz and the shocking truth came out that Melvin had abused her from the age of six to twelve, only leaving the country after she threatened to expose him if he didn't get on a plane and leave for good.

I have no idea how my sister had managed to keep secret something so momentous and it seemed incredible that none of us had suspected anything, although, as Fizz had frequently reminded us, why would we? Melvin was family and should have been trustworthy.

The revelation had rocked the whole family, but had hit my grandparents the hardest. Granddad had initially turned on Fizz, refusing to believe her. The stress of having to accept that his own son was capable of such depravity had taken its toll with a series of mini-strokes. His health had deteriorated so much this year that I feared he wouldn't be with us for much longer.

I also worried about my sister. She'd kept this huge secret and had put herself out there as this bubbly, friendly, quirky individual to hide her pain and I sometimes feared there were moments where she was still doing that. She'd repeatedly reassured us that she'd come to terms with what happened some time ago and the final piece of healing had been to let us know and see Melvin pay. There'd been a trial last year and it was complicated, with cases to answer in the UK and USA. Fizz had testified against him along with a handful of others and he was now behind bars, where he'd stay for a very long time. I hoped she had been able to move on like she said, but the bad stuff had a way of festering, no matter how hard you tried to push it away.

'Barney?' Fizz prompted. 'I know you too well. What's going on up there?' She tapped my forehead.

'You really don't want to know. Dark man-cave of weirdness.' It was a weak attempt at a joke and it didn't convince anyone.

'Barney?' she repeated.

'Okay, there *is* something going on. Promise you won't laugh.'

'I promise.'

'I'm lonely.' It felt strange saying the words out loud.

'Aw, Barney. Why would I laugh at that?'

'Because it's a bit pathetic.'

She shook her head. 'How long have you been feeling like this?'

'A few years, maybe. It's a big farmhouse for one person to rattle around in and I'm the only one who's ever done it alone. I knew Olivia wasn't the one, but...'

'You keep hoping you'll meet someone who is. I get it. Look, let's give *Love on the Farm* a try and, if they don't pick you, we'll try an app and, if that doesn't work, we'll try something else. She's out there somewhere. I'm certain of it.'

Fizz left shortly afterwards. I cleared the kitchen and let Bear and Harley out into the yard for one last sniff around before bedtime. Leaning against the doorframe, I breathed in the cool air and looked up at the night sky. A clear sky presented a blanket of stars and I couldn't help feeling insignificant under their vastness.

What I'd said to Fizz about feeling lonely was true, but I couldn't share that it was the situation with Melvin that had made me realise it. On the day I found out what he'd done to Fizz, I'd returned to the farm, jumped on the quad bike and raced up to Top Field, a roar building inside me, desperate for release. How could he have done that to my sister? How had none of us suspected a thing? How had she found the strength to fight that battle alone?

In the weeks that followed, we talked a lot as a family unit – Mum, Dad, Fizz and me – but I always came home to an empty house. Mum and Dad had each other, my grandparents did too, and that's when it hit me that I had no one. I couldn't talk to Joel and the lads about Fizz – not my story – but who else was there? I needed to talk about how guilty I felt that I hadn't been able to protect my little sister, how sick I felt that I'd idolised my uncle, how terrified I was about how it had and might continue to affect Fizz.

It had never felt like an option to talk to any of the women who'd passed through my life since that day. I doubted any of them would have been interested even if I had.

A gust of wind whipped round my legs, making me shiver.

'Bear! Harley!' I gave a low whistle and the pair of them bounded across the yard and into the boot room.

I took one last look up at the sky then closed and locked the door behind me. Had I really just let Fizz talk me into filling in an application form for a reality TV show? I hated being centre of attention. What had I been thinking? Just as well it wasn't likely to come to anything.

5

AMBER

I felt anxious at the studio all day on Wednesday and struggled to concentrate on the edits for the final winter episode of *Countryside Calendar*. It made no sense for me to be feeling that way. The edits had gone well, I was in my comfort zone, and the whole series had been a resounding success. All I kept coming back to was Sophie and the fear that, now that she'd done it once, it was only a matter of time before she auditioned for another role which would take her far away from her family and put her at risk.

I was walking back from the Tube to my flat when a FaceTime request came through.

'Hi, Soph,' I said, smiling brightly so she wouldn't pick up on my concerns.

'Where are you?'

'Walking back to my flat.'

'Have you passed the wine shop yet?'

'It's just ahead of me. Why?'

'Because you might want to get some bubbly to celebrate for me. I got the part!' Her squeal was so loud, a dog being walked over the road started barking.

'Erm, congratulations. But what part? I didn't know you'd had another audition.'

'I haven't. It's the same part from last week – Amelie in *The Book Sleuths*. Becca Scarsdale had been thinking about it all weekend and was worried she'd made the wrong decision. They called back the actor they'd cast as Amelie and asked her to audition for a different role which they decided was a better fit, so she's got that and I'm now Amelie! Isn't that amazing?'

I gulped as my stomach churned, but I forced another smile. 'Oh, wow, Sophie! Yes! So amazing! How do you feel?'

'Like all my birthdays have come at once. It's the best thing that's happened to me in years and I'm so ready for it. Amelie Kentish, here I come.'

The excitement in her voice should have been infectious but I felt sick with fear, my mind racing.

'When do you start?' I willed her to say next year to give us more time to get her prepared, but that wasn't how these things worked. Time would *not* be on our side.

'They're still casting a couple of the main characters and making some changes to the script, but filming begins in June.'

'I'm so chuffed for you. Give me a second. I'm back at the flat so I'm just going in.'

I typed in the entrance code on my three-storey block – one of four blocks on a former playing field – and set off up the stairs to the second floor, my footsteps echoing round the soulless staircase.

'So I guess you'll be moving to York then?' I asked.

She adopted a sarcastic thinking pose. 'I suppose I could stay at home. Hmm, Kent to York every day. Five hours by train or a 250-mile drive each way sounds like a reasonable commute to me. Perhaps I'll do that.'

'Hilarious,' I said, pulling a face at her. 'Why does it have to be York? It's so far away.'

'I dunno. Ask Becca Scarsdale. She wrote the script, not me.' She sighed. 'I had pretty much the same reaction earlier from Mum and Dad and, like I told them, I'll be fine.'

'Yes, of course you will. I'm delighted for you. It's a great opportunity.'

'Not being funny, but I can see why you never went down the acting route.'

'I genuinely am delighted for you. I'm just a bit... it's so far from home.'

'I know, but I can't keep hiding at Green Acres. It's time to face the world again. I'd better let you go. I'll speak to you later when I have more details. Bye!'

Before I had a chance to protest, she'd disconnected, and I sank down onto the stairs. Yorkshire. How could we protect her there?

My phone buzzed with a text message.

FROM MUM

Our baby girl's moving to York

The message was accompanied by three crying emojis and I responded with a broken heart. There had to be something I could do to be there for Sophie. Would I be anywhere near York over the summer months? I ran up the remaining stairs to my flat.

Opening my laptop, I looked at my production schedule for the year. In early June, I'd still be in Wales finishing *Countryside Calendar's* spring episodes and late June would be the summer season in the Lake District. Both of those locations were closer to York than London or Kent but, at between a two- and four-hour drive each, were hardly local.

But there was a job which might be.

I stared at the phone, chewing my lip. What choice did I have?

'Darling!' Esther gushed. 'I thought you weren't speaking to me.'

I ignored the dig. 'I need to ask you something. Have they secured a producer for *Love on the Farm*?'

'Not yet. I'm still hoping I can persuade you.'

'You said the first episode is all set up and the filming is in South Wales. What does the rest of the schedule look like?'

'Bear with me a moment.' I heard her long nails tapping on her keyboard. 'Wales in April, Devon and Cornwall in May and, let's see, it's—'

Impatience got the better of me. 'You mentioned Yorkshire before. When's that?'

'It's the final one in September.'

September was too late for me. If Sophie was going to struggle, it would be during her first month, so that was when I needed to be around.

'If they make it Yorkshire in June, I'll do it.' I could hardly believe I was saying that, but needs must.

'That's wonderful, darling! I knew you'd come round. But June in Yorkshire isn't possible. They didn't find anyone suitable from the original advert, so they've gone out again and Yorkshire needs to be last.'

'Then they'd better hope some good applicants come through quick sharp because, if they want me to do it, it has to be June for Yorkshire. That's my one condition. Non-negotiable. Well, my second condition. Not working with Parker Knowles is my other one, as always.'

'Is everything okay, Amber? You sound stressed. That's not like you.'

The softness and the concern in her voice brought tears rushing to my eyes and I blinked them away. We locked horns regularly over the business side of things – she was pushy, which brought out a stubborn streak in me – but Esther had been a good friend over the years and she did care, even if sometimes her haste to secure a contract suggested otherwise.

'I can't say anything yet, but I absolutely must be in Yorkshire then, so I need you to pull out all the stops for me to make that happen. You know I wouldn't make a demand like that without a good reason.'

'Okay. I'll try them now.'

'Thanks, Esther.'

'Don't you worry about a thing. You know me and my powers of persuasion. If early summer in Yorkshire is what my favourite client wants, early summer in Yorkshire is what she'll get. I'll come back to you as soon as it's confirmed.'

We said our goodbyes and I disconnected the call and closed my eyes for a moment, trying to calm myself. I had every confidence in Esther moving the Yorkshire filming forward to secure the deal, which meant I was about to do the one thing I swore I'd never do and produce a reality television show. How ironic that I was doing it to support my sister when reality TV was the reason she needed my support.

6

BARNEY

A week later, Joel was between shifts at the factory, so he called round at the farm in the evening. Ideally, we'd have met at the pub, but lambing season had started so I didn't drink and couldn't venture far.

Joel and I had been mates for about a decade. Aged eleven, we'd been placed in the same form class in our first year at senior school and had bonded over our contempt for PE.

'Sorry again about Olivia,' he said when I handed him a coffee and sat down opposite him at the kitchen table. Joel had been doing a stack of overtime recently, so we hadn't had a chance to meet in person since it ended.

'I'm not. It was never going to work. Fizz says I pick the wrong women, so you won't believe what she's signed me up to.'

I filled him in on the *Love on the Farm* application and I expected him to laugh at it for being a ridiculous idea, but he nodded his head.

'I hope you're picked. It's different, but it could work.' He smiled. 'It's very Fizz.'

I smiled back. 'Isn't it just?'

'When will you hear?'

'I don't know. The closing date for applications was a couple of days after we submitted mine, so any time now.'

'Nervous?'

'A bit, but every time I think about it, I tell myself there's no way they'd select me so I push it out my mind.' I took a slurp of my drink. 'What about you? Tilly giving you any more grief?'

He rubbed his hand across his face and it struck me how shattered he looked. 'Every. Single. Day.'

Each word was emphasised as a separate point and I felt his pain. Joel and Tilly had seemed like the perfect couple. They'd met seven years ago when she started work on the reception at Claybridge Fresh Foods. They started dating a couple of months later and were engaged within a year. I thought she was great and was so chuffed that Joel – who'd never made it past three dates with anyone before Tilly – had finally found love.

A fortnight before their wedding, Tilly had announced that the whole marriage and kids thing wasn't for her, which was a bit late because they might not have walked up the aisle yet but they already had Imogen, aged two at the time. Joel was devastated it was over and even more hurt when, a year later, the woman who wasn't interested in marriage and kids had married her ex-boyfriend Greg and was playing happy families with his young son. Since then, they'd had two more kids together.

Three years had passed since the break-up. Imogen was now five and Joel was still struggling with what had happened. After how badly she'd hurt him, I'd have expected Tilly to be kind when it came to their daughter, but it had been one fight after another.

'Same old?' I asked.

'Yep. Still refusing to fit round my shifts.'

Ever since the split, Joel had been battling with Tilly for time with Imogen. The lack of interest in having children had clearly been a throwaway comment because she'd been a devoted mother to Imogen while she was with Joel and, according to him, was great with all the kids. What she wasn't great at was letting Joel have the opportunity to be a good father. Working shifts meant he couldn't commit to spending set days every week with Imogen and, instead of giving him flexibility, Tilly denied him access. I dread to think how much money Joel had shelled out on solicitor fees over the years.

'I might have a solution,' Joel said, 'but it's a long shot. You know how Roger's retiring?'

I nodded. Roger was the production manager at work and, as the factory's leading supplier, I knew him well.

'Roger thinks I'd make a good replacement, so I've applied. It would mean a normal working day – no shifts and no weekends.'

'That's brilliant news. Have you mentioned it to Tilly?'

He vigorously shook his head. 'If I don't get it – and I think that's likely – she won't just be going on about my lack of commitment to looking after Imogen because I haven't left the factory, she'll be calling me a failure too.'

'That's not fair. And what does she think you'd do if you left work? All the factories round here work shift patterns.'

'She thinks I should re-train. Like it's that easy.'

'She's changed.'

'I'm glad you said that. I've been wondering if she was like this before and I just didn't see it.'

'No. She was a nice lass. Had us all fooled. I think she changed when—'

I broke off as my mobile started ringing with a number I didn't recognise. Joel indicated with a nod of his head that I should get it.

'Hello?'

A woman spoke. 'Hi there, is that Barney Kinsella?'

'It is.'

'Wonderful. My name's Tiffany and I'm calling from Clementine Creates, the production company behind *Love on the Farm*.'

My stomach lurched and I flicked onto speakerphone so Joel could listen.

'We've been working through all the application forms over the past week...' Tiffany continued in a sing-song voice, '...and we were particularly interested in yours. Would you be able to send us an audition video by the end of the weekend?'

I widened my eyes at Joel and he gave me a thumbs up.

'Erm... yes. What should I put on it?'

'We're looking for between five and ten minutes and it's mainly the same information we have on your application form – an introduction to you and why you've applied. If you can film it on the farm so we get a bit of a feel for what your environment looks like, that would be awesome. But I do need to emphasise the deadline of end of Sunday.'

'That's fine. I can do that.'

'Brilliant. I'll email you all the details over but, before I do, I need to let you know there's been a change in the schedule and we'll be filming the Yorkshire episode sooner than originally planned. It'll be June rather than September and members of the production team may need to meet you in late May. Would that present any problems?'

My stomach lurched once more. I genuinely hadn't expected to be shortlisted and now it was all feeling very real. And very sudden. I gulped and tried to sound confident.

'No. May and June are fine.'

'Awesome. Good to talk to you, Barney. Watch out for that email. Bye.'

The call disconnected and I looked at Joel.

He raised his eyebrows at me. 'What was that you were saying about no chance of being picked?'

'I'm stunned. Obviously I still have to pass the video part.'

'But you're a step closer. You need to believe in yourself more.'

I raised my eyebrows back at him. 'Tell yourself the same, Mr *I-have-no-chance-of-getting-Roger's-job*. If the outgoing production manager thinks you can do it, that's got to count for something. And their favourite pig farmer seconds it.'

He smiled at me. 'Cheers. I needed to hear that. So do you want some help making this video? I've got Imogen on Sunday – bloody miracle – but I know she'd love to come and see the animals and her Uncle Barney, of course.'

'That'd be great, thanks, and I'd love to see her too.'

My mind was racing. I should have asked Tiffany how many farmers had been asked to make a video, but maybe it was best not to know. Fizz would be dead chuffed. As soon as Joel left, I'd give her a call. She'd probably want to help with the video too and I was happy to take all the help I could get. Selling myself on paper was one thing, but selling myself on a video was another and I wanted to do my best because, suddenly, this all seemed possible.

A week had passed since Sophie's announcement of getting the part in *The Book Sleuths* and I felt like I'd barely paused for breath while my assistant Zara and I re-worked the production schedules on *Countryside Calendar* to provide space for the Yorkshire episode of *Love on the Farm*.

Tonight, I was back in London and meeting up with Matt Hambleton, the *Love on the Farm* director, for an early dinner then finally catching up with Dan for drinks. I hadn't seen him for several weeks.

After Parker, I'd sworn off men and had made my life all about my family and work. I had no interest in meeting someone new and risking getting my heart broken all over again, but I hadn't met someone 'new'. Dan was an actor and had played a teacher in Sophie's series, *Mercury's Rising*. Sophie had introduced us at an awards party eight years ago and we'd dated for about eighteen months. I'd cared deeply for him and who knows what might have happened if he hadn't secured a major part in a drama filming in Costa Rica for six months. We'd agreed to part amicably and see what happened – if it was meant to be, we'd find a way back to each other when he returned to the UK. It clearly wasn't meant to be back then because I met Parker and Dan started seeing the drama's costume designer, who he later married.

At the start of this year, our paths crossed once more after Brad and Tabs dragged me to a New Year's Eve party with them. My reluctance at being there soon drifted away when I spotted Dan. We fell into easy conversation and I discovered that he'd divorced a couple of years earlier after his wife had an affair. As midnight approached and the party guests piled out onto the roof terrace, Dan handed me a glass of champagne and said, 'Remember when we said we'd find a way back to each other if it was meant to be? I wasn't meant to be coming tonight and you didn't want to be here. I think that's fate. Don't you?'

With the fireworks of London exploding overhead, fireworks exploded inside me as we kissed.

Both free from filming commitments, we spent the next few days together and it felt as though we'd never been apart. The heartbreak we'd both experienced gave us a deeper connection. Our relationship had been good the first time round and this time, it was even better. The work schedule was a challenge, but he travelled to where I was filming when he could and I did the same for him. This usually meant an intense couple of days together followed by a couple of weeks apart, but we were both determined to make it work.

I felt bad about meeting Matt during my limited time back in London, but it was the only date we could both make, and an early meal meant I could still meet Dan afterwards.

Matt stood up and shook my hand when the waiter led me over to his table in the restaurant.

'So, reality television,' he said, his voice holding a trace of an American accent. 'Are you a fan?'

I winced. 'Would you judge me if I said no?'

He laughed. 'I'd say thank goodness! Luckily, *Love on the Farm* is less about what I dreaded and more about what I hoped. I'm really enjoying it.'

'It's a relief to hear you say that. So why did you get involved if you're not a fan of reality TV?'

'Would you judge me if I said money?'

We both laughed and I felt an instant warmth towards him. I could already tell we were going to work well together.

Matt explained that he was seeking to establish himself back in the UK after working in the USA for several years and *Love on the Farm* was his second project so far after working on a three-part thriller.

During the meal, we talked about our shared love of the countryside, and it was apparent we were on the same page around showcasing sunrises, sunsets and nature at its finest during the show. Matt agreed that there was a valuable opportunity to educate the viewers on how challenging – but also how rewarding – farming could be, and I was starting to think we'd end up with a series I'd be proud to say I worked on instead of one I conveniently missed off my CV.

'Just checking you know you won't be involved in the selection process for any of the farmers and matches,' Matt said when we moved onto discussing the filming of our first episode.

'Yes. And you haven't been either?'

'No. It was all done centrally by the experts. Part of your role will involve meeting the farmers and matches before filming. I've needed to do that for our Wales episode due to lack of time, but I'll hand the reins back to you for Yorkshire onwards.'

I hadn't realised the time had passed so quickly until I spotted Dan entering the restaurant and taking a seat at the bar. The sight of him always gave me a warm glow inside. At six foot two with broad shoulders, he had wavy dirty blond hair and warm grey eyes. I jokingly called him Clark Kent because he wore black-rimmed glasses rather than contact lenses when he wasn't filming and almost never got recognised. Take the glasses off and he got swamped. At the moment, he was even less recognisable as he'd grown a neat beard for his part, which was a first for him but really suited him.

Matt signalled for the bill. 'I'd better get back to my wife and kids and let you continue your evening.'

'Dan's at the bar,' I said when he'd paid. 'Can I introduce you?'

'That would be great.'

Dan slipped off his bar stool as we approached and I made the introductions. They shook hands and smiled.

'Have we met before?' Matt asked.

Dan shook his head slowly. 'I don't think so. Did Amber tell you I'm an actor? You might have seen me in something.'

'That's probably it. Good to meet you, Dan. Amber, it's been a pleasure and I look forward to working with you. You've got my number, so give me a shout if you have any questions, otherwise I'll see you in Wales next week.'

'He seems decent,' Dan said after Matt left.

'He is. We're going to make a good team. How was filming?' Dan had a major part in a period drama which had been fraught with problems and was way behind schedule.

'Still behind, but it's all good. We'll catch up eventually. You look gorgeous, by the way.' He placed a light kiss on my lips, making my heart leap.

'And you smell good,' I said. 'I didn't think you'd have time to go home and change.'

'I didn't, but I grabbed a shower on set. I've been riding a horse this afternoon and didn't think you'd appreciate eau de stables. Although, knowing your love of animals, maybe you would. Ready to go for a drink?'

'I am.'

He took my hand and we left the restaurant to find a bar. It was all so easy with Dan. He was fun, affectionate, good-natured – pretty much the opposite of Parker – and I really hoped we could make this work. Our work schedules so far had been challenging but not impossible. That was going to change in June when I started filming in Yorkshire. My biggest concern for now was how to tell him that I needed to spend any downtime with Sophie without making it sound like I didn't see him as important and without giving too much away. He knew her brush with reality TV hadn't gone well, but he didn't know the full story because she'd begged me not to tell him. She couldn't bear the thought of her former castmates knowing all the details, so Dan remained clueless for now and I really hoped *that* show didn't end up being the death of another relationship for me.

8

BARNEY

Sunday arrived – the day of filming my audition video – and I did my early morning rounds on the farm with my stomach in knots.

'I'm not sure about this TV show anymore,' I told Bear and Harley. 'Do you think it's a good idea?'

Bear licked his lips and Harley cocked her head to one side, both keeping their eyes focused on mine. I whistled for them to get on the back of the quad bike.

I'd felt so confident about it being a good idea when Joel came round on Wednesday, but I'd had time to over-think since then. I'd never followed any reality TV shows but I'd caught enough trailers and part-episodes to see a common link across them all – interviews with contestants where they were encouraged to bare their souls. 'Encouraged' was probably too polite a word. Did I really want to admit to thousands of strangers that I was lonely? And what if they asked about my past relationships but pushed beyond the more recent history? I didn't want to talk about Elle either. My family didn't know. Joel didn't know. That was how I wanted it to stay.

* * *

Joel arrived with Imogen around mid-morning. The others were coming over for lunch and we'd make the video afterwards.

'Uncle Barney!' Imogen called, running across the farmyard in her ladybird wellies, her high blonde ponytail swishing like a horse's tail.

I crouched down as she launched herself into my arms.

'You've grown so big,' I said, hugging her.

'I'm nearly six. Spin me!'

I gripped her hands in mine and turned in a circle in the farmyard, spinning her round as fast as I dared, laughing at her delighted squeals.

'I tried to do that earlier,' Joel said when I put her back down before we got too dizzy, 'but apparently I'm not as good at it as you are.'

'Uncle Barney goes faster,' Imogen declared. 'Can we see the horses?'

'Of course we can. How about you hold your dad's hand and mine and we do one, two and a three on the way to the stables?'

She grabbed a hand from each of us and we swung her arms forward to the count of one and two before lifting her in the air for a swing on the three.

'Again!'

We managed maybe eight swings before we reached the stables. Bear and Harley had joined us, so Imogen took some time to fuss round them before being lifted up to stroke the horses' manes and feed them a couple of Polo mints each, giggling as they licked her outstretched palm.

'Are you all set for this afternoon?' Joel asked in the kitchen a little later. I'd given Imogen some juice and she was playing with the dogs while I made coffee for Joel and me.

'I'm having second thoughts.'

'Why?'

I shrugged. 'Can you really see me on TV? I'm a farmer, not some attention-seeker who's hoping appearing on telly will launch my modelling career.'

Joel sniggered. 'You? A model?'

'Cheers for the vote of confidence. Okay, *not* a model but you know what I mean, yeah?' I handed him a mug and we settled at the table.

'Yeah, I get what you're saying but it's not like you're going into the *Big Brother* house or anything like that. This is you on your farm doing your everyday stuff.'

'But they quiz contestants. They get them to reveal their deepest secrets. They make them cry.'

'Just as well you don't have any deep secrets. Unless there's something I don't know about.' His tone was light, and he was smiling. He hadn't a clue.

I forced a smile in return. 'Nope. Nothing. Open book, me.'

'Then you've got nothing to worry about. Go for it! There's still a possibility you might not be picked, and I reckon you'd kick yourself later if you didn't try. And speaking of going for it, I've put my application in for the production manager job and Roger's put in a good word for me, so hopefully I'll be shortlisted for interview.'

'Nice one!' I crossed my fingers and held them up to him.

I glanced over at Imogen and lowered my voice. 'How was Tilly earlier?'

'Had a go at me for being early. We're talking two minutes. Moaned about farmyard smells and a pile of other stuff. I switched off, to be honest.'

'I'm sorry. That's crap.'

'At least she never badmouths me in front of Imogen. I just

don't get why she's so angry with me all the time. She was never like that when we were together.'

'Do you think it's Greg's influence?'

'Presumably.'

Imogen came running over with an empty beaker, requesting more juice and putting paid to any further discussion by clambering onto Joel's knee. If it was Greg, I didn't know what his problem was with Joel. Jealousy? Tilly had made it clear that she'd never loved Joel and it had always been Greg for her, but maybe he was jealous of them having a child together, not that that made sense when he also had a child from a previous relationship. I hoped the execs at Claybridge Fresh Foods would take a chance on Joel because being able to commit to regular days with Imogen would at least remove one of Tilly's many bugbears.

* * *

We hadn't told Imogen that Fizz, Phoebe and Darcie were joining us for lunch. She adored them all, particularly Darcie, and we'd have been questioned every five minutes as to when they were arriving. Imogen squealed with excitement when she spotted them piling out of Fizz's car and it was sweet watching her unable to decide who to cuddle first.

'All set for your film shoot?' Fizz asked, giving me a hug.

'Nervous and full of doubts about the whole thing.'

'Aw, don't be. You'll be awesome.'

'It'll be fun,' Phoebe said, handing me and Fizz a bag of food each. 'I think it's great what you're doing.'

'You do?'

'You're taking control, putting yourself out there and making things happen. It might not work, you might not find love, but at least you'll have tried.'

'Too right!' Fizz said. 'Never be afraid to fail. Only be afraid not to try.'

I rolled my eyes at another of her motivational quotes, but it was a valid point and it did lift me a little.

Twenty minutes later, the kitchen table was laden with the buffet Fizz and Phoebe had prepared and the room was full of laughter. I thought about sitting here all by myself only a fortnight ago, after Olivia left, thinking about how quiet it was and how alone I was. This was how it should be – noise, laughter, people, animals – and the only way I was going to make it happen was to put myself out there like Phoebe said. I *would* record the video and I'd throw myself into this fully. It might not work, but it had no chance of working if I didn't try it.

And if *Love on the Farm* didn't find me love, I'd search for it in another way. It was out there and I knew how good it could be because I'd had it once and I wanted it again.

9

AMBER

'I wish you didn't have to head to Wales straight after lunch,' Dan said, wrapping his arms round me late on Sunday morning while I was trying to pack.

'I wish I didn't too, but you know I like to get settled and up to speed.'

He kissed my neck teasingly. 'Can't we be late? Tell Brad and Tabs we hit bad traffic?'

We were meeting them for Sunday lunch in Windsor, west of London, after which I was driving to the Brecon Beacons National Park in South Wales and Dan was getting the train back to London after catching up with an old college friend in the area.

'They'll mainly be on the same roads as us, so I don't think we can get away with a lie about traffic.'

'Spoilsport,' he joked. 'I'm going to miss you.'

'I'm going to miss you too, but we'll see each other at the weekend. Zara's going home for her mum's birthday, so we'll have the cottage all to ourselves.'

'Perfect.' He kissed my neck once more then stepped back with a smile. 'I'd better leave the room. You're too irresistible.'

That gave me a warm glow. I'd never felt like I was irresistible to Parker. He'd never made me feel special. From seeing us together, I doubt anyone would even have placed us as a couple, never mind engaged and living together. He'd called it 'being professional' and I was all about the professionalism when we were working but, outside of work, I called the lack of affection 'being cold'. Of course, I'd never realised it at the time. It was funny how you could see a relationship so differently with a little time and space.

* * *

Over lunch, the conversation inevitably turned to Sophie's move to York in less than two months. I'd messaged Brad and Tabs this morning to remind them that Dan didn't know the full story about Sophie or that I'd specifically agreed to producing *Love on the Farm* just to be close to her. Tabs had messaged me back to assure me they wouldn't let anything slip.

'I spoke to Sophie a couple of nights ago,' Brad said. 'She sounds so excited about it.'

'I'm not surprised,' Dan said. 'I'd kill to be in a Becca Scarsdale series. She's a genius. My agent has always wanted to put me forward, but the timing's never been right around other commitments.'

'You'll have to see if Sophie can put in a good word for you,' Tabs suggested.

'I'll speak to her when I visit you in Yorkshire,' Dan said, smiling at me.

I wasn't going to get into a discussion in front of Brad and Tabs about potentially not seeing Dan while I was in Yorkshire – or at least not until I knew Sophie was settled and okay – so I took a sip of my drink and hoped somebody would change the subject.

'I'm sure she'll be fine,' Tabs said to me, 'but I'm glad you'll be close by. It's a long way from home.'

Dan looked round the table, frowning. 'She's nearly twenty-four. I don't get why her being in York is such a big issue.'

'She's our baby sister and we care about her.' Brad sounded jovial, but the tightness of his jaw suggested otherwise.

'It's the first time she's lived so far away,' Tabs added.

'Well, I think you're all being way too overprotective,' Dan said. 'Next thing you'll be telling me is that Amber only accepted this job so she could be near her.'

We all laughed with him. It was too loud and pitchy, but Dan didn't seem to notice. To tell him he'd hit the nail on the head would require the full story and, even though I was sure he could be trusted not to do anything to hurt me or my family by sharing it, there was that niggle of doubt. I'd thought Parker could be trusted not to do anything to hurt me or my family.

The subject changed and we had an enjoyable lunch. When we'd eaten, a call came through on Dan's phone from his producer, so he apologised and wandered off to speak outside.

'That was close,' Tabs said when he was out of earshot. 'Are you okay?'

'I feel like I'm lying to him.'

'You're not,' she said, gently. 'All Soph has ever wanted is to put it behind her and she can't do that if her colleagues know. If Dan knew, something would slip out to someone. He's a nice guy so it wouldn't be done intentionally or vindictively, but it *would* come out.'

'She's right,' Brad said. 'The acting world's too small. Everyone knows someone who knows someone.'

'Anyway, you and Dan.' Tabs grinned at me. 'Seems to be going well.'

I felt shy all of a sudden. 'It is. He's great.'

'Could he be the one?' she asked, leaning closer.

Could he? I glanced through the window, where I could see him with his phone held out in front of him, laughing.

'Early days,' I said.

'Don't be coy,' Tabs teased.

I looked back at her, smiling. 'The last time I jumped in feet first ended in disaster. I'm a little more cautious this time.'

'He's *nothing* like Parker Knowles,' Brad said. 'Chalk and cheese.'

'He's coming back,' Tabs whispered, 'but just so you're clear, we both approve and I'm available for bridesmaid services any time.'

I laughed, shaking my head at her. It was good to know they both liked Dan, not that I'd doubted it. They'd liked him first time round and, with it ending mutually and amicably, there'd been no need for anyone to get angry about him breaking my heart.

* * *

Dan said it would be quicker for him to walk to his friend's than have me drive, so we said goodbye in the car park. As I drove away, I felt quite emotional and needed to blink back the tears. That wasn't like me at all.

I couldn't stop thinking about Dan as I travelled west along the M4. Tabs had asked if he was the one. Maybe he was. We hadn't said we loved each other – both agreeing to take things slowly after being hurt – but I missed him when we were apart and I loved being with him. It hadn't been love last time. Was it now? It certainly felt like it was heading that way.

It was just after half five when I pulled up behind Zara's car outside the holiday cottage she'd booked on the outskirts of the pretty market town of Brecon. It had been Zara's birthday yesterday and her boyfriend Declan had booked a romantic weekend in a Cotswolds country hotel, so I hadn't been expecting her until late this evening.

I exited the car and smiled approvingly at the attractive white-washed cottage which would be our home for the next four weeks. I hated hotels. No, hated was a strong word. They were brilliant for holidays, but a life on the road had turned me against the often impersonal feel. Sometimes after a long day, all I wanted to do was make a plate of cheesy beans on toast and lie on the sofa with a good book or a film. The budget didn't stretch to suites and I'd soon learned it was a lot more comfortable staying in a holiday cottage or Airbnb. It was also much more conducive for work than Zara and I being in separate hotel bedrooms. It wasn't essential for her to be with me all the time, but she enjoyed the travel and it did make my job a lot easier having her on hand.

The front door opened and Zara waved at me, but she wasn't smiling, which wasn't like her. The cases could wait for a bit.

'Happy birthday for yesterday,' I said, hugging her. 'How was it?'

'The worst. Declan dumped me.'

'Oh, no!'

I followed her into the lounge and sat beside her on the sofa, oblivious to my new surroundings.

'What happened?' I asked gently.

'I got to the hotel and picked up a WhatsApp from him saying he was running late so I should check in. I did that and waited and waited. Eventually a message came through to say he wasn't running late – he wasn't coming at all.'

'Oh, Zara! That's awful.'

'I kept phoning him but he wasn't answering and eventually, after about an hour of trying, he sent me a message telling me to stop pestering him. I asked what was going on and he said *isn't it obvious?* I said no, so he sent me a GIF announcing *you're dumped.*'

'What? Who does that?'

'Declan, but apparently it doesn't make him a bad person because he did it the day before my birthday instead of on my actual birthday.'

'Did he say why?'

'No, but I soon found out. Some woman called Candi with an "i" tagged him into a load of photos on social media later that evening. They were all over each other and, considering she was wearing different outfits in each pic, it's safe to assume Candi and Declan have been seeing each other for quite some time.'

'I'm so sorry.'

'I'm such an idiot for trusting him. I knew he'd cheated on previous girlfriends, so why did I think I'd be any different, especially when I made it easy for him by being away so often? And to add insult to injury, he told me he'd paid for the hotel up front so I might as well spend the weekend there – call it a goodbye gift.'

I winced. 'But he hadn't paid.'

'Nope. So I spent my birthday weekend away on my own in some posh room with a four-poster bed and a bath for two and had to foot the bill myself.'

'What did you do all weekend?'

'I had a cry on Friday night but, after I saw the photos of him with Candi, I refused to waste any more tears on him. I had a lovely day on Saturday looking round some of the villages and I've been to the Forest of Dean this morning, which is probably much better than what I'd have done if Declan had been with me, but I could have done without the big hole in my bank balance. I do pick 'em, don't I?'

Declan was sadly the latest in a long line of bad boyfriends. Zara was a naturally beautiful woman with a heart-shaped face, full lips, high cheekbones and dark hair which she wore in a choppy shoulder-length style with a thick fringe. Her eyes – a mix of hazel and green – were captivating and black eyeliner all the way round emphasised them. She always drew attention when she was on set and she usually laughed it off and remained focused on her work. Occasionally the attraction was mutual, but it always seemed to end badly after a few months.

'How are you feeling now?' I asked.

'Still a bit angry, but I'm fine. I promise. Looking forward to some time on my own and playing matchmaker to a bunch of farmers instead.'

'You know I'm here for you if you want to talk some more.'

'I know, but I really am all right. Character building, they say.'

'It is, but it doesn't mean it doesn't hurt.'

She smiled at me. 'Thank you. Let's get your stuff out the car.'

And that was the conversation over again. I used to marvel at how strong Zara was, managing to pick herself up and brush it off each time a relationship ended, but I'd noticed the time between boyfriends was getting longer. Even though she swore she wasn't hurting, I knew she was. I could hear it in her voice. I could see it in her eyes. I could feel it in my heart.

10

BARNEY

I submitted my video for *Love on the Farm* on Sunday evening and tried to forget about it. Inviting everyone round had been a good move because they'd all contributed ideas and we'd had a right laugh making it. If it wasn't what the producers wanted, so be it. I'd done my best.

It was now late afternoon on Friday and I was with my full-time farmhand Milo in Middle Pig – my imaginative name for the middle of three pig fields – repairing one of the pens when my mobile rang. Nerves took hold as I recognised the number from before and my hands shook as I accepted the call.

'It's Tiffany from Clementine Creates. Is that Barney?'

'Yes. Hi, Tiffany.'

'Thank you for sending in your audition video. I have some fantastic news for you today. The team would love you to be one of the featured farmers on *Love on the Farm*, so congratulations! How do you feel about that?'

My stomach did a somersault and I felt a mix of panic and excitement. 'Erm... a bit shocked. I didn't expect to be picked.'

'Can I confirm your circumstances haven't changed this week and you are still eager to participate in *Love on the Farm*?'

'No change and yes to the show.' I couldn't quite believe I'd just said that.

'Wonderful! I'll send a document over for you to sign electronically to confirm that. If you could do that today, that would be appreciated. The producer's assistant, Zara Timmins, will be in touch early next week to confirm next steps. In the meantime, can you think about which family members, friends or colleagues we could interview about you as part of the show and ask them if they'd be willing to participate. Otherwise, please keep the news confidential.'

'Okay. How many people?'

'Ideally between two and four, although, if it's four, we can't guarantee we'll use all the footage. Congratulations again, Barney. I hope you enjoy this unique experience.'

'Thank you.'

I disconnected the call after we said goodbye and took a few deep calming breaths.

Milo was watching me, eyes narrowed. I could tell he had questions but knew he wouldn't voice them. He never started a conversation that wasn't connected to the farm.

'I've been selected to appear on that show I was telling you about,' I said, aware of a slight shake to my voice.

'Is that good?'

'I think so. I hope so.'

'Okay. Well done. Pen sixteen needs repairs too.'

Typical Milo, straight back to business.

'Just to reassure you, you won't need to appear on camera,' I told him, knowing it would be weighing on his mind.

'Good.' His shoulders visibly relaxed. He was so committed to his work that he'd have done anything I asked if he thought it was connected to the farm, but I'd never dream of asking him to go on camera.

'So, pen sixteen, eh? Let's do that now.'

As we worked on the repairs, my thoughts were all over the place, ranging from elation to panic and everything in between. This was it. This was really happening.

* * *

It was only right that Fizz be the next person to tell. I FaceTimed her when we'd finished in Middle Pig and she jumped up and down, squealing with excitement.

'Oh, my God! Barney! This is so awesome! Are you excited?'

'It hasn't quite sunk in. More nervous at the moment.'

'I can imagine. I'm nervous for you, but what an amazing opportunity.'

'I've got you to thank for that.'

'You certainly have. I'll have to think of an epic favour you can do for me in return.' She winked at the camera and I knew she'd expect nothing from me and had only done this to try to make me happy.

'I need some friends and family who can be interviewed on the show. Would you like to do it?'

She squealed again. 'Behave! I am so up for that. Who else have you asked?'

'You're the first person other than Milo I've told. I've been asked to come up with two to four people, so I'm thinking you, Mum or Dad, and Joel. I'd like to ask Granddad, but I'm not sure if he'd be well enough to come to the farm.'

She scrunched up her nose. 'Possibly not, but I think he'd be flattered to be asked.'

'Mum and Dad are coming over for tea tonight, so I'll ask them then and I'll bob over to see Granddad tomorrow. Can you keep it confidential in the meantime?'

'Can I tell Phoebe?'

'Okay, and I suppose it's okay to tell Samantha because you'll need time off for filming, but definitely nobody else.'

She nodded and did a zipping motion across her lips. 'I'm so thrilled for you, Barney. I've got a good feeling about this.'

After I'd finished work late the following afternoon, I drove over to Grandma and Granddad's bungalow in Cherry Brompton. Mum and Dad had been chuffed as anything about the news last night and either were willing to appear on screen, so it was time to ask Granddad.

'Barney! What a lovely surprise!' Grandma hugged me on the doorstep and welcomed me and the dogs in. They shot past her in search of their mum, Raven, who'd been a working dog on the farm but had moved to the bungalow on retirement.

'How are you today?' I asked as Grandma flicked the kettle on and tossed teabags into a large teapot.

'Very good. It's been a lovely day, so your granddad and I have spent most of it in the garden.'

'How is he?'

Her shoulders drooped. 'Today was a good day, but they're few and far between.'

'I'm sorry.'

'Me too, sweetheart. I wish things were different, but...' She sighed and shrugged. 'Age catches up with us all.'

She wouldn't catch my eye and I was fairly certain of what was running through her mind – would Granddad still have been fit and well if Melvin hadn't returned to the UK? We'd never know for sure.

Grandma pulled a striped knitted tea cosy over the pot, added three mugs and a jug of milk to the tray and I carried it outside. The three dogs were chasing each other in circles at the bottom of the large garden.

Halfway down was a greenhouse, pond and paved area with a wooden bench, low table and a couple of wooden deckchairs. Granddad was on the bench – his favourite spot – wearing a fleecy jacket with a picnic blanket draped across his legs. His eyes were closed and he was so still that my stomach lurched.

'Granddad?'

No response.

I laid the tray on the table.

'Granddad?' Louder this time, my heart pounding.

'Frank!' Grandma gave him a nudge and his eyes shot open.

'Barney! Have you been here long?'

'Just arrived. I thought you were...' I swallowed hard. I could hardly say what I really thought – that we'd lost him, '...asleep.'

I sat down on one of the deckchairs, my pulse rate back to normal, and Grandma poured the tea.

The dogs joined us and lay on the patio as we chatted about the weather and the work Grandma had done in the garden before I told them about *Love on the Farm*.

'It's certainly a different way to find the love of your life,' Grandma said, 'but it sounds like fun. I hope it works out for you.'

'What do you think, Granddad?' I asked.

'Bit weird if you ask me.' Granddad had never been one for filtering his opinions.

'I know it's not conventional, but I haven't had much success on my own so far. Meeting someone is harder than ever these days.'

'Well, good luck to you, son,' he said. 'You deserve to meet a nice lass, but I can't see that happening on a TV programme. You're sure you want to do this?'

'I've had a few wobbles but, yes, I'm sure.' I took a sip of my tea. 'I have a favour to ask. I need friends and family to come up to the farm and go on film saying a few words about me. Fizz and Mum or Dad are doing it and I'm going to ask Joel, but I wondered if you'd do it too.'

'Me? Why?' He looked and sounded aghast.

'Because you're my granddad and I inherited the farm from you and...'

I faltered at the vigorous shaking of his head.

'I'm not interested, son. Ask your grandma.'

I glanced across at Grandma and she shrugged.

'I'd really love *you* to do it, Granddad. Can you at least think about it?'

He pulled the blanket off his legs and slowly stood up. 'I've said no and I mean no,' he snapped. 'It's parky out here now. I'm going for a shower to warm up before my tea. Your grandma will see you out.'

'Sorry,' I whispered to Grandma as Granddad shuffled along the path to the back door. 'I didn't mean to upset anyone.'

'I'll have a word with him tomorrow.'

'No, don't. Just forget about it. It was a long shot. I'll head back to the farm and let you make your meal.'

'He's never been able to cope with being ill,' she said as I carried the tray back to the house, the three dogs following. 'Don't take it to heart.'

'I'm not.'

I hugged her goodbye and set off back to Bumblebee Barn. I wouldn't take a no to heart – it was the response I'd expected – but it hurt that he hadn't even been willing to discuss it. It hurt that his reaction to the whole thing had been so negative. And it hurt that he'd clearly wanted me to leave. Granddad had always been stubborn and opinionated, and we'd sometimes clashed on ideas for running the farm, but at least he'd been willing to listen to what I had to say instead of dismissing me outright like tonight.

11

AMBER

The first week of filming in South Wales went well. As anticipated, Matt Hambleton was a great director and a pleasure to work alongside. I felt like I'd found a friend and a colleague with whom I'd hopefully work again. As well as being on the same page about our visions for *Love on the Farm*, he shared the same work ethic as me and we worked brilliantly as a team.

I'd met Matt's adorable two little boys and his lovely wife Angelique when they visited the set one day. It was touching to see how close they all were, and I found myself wishing I had the same, which turned my thoughts to my relationship with Dan. Could this be us in the future? I hoped so.

I'd unexpectedly found myself warming to *Love on the Farm*. It fell into the tame end of reality TV, with genuine intentions to help farmers find love rather than putting the participants through ritual humiliation and manipulating the footage for shock value and ratings success. Real care appeared to have been taken to find good matches, with everyone involved completing personality and values profiles and exploring the outcomes with psychologists before filming. This might actually be a show I became proud of.

As the weekend approached, I felt on a high. Work was good and I was looking forward to a weekend with Dan, but he'd phoned last night to say they'd fallen even further behind with filming and everyone needed to work late. It was a blow but he'd promised he'd drive over first thing this morning and would message me when he set off, so I'd know his rough arrival time and not be trapped in the cottage waiting for him. Except it was now half eleven and I still hadn't heard anything.

I'd been up early as usual and had taken a walk along the River Usk before breakfast. To stop me clock-watching, I'd gone out again afterwards for a wander round the town and a walk alongside the canal. As the morning wore on, I'd phoned and texted Dan with no response and I was now back at the cottage catastrophising. Had he set off extra-early to surprise me and had an accident en route? Could he be shattered from a late night of filming and he'd slept in? Or was I about to go through what Zara had just been through with Declan?

Dan's name finally flashed up on my phone at 11.47 a.m.

'I hope you're nearly here,' I said the moment I answered.

'I wish. I'm stuck at the studio.' His voice sounded heavy with regret.

'You're still filming?'

'Got a call first thing about a re-shoot. I thought it would be quick and I could leave by mid-morning, but we're still at it and I can't see us getting out until late tonight. I could drive across then or first thing tomorrow.'

I wanted to say yes, but what was the point? We'd already lost most of the weekend. I tried to keep my tone light, despite being seriously fed up.

'No. You'll be shattered tonight and, if you drive over tomorrow, you'll get here and have to turn round and head back again. We'll have to leave it for now.'

'I'm so sorry. I was really looking forward to a whole weekend together.'

'Me too.' Tears pricked my eyes and I blinked them back. 'Can't be helped. I'd better not keep you.'

'You'll be okay on your own, yeah?'

'Of course! I'm used to it. Hope you get some sleep tonight.'

'Sleep isn't going to be high on the agenda. We'll catch up soon. Bye.'

I held the phone against my chest and released a frustrated sigh, annoyed with myself for not pre-empting this. Dan had talked so often about the problems on set that it was fairly obvious this would happen at some point, and I had two options for dealing with it. I could sit around the cottage feeling sorry for myself or I could take a leaf out of Zara's book and go exploring.

I'd visited the Brecon Beacons in my first year of producing *Countryside Calendar* and it was a beautiful part of the country. Some stunning views and country air would lift me, but walking would give me too much time to think. I needed an activity.

A little later, I set off to an activity centre where I'd managed to book the last place on an afternoon gorge-walking adventure. Even though I turned the music up loud, I couldn't quieten the troubled thoughts going round my mind. Dan's star was on the rise and there was so much I still wanted to do with my own career. We'd been reunited for less than four months, we still hadn't managed to spend a whole weekend together, and I had no idea when I'd be able to see him again. We had trust, a good past relationship history, and things were going well now, but were those things enough to hold a relationship together when we barely saw each other? I wanted a family. I wanted what Matt and Angelique had. Would Dan and I ever get to that place? Right now, I wasn't so sure.

12

AMBER

After a second week of filming in South Wales, we moved to North Wales for the first of our women – a sheep farmer in Caernarvonshire. The vast majority of farmers applying had been men, but three of the twelve who'd been chosen were women. There was a good mix of ages from twenty-four to sixty-six, we had a couple of divorcees and a widower, and one of the men was seeking a same-sex partner.

Visiting the different farms – a good mix of size and type – massively appealed to me but, after going through the process with our Brecon farmer, I was now really looking forward to meeting the participants looking for love in each episode. Somewhere inside me was a hopeless romantic, desperately willing for it to work out for them.

Our Brecon farmer – a divorcee in his mid-forties – hadn't found love with any of his matches but one of them had thought he'd be perfect for her best friend, and he'd agreed to her setting up a blind date. I was excited to discover how that panned out when we returned to film the follow-up in three months' time.

I spent the next three weeks in North Wales filming a

mixture of *Love on the Farm* and *Countryside Calendar* and didn't
see Dan in person during that time. With a five-hour round-trip
each just to meet halfway, it wasn't practical, not that our filming
commitments gave either of us the time to meet up. We Face-
Timed and spoke on the phone, albeit briefly, and we both reaf-
firmed our commitment to making this work somehow,
accepting that the current diary clashes wouldn't always be quite
so bad.

On the second Sunday in May, I drove through the villages and
countryside of the Yorkshire Wolds. It was one of only a few areas
in England I hadn't visited before, but first impressions were
extremely positive and I was excited about exploring somewhere
new to me over the coming weeks.

Although I was loving working with Matt and actually
enjoying the show, it was a little strange coming into the project so
late. Everything I was used to doing – securing the sponsorship
and finances, selecting the participants, exploring the locations,
pulling together the shooting schedule – had already been done
by my predecessor. Changes had been needed to move the Yorkshire filming forward but that had simply been a swap around of
two locations, the paperwork for which Zara had handled while
the production company, Clementine Creates, fast-tracked the
Yorkshire auditions.

Tomorrow I'd be meeting our first Yorkshire farmer – thirty-
one-year-old Barney Kinsella – at the unusually named
Bumblebee Barn in East Yorkshire. When filming with him was
complete, we'd be heading up to the northern part of the Yorkshire Dales to meet the eldest of our farmers.

I had a one-week break in filming *Countryside Calendar* so was
staying in East Yorkshire, where I'd spend part of the time meeting
with Barney and the three women who'd been lined up as his
potential matches. I'd also explore Bumblebee Barn for the best

filming locations so I could finalise the shooting schedule. The rest of the week would be spent researching a pet project of mine.

'Turn right in 100 metres and you have reached your destination.'

The sat nav cut into my thoughts and I slowed on the country road, watching for the turn-off. A large wooden sign for Hedgehog Hollow Wildlife Rescue Centre confirmed that I was in the right place, and I smiled at the cute illustration of a hedgehog family.

I'd been so excited when Zara emailed me a link to Meadow View, the smallest of four holiday cottages in the grounds of a farm and wildlife rescue centre. It couldn't be more perfect for me. Last year, we'd visited a wildlife rescue centre in Somerset with *Countryside Calendar*, which had triggered an idea for a documentary series featuring rescue centres around the country. My research had stalled and staying at Hedgehog Hollow for a few extra days should give me the nudge to pick it up again.

A tidy wooden fence ran along either side of the farm track and it warmed my heart to see a young hedgerow growing between the fence and fields. Far too many of our countryside's hedgerows had been removed over time, destroying vital habitat for our wildlife, and I felt a warm glow every time I saw a farm where hedges remained or were being re-established.

The track veered sharply to the left and dipped, revealing a beautiful three-storey ivy-clad farmhouse ahead of me. To the right were the rescue centre and holiday cottages – recognisable from the photos on the website – among other outbuildings.

'Perfect,' I whispered. 'Nice find, Zara.'

I parked in the farmyard beside an electric-blue Mini, stepped out, inhaled deeply, and looked around me. It was late afternoon and the sun was warm in a cornflower-blue sky with ribbons of cirrocumulus clouds – small white groups of clouds known as cloudlets grouped together high in the sky.

A grey and white tabby cat made a beeline for me and weaved round my ankles, purring.

'Hello, beautiful,' I said, bending down to stroke its back. I loved cats and longed to have my own but couldn't due to my extensive travel. Fortunately, I encountered many cats through work, so I grabbed my fix wherever I could.

'That's Misty-Blue.' A pretty young girl stopped beside me on a bike, removed her helmet and shook out her black curls. 'She's very friendly. And that's Luna.' She pointed to a black cat crouched beside the front wheel of a jeep. 'Do you have an animal for us to make better?'

I shook my head. 'No, I'm staying in one of the holiday cottages. My name's Amber. What's yours?'

'I'm Darcie and I'm ten and I live in the farmhouse.' She pointed towards the ivy-clad building. 'Which cottage are you staying in?'

'Meadow View. I'm a bit early. I said I wouldn't be here until six, but I set off earlier than planned.'

'Hold this and I'll tell Samantha you're here.'

She pressed the bike into my hand and ran across the gravel and into the barn. Moments later, she reappeared and ran back to me.

'Samantha says she won't be long. She's mending a hedgehog. You can come and see if you like.'

'Oh, I'd love to!'

Darcie took her bike and wheeled it over to the barn. Misty-Blue followed and so did the black cat, Luna, as though the little girl was the Pied Piper.

She pushed open the door and I stepped into the large barn. Two women – one with long brown hair in a high ponytail and the other with pink hair in two messy buns – were standing by a metal table, wearing surgical masks. They both looked up and waved.

'Come in,' called the brunette. 'I'm Samantha, this is Fizz. You're Amber?'

'Yes. Sorry, I'm really early.'

'Not a problem. We'll get you settled shortly. Are you squeamish?'

'No.'

'We're just about to sew up Thor. Grab a mask and you're welcome to watch if you want.'

I took a mask from the box she'd pointed to and approached the table. 'Thor?'

'We have name themes for the hedgehogs,' Fizz said. 'We've just changed to comic book characters.'

A large hedgehog was lying on the table with a tiny oxygen mask over his face and a slash across his side.

'What happened to him?' I asked.

Samantha tutted. 'Strimmer. I hate those things – one of the biggest threats to hedgehogs at this time of the year.'

'Thor's one of the lucky ones,' Fizz said. 'It looks nasty, but it's not too deep so we've cleaned him, we'll stitch him up, and he'll make a full recovery.'

She glanced towards Darcie, but the little girl had moved over to a sofa on the opposite side of the barn and was distracted playing with the two cats.

'We've seen some horrific strimmer injuries and, sadly, lots of fatalities,' Fizz added in a hushed voice. 'Right, Thor, let's get you sewn back together.'

Samantha indicated a stool tucked under the table, so I pulled it out and sat down, keeping silent while they worked.

'All done!' Fizz said, snipping off the stitches. 'He's had pain relief and antibiotics, so we'll slowly bring him round and get him settled in his crate.'

'You didn't need to take him to a vet?' I asked.

Samantha shook her head. 'My husband and dad run a veterinary practice and the rescue centre is the charitable side of it. Fizz is a veterinary nurse and we're both qualified to do some of the things other rescue centres would need to go to a vet for, although there's obviously plenty we still need to refer.'

'I've visited a few rescue centres, but I've not come across that set-up before.'

'We're special,' Fizz said. 'You must like animals then.'

'I love them. As soon as I discovered the holiday cottage was on a farm with a rescue centre, I had to book it.'

'A neighbouring farmer rents the fields, so it's not a working farm,' Samantha said, 'but you're very welcome to see more of what we do at the rescue centre if you have time during your stay.'

'I'd love to.'

'Fizz, are you okay to bring Thor round while I show Amber to her cottage?'

'No problem.'

After she'd removed her mask and washed her hands, Samantha retrieved a key from a small safe on the wall. 'Let's go!'

Fizz and Darcie called goodbye as we left the barn. I turned to wave to them and laughed at Darcie, who'd picked up Luna and was waving one of the cat's paws at me.

'You're welcome to leave your car here, but there's parking by the cottages so most guests use that,' Samantha said. 'You can either drive over now or we can walk together, have a tour, and you can move your car later.'

'I've been driving for hours, so a leg stretch would be great.'

We set off together across the farmyard.

'What brings you to the area?' Samantha asked.

'Mainly work, but I have some spare time, so I'd definitely like to take you up on that offer to see more of what you do.'

'Pop over to the barn any time you're free. Fizz and I both work full-time and we've got a team of volunteers, so there's nearly always somebody there. What sort of work is it?'

'A few meetings, a bit of research.' I hated sounding cagey, but we tried to stay under the radar. As soon as television was mentioned, the rumours would start. A subject change would work well. 'Darcie's sweet. Is she your daughter?'

'No. She's our found family, along with Phoebe, who adopted her. They both live with us.'

'I love the idea of family being whoever you want it to be.'

'Me too! So Fizz, who you just met, is Phoebe's partner. I'm married to Josh – the vet I mentioned – who's out on call at the moment. We have a son, Thomas, who's nearly eighteen months old, and a daughter, Lyra, who'll be five months old on Friday. They're at my mum's this afternoon so it's quieter here than it normally is.' She paused and laughed lightly. 'And that was a lot of information. I promise I won't quiz you later.'

I laughed with her, feeling drawn to her warmth and openness.

'I look forward to meeting them all. It sounds like you have a lovely family. I'm really close to mine too. I've got an older brother and a younger sister, but my brother's girlfriend has been around the family forever, so it feels like I have a big sister too.'

'Where's home?'

'The family home is near Maidstone in Kent, but my brother and I both live in London – different parts – and my sister is about to move to York.'

I heard the concern in my voice so wasn't surprised when Samantha picked up on it.

'You don't sound too convinced by that.'

'It's complicated.' I'd normally have left it there, but there was something so engaging about Samantha that I found myself expanding. 'She's got a new job which is a much bigger role than she's used to and would already have been a huge leap if she'd stayed down south but is a worry when she's leaving home too. We'd have preferred a few more baby steps, but it is what it is, so I've moved a few things around with my job and, when I'm back here next month, at least I'll be a bit more local to help her settle in.'

'Must be lovely to have a big sister looking out for you like that.'

'Or interfering. She's eleven years younger than me, so I can't help it.'

'York's a beautiful city. She's very lucky to be based there.'

'I've never been, but I'm looking forward to it.'

'We're here,' Samantha declared, stopping.

I'd read on the website that two derelict stone barns had been converted into four holiday cottages of varying sizes. From the outside, the conversion appeared to be beautifully done. Each cottage had a welcoming spring wreath hanging from a pale green wooden door and there were roses trailing up trellises around the doors.

'Meadow View, where you're staying, is the one on the end here and, if you look that way...' Samantha pointed behind us, '... you can see where the name comes from.'

Behind the rescue centre barn, stretching across to a row of trees to the right, was a beautiful wildflower meadow.

'It's bigger than you can see from here,' Samantha continued. 'It runs behind the barn and across part of the garden at the back of the farmhouse. It's really special to us. The original owners of the property, Thomas and Gwendoline Mickleby, sowed the meadow when they bought the farm.'

'It's beautiful.' I spotted a clearing beyond the barn with a white gazebo overlooking the meadow. 'You hold weddings here?'

'Yes. Josh and I were the first. We got married here just over three years ago and we've hosted maybe fifteen weddings since then. There's a building down the hill called Wildflower Byre, which was originally the dairy shed but is now a function room, so the wedding reception is held there and we've hired it out for loads of other events. All the profits from the holiday cottages and functions get ploughed back into running the rescue centre.'

'That's a brilliant idea.'

We headed down towards Wildflower Byre, but Samantha's phone started ringing before we reached it.

'It's Fizz. Sorry, I need to get this.'

I wandered away to give her some privacy, but the call was short.

'Hedgehog emergency,' she said. 'I'm needed back at the barn. You're welcome to keep exploring. The byre's open and if you follow the track to the left, you'll reach Crafty Hollow – the former stables where my cousin Chloe and Josh's Auntie Lauren run craft workshops. They'll have finished for the day, so it'll be locked up, but it's a beautiful building and worth looking at. Do you need anything other than this?'

She passed me the key to the cottage.

'I'm good, thanks. You have a stunning place here. I've never seen anything quite like it.'

'You should have seen it before. Completely dilapidated. I inherited it nearly four and a half years ago and there's a lot of work and a lot of love gone into creating what you see now.'

I could hear the pride in Samantha's voice and see it shining from her eyes, and rightly so.

'If you need anything, you've got my mobile number or pop over to the barn or farmhouse. Enjoy your wander.'

With a smile and a wave, she power-walked back up the hill towards the rescue centre and I continued down to Wildflower Byre. My mind was buzzing with ideas for my rescue centre series. If Samantha was willing to feature Hedgehog Hollow, there was so much about this place that I could explore. I was dying to know more of the story behind the rescue centre and how the different businesses supported it.

Birds chirped in the nearby trees, their song accompanied by crickets in the long grass. A cabbage white butterfly fluttered past me and a dragonfly flew in the opposite direction. What a haven for nature this place was. With all this beauty on my doorstep, I suspected I'd barely spend any time inside Meadow View.

I continued on the track past Wildflower Byre, intending to look inside on my way back. My phone buzzed with a WhatsApp message from Zara.

FROM ZARA

Let me know when you arrive. Just been exploring their Facebook page and I think you're going to move in and never want to leave! 😊

TO ZARA

Set off early so already here and having a wander. You found a gem. I love it!

FROM ZARA

Yay! Already excited for filming. Have double confirmed your meeting with Farmer Hottie at 10 tomorrow. Give me a call afterwards. Need to know if he's as cute in real life

She included a heart and a crying with laughter emoji, making me smile. She'd assigned affectionate nicknames to all twelve farmers and, although she had no problem remaining professional and referring to them by their proper names in all correspondence and face to face, I was terrified of making a slip-up. I'd already typed 'Farmer Hottie' into an email twice, but had thankfully spotted my error before sending it.

I clicked into my emails and brought up the photos of Barney

Kinsella. Was he a 'hottie'? I had to concede that he was probably the best looking of the men with his messy wavy dark hair and a cheeky smile, but I wasn't fooled by looks. I'd learned the hard way with Parker that appearance was superficial and it was 100 per cent about personality and aligned thinking. It turned out that Parker and I weren't just not on the same page – we weren't even in the same library.

Were Dan and I on the same page? I honestly didn't know. Four months into a relationship, most couples our age would have started to explore the future, but most couples would have spent more time together in a fortnight than we'd spent together in those four months. We'd agreed to take it slowly, but was there such a thing as too slow? I thought about Matt and Angelique and their family. The first time Dan and I had dated, we'd both been too young and career-focused to have those sorts of conversations. Would I be jumping the gun to initiate the having a family discussion now?

13

BARNEY

I felt my mobile ringing in my pocket as I rode the quad bike back to the barn on Monday morning. I suspected it would be Zara from *Love on the Farm* ringing about my meeting later this morning, confirming the arrangements for what felt like the tenth time. If it was her, she'd ring back or leave a message.

I parked in the barn and Harley and Bear jumped down when I cut the engine. My phone rang again but it wasn't Zara, it was Joel, and a wave of nerves swept over me. Joel *never* rang me when he was at work and today was his big interview. Maybe he wanted some last-minute reassurance before he went in.

'All right, mate?' I asked, connecting the call.

He didn't even say 'hello'.

'I've got my interview in ten minutes and my mind's gone blank. I can't remember anything I prepared, and I've stupidly left my notes at home.'

He was normally really calm, but I could hear the panic in his voice, which wasn't surprising. This was about more than securing a promotion.

'You don't need your notes. You've done stacks of prep and it's all in there. It'll come back to you when you need it.'

'What if it doesn't?'

'Then you wing it. Get yourself some fresh air and try to relax. You've got this, Joel. You'll be fine.'

I checked my watch after the call ended with Joel sounding much calmer. It was 9.45 a.m. and the TV producer was due in fifteen minutes, so I'd best stick around the farmyard in case she was early. I'd told Milo that she was coming. He wasn't good around strangers, so I'd wanted to warn him, but I swear it had gone in one ear and out the other. I unclipped my walkie-talkie and called for Milo.

'Quick reminder that the producer from that TV show is due here at ten,' I said when he answered. 'She'll be wanting a tour.'

'From me?' There was panic in his voice, and I could imagine the look of shock on his face. There was a reason Milo worked with animals. His social skills were shocking and he often proclaimed how much he hated people, which seemed pretty sad for someone in their mid-twenties. The upside of that was that he worked hard, was good at his job, and was reliable.

'No. I'll be the tour guide. I was just giving you a heads-up in case you wondered who I was with.'

I waited for a response – *fine, okay, thanks* – but none came.

'Good conversation, as always,' I muttered.

A courier van pulled into the farmyard so I rested the walkie-talkie on the quad bike seat and the dogs followed me as I retrieved a parcel.

'Go to the garage and stay,' I instructed Bear and Harley, pointing across the farmyard. 'I'll be back soon.'

They trotted across the yard and I took the parcel into the farmhouse. Nerves about my meeting escalated with each step and my palms were sweating so much that my hand slipped off the door handle and I had to wipe it down my boilersuit before I could open the door. Why was I so nervous? It wasn't like I was in front of the cameras today. This was a meeting with the show's producer who'd ask a few questions, give me some information, and have a tour of the farm. There was nothing difficult or nerve-racking about any of that, but the swirling in my gut suggested otherwise.

I took the parcel through to the snug which I used as an office. I hadn't ordered anything, so I ripped open the box, intrigued. There was a smaller box inside with a gift note stuck to the top. I put my glasses on to read it:

Congratulations on being chosen!
We're rooting for you to find your one.
Massive hugs and best wishes
Fizz, Phoebe & Darcie xxx

I opened the smaller box and lifted out a mug with a Mr Farmer figure on it from the *Mr Men* range, wearing a boilersuit, wellies and holding a pitchfork. I lifted out a second mug and laughed at the Mrs Farmer illustration. What were they like?

I placed both mugs on my desk, smiling. Why was I nervous about *Love on the Farm*? Because it mattered. This could be my chance to get what I longed for. Finally.

14

AMBER

I woke up in my bedroom at Meadow View early on Monday morning and, despite it being one of the nicest holiday cottages I'd ever stayed in and one of the loveliest settings too, I felt tense and tearful.

It happened on this day every year – the anniversary of my engagement to Parker five years ago and what would have been my wedding day a year later. I'd really hoped it wouldn't get to me this year, especially now that I was back with Dan, but the swirling emotions were just as strong as they'd always been.

Casting the duvet aside, I pulled on some clothes, made a mug of coffee and took it over to the meadow to watch the sun rising. We were in the golden hour – that time just after sunrise or just before sunset where the light is warm and gentle and there's a magical feel about it. I stepped up onto the wedding gazebo, breathing in the freshness of the new morning. It really was beautiful here.

I rested my arms on the back railings, taking slow deep breaths, trying to push Parker from my thoughts. It wasn't that I still loved him – my feelings towards Parker were quite the opposite. It was the anger and disbelief that I'd allowed myself to be dazzled by his looks, charm, confidence, status and had rushed headlong into an engagement with a man so completely unsuitable for me in every possible way. Of course, I'd thought he was perfect at the time. So perfect that I'd ignored the many red flags.

Stop thinking about him!

Glancing down, I noticed there was a pair of hedgehogs and a garland of flowers and hearts carved into the wood.

'So cute,' I whispered, lightly running my fingers across the artwork.

I took a photo to send to Zara at a reasonable hour then rested on the railings once more, looking out over the meadow. It had brightened enough for me to see the stunning mix of white, yellow, pink, purple and blue flowers and the occasional splash of red among the grasses. I recognised all the varieties and was so impressed with the diversity. It was a little early and a bit cool for butterflies, but I imagined there'd be a stack of butterflies and bees a little later.

I could easily have stayed there all day but there was work to be done, so I reluctantly tore myself away and returned to Meadow View to boil a couple of eggs for breakfast to eat with the loaf which had been baking in a bread maker when I arrived yesterday, making the cottage smell divine. There'd been a great selection of locally made supplies left for me including cheese, eggs and milk in a bottle from a neighbouring farm, a small box of chocolates, and some home-baked treats. The cottage was beautifully decorated and comfortable, but it was the extra touches and attention to detail I appreciated like the food, the extra-large bath sheets instead of tiny bath towels and locally sourced soap and hand cream.

I ate my breakfast on the patio out the back. Before going to Bumblebee Barn, I wanted to go over Barney Kinsella's application form, photos and audition video once more. It was too lovely to do that indoors, so I took my plate inside, made another coffee and retrieved my laptop, notepad and EarPods.

The crew were excited about Barney's episode because the camera loved him. He came across as warm, funny and extremely natural on screen, which boded well for filming. Add in his good looks and I agreed that he'd be a viewer favourite. I looked forward to delving deeper and finding out more about what made him tick.

* * *

Mum often joked that I must have been a farmer in a previous life because the moment I set foot on a farm, I felt flooded with warmth and peace, as though I was where I was always meant to be. I loved everything about life on a farm and even the aspects some might find less appealing – early mornings, mud, working outdoors in all weathers – didn't bother me.

A couple of years back, Sophie asked me why I didn't become a farmer instead of spending my days filming other people on their farms, living out my dream existence. I'd responded, 'I get the best of both worlds doing what I do – experiencing farming without the financial worries or responsibilities.'

But that wasn't the truth. I'd filmed enough episodes of *Countryside Calendar* to know that farming was tough and especially so when tackled alone – something which filming *Love on the Farm* had already emphasised after only meeting two farmers. When the farmhands went home at the end of the day, the single farmer was on their own and it could be so lonely and isolating. Even though I was an introvert who was comfortable in my own company, I couldn't live like that.

When Sophie asked me the question, I'd been single and

unable to see myself meeting anyone in the future. Parker Knowles had destroyed my ability to trust, and I didn't think I'd ever be able to let someone in again. Then Dan had come back into my life. I already knew I could trust him, but Dan was a city boy at heart. He enjoyed an amble through the countryside and he loved a village pub, but could I see him settling down outside a city? Definitely not.

At that moment, I realised that we wanted different things, different lifestyles. Was there any way of finding a compromise between our two worlds?

* * *

As I approached Bumblebee Barn later that morning, I slowed down and smiled at the large white sign showing an illustration of a round bee pollinating a stem of lavender. I'd have to ask Barney where the farm name came from as, in the information Zara had pulled together, I couldn't see any obvious connections to bees of any variety.

In the farmyard, I parked where I wouldn't be blocking any of the barns. Two Border Collies ran over to me, tails wagging, and I bent down beside them and let them sniff my hands before giving them a stroke.

'You must be Bear and Harley,' I said, remembering their names from Barney's video. 'Where's your owner?'

A few hens pecked across the farmyard, but I couldn't see any humans. There was a pretty whitewashed farmhouse in front of me with dormer windows set into a red tiled roof and various barns and outbuildings surrounding the farmyard.

'Hello?' I called.

Silence.

I shouted a bit louder but there was still no response, so I pulled on my wellies and headed over to the barn from which the dogs had emerged. There were a couple of quad bikes parked beside a tractor, but no sign of human life. I glanced down at my phone. I was a smidge early, so it was possible Barney was working in the fields and would come and find me at ten.

A tall, slim dark-haired man strode into the farmyard, head down, shoulders slumped, hands in the pockets of his navy-blue boilersuit. He definitely wasn't Barney, but I approached him anyway.

'Hi there,' I said. 'I'm looking for Barney Kinsella.'

He kicked at a pebble and kept his eyes down. 'Should be round here somewhere.'

'I've got a meeting with him at ten. My name's Amber Crawford.'

When he didn't respond, I asked, 'Do you think you could find him for me?'

He sighed as he unhooked a walkie-talkie. 'Barney. Your visitor's here.'

There was no response.

'Barney! Visitor!'

I could hear an echo of his words from across the farmyard. With a shrug, the man who was maybe in his mid-twenties – although it was hard to tell with an unruly mop of dark hair covering half his face – headed towards the barn with the vehicles in it from where the echo had sounded.

'What's your name?' I asked, following him.

'Milo.'

'How long have you worked here?'

'Ten years.'

'Ten years? You don't look old enough.'

'Weekend job when I were fourteen.'

Milo had long legs that covered the ground at an alarming

pace and I had to run alongside him to keep up. He didn't strike me as a conversationalist, but I wasn't going to stand in the farmyard like a lemon when I had an opportunity to get to know more about the farm.

'Do you like working here, Milo?'

'Yep.'

'What's your favourite part of the job?'

'Animals.'

'And your least favourite?'

He finally looked at me with a pointed stare. 'Humans.'

Oh! That was me told!

He pointed to a walkie-talkie on the seat of a quad bike. 'Idiot.'

I wasn't sure whether he meant himself, Barney or me, and I wasn't going to ask.

'Hi! You must be Amber.'

I turned at the sound of a familiar, friendly voice to face the man from the video I'd watched so many times striding towards me, smiling widely. I knew from his application form that he was six foot four, but he somehow looked even taller than that in real life, with broader shoulders than I'd expected.

'Yes, Amber Crawford. Good to meet you, Barney.'

I held my hand out and he gave it a strong shake. The movement made his dark hair flop over his forehead and he swept it back from his face.

'Good to meet you too.'

'Your dogs are gorgeous,' I said as one of them pressed against my leg. 'Which one's which?'

'The one by your leg is Bear. He's bigger than Harley and has brown eyes. Harley's are grey. They're brother and sister and they're five. Their mum, Raven, used to work on the farm but she's enjoying retirement with my grandparents.'

'You left this on the bike.' Milo thrust the walkie-talkie into Barney's hand. 'Really helpful when your visitor was due.'

'I hadn't gone far,' Barney said, clipping it onto his pocket. 'I was only taking a parcel inside.'

With a shrug, Milo strode off across the car park. Barney turned to me with an apologetic smile. 'He's amazing with animals.'

I smiled back. 'Pleased to hear it. Should we get started?'

'Do you want a tour first or last?'

'Let's go inside and do the formal stuff and then you can give me a tour, if that works for you.'

'That's fine.'

I retrieved my bag from the front passenger footwell on the way. At the back of the house, Barney pushed open the nearest of two doors, the furthest being on what appeared to be an extension jutting out from the end.

'Make yourself comfortable at the table,' he said. 'I'm going in through the boot room.'

He closed the door behind me and headed down to the extension with the dogs. I looked round the kitchen and smiled appreciatively. One of the things I loved to do in any rare downtime was design my perfect farmhouse on Pinterest and Barney's kitchen was like my Pinterest board in real life. It was huge, running the full length of the house. The traditional elements – beams on the ceiling and a stone-flagged floor – complemented the modern log burner, cream units and an enormous cream fridge.

There was a wooden table with benches down the long sides and a chair at each end, so I perched on one of the benches. I could hear Barney talking to the dogs in the boot room at the end.

'Can I get you a drink?' he asked, stepping into the kitchen.

'Coffee would be great, thanks. White, no sugar.'

Bear and Harley slurped from a water bowl while Barney put the kettle on. I dug out my iPad and scanned down my questions.

'Hope that's not too strong,' he said, placing two mugs on the table. He sat down on the bench opposite me and the dogs settled at his feet with a chew each.

'It looks great. Thank you. So the purpose of today is to ask you a few questions and to explain more about the filming process. I know Zara has already gone through some details over the phone, but it can be a lot to take in first time round which is why I like to go through it again in person.'

'Okay.'

'I've read your application form and watched your video several times, but nothing beats hearing it from the horse's mouth, so my first question is this: what do you hope to get from the show?'

It was a subtle rephrasing of what the participants had already been asked – *why are you interested in appearing on* Love on the Farm? – but I found it a much better question for tapping into their true motivations and uncovering any red flags.

'I dunno. It's something different to do – never been on TV before. Should be a laugh.'

It was a fairly standard answer, but it disappointed me. I'd hoped there'd be a more significant motivation for him than just for the laughs.

I smiled politely. 'It's a unique opportunity and, yes, we hope to have some fun with the show. But my question was about what you're hoping to get out of it. You're putting yourself out there on national television in a search for love. What's your motivation behind that? What do you hope the outcome will be?'

'I guess it'd be great if you managed to find a match.'

I held his gaze. He had really dark brown eyes, warm like pools of chocolate. 'Why?'

There was a flicker of something in his eyes which I couldn't quite place. My first instinct was fear, but that made no sense. He lowered his eyes to his coffee.

'Erm... don't most people hope to find love?' He looked up and shrugged. 'I've not got a great track record. My sister reckons I'm attracted to a particular type who's never suited to farm life.'

'Do you think you have a type?'

'I didn't, but I was looking through my photos last week and I think she's right. I'll show you.'

He scrolled through his phone for a moment before holding it out to me. An attractive but heavily made-up woman with long blonde hair smiled at the camera.

'That's Olivia. She dumped me just before I applied for the show. It was the early mornings that killed that one.'

He scrolled again and, with each photo, came a farm-related reason for the relationship ending.

'Hope hated the smells, Jenna hated the dogs, Suzie hated all animals...'

'Okay, you can stop scrolling. And your sister was right. I don't know about personality but looks-wise, there's a definite type. You have a thing for blondes?'

That expression was there again for a fleeting moment before he shrugged. 'I guess so.'

I'd be meeting his matches this week, but I knew from their application photos and videos that only one of them, Tayla, was blonde and her style was a short choppy bob. Hopefully Barney wasn't as shallow as the carbon-copy girlfriends suggested and was attracted by more than physical appearance.

'I can't give anything away about your matches, as I'm sure you can appreciate but, hypothetically, how would you react if none of them were anything like your previous girlfriends?'

'I'd probably say we're probably wasting each other's time and how do I pull out of it?'

Barney laughed as he said it and I was fairly sure he was joking, but I felt another stab of disappointment. I really wanted him to be so much more than 'Farmer Hottie', but early indications weren't positive.

15

BARNEY

Across the kitchen table from me, Amber didn't look impressed and who could blame her? What a stupid, flippant thing to say. Fizz had warned me about using humour as a defence mechanism when I was nervous, but I could never seem to help myself.

'I'm kidding,' I said, flashing Amber my most charming smile. I remembered the conversation I'd had with Fizz the night she'd convinced me to apply and decided to call on her wisdom instead of my stupidity. 'They say the definition of insanity is doing the same thing and expecting a different result. Clearly my approach to dating hasn't been working. It's time to try something different.'

I cringed inwardly. It had sounded good coming from Fizz, but somehow sounded like a pile of insincere bollocks coming from me.

Amber stared at me for a moment, her brow furrowed. No doubt wondering what the hell she'd been landed with.

'I *do* want to meet someone,' I said, trying to recover things, 'and I'm hoping that, even if one of the three doesn't end up being the one, I'll learn something about myself and what I've been doing wrong so far. My ultimate goal is to get married and have children. I want someone to pass the farm down to. I want the happy ever after my parents and grandparents have.'

Amber grasped at a silver heart-shaped locket dangling from her neck and fiddled with the clasp, opening and closing it a couple of times. Her frown faded and she smiled instead, her fingers slipping from the necklace.

'We can't make any promises, but we'll do our best. If you answered the questionnaires fully and honestly, the matches should be good.'

I returned her smile, but my stomach did a loop-the-loop. Had I answered honestly? I'd tried to, but it hadn't been easy when I couldn't be honest with myself.

'I believe that Tiffany from the central team spoke to you about including friends and family in the show,' Amber said, thankfully changing the subject. 'Did you line up any willing volunteers?'

'Yes. Do they need to be confident and able to come across well on TV?'

'Ideally, but we recognise this is new to most people so we can give some pointers and do several takes.'

'I've got the ideal person and you've already met him.' I grinned at her. 'I was thinking Milo.'

Amber laughed at that, making her eyes sparkle and bringing pink tinges to her cheeks.

'I said pointers, not miracles. Please tell me you have other options.'

'Yes, I do. My best mate Joel has said yes and so have my parents, depending on their work commitments. And, because she's the one who convinced me to apply, I've asked my sister, Fizz.'

Her eyes widened. 'Your sister's called Fizz?'

'Yeah, I know, it's unusual. It's short for Felicity which she hates but not as much as I hate my real name – Barnaby. We have no idea what our parents were thinking.'

'I've met a Fizz this week,' she said, 'and I can't imagine there are two in the area. Does she work at Hedgehog Hollow?'

'She does! How do you know Hedgehog Hollow?'

'I'm staying in a holiday cottage there. Your sister's lovely. I haven't mentioned the show – we try to keep these things quiet – but you're welcome to tell her, or I will if I see her first.'

'Small world.'

Amber scribbled a couple of notes onto her iPad. 'So that's your parents, best friend and sister. Is that everyone?'

'I think so. I was hoping my granddad would say yes – the farm passed down from him to me – but he's not been well lately so it's a no from him.'

'It's not for everyone and it's great that you have four who've said yes.' She took a sip of her coffee, her eyes scanning down her screen before she looked up at me again. 'Do you mind me asking a question? Was there a reason why the farm passed from your granddad straight to you and skipped your parents' generation?'

'Mum's brother Melvin was poised to take over, but he went to America and now...' I winced and looked down into my coffee as a thought struck me. Would they still want me on the show if they knew what Melvin had done?

As though picking up on my anxiety, Bear placed his head in my lap and I stroked his fur, drawing comfort from the softness.

'Are you okay, Barney?' Amber's tone was soft with compassion and, when I looked up, I saw that matched in her expression. I couldn't tell her about what he'd done to Fizz, but I could tell her where he was.

'Melvin's no longer part of our family. He's in prison. So if you or your production company need to distance yourselves, I get that. It never entered my head before. There weren't any questions about it on the form.'

My voice cracked and I felt my eyes burning. Fearing I might actually break down in tears in front of Amber, I picked up my mug and poured the dregs down the sink. Even though I had a dishwasher, I washed it to allow time to compose myself before returning to her.

'Whatever your uncle did has obviously had repercussions on your family and I'm very sorry to hear that, but I'm not going to ask you any more about it, so please don't concern yourself. It's completely separate to your quest for love, but I do appreciate you giving me a heads-up. Believe me, Barney, if we ruled out every person who had a connection to someone undesirable, no TV programmes would ever get made.'

She smiled warmly and I felt reassured. The lump was still in my throat, so I swallowed hard. 'Was there anything else you wanted to ask me?'

'Nothing to do with the show, but I was wondering about the name of the farm. Bumblebee Barn is lovely and I wondered where it came from.'

The lump eased with the move onto a different topic of conversation.

'There's a story to it. It used to be called Middleditch Farm, but my great-grandfather officially changed it to Bumblebee Barn in the sixties as a tribute to his daughter. My great-grandparents had always wanted a big family but, after having my granddad, nothing happened. They'd accepted it was never going to and were stunned to discover my great-grandmother was expecting again when my granddad was fourteen. They had a girl – Jennifer – but she wasn't well, and they knew her life would be short. She died when she was only six.'

'Aw, that's so sad. What was wrong with her?'

'I honestly don't know. Granddad won't talk about it and Grandma met him a year after Jennifer died so she doesn't know any details either. All we know is why the farm name changed. Jennifer loved to sit in the garden and watch bees buzzing round the flowers. The summer before she died, Granddad found a bumblebee nest in one of the barns and he carried his sister there every day so she could see it. She christened the barn Bumblebee Barn and loved her visits to the nest so, on what would have been her seventh birthday, my great-grandfather surprised my great-grandmother by legally renaming the farm Bumblebee Barn in Jennifer's honour.'

Amber's eyes glistened and she played with the locket again. 'That's a heart-breaking story, but so lovely too.'

'He had a wooden sign made with a bee carved on it and it stayed up at the end of the farm track for decades, but I got the new one made a few years back for what would have been my Great-Aunt Jennifer's sixtieth birthday.'

'That's lovely too,' she said, her voice soft. 'Will you show me the barn when you give me the tour?'

'Sure. It was actually the barn I met you in earlier, but I can take you back in there and point out where the nest was.'

'Thank you. I'd like that.'

'Was there anything else you wanted to ask me?'

'I think I'm done for now, so I'll just run through some more details about filming, then we can have that tour.'

'Fire away.'

* * *

Sometime later, Amber packed up her iPad. I pulled on my boots and met her in the yard so I could show her the original Bumblebee Barn.

'I don't know what it was used for back then but it's my garage now – home to the quad bikes and tractor. The nest was in that far corner, although I've put shelving up there now.'

Amber looked to where I pointed, nodding slowly.

'Thanks for sharing Jennifer's story with me,' she said, her voice soft. 'It's really touched me.'

'You're welcome. You might like this too.'

I led her over to a thick wooden pillar in the middle of the barn.

'Is this the original sign?' she asked, running her fingers over the bumblebee carving.

'Yeah. I couldn't bring myself to get rid of it, so I cleaned it up and put it up in here where it belongs.'

Her gaze lifted to the framed photograph of a young girl sniffing some stems of lavender while a couple of bees buzzed round.

'That's Jennifer? She's beautiful.'

'That photo was the inspiration for the new sign.'

My walkie-talkie crackled and Milo's dulcet tones echoed round the barn. 'You're needed.'

'Okay. Where are you?'

'Top Field.'

'I'll be with you shortly. Do I need to bring anything?'

'No.'

'Anything I need to know?'

'No.'

I switched the walkie-talkie off and rolled my eyes at Amber. 'It's probably hard to imagine why I'd like to meet someone when Milo and I have such in-depth conversations.'

'Does he talk much about the animals?'

'Nope. He talks *to* the animals – but not to me about them. He's always been like that, so I'm used to it, and I couldn't imagine this place running as well as it does without him. He's a good lad. I was going to suggest we start the tour in Top Field anyway, so we'll go up there and see what he wants.'

Milo was extremely self-sufficient, so I did know that, whenever he called me, he genuinely needed help.

Bear and Harley jumped on the back of the quad bike and we set off to meet Milo, with Amber following behind in her 4x4. I couldn't quite work her out. She'd been so warm and friendly when we met but, when we'd been talking about my motivations for the show, I felt like I'd said the wrong thing – if there was a 'wrong' thing to say. She'd seemed distant, as though everything I said disappointed her. Or maybe she'd heard it all before and was weary of reality TV show contestants churning out the same old thing. But after I talked about Melvin, it was like a switch had been flicked back and I felt that warmth again, which grew stronger as I told Jennifer's story. Even if she hadn't shared that it had touched her, I could tell it had from the tears in her eyes and the way she kept playing with that locket round her neck.

I couldn't believe that I'd nearly cried in front of her when I mentioned Melvin. Where had that come from? I didn't do tears. When I found out what he'd done to Fizz, I'd been overcome with anger and guilt but, as those emotions eased, the tears hadn't come. So why had it affected me so strongly nearly eighteen months after we learned the truth?

Talking about the name of the farm had felt emotional too. Although it was sad that Great-Aunt Jennifer had died, I'd never felt upset by the story before. Could my reaction have been because of how it seemed to affect Amber? But why would it? I barely knew her, so there was no reason for her emotions to affect me so much. Must be just the nerves getting to me.

16

AMBER

Bumblebee Barn was set on a gentle slope, with Barney telling me that Top Field where we met Milo was one of the highest points. I didn't want to crowd Milo when he wasn't a people person, so I stayed by the gate while Barney took the quad bike across to find out what the problem was.

The view over the farm was stunning. Top Field itself and the one below it were full of grazing Swaledale sheep with their white fleeces and black and white faces, and the fields we'd ridden past were dotted with goats and pigs. I could see the farmhouse in the distance – T-shaped with a garden out the front – and various barns, stables and other outbuildings. The fields to the other side of the farmhouse were all crops and I recognised wheat – a carpet of pale gold – alongside spring barley and oilseed rape, the green stalks of the barley contrasting against the brilliant yellow of the rape.

To my left, I could see another farmhouse in the distance, so presumably that signalled the boundaries of Barney's land.

'Nothing to worry about,' Barney said, returning to me. 'Milo was concerned that one of the sheep might have a foot problem, so we'll keep an eye on that.'

'I've been admiring your view.'

He grinned at me. 'Not too shabby, eh?'

'I presume that's the end of your land by that other farm.' I pointed to the left.

'It used to be, but that's Whisperwood Farm, which my granddad bought. My grandparents keep it as a holiday let but I own the fields around it. I keep them arable to avoid animal noises and smells for the guests. There's another field behind us called Double Top Field which was part of Whisperwood and there's more sheep in there and, as you can see, we've got goats further down and three fields of pigs – Top Pig, Middle Pig and Bottom Pig.' He gave me a cheeky wink. 'It took hours of creative thought to come up with the field names. Fancy meeting the goats?'

* * *

A call came through as I drove back to Hedgehog Hollow, smiling contentedly from a lovely hour or so touring Bumblebee Barn.

'Hi, Zara,' I said, connecting via Bluetooth.

'Amber! I was expecting to leave a message on your voicemail. Have you finished at the farm?'

'Yes. Just on my way back now.'

'What was he like? Hottie in real life?'

I should have known that would be her first question. 'Still don't like the word *hottie*, but he *is* very good-looking in real life.'

'Yes! I knew it! And looks aside?'

'Erm, interesting.'

'Uh-oh, that's not good.'

'No, it is, I think. I thought he might be one of the lads, all about the jokes and banter. He showed me photos of his last four identical girlfriends and I was starting to think he was shallow, but now I think our farmer may have depths.'

'That *is* interesting. Depths in what way?'

'I'm not sure at the minute. There were a couple of things that came out which made me think he might be really sensitive. We'll see. Anyway, what were you going to chat to my voicemail about?'

'Just a small change of plan for tomorrow afternoon. Tayla Kenzie rang and asked if it was possible to meet you an hour later at two instead of one. I didn't think it would be a problem, but wanted to check with you first.'

I was meeting two of Barney's matches tomorrow – Bree and Tayla – and the third, Claire, on Wednesday.

'It's probably a better time for me. Gives me more flexibility if my meeting with Bree runs over.'

'Great. I'll adjust your diary and confirm it back to her. I've got a video call in five minutes, so I'll call you later to find out more about Farmer Hottie.'

I shook my head, smiling as the call disconnected.

Although first impressions of Barney had been a bit hit and miss, I'd found myself really warming to him. He spoke with passion about the history of the farm and with modesty about the changes he'd implemented since taking over from his granddad. He had a great sense of humour, but it was also clear he was extremely serious and knowledgeable about farming, and I liked that combination a lot. I only hoped that Bree, Claire and Tayla did too.

By the time I returned to Hedgehog Hollow, I realised that my melancholy about today's anniversary had completely lifted. It was amazing how some time spent on a farm in good company could push those dark clouds away.

17

AMBER

On Thursday morning, I sat at the dining table in Meadow View with the paper profiles for Barney and his three potential matches – Bree, Claire and Tayla – fanned out in front of me. I chewed thoughtfully on my pen as I scanned down the notes I'd made on my iPad.

I'd enjoyed meeting with them over the past couple of days, but I wasn't convinced that any of them were quite right for Barney. It didn't seem as though the same care and attention had gone into these matches as it had with the Wales ones. Was that my fault? By changing the schedule, they'd had far less time to devote to the selection process.

A call came through from Zara.

'Grant Lennon's PA just rang me,' she said after we'd exchanged pleasantries. 'Grant and Liza want an urgent video call with you at noon today.'

Grant and Liza Lennon were the husband-and-wife team who ran Clementine Creates – the production company behind *Love on the Farm*.

'Urgent? Why? Should I be worried?'

'She didn't know the reason.'

If they both wanted to speak to me, it couldn't be good news. They'd been sent the rough edits of the Wales shoot at the start of the week, so presumably it was connected with that. My guess was that, despite us following their brief to the letter, it wasn't what they wanted.

'Is there anything I need to prepare?'

'No, but ring me afterwards.'

We said our goodbyes and I released a loud sigh. I could just about cope with Grant and Liza separately, but they were formidable as a partnership and the thought of a video call with them both was intimidating.

'No point speculating,' I muttered to myself, returning to the profiles.

A few minutes later, I pushed my chair back, shaking my head. I couldn't concentrate. The only logical reason for an urgent video call with both of them was that they wanted to pull the plug and the idea of that made me feel nauseous. Despite fighting not to be involved in this project, I'd grown to really like it and I wanted to see it through.

It was just past nine now and I was officially meant to be on a day's holiday, so I might as well stop fretting and focus on my research project. Samantha had said I'd be welcome over at the rescue centre any time and this was my first opportunity to take her up on that offer.

I pulled on my trainers and headed over to the barn, avoiding the puddles. Last night, we'd had torrential rain, and today had dawned as dull and overcast with more rain expected around lunchtime.

Fizz was standing by the kettle, dropping teabags into a couple of mugs. 'Amber! Perfect timing. Fancy a brew?'

'Yes please.'

I joined her and scanned the large selection of teas in the drawer, choosing a strawberry and elderflower one. As I handed it to Fizz, the door opened and Samantha came in, pushing a double buggy.

'Amber! Great to see you.'

'Are these your two?' I asked, crouching down beside the buggy.

'Yes, this is Thomas and Lyra. Officially I'm still on maternity leave with Lyra until after the half-term holiday, but—'

'She can't stay away from the place,' Fizz interrupted, obvious affection in her voice.

Fizz handed me my mug and picked up hers and Samantha's. I followed them over to the other side of the barn, where there were a pair of sofas either side of a coffee table. Samantha pulled out a large play pen, added some toys, then lifted Thomas into it. In the meantime, Fizz laid a play mat beside the pen and laid Lyra on her back under a baby gym.

'They're both gorgeous,' I said, gazing admiringly at Thomas's thick dark hair and Lyra's slightly lighter brown hair, curling at the ends. 'And those outfits are adorable.'

Thomas was wearing cute fox dungarees and Lyra sported a pinafore dress with an embroidered hedgehog on the bib.

'They have a lot of outfits with animals on,' Samantha said, picking up her mug and settling onto the sofa opposite me. 'Especially hedgehogs. But so do I.'

'Me too,' Fizz said. 'And unicorns. They're my number one love, although we've yet to rescue one.' She winked at me. 'So how are you enjoying your stay?'

'I love this place. I'm so glad I'm coming back and staying for a whole month, although you might struggle to get rid of me after that.'

'You have a friend staying with you then?' Samantha asked.

'Yes, my assistant Zara will be here for some of the time.'

'Barney told us who you are,' Fizz said, beaming at me. 'I can't believe you're a TV producer. That's awesome!'

'Must be a fascinating job,' Samantha added.

'It is. I'm lucky to do what I do.'

'What did you think of my brother?' Fizz asked. 'Have you met his matches? Do you think it'll work for him? Sorry! That's a lot of questions, but I'm so excited about it.'

I smiled at her. 'Your brother's great and I love the farm. Yes, I've met his matches, but I can't give anything away. As for it working, there's a rigorous selection process but that can only go so far. Who knows what will happen when they meet?'

'I hope it works out for him,' Fizz said. 'He's so lovely and caring and he deserves to find someone special. I know I'm biased, but you agree, don't you, Sam?'

'All the way. Barney's amazing. He's kind, considerate, great fun, passionate about what he does and extremely knowledgeable. He'd make someone a great husband one day.'

Fizz nodded enthusiastically. I'd told Zara on Monday that I thought Barney might have depths and here were two women who knew him really well confirming it. Yes, Fizz was potentially biased, but Samantha clearly thought the world of him too.

'Then let's hope we've done our job and we find love for him,' I said. 'While the drinks are cooling, could I bother you for a tour of the rescue centre?'

Fizz jumped up. 'Tour guide at your service. We've got two floors, but most of what we do is on the ground floor. We started off only rescuing hedgehogs but our good friend Terry, who's sadly no longer with us, brought in a fox cub a couple of years back and that triggered conversations about expanding. So we did. Last year, we added in another couple of treatment tables and expanded the resting space where we were just sitting to accommodate more volunteers...'

I could happily have stayed all day but had to return to Meadow View for my video call with Grant and Liza, so I reluctantly said goodbye ten minutes before it. I'd loved looking around and hearing the history of how Samantha had inherited Hedgehog Hollow after saving the owner's life as well as the story of how Fizz had become involved. They'd be perfect to include in my documentary, but I wanted more time to develop my proposal before I sounded them out about it.

* * *

'Good afternoon, Amber!' Grant's booming voice filled the lounge, and I turned down the volume on my laptop.

'Hi, Grant and Liza, how are you?' They were both connected to the call independently, although they were likely in the same building, probably even in offices next door to each other.

'We're fine, but we have a serious problem,' Liza answered.

My stomach sank.

'Before we get onto that,' Grant said, 'how's this Yorkshire farmer? What's his name?' He shuffled some papers on his desk. 'Oh, yes! Barney. You've met him this week?'

'Yes. We met on Monday.'

'And what did you find out about him? Anything that's not on his application form or video?'

I wasn't sure what Grant's angle was and I felt strangely protective towards Barney. 'Not really. He seemed friendly and genuine. His farm's gorgeous. He's got a lovely family. His sister works at the rescue centre where I'm staying.'

'It was his sister who talked him into applying, yes?' Liza asked. 'Why was that?'

'Fizz was concerned about him having a type – completely unsuitable for farming – and she wanted him to break the mould and try something different.'

Liza tapped her pen against her lips thoughtfully. 'Interesting. Well, we've watched the first episode of *Love on the Farm* and it's—'

'Absolutely shite,' Grant finished for her.

My stomach sank even further.

'Not the word I was going to use,' Liza said, 'but it's no good.'

'What is it that concerns you?' I asked, trying to keep the frustration out of my tone. I wanted to add that we'd followed the brief exactly, but I'd sound defensive if I said that. Best to leave it as an open question.

'It's far too tame,' Grant said, disgust in his tone. 'Viewers are going to hate it.'

I disagreed, but getting into an argument with someone of Grant's influence was potentially career-limiting and I wasn't that foolish.

'I'll put my hands up to this one,' Liza said, raising her hands on the screen. 'This was my baby. I wanted to rise to the challenge around reality shows being deceptive and staged and show the nation something a bit gentler, but we think we've gone too far the other way. This is more like an episode of *Countryside Calendar* with dating.'

She actually curled her lip up as she said *Countryside Calendar* and it was obvious to me that she was a TV snob about the value of family-friendly shows like that. I liked to keep the peace, but I couldn't let her disdain of my beloved programme slide.

'I thought the reason you wanted me to produce *Love on the Farm* was because I produce *Countryside Calendar*.' I paused to let that sink in and was sure I detected a flush creeping up Liza's neck. 'From the brief, I understood that you wanted me to bring that family-friendly appeal, so it was effectively *Countryside Calendar* with dating that you were after.'

'Yes, yes, but we've changed our minds,' Grant said. 'We thought about axing it, but Liza's convinced there's still mileage in it so we're sticking with it but taking it in a different direction. We need more drama and grit.'

'We need *Tropical Heat* on a farm,' Liza declared.

Urgh! *Tropical Heat* was Clementine Creates' longest running and most successful reality TV show, where beautiful people living on a Caribbean island for six weeks would fight elimination by coupling up. It represented everything I detested about reality television – forced tension, contestants deliberately pitted against each other and manipulated editing – but it was a ratings winner among the age sixteen-to-thirty-four demographic; a demographic at whom we weren't meant to be aiming *Love on the Farm*.

'What would *Tropical Heat* on a farm look like for you?' I asked, dreading the answer. 'We can't introduce challenges. The contestant details specifically stated there'd be nothing like that.'

'And our legal team say we're bound by that.' The tut Grant added suggested he wasn't impressed with the outcome of that conversation. 'But we can still shake it up and the way to do that is the matches. We want some conflict in there.'

'You mentioned that Barney goes for the same type of woman and they're not suited to farming,' Liza said. 'That's what we want.'

'But that would go against the profiling.'

Liza shook her head. 'Not if there's at least one match done through the profiling route. The others will be there to add some flavour. Some spice.'

My head was spinning. 'Are you saying you're not going to use the women I've already met?'

Liza shook her head once more. 'We'll use one of them. Have a think about who has the most chance of winning young Barney's heart and let Tiffany know by the end of today. We'll select a couple of wildcards. What does Barney's type look like?'

I didn't want to respond, but didn't feel I had much choice. They wouldn't accept a vague answer.

'Tall, great figure, long blonde hair, lots of make-up. But I—'

'We'll be in touch with details of the replacements,' Grant said. Then they were both gone and I was left staring at a blank screen, struggling to process what had just happened.

I closed my laptop, propped my elbows on the table, and rested my head in my hands. What had I got myself into?

I have no idea how long I sat there, my head spinning, but my mobile phone ringing made me jump. I assumed it would be Zara, eager for an update, but Matt Hambleton's name flashed up. I'd never thought to ask Grant and Liza whether Matt already knew their plans and what he thought of them, although they had cut the video call before I could form any questions.

'Hi, Matt,' I said. 'I take it you've heard?'

'Yeah, and you sound as enamoured by the idea as I am.'

I sighed. 'I think they're making a huge mistake.'

'Me too, and they weren't impressed when I said so. They told me I didn't have to stay on the project if I wasn't bought into it.'

'Don't tell me you've walked.'

'No, but I can't guarantee I won't. What about you?'

'Still on the team too, but I don't believe in it anymore. They told me they wanted *Tropical Heat* on a farm.'

'I thought the whole point of this was to showcase a non-manipulated side to reality TV.'

'It was, but it appears that Grant and Liza are all about the manipulation. I can't believe we're only going to use one of Barney's proper matches and they're going to pick two unsuitable ones. It's not what any of us signed up to. Did they say anything about re-shooting the Wales episode? I didn't get a chance to ask.'

'They're going to decide by the end of the week whether to re-shoot or ditch it and make five episodes instead of six. It's so wrong.'

'It's a mess, but at least you're going to stick around.'

'For now. I'm not happy about it, but I'm a team player and I don't want to leave anyone in the lurch so I'll see it through as long as they don't throw any more curveballs at us. As least we share the same thoughts on it and can sound off to each other.'

'Let me know if you hear anything else, Matt. We'll get through it together.'

'Same here. Enjoy the rest of your week.'

'That might be difficult after this bombshell, but I'll try.'

After ending the call, I knew it was only fair to let Zara know, but I clicked into my emails first to see whether anything had come through from Clementine Creates. There was one email and I ground my teeth as I read through it. It pretty much clarified what they'd already told me, but it was the line across the top in bright red capitals that annoyed me the most:

YOU MUST NOT REVEAL ANY OF THIS INFORMATION TO PARTICI-PANTS. TO DO SO WILL BE A BREACH OF CONTRACT AND THERE WILL BE FINANCIAL REPERCUSSIONS.

I closed my laptop, grabbed my phone and pulled on my jacket. I needed some air, but I'd spotted a few drops of rain on the lounge windowpane.

It was spitting outside so I speed-walked over to the wedding gazebo. A few deep calming breaths while looking out over the meadow further calmed me enough to call Zara.

'I'm not surprised you and Matt are so peed off,' she said, after I'd filled her in. 'It all seems so dishonest.'

'It is and I don't feel comfortable about it at all.'

'Do you know which of the matches you're going to recommend?'

'No. I'm not convinced there's a frontrunner among them. If I'd known I was going to have to whittle them down, I'd have asked all of them – Barney included – way more questions.'

'You can't feasibly see the matches again, but could you go back to the farm under the pretence of needing to ask Barney a few more questions? I can set up another meeting if you like.'

I pondered on it. It was tempting, but it carried risks, especially after the warning in the email.

'Better not. If I did and the Lennons somehow got wind of it, they'd think I'd warned him and, the way I'm feeling about it, I'm not sure I'd be able to help myself.'

'Good point. You said his sister knows who you are now and that she's really close to Barney. Could you quiz her?'

'Zara! That's genius. I'll catch you later.'

18

AMBER

As I crossed the farmyard, Fizz emerged from the rescue centre with a pet carrier in one hand and a plastic crate tucked under her arm.

'Are you on your way out?' I asked, joining her as she loaded the items into her Mini.

'Hedgehog rescue. We've just had a call from a building site. They've found a hedgehog in some foundations and, every time they try to reach for it, it disappears into a pipe.'

'Aw, bless it. Hope it's okay. Do you mind if I pop over when you get back? I'd love to ask you a few questions about your brother.'

'You can come and help me if you like and ask me on the way.'

'Really? Oh, wow. That would be amazing. Thank you.'

'Hop in.'

I got into the passenger side, excitement bubbling in my stomach at the thought of helping with a hedgehog rescue. Fizz closed the boot and got in beside me.

'The building site is on the outskirts of Reddfield, so it'll take us about twenty minutes to get there.'

She turned the car round and we set off down the farm track.

'So what do you want to know about Barney?'

'Barney says you think he has a type. He showed me photos of his last few girlfriends and I have to agree.'

Fizz laughed. 'They look like they've come off a production line, don't they? I jokingly call them Barney's Barbies. Don't get me wrong, they're all stunning, but I don't get it. Barney isn't into superficial stuff like looks, yet he keeps picking the same sort of girlfriend. I know you can't tell me anything about the matches, but I'm hoping they're nothing like his exes.'

My cheeks flushed and I turned to look out the window at the passing countryside. They hadn't been, but it was very likely they would be now, and it was my fault for revealing that detail to Grant and Liza.

'If it was up to you to make a match for your brother, what sort of woman would you pick?'

'Ooh, great question! Looks wouldn't enter into it and, on that note, the issue I have with Barney's ex-girlfriends isn't about their looks – it's about their suitability. His ideal woman may well look exactly like one of them, but her personality would need to be different. She'd love the outdoors and be passionate about the countryside, happy to be out and about whatever the weather. She'd love animals but would understand that the sheep and pigs aren't pets so she probably wouldn't be a vegetarian or vegan. She'd get that farming is about early starts, long hours, hard work, smells, mud, and financial pressures.'

She glanced at me, smiling. 'That's a pretty big list so far.'

I smiled back. 'I don't think any of it is unreasonable. Keep going.'

'She doesn't have to give up her job, friends or interests, but I'd hope she'd be a partner for Barney, willing to help out and ease the burden on him, which might mean some compromises at certain times of year. An optimist would be good, but balanced with realism. Is that a contradiction? Ooh, and Barney's really into innovation and the environment so it would be good if she is too, even if she has different views. A bit of healthy debate never hurt anyone. But the absolute most important thing is that she needs to love my brother for who he is and not try to change him because I think he's pretty damn perfect.'

Her voice cracked and she took a deep breath. 'Sorry. Getting all emotional there. He's such an amazing brother and I can't bear the thought of him being lonely.'

Her words hit me like a punch in the stomach and I instinctively reached for my locket. 'Barney's lonely?'

Fizz took a sharp intake of breath. 'He told me that in confidence. You won't let on, will you?'

'I won't breathe a word.'

'Thank you. It breaks my heart thinking of him all alone at the farm. He deserves to find someone special. I really hope this works for him.'

'I'll do my best for your brother,' I said gently, while guilt washed over me at how unlikely that now seemed. 'Sounds like he deserves a break.'

'He deserves the world. He's not just my big brother, he's my friend too. He's been there for me through some really tough times. I know you can't work miracles and the odds of meeting Miss Right on a TV show must be phenomenally high, but it's worth a shot, right?'

She glanced at me and the tears shining in her eyes were so moving, I wished I could hug her and reassure her it would work. Truth was, the likelihood of it working with three matches was already remote and now I was only permitted to choose one of those three. The pressure was on to make it the right one.

* * *

We arrived at the building site and I'd anticipated a hubbub of activity, but there was only one man in a hi-vis vest and hardhat standing by the site entrance. Fizz wound her window down.

'Are you the hedgehog rescuer?' the man asked.

'Yes. I'm Fizz and this is Amber.'

'I'm Barry, the foreman. The site's been closed for the past fortnight, but I dropped by earlier to make sure the rain last night hadn't done any damage and that's when I spotted the hedgehog. I tried to get it out, but it kept retreating and I didn't want to scare it or hurt it.'

He pushed open the metal gates and indicated we should drive through and park to one side while he locked them behind us.

'I'll grab you a couple of hardhats then show you where it is.'

'You might want to pull this on,' Fizz said, handing me a navy boilersuit. 'I keep several in the boot.'

When I'd pulled it on, she handed me the pet carrier, a child's fishing net and a couple of other poles which appeared to be homemade rescuing devices, and grabbed the crate herself.

We followed Barry into the site and, after a few minutes, stopped beside a deep trench. A piece of plastic pipe – roughly eight feet long – was lying in it with one end up against the corner. There were also planks of wood, smaller pipes and other pieces of debris in the trench.

'None of that stuff should be in there,' Barry said. 'It must have all got blown in or washed in by the rain. Every time I tried to get the hedgehog out, it ran back into that big pipe. I was going to try and lift the pipe out but I could hear squeaking. I think there might be more than one hedgehog in there.'

'It could be hoglets – baby hedgehogs,' Fizz said. 'We haven't had any admitted yet, but it's the right time of year for the first ones. There's probably a nest in the pipe.'

She lay down on the mud and eased her hardhat away from her ear.

'Amber, you might want to lie down and listen.'

I copied her and could hear the squeaking Barry had mentioned – a bit like a baby bird.

'We call that sound peeping and it's hungry hoglets calling for food. I reckon some of that debris created a ramp which is why the mum nested in the pipe, but the ramp collapsed in the bad weather, trapping her and stopping her from getting any food.'

Fizz changed position onto her knees, hands on her hips as she looked thoughtfully between the pipe and trench.

'My gut feeling is that a nest will be at the far end by the corner, so there's no point trying to go in at the open end. We need to ease the pipe away from the corner carefully and slowly to check.'

She looked from me to Barry and we both nodded our approval.

'Really slowly,' she emphasised as we took hold of the pipe. 'Go!'

The pipe wasn't particularly heavy, nor was it stuck, so it moved easily.

'They're not at this end,' Fizz said, sounding disappointed. 'I can't see all the way through either, so I suggest we lift the pipe out of the trench so we can at least see where they are but, Barry, keep a close eye on that end. Last thing we want is a hedgehog taking a flying leap out of there.'

Even though they both kept the end close to their bodies so there was no danger of any hedgehogs or hoglets slipping out, it didn't stop my heart from pounding as Barry lifted one end and Fizz the other.

Fizz lay flat on her stomach and peered into the pipe. 'There's a nest about a third of the way in and I think I see hoglets. Mum's curled up.'

Fizz didn't want to stick anything into the pipe in case she hurt one of the hoglets, but she hoped a gentle easing up of one end of the pipe would help it slip out. It took a few attempts but eventually the nest dislodged.

'Got them!' Fizz called, placing a mass of straw and leaves in the pet carrier. 'Can you count them, Amber, while I check the pipe?'

There were four tiny hoglets, but only three of them were moving.

'Four, but I think one's dead.'

'Okay. There's only Mum left in the pipe, which is good. I was worried there might be a hoglet out of the nest. I'll try to get Mum with the net.'

That worked first time round and Fizz added the hedgehog to the pet carrier.

'There's definitely nothing else in there,' Barry said as I closed the top of the carrier. 'That was impressive.'

'Teamwork!' Fizz gave us both fist bumps. 'Thanks so much for the call, Barry. You're quite literally a lifesaver. I need to transfer them into our travel incubator and get some fluids into them back at the car, so are you okay to stick around for a while?'

'Whatever's needed. My kids think my job's boring, but they're going to love hearing about this.'

We arrived back at Fizz's car and I watched in awe as she set up a mini workstation in the boot. She confirmed my suspicions that one of the hoglets had died and placed it in a tiny box. She weighed the others and their mum to ensure she measured out the right level of subcutaneous fluids to help rehydrate them.

At Fizz's invite, Barry took photos to show his children and, with the family warming in the incubator, we returned to Hedgehog Hollow.

'That was amazing,' I said. 'You were so quick.'

'Speed's essential for survival and I've been doing this for a few years now, so it's second nature to me. How do you feel? You've just helped save a hedgehog family.'

'I'm buzzing. That video call earlier didn't go well, and I was feeling pretty low, but that's just made my day.'

She smiled at me. 'I honestly can't think of anything more rewarding than working with animals. Every day's different and every day's special. I couldn't imagine ever wanting to do anything different.'

As we drew closer to Hedgehog Hollow, her words swam round my head. I absolutely loved my job and, like Fizz's, every day was different. The reward for me was spending time in the beautiful countryside seeing stunning views, meeting inspiring people and gorgeous animals. Could I see myself doing it forever? The job, definitely, but what about the lifestyle?

Back at Meadow View, I reflected on Fizz's comments about Barney feeling lonely and thought back to the expression on his face on Monday when I'd pushed him on why he wanted to meet someone. At the time, I'd thought I'd detected fear but had been unable to work out why. Perhaps it really had been fear – fear of confessing how lonely he really was? More than ever before, I wanted to find him love. I just wasn't convinced that it would happen on *Love on the Farm*.

That feeling of loneliness was a heavy relate for me. After what Parker did, it was the reason I packed my diary with back-to-back projects so that I'd be too busy working to focus on how lost and lonely I felt. It was why I encouraged Zara to join me on my travels as much as she wanted, even though it wasn't always necessary for her to be on site.

What I needed to work out now was whether I was keeping things going with Dan because I was falling in love with him and could see us getting married and having children, or whether having that connection with him helped ease the loneliness.

19

BARNEY

On Tuesday – the day after I met Amber – Joel sent me a message to say he hadn't got the production manager job. I was gutted for him. He'd been working nights, so we couldn't catch up immediately, but he was coming round to the farm this evening. I had an idea to help him let off steam and raise his spirits, and the recent heavy rain couldn't have been better timed.

'Barney Kinsella, you're an absolute legend.' Joel ran his hand along the side of my second quad bike – the one Milo sometimes used – his eyes shining with excitement. 'This is just what I need.'

'Get these on.'

I tossed him a spare pair of waterproof overalls and within five minutes, we were on the bikes and heading up the track towards The Quad. It was a large undulating piece of land by Top Field which had originally been part of Whisperwood Farm. I sometimes used it for grazing but preferred to keep it empty as it was my favourite area for off-roading on the quad bike. Several years ago, Joel and I had created some hills and a few obstacles and had often taken the bikes out, but life had got in the way and I couldn't remember the last time we'd had a ride for fun.

There was a swamp area at the bottom of The Quad which was brilliant to ride through if you didn't mind getting mucky, and this evening was going to be all about the mud.

We paused at the entrance to The Quad and I flicked the visor up on my helmet. 'Race you to the swamp?'

'You're on!'

I closed my visor and held up my gloved hand, counting off three on my fingers before we accelerated, both determined to be the first to the swamp. I couldn't see his face, but I knew Joel would be laughing. I couldn't change the interview outcome or the situation with Tilly, but I could take his mind off it temporarily.

Joel made it to the swamp first after I misjudged a jump and swerved. He rode through it at speed, water spraying out either side, and did a U-turn at the other side before riding back through. I did the same and we chased each other round The Quad, over hills, through puddles, round obstacles, before taking a rest at the top to catch our breath.

'I needed that,' Joel said, smoothing his hair back after he removed his helmet.

'I thought you might. I'm sorry about the job.'

'It was grim. Worst interview I've ever done. I kept having to ask them to repeat the questions and every answer I gave was a jumbled mess. It was always a long shot, but I'd prepared so hard and I let the nerves get to me.'

'Don't be so hard on yourself. There'll be other chances.'

'I hope so. What about you? How did Monday go?'

'Good, I think. The producer, Amber, was a bit hard to work out at first. I don't think she really liked me.'

'What makes you say that?'

I shrugged as I recalled my meeting. 'Just a sense that she was disappointed with some of my answers. I might have come across as a bit flippant and desperate for my fifteen minutes of fame. I think I brought her round. She liked the story behind the farm name and she loved the farm when I gave her the tour.'

'Be hard not to.'

We both looked down over the land. The Quad was one of the higher points of the farm so the views were amazing, even on a dull day like today. I was so lucky to have all of this. It was damn hard work, but I loved it.

'Are you nervous about the filming?' Joel asked.

'Not yet. Still doesn't feel real and probably won't until the cameras arrive.'

'Do you think it'll work?'

'No, but I'm going into it open-minded and hoping I'll be proved wrong.'

20

AMBER

I sat on the sofa and tucked into a mini quiche and salad later that evening, reflecting on the events of the day. What an honour it had been to join Fizz on that hedgehog rescue. Sticking with the superhero theme, they'd named the adult Diana after Wonder Woman. Superman had provided the inspiration for the hoglets, with two boys christened Clark and Kent and a girl named Lois. They were tiny and, even though they took the formula we fed them, Fizz had warned me that mortality rates were high at their age – likely eight to ten days because of their size and their eyes still being closed.

I was still buzzing from the rescue and praying that Clark, Kent and Lois would make it through the night. But there was something I needed to do right now which was going to kill my buzz.

With a sigh, I fanned out the profiles of our three matches once more. I couldn't delay it any longer. After what I'd learned from Fizz about Barney, I didn't want to mess this up, so I opened a Word document and created a table listing everything Fizz had said about the ideal match for her brother, awarding Bree, Claire and Tayla up to five points based on how strongly they met each criteria.

An hour later, I sank back on the sofa. Tayla Kenzie, the one with the blonde bob, had come out on top and my gut supported that. But my gut still told me that none of them were quite right for Barney. I scanned down the table once more, disappointed at the limited number of fives.

I moved the profiles of the women aside to reveal Barney's. On the first page, there was a posed photo of him on the quad bike with Bear and Harley, but the first image inside was a candid one, playing fetch with them. The sun was setting and the meadow was bathed in a warm orange glow. Bear was in the air and Barney was poised to throw the ball. His hair was messy, he hadn't shaved, and his smile was captivating. Butterflies unexpectedly stirred in my stomach.

'Stop it!' I reprimanded myself, closing the folder and covering it with the others. 'Tayla Kenzie it is. Let's get this email written.'

* * *

My week at Hedgehog Hollow was followed by an intensive six days of working on *Countryside Calendar* in Wales. Filming came to a close on Saturday evening and the producer and crew headed home. I was meeting Dan in Cheltenham tomorrow, so I was staying in the cottage tonight. Still licking her wounds from her break-up with Declan, Zara was in no rush to go anywhere, so she decided to keep me company and we booked into the local pub for a relaxing meal and bottle of wine.

'To another great week of filming,' I said, clinking my glass against Zara's. 'I can't believe there's only one week left here and then it's back to *Love on the Farm.*'

'How's the love for *Love on the Farm*?' she asked.

I rolled my eyes at her. 'Ask me again when we find out who's replacing Bree and Claire.'

'You really think they'll go for TV gold instead of good matches?'

'I'm sure of it and so's Matt. He's scarily close to walking out.'

Her eyes widened. 'Did he tell you that this morning?'

I'd had a video call with Matt before filming today.

'Yes. He's not happy. He's spoken to Grant a couple of times this week to try to get him to change his mind about the matches and about ditching the Wales episode but there's no budging. Matt said there was steam coming out of his ears each time the call ended.'

'I really like Matt. I hope he doesn't leave.'

'Me too.'

'Have they chosen the replacements?'

'Matt says they've narrowed it down to five.'

'Can't you make the final decision? You're the only one who's met Farmer Hottie.'

That name still made me smile. 'Matt suggested that to Grant, but it's a no because that would introduce a bias that hasn't been there with any of the others.'

'And because you'd pick the ones who actually have potential instead of the ones best for car-crash TV.'

I sighed as I nodded. 'Exactly.'

'That's so bad.' She took a glug on her wine. 'Anyway, cheerier subject, what have you got planned with Dan tomorrow?'

'I'm not sure. I've filmed around Cheltenham, but have never been into the town itself.'

Tomorrow would signify a whopping six weeks since I'd last seen Dan, although being so busy with work had meant it hadn't felt nearly that long. Cheltenham had been chosen for being roughly halfway between us both and I'd originally made a two-night booking. Disappointingly, Dan had to return to London first thing on Monday for a family birthday, so I'd changed it to one night only.

'Do you think it'll be weird seeing him after so long apart?' Zara asked.

'Nah! It's Dan. We'll be fine.' But as I said the words, butterflies rose in my stomach. Six weeks apart *was* a long time, and many couples wouldn't have survived it. Would we find the weekend a strain?

'You must have missed him so much.'

The butterflies intensified. Had I?

* * *

The following morning, as I drove towards Cheltenham, I couldn't stop thinking about last night's conversation with Zara. The truth was I hadn't really missed Dan and I was grappling with why. Was it because I'd been so busy with work that there'd been no time to miss him? Was it because I was used to us being apart this time around and I'd accepted it was how our relationship worked? Or was it because I didn't care enough? And if it was the latter, why were we together?

By the time I reached the outskirts of Cheltenham, I hadn't resolved anything, but I had decided to throw myself into the weekend, which could well turn out to be a make or break one.

Dan was travelling by train and I'd timed my journey to arrive at Cheltenham Spa train station to pick him up just after half eleven. I pulled into a parking space ten minutes before his train was due in and checked my phone. There were no messages telling me he'd set off or made his connection and I felt a flicker of panic. What if he was about to do a Declan on me and, like Zara, I was going to spend a romantic weekend for two all on my own?

'Dan's not like that,' I said out loud, hoping it would convince me, but I felt a little nauseous as I entered the train station and checked the information board. Dan's train was running on time. But was he on it?

The train pulled into the station and I watched anxiously for any sign of Dan moving towards the door, but the figures were too much of a blur as the carriages passed. I stood back, heart thumping, as the doors opened and travellers filed out onto the platform and others boarded the train. No Dan. My stomach sank. Either he'd missed his train, or I'd been stood up.

Train staff had closed the doors and the train was readying to depart. With a sigh, I took my phone out to ring Dan when one of the doors burst open and there he was. He hitched his backpack onto his shoulder and glanced down the platform, breaking into a run when he spotted me.

'I nearly missed my stop!'

Before I could ask how, he gathered me into his arms and drew me into a passionate kiss which took my breath away.

'It's been a long six weeks waiting to do that,' he said, drawing back and drinking me in. 'You look amazing.'

'I thought you'd stood me up.'

'Never! I fell asleep. It was only when someone nudged me telling me I was in their reserved seat that I realised we'd arrived.'

He kissed me again and my earlier worries drifted away. It was going to be fine. We were going to be fine.

21

BARNEY

It was the last Sunday in May, meaning a full family gathering for lunch at the farm, but there'd been a slight change of plan this month. Grandma had phoned last night to say that Granddad hadn't had a great week and wasn't up to venturing out, so was there any chance we could dine at theirs instead.

I'd been to their bungalow twice since the awkward incident where he'd refused to be filmed and had wanted me to leave. There'd been tension both times. I'd mentioned the show – to fill them in on what I was doing rather than to try to talk Granddad into filming – but he'd walked off the first time and had closed down the discussion the second time. I didn't think that was very fair to me, nor was it fair that Grandma had felt the need to apologise for his behaviour, so I was a little apprehensive about today. I wasn't going to raise the subject, but filming for *Love on the Farm* would start a week tomorrow, so it was inevitable that somebody would.

That 'somebody' was Fizz. 'I can't believe filming starts in just over a week,' she gushed as soon as we started eating. 'Just think, next time we sit down for Sunday lunch together, you might have found Miss Right.'

'You're still going ahead with that nonsense?' Granddad asked, his voice gruff.

I felt all eyes on me and was grateful I'd just picked up the gravy boat. Pouring gravy and passing it on would give me time to compose a response other than the one that had popped into my head: *Why do you have such a problem with this? I know you don't want to go on video and I accepted that first time. Get over it!*

I cleared my throat as I passed the gravy boat to Dad. 'I'm sorry you feel it's nonsense, Granddad. You were so lucky that you met Grandma before you took over the farm. I haven't been that lucky, so I'm trying something different.'

'But a TV show? You surely can't think that will work.'

'Maybe it will and maybe it won't, but I'll never know if I don't give it a try. Nothing else is working.'

My voice cracked on the last sentence and my eyes burned. I put my head down and busied myself cutting up my beef, hoping I wasn't about to cry in front of my whole family.

'I think it's a brilliant idea,' Mum declared brightly. 'I'm really proud of Barney for putting himself out there like this. The dating world these days is so different from what it was in your time, Dad. Give this a chance.'

'But I just don't see how anyone's going to meet their future wife on a television programme.'

'Then I suggest you keep your opinions to yourself, Frank,' Grandma said, giving Granddad a pointed look despite her soft tone. 'Don't fall out over this. Barney knows what he's doing.'

Granddad rolled his eyes, but he didn't respond. An awkward silence settled round the table, each scrape of a knife or fork on a plate cutting through me. A subject change was needed. Fast.

'Erm, Granddad, I was thinking about expanding the

Swaledales, but it would mean moving the goats. What do you think?'

'I didn't think my opinion was welcome,' he muttered, pushing aside his plate. 'I need a nap. I'll eat this later.'

'Granddad, that's not—'

From across the table, Grandma shook her head at me and held a finger against her lips while Granddad shuffled out of the room.

'I'm so sorry,' I said when the lounge door closed.

'Don't be, Barney. It's not about the show.'

'What is it about, then?'

She placed her cutlery down, put her elbows on the table, and rested her chin on her clasped hands. 'He's scared. He knows he's not long for this world and you talking about finding love makes him think about how he's not going to be around to see you get married or have children. Same for you, Fizz. I know his behaviour's not logical because he's pushing you both away, but it's a protective mechanism.'

'Is there something we don't know?' Mum asked. 'Has the doctor said something?'

Grandma shook her head and stroked Raven, who'd appeared beside her. 'Nothing like that. This is all on the back of the strokes and his general health. He gets tired easily and his appetite isn't what it was. Much as we don't want to accept it, we can't kid ourselves we have years left together.'

Fizz sniffed beside me and dabbed her eyes with her serviette.

'Please don't let on that I've told any of you this,' Grandma continued.

'We won't,' I said, pushing down the lump in my throat. 'Is there anything we can do?'

'I liked what you asked him about the farm. I know he left the table, but that was him just lashing out at the other stuff. He's feeling a bit useless. His mind's sharp but his body's letting him down. I'll be surprised if he doesn't come back later and start a conversation about the Swaledales.'

Lunch was sombre after that. Fizz told us about the latest admissions at the rescue centre and Mum talked about a couple of recent event bookings, but it was small talk while we processed what Grandma had revealed.

An hour or so after lunch, I was getting ready to head back to the farm when Granddad reappeared. Grandma heated up his lunch and brought it through to the lounge on a tray.

'So, Barney, how many Swaledales are you thinking of adding in?' Granddad asked as he tucked in to his meal.

Grandma patted my knee as she sat down beside me, as though to say *I told you so*. I was glad she was right about the conversation, but prayed she was wrong about Granddad having little time left.

22

AMBER

I opened my eyes on Monday morning and smiled at Dan, propped up on one arm, looking down at me.

'What time is it?' I asked, noting that he was already dressed.

'Just after seven.'

I rubbed my sleepy eyes. 'You're going?'

'I'd rather be staying with you.'

'Me too.'

He brushed my hair back from my face and kissed me slowly and tenderly, sighing as he pulled away.

Moments later, he was gone, and I lay back against the pillow feeling a little lost.

Yesterday had been amazing. After checking in at the hotel, we spent the afternoon in Pittville Park, walking hand in hand and talking. We hired a rowing boat on the lake and Dan recited a romantic speech from his period drama which was quite beautiful. On the evening, we dined in the Montpellier District and I felt closer to him than I'd done since we reunited at New Year. We shared such an easy friendship, but had that added spark of attraction which the time apart had intensified. I felt reassured that we could make this work and there'd been no need for me to have a wobble. I'd probably only felt that way because of everything going wrong on *Love on the Farm* and my concerns about Sophie.

After breakfast, I drove back to the holiday cottage near Flint in North Wales, arriving just after lunch. I messaged Mum and Dad to let them know I was back and to see when they were free for a catch-up. I knew that Brad and Tabs had travelled across last night and stayed over, so I was conscious they might have plans for the day.

My phone rang moments later with a FaceTime request from Mum. When I accepted, Dad was also on the screen, and I could see they were on the deck out the back of Green Acres.

'How was your weekend with Dan?' Mum asked after we'd exchanged greetings.

'Really good. Too short, but we still managed to pack a lot in. How's everyone doing?'

'All fine,' Mum said. 'Sophie's decided she has no clothes, so Tabs has taken her to Maidstone on an emergency shopping trip, and Brad's gone for a run.'

'I can't believe she only has four more nights at home. How are you both feeling?'

'Trying not to think about it,' Dad said, in a strained voice. 'But she seems happier than we've seen her in a long time.'

I thought about what Dan had said at the pub in Windsor six weeks ago. 'Do you think we're being too protective of her and she's made better progress than we've given her credit for?'

They exchanged glances and shrugged.

'I don't know,' Mum said. 'It's possible. She's been so positive since she got the part.'

'Then maybe this part and the move to York will be the making of her.' I held my crossed fingers up to the camera. I really hoped it would but only time would tell.

Mum shook her head and tears filled her eyes. 'Sorry. I'm so worried. If you weren't there...'

'But I will be there and I'll watch out for her. Has she questioned me being local?'

'She's made a couple of comments,' Dad said, 'but she hasn't directly asked if she's the reason you're doing the show. I think she quite likes the idea of you being on hand just in case.'

Mum placed her hand over her heart. 'What you're doing for your sister means the world to us. I know it can't be easy.'

'Don't worry about me. There are plenty of upsides. I get to spend my days at Bumblebee Barn and my evenings at Hedgehog Hollow and they're both stunning. I get to work with a great director and crew and hopefully I'll help some farmers find love. That has to be worthwhile.'

The changes to the format were the sort of thing I'd normally have talked to my parents about, but I held back. They were worried enough about Sophie's new venture without me giving them cause for concern about me too. Whether Matt stayed or left, I'd go into work with a smile on my face each day and try to salvage what I could.

23

AMBER

The following week flew past with filming for *Countryside Calendar*. I spoke to Sophie a couple of times and she was becoming more excited with each passing day. I'd offered to join her in York today, but she wouldn't hear of it.

'I know it's only because you care, but you're all building this up to be something bigger than it is,' she'd protested. 'I want to do this on my own. I need to. If I was eighteen and heading off to university for the first time, I'd want someone with me, but I'm twenty-three and it's time to stand on my own two feet.'

So she'd got her way and, as I drove across the country this morning towards Hedgehog Hollow, I thought of my sister driving north and hoped she was still feeling positive now that it was actually happening.

Sophie had told me that the main cast members and senior crew were staying in a boutique city centre hotel and everyone else was in a nearby chain hotel. I'd been hoping they might be in a shared house to reduce loneliness and homesickness, although maybe it was better she had her own completely private space. Shared accommodation carried echoes of before.

* * *

'Welcome back!' Samantha must have spotted me arriving from the barn window and gave me a hug as soon as I exited the car. 'It's great to see you again.'

'And you. It's so good to be back. I've missed this place.'

She handed me the key to Meadow View. 'I saw Barney yesterday. He's really nervous.'

'Is he? He'll be fine.' I hoped. I still hadn't had any details through about the two replacement matches, so I had no idea what lay in store.

'He says he won't get to meet his first match until Thursday.'

'That's right. The start of the week is all about filming him doing his normal activities on the farm, plus the family and friend interviews. We'll then leave him in peace for a bit and do a similar thing with the three matches. It's important to do those interviews before their paths cross so there's nothing influencing what they say.'

'It all sounds fascinating.'

'Let's hope the viewers think so. There's always an element of uncertainty working with a new format.' *Especially one that's been messed with to add a little spice.*

'I'm off out for the afternoon with Josh and the kids, but Fizz is in the barn if you need anything.'

'Thanks. Enjoy your day.'

I clambered back into the driver's seat and drove the short distance to the cottage. Zara would be joining me early this afternoon.

There was no word from Sophie but, as she'd had a halfway stopover last night to avoid the long drive in one go, she had to have arrived in York by now. I didn't want to pester her by

messaging but was relieved when a message finally pinged
through on the family WhatsApp.

FROM SOPHIE

> Arrived a couple of hours ago and was the first
> here so I could pick my bedroom. It has amazing
> views over York Minster. I haven't seen anyone
> else yet but they've organised a drinks reception
> for the cast at 6pm so plenty of time to unpack
> first. Very excited xx

I was about to type in a reply when another message came
through.

FROM SOPHIE

> STOP WORRYING ABOUT ME!!!!

It was accompanied by several rolling on the floor laughing
emojis.

TO SOPHIE

> Glad you've arrived safely and bagged the best
> room Enjoy your drinks reception tonight. And I'll
> always worry about you. That's what big sisters
> do xx

FROM BRAD

> What Amber said. Except with brothers at the
> end x

FROM TABS

> Photo of drinks reception outfit needed. Enjoy xx

FROM DAD

> Dads will always worry too x

FROM MUM

And mums. It's the law. Have fun tonight, baby
girl xx

From the speed of the responses, I couldn't help thinking that
everyone had, like me, been checking their phones continuously,
anxiously awaiting news.

'Everything's going to be all right,' I said as I took my toiletries
into the en suite. 'Sophie has the part of a lifetime in a beautiful
city and I'm, well, I'm staying somewhere fantastic. Think positive
thoughts.'

But as I settled down to sleep later that evening, my thoughts
were troubled. All I could picture was Sophie's pale face, her eyes
red, her cheeks blotchy from tears, rocking back and forth on the
hospital bed five years ago. All I could hear were Parker's pleas. *It's
not my fault. I didn't know what was going to happen. You can't
blame me.*

I could and I did blame him. He'd been the director and he'd
been the one who'd taken things too far. My baby sister had been a
sweet, trusting eighteen-year-old and he'd taken that from her.
What happened on *that show* had been unforgivable, especially
when he'd been my fiancé and we'd all trusted him to take care of
her, and not to manipulate things. To spice it up. To attract more
viewers. It was sick.

24

BARNEY

It was extremely rare for me to struggle to sleep – fresh air and a physical job usually wiped me out – but I'd barely slept a wink last night. Two things weighed heavily on my mind.

The first thing was *Love on the Farm*. Amber and Zara had briefed me well several times over, but I still felt like I hadn't a clue what to expect from the first day of filming. Why the hell had I agreed to do this? A dating app probably had more chance of finding a suitable match and there wouldn't be family, friends and thousands of strangers watching every move I made. Even though Grandma had told us that Granddad's comments had nothing to do with the show, I couldn't help wondering if he was right about it being a load of 'nonsense'.

The second – and more worrying – thing was the farm. I had no idea how I was going to manage around filming. Milo had agreed to overtime but he'd fallen off his bike cycling home from the farm on Saturday and had broken his wrist. His arm would be in plaster for the next six to eight weeks while the bone healed. I was relieved for Milo that the fall hadn't been worse, and it had been a clean break which the doctors assured him would heal well, but him being out of action presented me with a major problem.

This week wouldn't be too horrendous as the crew would only be with me today and Friday and Mum, Dad, Fizz and Joel had all offered their support. They'd be here today anyway for the family and friends videos so could work on the farm around their interviews. Fizz and Mum were both free on Friday, so we had it covered, but next week was a nightmare. Filming was scheduled every day from Monday through to Friday and again the following Monday. I had no idea how I was going to cope then. Mum had offered to pull together a rota, but I couldn't expect everyone to take time off from their own demanding jobs to run the farm for me. I'd have to hope the filming wouldn't take all day every day and I'd be able to work first thing and last thing. Just as well it was June and light until late, which made working into the evening quicker and easier.

I was in the kitchen at 5.30 a.m., already on my third coffee, when I heard laughter from outside. Bear and Harley's ears had pricked up, but their tails were wagging so they clearly knew whoever had arrived.

Opening the door to investigate, I was stunned to see Mum, Dad, Fizz and Joel gathered in the farmyard. Bear and Harley shoved past me to welcome them.

'What are you all doing here so early?' I called.

'We figured we could take the pressure off and get ahead if we had an early start,' Dad responded.

'But...' I was so touched that I couldn't find any words.

'I'll make coffee and you have fifteen minutes to decide how best to use us today,' Fizz said, giving me a gentle nudge in the stomach as she walked past.

'And we *will* sort that rota for next week,' Mum added, giving me a hug. 'No more arguments.'

* * *

We were having a break for bacon butties at half eight when I recognised Amber's 4x4 pulling into the farmyard. A wave of nerves swept through me as I pulled my wellies back on and went outside to greet her.

'Good morning, Barney!' she called, pulling on a black baseball cap with her name and the word 'Producer' across the front in white lettering. 'Happy filming day. How are you feeling?'

'Bricking it.'

'That's completely normal. We'll soon have you relaxed and enjoying it. This is Zara.'

A younger woman – maybe in her mid to late twenties – looked up from the boot, where she was pulling on a pair of bright yellow wellies with daisies all over them. She had medium-length messy dark hair with a thick fringe and, although her make-up was minimal, black eyeliner rimmed her eyes. I couldn't take my eyes off her. She looked a lot like... I shook my head to dislodge that thought. Today of all days, I definitely didn't want to go there.

'Great to meet you in person,' she said, giving me a smile and a wave.

Realising I was staring, I said the first thing that came into my head. 'Thanks for all the helpful information.'

Her smile widened. 'Absolute pleasure. Helpful information is my speciality. Love a bit of detail. Do you like the hat?'

She pulled on a baseball cap like Amber's with 'Producer's Assistant' across the front under her name.

'It's, erm...'

'It's lame,' she said, laughing, 'but it serves a purpose.'

'We all wear them while filming,' Amber said. 'It helps us get to know each other and it's easier for the cast.'

'Although there's always some muppet who forgets or loses theirs,' Zara said.

'Or the jokers who swap them,' Amber added. 'The director, Matt, will be here in about half an hour and the rest of the crew will arrive around ten. Do you mind if I show Zara round?'

'Feel free, but there's coffee and bacon butties in the kitchen if you want.'

'You don't need to ask twice,' Amber said. 'Lead on!'

25

AMBER

Zara and I had already eaten, but the bacon butties smelled so good that we gave in to temptation. It gave us an opportunity to get to know Barney's parents and best friend on a more informal basis and they were so warm and welcoming, not that I'd have expected anything else, having already met Barney and Fizz.

Barney's mum, Natasha, was telling me about her events and catering business when Zara tapped me on the shoulder.

'So sorry to interrupt,' she said, 'but Matt's just pulled in.'

'That's our director,' I said to Natasha, 'and our cue to say goodbye for now. Thanks for the butties and coffee.'

I looked round but couldn't see Barney.

'He got a phone call,' Natasha said. 'I'll tell him you've gone.'

I thanked her and left with Zara. Matt was pacing up and down beside his car, holding his phone out in front of him. He spotted us and pointed to his EarPods, indicating he was on a call.

'We'll wander over to the original Bumblebee Barn,' I told Zara, leading her across the yard. 'So what do you make of Barney?'

'The photos don't do him justice. Definitely Farmer Hottie with a hot bezzie mate.'

'You like Joel?' With a broad-shouldered rugby player physique and dirty blond hair, he looked nothing like any of Zara's previous boyfriends.

'Hell yeah. Did you see his eyes? I could melt in them.'

I'd forgotten it was always the eyes that drew Zara in.

'Barney's gorgeous,' she continued, 'but Joel does it for me, which is just as well 'cos I think Farmer Hottie likes you.'

'Behave! Of course he doesn't!'

'The whole time we were in the kitchen, he couldn't take his eyes off you.'

'Stop it! We're here to find Barney's Miss Right and it's not me because I'm already taken.'

My tone was perhaps a little sterner than I'd intended, but the suggestion that Barney might be interested in me had thrown me. As if things weren't bad enough already, the last thing I needed was misguided attention. Alarmingly, Zara tended to have a sixth sense about these things. Hopefully it was wrong on this occasion.

'Okay, okay.' Zara put her hands up in surrender but was smiling. And then her smile faded. 'Uh-oh, Matt doesn't look happy.'

She wasn't wrong. The hunch of his shoulders as he approached us gave me that sinking feeling and I prepared for bad news.

'Good morning!' I called brightly.

'It might be morning,' he said, his tone flat, 'but there's sod all good about it. I've got some news for you from HQ and, on the back of it, I've just quit the show.'

Zara gasped.

'Aw, Matt. No!' I cried. 'We haven't even started filming.'

'I know, but that was Grant Lennon and he's changed the rules yet again.'

'You're joking! What now?'

At the sound of voices, he looked over his shoulder. Barney and the others had spilled out into the yard but they split up and headed off in different directions. Matt waited until they were out of earshot before continuing.

'Firstly, they're definitely scrapping the Wales episode because they reckon it doesn't fit anymore, so that was a right waste of time and effort. Secondly – and you're both going to hate this – they want us to manipulate the footage.'

I closed my eyes for a moment, my forehead scrunched as I let that news sink in. 'During filming or during editing?'

'Both.'

'So basically they've had an about turn on everything that was promised to us and the participants?'

'Yes, and I can't be part of that. I'm sorry.'

I shook my head. 'Don't be, Matt. Believe me, if I could, I'd be walking away too. What happens now?'

'They want the next four days to go ahead as planned and, because I like and respect you and don't want to leave you in the lurch, I've agreed to see this week out. They want to make sure they get what they need out of the interviews, so some questions will be emailed to us, and we have to ask them all.'

'What about next week?' Zara asked.

'There'll be a new director. One who doesn't have any scruples.'

Zara glanced at me, her eyes wide, and my heart started pounding. We both knew who fit that bill, but there was no way they'd do that to me. Would they?

'Did they say who?' I ventured.

'No, but I'm sure they'll have someone in mind and probably even approached them after our first bust-up.'

Much as I wanted to retreat into the darkest corner of the barn to process this, the crew would be arriving shortly and I had a job to do. Crisis-handling mode kicked in.

'Thanks for sticking around this week, Matt. I really appreciate it. I'd better give you both a tour before the crew arrive.'

* * *

Ninety minutes later, the farm was a hive of activity. I'd given Matt suggestions of good locations for filming the interviews with Barney, his family and Joel. He approved of them all and confirmed who he wanted to film where. A marquee had been erected in a field near the barns with wooden folding chairs, tables and refreshments. It would be the base for the crew and participants between filming.

Although the interview questions had changed, the format hadn't. I was still playing question-master but wouldn't appear on camera and my question would be edited out.

Our first interview was with Barney's mum, Natasha. With his dad, Hadrian, also being available today, Matt and I had intended to film both parents together, but that wasn't what the Lennons wanted and I could guess why – they'd be hoping there'd be differences in their answers and they'd manipulate the footage to suggest conflict where there really wasn't any.

I briefed all participants to either repeat the question or to phrase their answer in a way that incorporated the question and therefore made sense with my voice cut out.

'How would I describe Barney's love life?' Natasha repeated, grimacing. 'Non-existent. No, that's not true. He's had girlfriends from time to time, but they don't tend to be in his life long enough for us to meet them.'

'When was the last time you met one of his girlfriends?'

'The last time we met a girlfriend was...' She frowned. 'I

honestly can't remember. We were going to have Sunday lunch with his most recent, but she ended it the day before. I'm hoping we didn't jinx it.'

'Has Barney had any long-term relationships?'

Natasha was silent, so I gave her the thinking time. 'No. Well, he did have a girlfriend at school but, you know, they were very young. They dated during school and college, but it was never serious.'

'What makes you say that?'

She shrugged. 'There could never be a future in it. Her dad was Italian and her mum half-Spanish, so she was multi-lingual. She wanted to travel the world and work overseas and Barney only ever wanted to run the farm. They both knew it would end when she went to university.'

'And he was okay with that?'

'Barney said he was okay with it and we had no reason at the time not to believe him.'

'Did they stay in touch?'

'No, that was the end for them. She went to university in Europe – can't remember where now – and Barney stayed here and took over the farm a few years later.'

I continued working through the questions we'd been emailed, exploring Barney's best qualities, what he was like growing up, what she thought he could bring to a relationship, what sort of woman she thought would make the perfect partner, what she hoped for the future and any aspirations on her part to become a grandparent.

The new questions weren't contentious, but it was how the answers would be spliced in editing that concerned me.

When Matt was happy we'd captured everything, I told Natasha she could go but not before I asked the name of Barney's school girlfriend.

'Elmira,' she said. 'Pretty name. Arabic origins, I think.'

I thanked her for her time and we prepared to move location for the interview with Hadrian.

'Did you know about the school girlfriend?' Zara asked as the camera crew packed up.

'No, but I've never asked the question.'

'Must be weird being in a long-term relationship like that, knowing it has an expiry date. I don't think I could do it. What's the point of being together when you know it can't go anywhere and is going to end soon?'

'Maybe each one hoped the other would change their mind.'

'Maybe. Are you going to ask him about it?'

I removed my cap and brushed a few strands of hair back from my forehead. 'I'll have to. There's no way the Lennons will let that slip.'

I hoped that the relationship had been as easy to cast aside as Natasha seemed to think because I really didn't want to open up an old wound about the one that got away. That wasn't what I was here for. Or it hadn't been until the rules of the game changed.

26

BARNEY

'Barney? Are you okay?'

I glanced at Amber and nodded numbly.

'Should I repeat the question?'

I nodded once more, to buy thinking time more than anything. It had been going so well until that question. She'd asked me what I loved about being a farmer and to share some of the history of Bumblebee Barn. We'd discussed my lack of success with women and I'd joked about some of the reasons I'd been dumped. I'd made the crew laugh. It was all good. Until...

'I wondered if you could tell me more about your long-term girlfriend from school,' she repeated. 'Elmira, was it?'

Goosebumps pricked my arms despite the warmth of the June afternoon. Elmira De Luca. Elle. Nobody had said that name in such a long time and it had floored me just now. I hadn't mentioned her in my application form, video or any of the conversations I'd had with Amber or Zara.

'How do you know about her?' I finally managed, the words coming out all deep and husky.

'We asked your mum if you'd had any long-term relationships and Elmira was mentioned.'

I couldn't blame Mum for mentioning her. She didn't know what had happened.

'It was years ago,' I said in an effort to deflect the line of questioning.

'So I understand but, as you haven't had any long-term relationships since Elmira, I wondered if you could tell us a bit about her.'

'There's nothing to say. Elle and I hung out, but she moved to Paris when she finished college. We didn't stay in touch after that.'

'Would you say she was the one who got away?'

'No. We both wanted different things, so it was never serious.'

Why did I suddenly feel like Amber was a tabloid journalist trying to dig for scandal? *Nothing to see here. Move along. Next question.*

'And you didn't date anyone for a long time after that?'

'That's right, but I had no time for a girlfriend. I was busy getting ready to take over the farm. Granddad should have retired a few years earlier, but it got put on hold. He was worried I was too young to run it on my own and he might have to delay his retirement even more. I wanted to prove I was capable so he could finally get the retirement he deserved.'

Amber wandered over to Matt and there was lots of nodding and shrugging as they spoke in hushed tones. I looked over at Zara, but she was distracted watching them. Whatever Matt said to her, it didn't look like Amber was too happy about it. She seemed agitated as she came closer, removing her baseball cap, smoothing her hair back, and replacing the cap. The locket was fished out of her T-shirt and she twiddled it back and forth on the chain.

'Just one more question about Elmira,' she said. 'What did she look like?'

I gulped. 'What does that have to do with anything?'

'Can you just answer the question, please?'

I didn't want to but if I evaded it, they'd keep digging, convinced I was hiding something. And they'd be right.

'My ex-girlfriend had long dark hair and dark eyes,' I said, my tone flat. 'We split up thirteen years ago. It was a good relationship, but we were just teenagers and she wasn't the love of my life, she wasn't the one who got away and the fact that my more recent girlfriends look nothing like her is purely coincidence.' I glanced at Matt then back to Amber. 'Are we done now?'

'Yes. The guys will remove your mic pack. Thank you.'

I stood rigid as they unhooked the pack from my jeans and unthreaded the cable from my T-shirt. I wanted nothing more than to jump on the quad bike and escape to The Quad away from everyone, but Joel was out on my bike and Dad had taken the other after his interview. Besides, I could hardly disappear for some time out when everyone was gathered at the farm to do me a favour.

I still needed a moment. There shouldn't be anyone near the goats. Watching their antics never failed to cheer me up so, keeping my head high, I strode off in that direction.

I hadn't got far when Amber called my name. I paused for a moment then kicked myself for doing so. I could have pretended I hadn't heard her, although she'd only have called again and would probably have run to catch me.

'More intrusive questions?' I asked, turning with my eyebrows raised.

She'd removed her baseball cap.

'I'm sorry about the questions. I didn't mean to hit a nerve.'

'You didn't.'

'Your face when I said her name.' Her tone was gentle, apologetic, but I wasn't going to give anything away.

'I was surprised. That's all. Elle's a blast from the distant past who I wasn't expecting to talk about today.'

'I got the impression she might have meant a bit more than you'd let on.'

'Well, she didn't. Can I go now?'

'Yes, of course. Sorry.'

I took a couple of steps away then stopped and returned to her side. 'And if you're trying to read something into my reaction just now, I can save you the trouble. I'm a bit on edge because Milo broke his wrist so, not only am I worried about him, but he's out of action for a while and I've had to rope in my family and Joel to help out. I could really have done with pulling out of the show, but I'm not someone who goes back on their word. It's all been pretty stressful, and I'm knackered, so being questioned about my child-hood girlfriend threw me.'

'I'm sorry about Milo. I can imagine how much you'd miss him.'

'Yeah, well, it's ridiculously quiet round here without his constant jabber.' I smiled weakly at her. 'Look, I know you're only doing your job.'

'My job isn't to make anyone feel uncomfortable.'

'You didn't. It's me. As I said, I'm tired and you took me by surprise. I thought we were meant to be finding my future, not raking over my past.'

'But to find the right person for your future, we need to under-stand how your past has influenced you. Surely you can see that.'

'I suppose so. But you're barking up the wrong tree. Elle and I... it was never going to be forever and we went into the relation-ship both knowing that. It was fun while it lasted, but there's no broken heart or deep scars that have never healed.'

'Okay. I'm sorry. Are we good?'

'We're fine. But can we leave Elle out of it? If you're wanting to play it for laughs and make me look stupid, isn't my track record of being perpetually dumped enough? I can re-record those segments if you want. I can add detail. I've got other examples.'

Amber reached for her necklace. She'd be a hopeless poker player. She'd just revealed that I'd nailed it about the plan. I should have known there'd be a hidden agenda.

'Why would you think we're trying to make you look stupid?'

'Isn't that how these sorts of shows work?'

Her grip tightened round the locket, and she lowered her eyes. 'Some of them.'

'But not this one?'

Silence.

I sighed. 'It was a long shot anyway. Who finds their perfect partner on a TV show?'

Amber looked up, her eyes sorrowful. 'It *can* happen and we really do hope it'll happen for you.'

I held her gaze and noticed how stunning her eyes were – green with dark rims and hazel round the iris – and how long and thick her lashes were. The sun bounced off her red hair and I wondered how she looked with her hair down. I'd only ever seen it tied back.

She loosened her grip on her locket, but kept her fingers pressed against it as her eyes searched my face. One of us needed to speak. Probably me. But I had nothing.

A bee buzzing past broke whatever spell there was between us, and Amber took a step away from me. 'So, erm... that's a good idea to focus on some more girlfriend disaster stories. Only if you don't mind. I mean, you suggested it, but you might not really want to do it.'

'I don't mind. You can film it later or when you're back on Friday if you prefer.'

'Thanks. I'll have a word with Matt and let you know. I'd better let you get on.'

'Who do you need next?'

'Joel, but give us half an hour.'

I watched until she disappeared from view then rang Joel to let him know what time he was needed.

'How did it go?' he asked.

'It was okay at first, but then they asked me about Elle.'

'Elle? Why would they ask about her?'

'Chasing a story that isn't there, I think. If they ask you about her, can you do me a favour and not tell them anything?'

'Okay, but I didn't think there was anything to tell.'

'There isn't, but they seem to think there is and I don't see the point in discussing something that meant nothing and happened so long ago.'

'No worries. I'll keep schtum.'

I put my phone back in my jeans pocket, looked around me and shook my head in despair. Of all the places on the farm I could have stopped, why did it have to be next to Spring Field? I shielded my eyes from the sun as I looked towards the remains of the stone shelter, memories swirling in my mind, anger taking hold. I kicked at a nearby thistle until I'd uprooted it then sank onto the verge with my head in my hands.

It was never going to be forever and we went into the relationship both knowing that. It was fun while it lasted, but there's no broken heart or deep scars that have never healed.

Who was I kidding?

27

BARNEY

Thirteen years ago

I paced up and down inside the old stone shelter in Spring Field – named because of the underground spring below the well – pausing in the doorway every so often to look across the meadow. She was late.

A sudden gust of wind sent ripples over the long grass and a chill through me. It had been muggy all week, but a storm was brewing and expected to break within the hour. I hoped we didn't get caught in it, but at least the shelter would give some protection.

A beep from my mobile set my heart racing.

FROM ELLE

Sorry I'm late. Just parked. With you soon xx

TO ELLE

Was beginning to think you weren't coming xx

FROM ELLE

You know I can't stay away from you xxxxxx

A follow-up text made me laugh.

FROM ELLE

Plus, you have my birthday present. Of course I
was going to come! xx

I'd been captivated by Elmira 'Elle' De Luca from the moment
she sat down next to me in my first ever French lesson at
secondary school, aged eleven. While our French teacher tried to
settle the unruly class, Elle grabbed my blank exercise book,
flipped to the back inside cover and scribbled something. She
closed the book, pressed her finger to her lips in a 'shh' motion,
winked at me and whispered, 'Later.'

All lesson, my fingers twitched, desperate to know what she'd
written. As we filed out of the classroom at the end of the lesson, I
opened the book:

*Le français est la langue de l'amour. Je suis ravie de l'apprendre
avec toi, mon magnifique nouvel ami.*

I fished out my exercise book and French dictionary the
moment I exited the gates, eager for a translation:

*French is the language of love. I'm excited to be learning it with
you, my gorgeous new friend.*

Gorgeous? With my long limbs and slim frame, nobody had
ever called me that before. I looked up, frowning. Was she taking
the piss? I spotted her nearby and she beckoned me over.

'You know what it says now?' she asked, looking up at me through her dark lashes.

'Yeah, but you can't mean it.'

'I mean every word. *C'est vrai. Je pense que tu es magnifique.*' She lightly kissed me on the cheek then ran off towards the car park.

I looked round me, wanting some sort of reassurance from the other students that the kiss had actually happened, but nobody was paying any attention. I had no idea who she was or why she'd picked me, but I'd already fallen a little bit in love with her.

Elle was completely different to any of the other girls at school. She looked nothing like them with her dark eyeliner-rimmed eyes, thick dark hair and olive complexion, but it was so much more than looks that made her stand out. She had an air of confidence and a level of maturity. Engaging in gossip and spreading rumours was beneath her and she spent her breaks in the library studying. She was every teacher's dream – a bright, curious student who excelled in every academic subject and in sports too – and she was my dream. Our friendship grew over the next couple of years, helped by her parents stabling their horses at the farm, making her a regular visitor to go riding.

Her thirteenth birthday in mid-June fell on a Saturday and she came to the farm for an early-evening ride with me before going out for a meal with her parents. We rested the horses by the drinking trough in Spring Field and sat in the entrance to the old shelter.

'Happy birthday,' I said, passing her a small paper bag. I'd wanted to get her a birthday present but hadn't known what to buy, so I'd asked Fizz to make her a friendship bracelet.

Elle's eyes sparkled and I thought she was going to cry as she removed the deep maroon bracelet from the bag. 'It's beautiful, Barney. You made this?'

'I tried but mine fell apart. Fizz did it but I picked the colour and pattern.'

She held her arm out and I fastened it round her wrist. She ran her finger over the cream heart in the middle.

'A heart for friendship?' she asked, her eyes fixed on mine.

'If that's what you want.'

She gazed back down at the bracelet and I wondered if I should have just said 'yes', but that would be a lie.

'I'd like another birthday gift from you,' she said, her eyes meeting mine once more. 'A kiss.'

My heart soared then plummeted as she tapped her cheek. I shuffled closer and moved to kiss her on the cheek, but she whipped her head round and our lips met instead. I expected her to laugh and pull away, but she shuffled closer still and slid her hands into my hair.

We shared thousands of kisses after that. The shelter where I was waiting now had become our special place – the place we first kissed, where we first said 'I love you' and where I was hopefully going to secure my future this evening.

I had no idea how she was going to react, but I had to give it a try. It felt right to me, but I wouldn't be the one giving up on my plans. And I wouldn't be expecting her to sacrifice everything. She could still study abroad. She could still travel. The only difference would be that she'd be coming home to me each time instead of us saying goodbye at the end of August and never seeing each other again. That had to be right for both of us. She loved me – from the day she'd scribbled in my French book, she later told me – and people who loved each other as deeply as we did deserved a future together.

Elle waved as she clambered over the five-bar gate at the edge of the field and ran through the meadow towards me, her long hair fanning out behind her, her tanned legs seeming to stretch out forever beneath a sunflower-yellow minidress.

'Last exam aced!' she squealed, jumping up and wrapping her legs round my hips as she smothered me with kisses.

Keeping tight hold of her, I moved inside the cooler shelter, responding to her with enthusiasm.

'Happy eighteenth,' I murmured between kisses. 'Would you like your gift?'

'Is this not it?'

She lowered her feet to the ground and pushed my T-shirt up, trailing kisses across my stomach and chest.

'You've got too many clothes on for this heat,' she said, her voice low and teasing.

As she lifted my T-shirt over my head, I heard a rumble of thunder and we smiled at each other. We both loved storms.

I reached for the small box wrapped in a bow I'd placed in a cubby hole earlier.

'I thought it was time we upgraded the friendship bracelet,' I said, as she opened the box to reveal a silver charm bracelet.

'Oh, Barney, it's beautiful. But it must have cost you a fortune.'

'You're worth it,' I said, removing the bracelet and fastening it onto her wrist next to the original friendship bracelet.

'One day, I'll fill it with charms, but there are four for now.' I spun the bracelet round to explain each. 'The apple's for school where we met, the birthstone's for your birthday – when we first kissed, the heart is how I feel about you, and the infinity symbol is for how long that love will last.'

'That is so romantic. I love it and I love you.'

As the barn darkened, only to be lit by a flash of lightning, Elle kissed me with a greater longing than ever before, taking my breath away as she ran her nails down my back.

'There's something else I want from you for my birthday,' she whispered breathlessly as the barn lit up again and thunder crashed overhead. 'I want you to make love to me.'

I gulped. There was nothing I wanted more, but we'd made a promise to each other that we would never take it that far. The way she'd described it, so much more poetically than me, was that we'd given each other our hearts and souls and, if we gave our bodies too, all the pieces of us would be broken when we parted forever at the end of August. It hadn't stopped us having fun and we'd come close so many times, but one of us had always remained strong.

'Why now?' I asked, kicking myself for trying to talk her out of it.

'Because it's my birthday and the only thing I really want is you.'

'You've already got me.'

She turned her back to me. 'Unzip me.'

'Elle, you have no idea how much I want to, but...'

'Unzip me,' she repeated. 'Or I will.'

Protesting was fruitless. When Elle really set her mind to something, nothing could sway her, and I suspected she'd have been planning this day for a long time.

With shaking hands, I slowly unzipped her dress and gasped when I realised she wasn't wearing anything underneath. The dress slid to the ground and she turned to face me. Keeping her eyes on mine, she unfastened my jeans.

Another flash of lightning illuminated the barn, followed by the heavens opening. As rain poured through the gaps in the slates, Elle and I lowered ourselves onto a picnic blanket and fully surrendered to each other for the first time.

She'd said we could never give our bodies to each other because that would mean we could never separate. Which had to mean that the answer to the question I planned to ask her was 'yes'. Hadn't it?

28

AMBER

Present day

'I sent Zara and the crew to the next location,' Matt said when I returned to where we'd been filming Barney. 'How was he?'

'Angry. Confused.'

'And you?'

'The same. How do people do it, Matt? How does anyone keep digging like that, knowing they're going somewhere the participant clearly doesn't want to go?'

'Honest answer? Because they don't care. They see the participants as entertainment, not as people.'

'I hate it. This isn't me. That shocked look on his face the minute I mentioned Elmira! It was obvious his mum hadn't a clue what they'd meant to each other and there's a story there. I had Grant and Liza's voices in my head with all these intrusive questions and I couldn't do it. The ones I asked were bad enough.'

'Did he say anything about Elmira?'

'No. He was adamant there's no story, no scars, no broken heart, which confirmed to me that there is and it cuts even deeper than I initially thought. Even if he'd admitted it all off-camera, I'd have still let it go.'

'I know you would. Tell you what, how about we edit those parts out? The Lennons won't hear about the ghost of girlfriend past from me. I feel just as bad as you about the way this is going.'

I gave him an appreciative smile. 'That would be great. Barney said he doesn't mind sharing some more dumping disasters with us. I think we should go down that route. Some of those are really funny and I think seeing a good-looking farmer laughing at himself is endearing and surely a much better ratings winner than ripping his heart out and leaving him to pick up the pieces. Barney's got a great sense of humour. Let's showcase that.'

'I'm all over that,' Matt said. 'We'd better head over to meet the others for Joel's interview. You're okay with things now?'

'I'm good. If we have to go in a new direction, let's make it a positive one.'

Whatever had gone down between Barney and his ex, he didn't deserve to have it painfully re-lived on reality TV. He deserved love and, as it was fairly unlikely he'd find that from his matches, I'd do my best to ensure he got it from the public. It wasn't unheard of for a star of a show like this to find a connection afterwards through social media. Maybe Barney would find love that way instead.

29

BARNEY

Dad lit the barbeque after the *Love on the Farm* crew left for the day. I went into the kitchen with Mum and we sat opposite each other at the table, chopping the salad.

'That was a different day,' she said, passing me a cucumber and pulling a dish of beef tomatoes towards her. 'Are you pleased with how it went?'

'Hard to say. Depends which parts they show on TV. I'll probably come across as a right numpty.'

'So what if you do? If you find love, you'll have the last laugh. If you don't, you've lost nothing and you've had a rare chance to do something completely different.'

Mum had always been an optimist and I tried to channel her positivity. Most of the time, I managed.

* * *

By 9.30 p.m., there was only Joel left. Mum and Dad had left about half an hour ago, and I'd just waved Fizz off.

'You look like you need another of these,' Joel said, handing me an opened bottle of lager.

We took our drinks over to the kitchen table where Bear draped himself across my feet and Harley did the same to Joel. I was pretty sure I knew why he'd hung back and perhaps it was time.

'They didn't ask me anything about Elle,' he said. 'That's a blast from the past, eh?'

'Too right. I haven't thought about her in years.'

'Bullshit! What *really* happened between you?'

'You know what happened.'

'I know what you told me and everyone else. Not serious, always knew it was ending, you were fine with it. I didn't buy it at the time and I'm definitely not buying it now.'

I took a couple of deep glugs of my drink and peeled the corner of the label back with my thumbnail, debating whether to tell him everything.

'I thought Zara looked a bit like her,' he said. 'You noticed too, didn't you?'

'Yes.' I took a deep breath. Sod it! It was time.

'I asked Elle to marry me,' I said. 'It was on her eighteenth birthday.'

He winced. 'And she said no?'

'Actually, she said yes.'

30

BARNEY

Thirteen years ago

The storm had passed but the shelter was damp and the air cool. Elle shivered in my arms, so I draped my T-shirt round her shoulders.

'You'll freeze,' she protested.

'I'm good in the cold. Comes with the job.'

I pulled my jeans on and patted the right pocket to make sure the ring hadn't slipped out.

'I have something else for you,' I said as we leaned against either side of the entrance, looking out over the freshly drenched fields. I reached for her hand and brushed my thumb over her knuckles. 'I know you have plans to study in France and to travel and I'd never ask you to give that up for me, but I don't see why achieving your dreams means saying goodbye to ours. We love each other and we want to be together.'

Her smile slipped. 'Barney, don't. There's no way it can work.'

I shook my head. 'How can you say that when we haven't even tried?'

'We don't have to!' She snatched her hand away and folded her arms across her chest, glaring at me. 'Distance relationships are too hard.'

'I'm not saying it won't be hard, but surely it's worth a try. Your parents had one and they're still together.'

'Yeah, but they split up several times first.'

I cupped her face and gently kissed her pouting lips.

'But your parents reunited each time because they knew they had to be together, just like us. You know we're great together.'

'Yes, but... I don't know.'

She'd dropped her arms back to her sides and I could see she was wavering, struggling to come up with further objections, and I took my chance.

'Well, I *do* know.' I bent down onto one knee and held the ring out in front of me. 'I love you, Elle. I can't speak five languages like you and I've hardly travelled anywhere, but *je pense que tu es magnifique.*'

She smiled at the repeat of our first conversation. If she liked that, she was going to love the rest, even if she didn't love my appalling pronunciation or any misapplication of gender or tense. It would be a miracle if I managed to get all the words in the right order.

'*Quiero pasar el resto de mi vida contigo...*' I want to spend the rest of my life with you in Spanish...

'*Sono certo che possiamo falo funzionare...*' I'm certain we can make this work in Italian...

'*Ich bin bereit, alles zu tun, um dich so glücklich zu machen, wie du mich gemacht hast...*' I'm willing to do anything to make you as happy as you have made me in German...

'So please, please, please say yes to my next question. Will you marry me?'

She pressed her hand across her mouth, her eyes sparkling. 'I can't believe you learned all that.'

'I'm sorry about the pronunciation. It was—'

'It was perfect,' she said, shaking her head. 'You're perfect. *Oui, sí, sì, ja*, yes!'

She held out her left hand and I slipped the ring on her finger. With a squeal, she flung her arms round me.

* * *

That night, we decided it would be best not to tell our parents until after Elle had received her A level results. Her parents had been worried about us getting involved and messing up her future plans, so they thought we were just friends. Mine thought we were more than friends but that it wasn't serious and we only saw each other occasionally. Neither had any idea how often we met up in the shelter.

I walked her back to her car, hand in hand, so she could go out for her birthday meal with her parents and sister. She kept gazing down at her ring then back up at me, a wide smile on her face.

'We really will find a way to make it work,' I said when we reached her car. I ran my fingers into her hair and brushed my lips against hers. 'I promise you.'

'I believe you.'

She backed up against the side of the car and pulled me closer.

'We need to celebrate our engagement,' she said, her eyes hungry with desire as she unfastened my belt.

* * *

On the last Saturday in July – six weeks after I proposed – Elle and I were meant to be going for a horse ride but she texted me asking me to meet her at our shelter instead.

She was sitting on a boulder outside as I approached, legs drawn up to her chest, head dipped.

'Elle? Are you okay?' I asked, crouching down beside her.

She sniffed loudly.

'Elle?'

I pushed her hair back from her face and gently lifted her chin. Her cheeks were flushed and streaked with tears and her eyes were red. I'd only seen her cry once before – very recently – and something had clearly broken her again.

'Has something happened to your nonno?'

In the early hours of the morning after Elle's eighteenth, her dad had received a phone call to say that his mother – Elle's grandma or nonna – had collapsed with breathing difficulties. The family had rushed to Italy, just in time to say their goodbyes. Nonna passed away that evening. I therefore hadn't seen Elle again until one evening after the funeral when she'd sobbed in my arms. She'd shared her fears that her grandfather – her nonno – wouldn't be long for this world, desperate to be reunited with the love of his life and I thought that time might have come.

'Not Nonno,' she whispered. 'Me. I'm pregnant.'

I opened my mouth, but nothing came out. *Pregnant? Shit!*

'And before you ask, yes, I'm sure. I've taken four tests.' Her words were a little louder with a harsh edge to them although, to be fair, the question poised on my lips had been to ask if she was sure.

'How?' I eventually managed, wishing I'd stayed silent instead.

She wiped her cheeks and arched an eyebrow. 'Do I need to draw a diagram?'

'No, I mean... you were going to take the day after pill because we...' I shook my head. 'Of course. You flew out to be with your nonna.'

'It was such a rush to get there on time so getting the pill went clean out my mind. I'm sorry.'

A fresh torrent of tears rained down her cheeks and I gathered her into my arms. The thought of becoming a dad at eighteen terrified me. The thought of telling Elle's dad was even scarier.

'It'll be all right,' I reassured her. 'This doesn't have to stop things. It'll just change plans a bit.'

'A lot,' she wailed, shaking in my arms.

'Okay, a lot, but it's nothing we can't deal with. You want children and so do I. It's earlier than we'd have planned, but—'

'Ten to fifteen years earlier.' She pulled back and stared at me, eyes wide. 'That's huge and it ruins everything. If we have this baby, I can't go to France.'

I pushed aside the 'if' – not an option I wanted to consider – and focused on the rest of the sentence.

'You can still go to France. Maybe not this year, but you could go next year or the one after.'

'And leave you on your own with the baby?'

'I don't need to be on my own. I've got my parents and Fizz. I'm sure they'd help out. Or I could even come to France with you.'

I had no idea how or if that would work. I was thinking on my feet here, anxious to calm her down.

Her expression softened and she took my hand in hers. 'You'd really leave the farm for me?'

'In these circumstances, of course I would.'

She snatched her hand away, glaring at me, the softness gone. 'But you wouldn't leave the farm if there was no baby.'

I narrowed my eyes at her, not sure I was getting her point.

'I don't know why you're looking all confused,' she snapped. 'You just said you'd leave the farm and come to France to look after our baby while I study, but in all the other conversations we've had about the future, you've never once offered to come abroad with me. It's always been about your granddad retiring and you taking over the farm. So you're basically saying you *wouldn't* leave the farm for me but you *would* for our baby.'

I could see why she was angry. It sounded bad when she put it like that.

'I don't know, Elle. I've only just found out, so this is me thinking out loud and making a mess of it.'

She stood up with such force that I tumbled backwards.

'So you're saying what you think I want to hear,' she cried, towering over me before storming off across the field.

'No!' I scrambled to my feet and chased after her. 'I love you, Elle. I'm just trying to find a way to make this work.'

'Sometimes things just don't work and we have to accept it.'

She sped up and was soon sprinting across the field. I couldn't keep up.

'Elle! Stop!'

But she made it to her car and sped off without a sideways glance.

I sank to my knees in the meadow. What did this mean? Was it over? I ran through everything I'd said, cursing myself for every stupid word. I'd jumped into finding a solution without once asking her what she wanted. I deserved that reaction. Bloody idiot.

* * *

The rest of the weekend was agony. Elle texted me to say she thought we needed a couple of days apart to calm down and we'd talk again the following week.

It was the Wednesday before I saw her again and, this time, I let her talk. She was scared, understandably. As well as her long-held future plans being in jeopardy, she feared that we weren't ready for a family. We were still teenagers and, although I was earning, my wage was minimal and we both still lived with our parents.

Those same worries had hounded me too, but we were in a better position than many – I did at least have a job and I was about to inherit the farm. We wouldn't have the mortgage or rent worries that burdened most young families and Bumblebee Barn would be the perfect place to raise a family, as it had been in the past.

I took care not to dismiss any of Elle's objections but, for each one, I helped her find a positive and I could tell she was coming around.

Over the weeks that followed, we saw each other as often as we could. Sometimes all she wanted was us to cuddle in silence, and other times she had something a little more active on her mind. We talked a lot – about the practicalities of having a baby, about her still studying abroad, about travelling in the future. She'd always wanted to use her languages and had even looked into teaching as a way of doing that – her idea rather than my suggestion – which was encouraging. It wasn't what she'd planned, but it was an option and she seemed excited about it.

I regularly painted a picture of what life could be like on the farm, happily married with children running around, teaching them to ride, having them feed the animals, and Elle spoke with increasing enthusiasm about teaching. We even moved onto speculation about whether she was expecting a boy or a girl and she made me laugh with what she thought were some of the worst Italian and Spanish names.

There was one dark day when we talked about other options. I found that conversation exceptionally hard. In a short time, I'd already come round to the idea of being a dad, and I didn't want that taking away from me. Elle was dead set against adoption. She didn't see the point in going through with a pregnancy only to give the baby away and then spend the rest of her life thinking that she had a son or daughter out there who might track her down one day wanting answers. For Elle, there were only two options – continue with the pregnancy and be a parent. Or don't continue. The following day, I fought back tears of relief when she told me she wanted to continue.

Towards the end of the middle week in August, the A level results were due. I saw Elle on the Tuesday, two days before results day, and she was quieter than usual. When I asked if everything was all right, she told me she was nervous about the results. What if she hadn't aced them after all?

Results day arrived and I was anxious for her. Her GCSEs had been top marks across the board, and I was certain she'd have repeated that for her A levels. She was going to college to pick up her results any time after ten and had said she'd text me as soon as she knew. By the time I broke for lunch at 1 p.m., there was still no word from her. I hoped that didn't mean she'd flunked them. I texted her to reassure her that I was there for her whatever the results were. I called too but went straight to voicemail.

It was after 9 p.m. and getting dark when she finally texted me, asking me to meet her at half nine at the village green in Benton-bray – one of the largest villages in the area.

I spotted her car as I pulled up near April's Tea Parlour and I found her on a bench overlooking the playground.

'You had me worried,' I said, sitting down beside her. I'd have held her hand, but she had both hands shoved in the pockets of her denim jacket and I could feel tension emanating from her. My stomach lurched. Had she failed her exams?

'How did you do?' I asked tentatively.

'All As.' There was no enthusiasm in her voice and her face was expressionless.

'That's awesome, isn't it?'

She remained still and silent.

'Are you okay?' I asked, almost afraid to hear the answer.

'The baby's gone.'

It took a few moments for me to make sense of the words. In our many conversations about the baby, we hadn't spoken about the possibility of a miscarriage.

'I'm so sorry. When did it happen?'

'I had an appointment after I picked up my results.'

Again, it took a few moments for the words to register – moments in which she shuffled along the bench, placing a gap the size of a person between us.

'An appointment?'

'I scheduled it for after the results. I wasn't sure if I'd go through with it but, when I saw those As on the page, I knew I had to.'

I felt sick. 'You aborted our baby?'

She finally looked at me and spoke each word slowly and deliberately with massive emphasis on the third one. 'I terminated *my* pregnancy.'

Abortion, termination, ours, hers, it all amounted to the same thing. She'd made the decision without discussing it with me. It wasn't like the subject hadn't been raised before but she'd been the one who'd decided to continue with the pregnancy and there'd been no suggestion since then that she was doubting that decision.

'I don't understand. I thought we were going to make this work.'

'And *I* decided that it couldn't.'

I didn't trust myself to say anything else because I could never take back whatever I spilled out and the only words coming to mind were angry, bitter, accusatory.

'These are yours.'

She removed her right hand from her pocket and placed something on the wooden bench between us. Darkness had fallen but there was a streetlight nearby which cast a pale glow over the items: the engagement ring, the charm bracelet and the friendship bracelet. I picked up the latter. The tie cord was frayed where she'd cut it to remove it. No baby, no marriage, no friendship.

'So it's over?' I asked, my voice cracking. 'No discussion.'

'How can it not be over? Do you think it's possible for us to recover from what I've done today?'

I had no response to that. I was too numb, too shocked.

'No, I thought not,' she said stiffly.

We sat in silence. A light wind pushed her hair across her face, an owl hooted and a couple of dogs barked somewhere in the distance.

'Why did you do it?' I asked eventually.

'Because this is *your* dream, Barney, not mine. I *don't* want to be a teacher. I *don't* want to defer my studies or travel later because we both know it won't happen. I *don't* want to live on a farm. I don't even want to live in England. And I'm not sure that I even want children. Ever. As soon as I saw my results, I knew I couldn't do any of it.'

'So the answer was an abortion and it never crossed your mind to talk to me first?' It was a battle not to shout the words.

'Of course it did! But I ruled it out because you'd have begged me to reconsider, to stay, to make it work. And for what? A couple of days would have passed and I'd be back to feeling exactly the same.'

'I could have raised the baby on my own.'

She shook her head vigorously. 'Too messy. Too emotional.

You'd always have been hoping that one day I'd come back to play happy families and I'd never feel free.'

I glanced at the ring and bracelets on the bench between us, pushing down the lump in my throat. 'I guess you're free now. Like you always wanted to be.'

'I'm sorry, but you always knew what the end point was going to be.'

'Yeah, well, stupid me for thinking that love conquers all.'

'Bitterness doesn't suit you.'

'Oh, I'm sorry, Elle, should I be happy about this?'

'Neither does sarcasm.' She stood up. 'I really am sorry. I know I've hurt you.'

Hurt me? It seemed so inadequate a word for what she'd just done. Ripped my heart out and stomped on it, more like.

We stared at each other. Where I'd once seen warmth and love in her eyes, all I saw now was coldness. She shrugged and walked away.

'Did you love me?' I called after her.

She stopped and turned to face me. 'Yes. I've always been honest with you, Barney.'

'Until today.'

'Still being honest with you. I could have said I'd had a miscarriage or it had been a false alarm. I could have left the country without a word. But I came here and I told you the truth.'

'Yes, you did. But the truth would have been telling me earlier this week or last week, or whenever it was that you considered this the endgame. Because if you'd trusted me with the truth, I'd actually have supported you. I'm not some neanderthal with no respect for women. It isn't what I'd have chosen, but I'd have supported your right to make that decision – your body, your choice.'

I snatched up the returned items and stood up, clenching them in my hand.

'You asked how it would be possible to recover from what you'd done today. I say it *would* have been possible if you'd involved me. I'd have gone to the clinic with you, held your hand, and we'd have got through it because we love each other. But you didn't involve me. You went right ahead and made every decision yourself. That's not a relationship. It's not even a friendship.'

I opened out my fist to reveal her gifts. 'But I guess you already knew that when you removed these. Didn't you?'

She looked at the items, then me, but she didn't speak. It was over.

I shoved them in my pocket and walked away. She didn't follow me. She didn't even call my name.

31

AMBER

Present day

On Tuesday morning, Zara and I travelled forty-five minutes to Wilbersgate – a market town between Reddfield and Hull. Our filming focus for today was the first of Grant and Liza's replacements, twenty-one-year-old Rayn Masterson.

I'd only been emailed her profile last night so Zara and I had put in a late one studying it and planning what we wanted to ask her over and above the questions we'd been instructed to ask.

Rayn lived with her mum, stepdad and three younger siblings in a large townhouse with a long walled back garden. A wooden bench below a rose-strewn pergola at the far end provided the perfect backdrop for filming – a tranquil pocket of nature away from any traffic noise and children playing.

Oozing with confidence, Rayn's dream was to perform in the West End. She'd just graduated with a first-class honours drama and theatre degree from Lancaster University and had an impressive CV of lead roles in local productions.

After we'd filmed various introductory soundbites, we moved on to the show, starting with an easy question.

'What do you think of the countryside?' I asked, smiling at her.

'I love the countryside,' she gushed, her ice-blue eyes sparkling. 'Running up to the top of a hill, flinging my arms out wide and belting out "The Hills Are Alive" is so magical. Or if it's winter and there's snow on the ground, I love to go into a wide-open space and channel Elsa. Everyone thinks of "Let It Go" and, don't get me wrong, it's a banger of a tune, but I love "Into the Unknown" best. Do you know it? It's from *Frozen II*.'

Before I could respond, she rose from the garden bench and burst into song, complete with dramatic gestures and exaggerated facial expressions. Zara disappeared off up the lawn and I knew she'd had to do that to compose herself. I was struggling to keep a straight face myself and, looking round the crew, I clearly wasn't the only one. It wasn't that she was bad; it was just so unexpected. Rayn's singing voice was actually quite stunning, and I had no doubt that she could hold her own on a West End stage, but was this show going to help catapult her there? Doubtful.

'I'm a Disney princess,' she announced, positioning herself back on the bench after her song and looking coyly at the camera.

'You're a what?'

'Oh, not for real.' Her laugh was more like a small child's giggle. 'I do children's parties and other events. Elsa, of course. Already got the hair.' That warranted a massive flick of her long blonde waves as though she was in a shampoo advert.

She pointed at me. 'You'd make an awesome Anna with that gorgeous red hair. Can you sing?'

'Erm, only in my car when I'm alone. Ears would be bleeding if there was anyone with me.' Sophie was the only talented singer in our family.

'Aw, you poor thing.' Rayn clutched her hand across her heart. 'We can't all have the gift. I'm sure there are plenty of other things you're good at.'

Zara had only just returned and had to leave again. I swear I could hear her snorts of laughter.

'What about spending time in the countryside but not singing?' I asked, hoping to get a sensible answer this time.

'I'm not really a countryside kind of girl,' she said, wrinkling her nose. 'Too many creepy crawlies and nothing to do on an evening. I'm definitely a city girl.'

Beside me, Matt tutted. I didn't dare look at him.

'So, Rayn, this programme is called *Love on the Farm* and it's all about matching you up with a farmer. Our farmer lives deep in the Yorkshire Wolds countryside, nowhere near a city, so we were expecting some answers that perhaps indicated a love for the countryside.'

She'd leaned forward, her brow creased, and appeared to be listening to me intently, nodding frequently.

'Give me a bit more,' she said, beckoning the information with both hands.

'Erm, well...' I glanced at Matt, but he shrugged. 'Erm, maybe you have some fond memories of time spent in the countryside or visiting a farm. Perhaps you have favourite animals.'

'This farmer has animals?'

'Yes. He has a mixed farm so some crops and some animals.'

'What sort of animals?'

'Sorry, but I can't give anything else away. It's meant to be a surprise when you meet him next week.'

'Okay. Understood. Crops and farm animals.' She rubbed her

temples as though that helped her take in what I was saying. 'Yes, I can work with that. Do you mind if we take five?'

I glanced up at Matt.

'That's fine,' he said. 'Take fifteen. We'll have a coffee break and resume filming at quarter past eleven.'

I planted my hands on my hips, shaking my head in disbelief as I watched Rayn sauntering up the garden. Her mum approached her and they were soon deep in conversation with lots of pacing and waving around of the arms.

'Do you think she even applied for this show?' Matt asked. 'Could they have plucked her out of the applicants for *Tropical Heat* or something like that?'

'Nothing would surprise me anymore.' I reached for my flask. 'Wish we had something stronger than coffee.'

After our drinks, we prepared for filming again. Rayn asked if her mother could watch. Neither Matt nor I had a problem with that as long as she kept quiet and her presence didn't distract Rayn.

Rayn settled onto the bench again and threw me a dazzling smile. 'Ask me that question about what I think about the countryside again. I've worked on my part and have an awesome answer prepared.'

Her part? Oh, God! But we were going to just have to go with it.

'What do you think of the countryside?' I asked.

She beamed at the camera, eyes sparkling. 'I absolutely *love* the countryside. I live in a market town, but it's surrounded by fields and hills so it's almost like I live in the country. My grandparents on my dad's side of the family used to have a smallholding and I loved staying there as a child. I'd collect the eggs from the henhouse on a morning and help feed the other animals.'

Her smile slipped and her eyes filled with tears. 'They passed eight years ago within a couple of weeks of each other. There isn't a day that goes by when I don't miss them and their beautiful home.'

A tear slipped down her cheek and I actually felt a lump in my throat, even though I was fairly sure it was all an act.

'Cut!' Matt instructed.

Rayn beamed at me once more and wiped away the rogue tear.

'Darling, that was fabulous,' her mother cried, rushing towards her with a bag of make-up and checking the tear streak hadn't done any damage.

'Was that the kind of thing you were looking for?' Rayn asked. 'Because we can explore a different angle if you prefer.'

'It was great,' Matt said. 'Amber'll run through the rest of the questions with you now.'

The rest of the filming went smoothly. A natural in front of the camera, we managed most questions in the first take. Rayn occasionally asked for the type of answer we were seeking, took five for a conversation with her mother, then came back and delivered a dream response.

We interviewed her mother and her siblings – the youngest boy and girl together and the older boy on his own – and her best friend. All of them were into the performing arts and able to follow directions and work with the camera easily, which made our jobs so much smoother.

While the crew were packing up – earlier than expected due to so few takes being needed – Zara and I sat down with Rayn and ran through the plans for filming at Bumblebee Barn the following week.

'Today has been a-may-zing,' she said when we'd finished. 'I've learned so much. I can't thank you enough.'

'It's our pleasure and it's been lovely to meet you.' I wasn't lying. She was a lovely young woman – vibrant, warm, engaging and fun – but in terms of the purpose of the show (or rather the *original* purpose of the show – who knew what the point was now?), today had been a waste of time. She couldn't be less suitable for Barney.

Although we'd finished for today and it was time to head back to Hedgehog Hollow, there was one question I had to ask, or it was going to niggle away at me.

'That stuff about your grandparents and the smallholding, was it true?'

'Elements of it. It was more of an allotment than a smallholding, and a scabby one at that. I hated visiting. Granny and Granddad Maggots would send me for eggs and the henhouse was always covered in shit and the hens would go for me. One day, a fox had got in and slaughtered them all. Traumatised me for life, that did.'

'What did you say their names were?' Zara asked.

Rayn laughed, a deeper sound than earlier, bordering on a cackle. 'Granny and Granddad Maggots. They wouldn't throw food away, even when it was past its best and mouldy. Next stage was maggots, so the name stuck. Suited them.' She shuddered. 'He's dead – died before my birth dad buggered off with that little slapper from his office – and I don't know and don't care about Granny Maggots. Good riddance. She was such a bitch.'

'So you don't like the countryside?' I asked.

'Bloody hate it. Like I said to you before, it's full of creepy crawlies and bad memories from being forced to stay with those two nutters. No wonder my birth dad was tapped.' She patted above her temple with her finger to emphasise her point. 'With loony parents like that, what chance did he have?'

Her tone dripped with bitterness and her lip was curled in disgust and then, as though a switch had been flicked, that radiant smile returned with the soft voice.

'Is there anything else you need from me today?'

'No, we're good.' I stood up. 'Thank you.'

'If you have any questions between now and Monday, drop me an email or give me a call,' Zara said.

We moved away from the table and towards the back door. I couldn't wait to get in the car and analyse what had just happened, but Zara paused and turned back to Rayn.

'Sorry, but I have one more question. If you hate the countryside so much, what will you do if our farmer picks you as his perfect match?' She leaned in conspiratorially. 'Off the record, of course.'

'Play along for the camera, have a bit of fun with him for the rest of the summer if he's fit, and then move to London as planned.'

I gasped. 'You're moving to London?'

'Yep. A few of us from uni have got a flat lined up. Best place to be for acting jobs.'

I had no idea how to respond to that, so I smiled politely and ushered Zara back towards the house to beat a hasty retreat. I knew Zara would be bursting to talk about it – as was I – but she remained professional until we'd pulled away from the house and out of the street.

'What just happened?' she cried.

'I have no idea.'

'Will the real Rayn Masterson please step forward? How many personalities did she have?'

'That was the weirdest experience ever,' I agreed. 'Scary thing is that I think the woman talking about Granny Maggots might be the real Rayn and everything else was an act.'

'And that thing about moving to London in September? What's that all about?'

'It's about a wannabe applying to every show that exists,

seeking her fifteen minutes of fame and hoping it will open a few doors.'

'Poor Barney.'

'Yep. One down, two to go.'

Rayn Masterson would absolutely ace the audition as one of Barney's Barbies on looks alone but she also represented everything wrong with all the other women in that club; zero interest in farming or the countryside. Plus, there was one thing that the others had over Rayn – honesty. They'd been themselves in front of Barney and my fear was that the part that Rayn was acting – very effectively – might just win him over. We'd have to hope that she couldn't sustain it for the time she'd be spending at the farm or that Marley or Tayla shone more brightly.

32

AMBER

When Zara and I returned to Hedgehog Hollow, Fizz was in the farmyard with her car boot open. I wondered if she was on her way out to a rescue or maybe returning from one. She looked up and signalled for us to stop.

'I know you can't tell me anything, so I won't ask how filming went today,' she said, bending down by the passenger side door. 'Reason I stopped you is to say that Phoebe and I are off to the cinema tonight. You're both welcome to join us if you fancy it.'

She named an action film I really fancied seeing but I'd called Matt on the journey to fill him in on the final strange conversation with Rayn and we'd agreed he'd join me to action plan for the next two days. I really appreciated that, even though he'd resigned, he hadn't detached himself from the project.

'I'd love to, but I've got a meeting with the director, but you can go if you want, Zara.'

'You don't need me?'

'I always need you, but we can survive without you and I'll fill you in on the plan when I get back. You deserve an evening off.'

'Brilliant. I'm in.'

* * *

I approached filming the following day with a smile and a positive attitude. Spending time with Matt last night had been incredibly useful. He'd told me that knowing he was walking away at the end of the week had helped him get some perspective and his advice to me was not to take any of it to heart and, while the whole concept didn't sit comfortably with either of us, most of the participants who put themselves forward for reality TV had some inkling as to what they were letting themselves in for and ulterior motives for doing it, as Rayn had demonstrated yesterday.

His advice made sense when it came to the matches – particularly if they were anything like Rayn – but it didn't help me with Barney. Unlike our Queen Elsa wannabe with her many personas, I believed him to be a genuine human being. It wasn't an unfounded feeling either. Everything I'd seen and heard so far backed that up – what a delight his sister was, the devotion from the rest of his family, the high regard in which Joel held him, and the concern he'd shown for Milo when he'd told me about his farmhand's broken wrist. And, of course, that broken heart he was doing his best to hide.

We hadn't been sent the application form for the second replacement match yet. All I knew was that twenty-two-year-old Marley Brambles – loving that name – rented a flat with her best friend above an estate agency in the seaside town of Whitsborough Bay which was unsuitable for filming. Fortunately, her auntie and uncle ran a riding stables near Claybridge between Whitsborough Bay and York, so that was our destination for today.

I hoped that the equestrian side to the family had rubbed off on Marley so, if nothing else, she'd have a love of horses in common with Barney.

As soon as I saw her, it was obvious why she'd been selected.

Just like Rayn yesterday, Marley would have sailed through the auditions for Barney's Barbies and, again, I wished I hadn't let that slip to the Lennons.

Marley's long blonde hair was straight. A few layers shaped round her face softened the look. Her eyes were deep blue and, like Rayn, her make-up was immaculate. When Marley was out of earshot, Zara whispered something about expert contouring. I nodded, although I had no idea what contouring meant or how to spot it. I was surprised anyone would notice Marley's face when she had other assets so prominently displayed. She'd already proudly announced she was a 34G as she adjusted the lace edging on her skin-tight vest top, immediately followed by, 'Just had them done.' I wasn't convinced that breast enlargement and riding would go hand in hand, unless she had a super-strong sports bra, and could feel my hopes about a horse connection fading away.

'Hi, I'm Marley,' she said, smiling at the camera for her introduction. 'I've got a first-class degree in psychology, a master's with distinction in neuroscience, I'm about to embark on a PhD in neuropsychology and, when I'm not studying, I'm a lingerie model. Who says you can't have looks *and* brains?'

There was a stunned silence and I could tell from the smug expression on Marley's face that she loved the reaction. Assumptions were probably made about her all the time and I was annoyed at myself for being guilty of making several.

'So, Marley,' I said, managing to compose myself. 'Tell us what you think about the countryside.'

'I was raised in Whitsborough Bay on the coast, so I have to confess that my first love is the sea, but Whitsborough Bay is surrounded by stunning countryside, so it comes a close second. I love hiking. I've completed all the major walks in the area several times – the Wolds Way, the Cleveland Way, the Esk Valley Walk and a stack of others. I've also done Wainwright's Coast to Coast – 190 miles through the most beautiful scenery.'

I glanced at Matt and he gave me a thumbs up. This was starting to sound promising.

'My auntie and uncle run an equestrian centre,' Marley continued. 'I've been round horses since I was tiny and I was originally planning on being a jockey, but I had a bad fall when I was fifteen and, although I can still ride, I can't ride competitively.'

'I'm sorry about your fall. What happened?'

'A deer ran out, spooked my horse Cleo, she reared and I woke up in hospital. Thankfully Cleo was fine but I'm now part bone, part metal.'

The Lennons would want to milk this. They'd be after emotion and ideally tears.

'And how did that affect you, having your future plans crushed like that?'

She waved her hand dismissively. 'People have to change their plans all the time. It was disappointing but I wasn't going to wallow and, at first, I was more concerned about Cleo than myself. When I knew she was unscathed, I focused on getting better. I've been round horses and jockeys long enough to be realistic about the impact of a fall, so I'd already thought about alternatives when I got my prognosis. As it happens, I love what I do and I'll have a career for life as a result. You can't be a jockey forever.'

We definitely weren't going to have tears from Marley. She was clearly made of stern stuff, practical and optimistic.

'And what are your thoughts on farms?'

'I know stacks of farms and farmers. Comes with the equestrian world. I love farms and animals and would happily live on one. I'm used to early mornings, hard work, mud, manure, and crazy weather, but there is one absolute no-no for me...'

I held my breath, dreading to know what was coming.

'Pigs,' she declared. 'I know it might sound ridiculous, but I have an irrational fear of them. It's a phobia, actually. My parents took me and my brother to a petting zoo when we were little and one chased me and pushed me over and... urgh...' she shuddered, '...I'm sweating just thinking about it. So I hope the farmer you've matched me with doesn't have any pigs. Does he? He doesn't, does he?'

I fought to maintain a poker face. 'We can't give out any details. It needs to be a surprise when you meet him next week.'

'I understand. I put this on my application form. They'll have seen that. They wouldn't be mean enough to match me with a pig farmer, would they?'

I smiled politely while cringing inside. Yes, they absolutely would. Now the choice of Marley with her looks, brains, passion for horses and love of the countryside made absolute sense. A woman with a phobia of pigs matched with a pig farmer was car-crash television. I could picture Grant and Liza rubbing their hands together with glee when they'd discovered that.

33

BARNEY

On Wednesday evening, I went into the office to catch up on some admin. It had been muggy all day and, despite pushing the window wide open, there was no air coming through and the small room felt oppressive.

It was tempting to leave my admin and lie on the sofa with a cold drink, but time wasn't on my side. Mum had drawn up a rota for next week for the farm tasks and we could probably hold it together between us, but I couldn't expect anyone to do the admin, so I not only needed to catch up – I needed to get ahead.

'I need a fan,' I muttered to myself. 'I'm sure I've got one somewhere.'

Harley came to see what I was doing.

'Have you seen my fan anywhere?' I asked her.

The heat in the room must have hit her because she padded straight out again. Either that or she was bored by my question.

It wasn't in the office, so it had to be in one of the four spare bedrooms. I'd done up the master bedroom and en suite when I took over the farm and I'd had the second bedroom decorated too so my parents, Fizz or Joel could stay over, but I'd never touched the other three. They were still exactly how I remembered them from childhood visits to the farm, with floral wallpaper and tired-looking fitted wardrobes. These days they acted as dumping grounds for anything I couldn't be bothered to sort through, sell, give away and the sort of items that would normally go into an attic – something the farmhouse didn't have – like suitcases, Christmas decorations, an old exercise bike, childhood board games.

'Come out, come out, wherever you are.'

I opened the double doors to a fitted wardrobe in one of the spare rooms. My old school blazer and tie hung on a solitary hanger and plastic carrier bags of what looked like old clothes and bedding were lined up across the bottom. I moved one of the bags and it disintegrated in my hands. Obviously been in there far too long.

There was another cupboard above it, fitted up to the top of the sloped ceiling. The handles were at the bottom corners, so I could open it with ease, and there was the fan on the top shelf. Unfortunately, the shelf was too great a stretch for me. I looked around the room but there weren't any chairs. Feeling too hot and lazy to go downstairs for a stepladder, I tugged at the dangling cable and the fan wobbled closer to the edge.

'Bit further.'

I tugged again until the fan was balanced precariously. Another tug and it was free. Falling. And bringing an avalanche of papers with it. I caught the fan and leapt backwards to avoid death by paper cuts, shaking my head as the papers kept on coming.

I didn't have the time or energy to clear up this evening, but my curiosity was piqued as to what it all was. Placing the fan on the floor, I knelt down and picked up the first pile – statements from my very first bank account. I'd closed it years ago, so they could all be destroyed. There were school reports and swimming certificates. Shuffling everything into a pile against the wardrobe, my fingers brushed against a black A5-sized plastic folder.

Nothing else was organised into folders, so I opened the popper, peered inside and lifted the items out one at a time. Charm bracelet. Friendship bracelet. Engagement ring. I couldn't remember placing them in there, but I remembered Elle hadn't returned the boxes.

Staring at the items in my palm, I expected to feel something – anger, sadness, regret – but I felt empty. Had sharing my story with Joel on Monday night somehow managed to unburden me of the pain I'd been shouldering for thirteen years?

I ran downstairs to the office and logged onto Facebook. I'd thought about looking for her online so many times over the years, even though I had no idea what I'd do if I found her, but I'd only ever got as far as typing in 'El' before reprimanding myself and walking away. This time, I typed in her full name, then again as Elle, but it didn't generate any results. She could have got married and changed her name, if she was even on social media at all. She'd never bothered with Facebook while we were seeing each other. Would Instagram be more her style?

I typed in her name and gasped. First result. Elmira De Luca @Trav_Elle.

Each photograph on her profile was like a slice of perfection. She appeared in most of the shots, often with her back to the camera or only showing her side profile, presumably to keep the follower's focus on the stunning scenery while showing she was actually there. Even if there hadn't been the occasional shot of her face, I'd have recognised her.

Wearing floral dresses or sculpted swimwear, with big straw hats and sunglasses, she showcased turquoise oceans, infinity pools, delectable cuisine, sand dunes...

'Travel influencer,' I whispered. 'Three point seven million followers. Wow!'

She'd done it. She'd travelled the world – perhaps several times over – and she was living her dream. There were no children in the pictures or any sign of a partner, but that didn't mean they didn't exist.

I scrolled down further, through winter shots of the Northern Lights, glaciers, hot springs and Christmas lights, through autumn and back to summer once more. I sat forward in my chair, scrolling back through another year – more stunning photos in incredible locations – and I experienced a moment of clarity. Elle had been right all along. It could *never* have worked between us. My world was my family and the farm, but her world quite literally was the whole world. The compromise I'd offered her would never have been enough. If she'd stayed, she'd have been like a caged animal, and we'd have ended up resenting each other. She really had needed to be free.

'I hope freedom brought happiness,' I whispered, closing down Instagram then shutting the laptop.

There was one more thing I needed to do before I tackled the admin. I called for the dogs and took the quad bike up to Spring Field, where I chucked tennis balls to them as we made our way across the field to the shelter. The sun was low in the sky and trails of peach-tinged clouds held the promise of a beautiful sunset.

Bear and Harley flopped outside the shelter, each with a ball between their front paws, catching their breath as I stepped inside our special place for the first time in thirteen years. More tiles had fallen in or slipped off the roof and several stones had crumbled as the weeds pushed their way to the light, but it was still how I remembered. The picnic blanket was heaped in the corner, probably home now to thousands of bugs.

What date was it? I checked my phone – 5 June – and did a

swift calculation. A week on Monday, it would be Elle's thirty-first birthday, and exactly thirteen years since I proposed. I could still remember every little thing about that day – the nerves-infused excitement I felt when she said she wanted to take our relationship to the next level, the physical excitement when I granted her wish, and the elation when she finally agreed to marry me. I could also still remember the day it ended.

The pain had gone and, with it, an even stronger emotion.

Guilt.

Guilt that I'd said yes to the one thing we'd promised we wouldn't do for fear of complications. Guilt that I'd tried to make her stay when I knew she needed to be free. Guilt that both those actions resulted in an unwanted pregnancy and a life-changing decision.

I took one last look round the shelter then sat in the doorway, breathing in the warm air. Harley placed her paw on my thigh then settled down beside me, her warm body pressed against my leg. Bear rested his head on my other thigh. I stroked them both and we sat there in silence as the sun slowly melted onto the horizon. Elle and I were never meant to stay together. As she'd frequently told me, sometimes things just didn't work.

And, right now, I finally accepted that.

34

AMBER

After the revelations from Rayn and Marley, our hopes were pinned on twenty-six-year-old Tayla Kenzie – the only one in the mix from the original matches.

On Thursday morning, Zara and I headed to the coast to a village called Little Fraisby, near the small seaside town of Fellingthorpe. Tayla's father had some health and mobility challenges, so she lived with her parents, helping her mother care for her father. They had a pretty bungalow with a small but beautifully maintained back garden with views of the North Sea beyond.

The sea breeze took the edge off the mugginess that had been building across the week, making for pleasant filming conditions.

While I hadn't considered Tayla to be a perfect match for Barney, I had at least met her and knew that her reasons for taking part were genuine. She loved the countryside and had been raised on a farm until ill health meant her father needed to sell up. She worked in a farm shop and was genuinely looking for love. No desire to be famous and definitely no pig phobias.

My concerns for the match hadn't therefore been a lack of shared interests or even her looks – she was still blonde, after all, even if her hair was short and her make-up natural. I'd been worried about the personality match – or lack of it. Tayla was shy, quiet, lacking in self-confidence and perhaps a little too serious for Barney, who was none of those things. Last time I met her, I'd challenged her on her lack of self-confidence and how that tallied with appearing on television – usually the domain of those brimming with confidence – but she said it was something she was trying hard to work on and she saw this as a way of challenging herself.

As Barney's opposite, Tayla might complement him or it might be a disaster, but I still stood by her being the best chance of a love match out of the original three.

Filming with Tayla couldn't have been more different to our first day with Rayn. She was extremely nervous, stumbling over her words, nibbling on her nails and looking absolutely terrified. After we hit double figures on the takes to get her introduction right, Matt and I were concerned she might break down in tears and suggested a time-out. I admired her for wanting to push herself out of her comfort zone to build her confidence, but suspected this might have been a step too far.

Tayla went into the bungalow with the three family members and friends we were filming later that day: her mother, the manager at the farm shop where she worked, and her sister-in-law – the person who'd convinced her to apply. Whatever they said to her, it worked, as she emerged much calmer and we eventually had some footage we could use.

With each hour that passed, Tayla seemed more settled. She had a beautiful smile which we saw more frequently and a quick-witted sense of humour emerged. By the end of filming, I believed once more that it could work between her and Barney if she managed to relax and let that sense of humour and fun personality shine from the start.

After filming, Zara and I sat down with Tayla to go through the arrangements for next week, but she seemed nervous once more, which was odd considering the cameras were off. Her right leg bounced up and down and I wished I could gift her a massive slice of self-belief.

'I'm sure he won't, but what happens if the farmer chooses me?' she asked.

'If he chooses you, you'll go on the big date the following week, but I can't tell you anything about what or where that will be. It'll just be the two of you... and Zara, our director, me, the camera crew...'

She didn't laugh. It wasn't the greatest of jokes, but it deserved something.

'After that, it's up to the two of you,' I continued. 'The only further commitment to *Love on the Farm* is that, three months down the line, we return to the area, catch up with you both, and do a reveal to the viewers as to whether or not the match worked.'

'What about the big date? Again, I'm sure he wouldn't pick me but, if he did, would I be expected to kiss him?' Both legs were bouncing now.

'Gosh, no. We're not that sort of show, Tayla.' Although I still wasn't quite sure what kind of show we were. 'If there's mutual chemistry and it feels right and comfortable for you both, then we'd absolutely encourage a kiss – the perfect demonstration of success in finding love on the farm – but there'll be no pressure for anyone to kiss if those feelings aren't there or it doesn't feel right.'

I had no idea what the new director's take would be on that, but mutual consent was something I felt very strongly about, and I'd argue tooth and nail about it if they suggested otherwise.

She smiled weakly. 'That's okay then. Thank you.'

Zara looked very thoughtful, chewing her lip as she studied Tayla.

'You look poised for a question, Zara,' I prompted when she didn't say anything. If she'd picked up on something which I hadn't, I wanted to explore it.

'It's probably nothing,' Zara said with a shrug. 'It's just that I've seen your application video, Tayla, read your application form, and gone over Amber's notes from your face-to-face like a gazillion times and I'm picking up some hesitancy around the match which I didn't detect before. I wondered if there was a reason for that.'

Gosh, she was good. How had I missed that? In my face-to-face interview, I'd asked her about her ideal date if she was chosen, and she'd described it ending with a kiss. It was possible that, after a day of being surrounded by cameras, the idea of sharing a kiss on screen was intimidating, but what if there was something else going on?'

Tayla hung her head and mumbled something neither Zara nor I could catch.

'Can you repeat that?' I asked gently.

'I don't want him to pick me.' It was still a mumble, but the words were clearer.

'Can I ask why?'

Silence.

'Tayla? Is there something you want to tell us?'

She looked up, her eyes darting from me to Zara then back to me.

'I'm really sorry. I never expected it to happen, but I've met someone.'

* * *

'You look like you could do with this.' Zara placed a large glass of icy cold rosé wine on the patio table beside my laptop.

I looked up at her and nodded gratefully. 'You're a star.

Although the way I'm feeling right now, you'd be better off giving me the whole bottle and a straw.'

She pulled out the chair beside me and took a sip from her glass before sitting down. 'What's the plan?'

'Pack up our stuff and run for the hills?' I accompanied that with a laugh which bordered on hysterical, so I grabbed my wine and downed a couple of gulps.

I picked up Rayn's profile. 'Hates the countryside unless she's pretending to be Maria von Trapp or Queen Elsa, not a particularly nice person, only in it for the fame, and is moving to London in September. Computer says no.'

I dropped her profile back on the table and picked up Marley's, which we'd finally been emailed after her interview. 'Loves the countryside, loves animals, is terrified of pigs. Computer also says no.'

'And today's last chance saloon was Ms Tayla Kenzie.' I picked up her profile. 'Took a lot of warming up but a beautiful butterfly began to emerge from the chrysalis and it looked like we had a winner. Except Mr Right, Aston, who she's had a secret crush on for over a year, finally asked her out and they're already choosing a puppy together. Computer says yes. Contestant says no.'

I slapped her profile down on the table a little too hard, making Zara jump.

'There's no way Barney's going to pick her,' I continued, tapping my finger on Tayla's profile. 'It took her ages to warm up to us and she doesn't want to warm up to him because she's already got the man of her dreams. The whole thing's a disaster.'

'I really was single and looking for love when I applied and even when we met,' Tayla had insisted, tears pooling in her eyes. 'I feel so guilty. If you want to replace me, I completely understand.'

In an ideal world, we would have replaced her, knowing what

we now knew, but it was too late. She'd signed a contract and the window for withdrawing had already passed.

Aston knew all about the show and was happy for her to take part because her father was so excited about seeing his daughter on TV and, with his health in rapid decline, they were eager to give him something to look forward when the programme aired.

I'd assured her that there'd be no replacing and that the risk of reality television was that, because of the passage of time between applying and filming, people's circumstances often did change. Besides, even if we could have replaced her at the eleventh hour, who with? Somebody else completely unsuitable brought in for viewing figures instead of love? Somebody who'd make a fool out of Barney? I wasn't prepared to put him through that.

'I'm so gutted about Tayla.' I took another glug from my wine. 'Obviously not for her as she's found love, but for Barney. There's nothing we can do, though.'

Zara gathered up the profiles and moved them to the other end of the table out of reach.

'Even if Tayla had still been single,' she said, 'there's no guarantee there'd have been any chemistry between her and Barney.'

'True. But she was the only option out of the three.'

'Agreed. But, before today's revelation, you already had your doubts about her and it wasn't looking good first thing. I know she got better but, boyfriend aside, she's not the right personality type for Barney and you know it. She was the best of a bad bunch and now she's out of the race.'

'I feel so guilty for him that we have nobody.'

'Don't. It was always a long shot and I'm sure all the farmers know that. Even if the Lennons hadn't mixed things up, what were the odds for a match among the original three women and of Barney picking that right person after less than two days together? It didn't happen in Wales for either of our farmers.'

No, it didn't, and both of them had three good matches instead of one chosen by me under duress and two picked by the Lennons to add spice.

'Even without the meddling, I don't think it would have happened for Barney and I know you feel the same. You struggled to narrow the original three down to one and that wasn't because you were spoilt for choice.'

'I need to let it go, don't I?' I said, laughing as Zara burst into the *Frozen* song, mirroring Rayn's dramatic arms and facial expressions from her *Frozen II* rendition on Tuesday.

Everything Zara said made perfect sense and I wasn't naïve enough to think that all the stars would align to have any of the couples still together three months later, but the romantic in me wanted it to work. Especially for Barney. I wanted to break the cycle and heal his broken heart.

A FaceTime request came through from Sophie, so Zara said she'd head inside to start preparing our dinner while I spoke to my sister.

'Hi, you, how's it going?' I asked when I accepted the request.

'Becca Scarsdale is such a gifted scriptwriter. All the characters are so well developed.'

'She deserves all those awards.'

'She absolutely does. I'm so lucky to be involved.'

The words were positive, but she wasn't smiling, setting off alarm bells.

'How are you getting on with the rest of the cast?' I asked. 'Made any new friends?'

'Not really. A few of them have worked together before so I feel like the new kid at school. And they're all so experienced. I've done nothing since *Mercury's Rising.*'

Was that the reason for the downcast expression?

'That's not true, Soph. You've had loads of roles since *Mercury's*

Rising and you know it takes a talented actor to deliver a memo-rable performance as a guest star.'

'I suppose.'

'And Becca Scarsdale is known for her exemplary casting deci-sions. There's no way she'd have cast you if she thought you could be a weak link. Has anyone said anything to you?'

She shook her head. 'It's me. I'm being silly.'

'It's not silly at all. You're in a strange place with new people doing something you haven't done for a lot of years. It's a different beast and it'll take time to settle in.'

'Yeah, you're right. The rest of the cast are nice. They're not leaving me out or anything like that. I just...' She clapped her hand to her cheek and rolled her eyes. 'I'm making a mountain out of a molehill.'

'You're having a few wobbles. It happens to us all.' It would be an appropriate moment to share that my time on *Life on the Farm* had been one wobble after another, but she had no idea I'd taken the part to be near her and, if I shared any of my concerns, that was bound to come out.

'Anything else bothering you?' I asked.

'Nothing.'

'Sophie! I know you too well. Spill!'

To my horror, she burst into tears.

'Oh, my God, Soph! What's happened?'

She tried to speak but her sobs drowned the words. She put the phone down, giving me a view of the ceiling and I heard her blowing her nose in the background so presumably she'd gone for tissues. All I could do was wait.

'I don't know where that came from,' she managed eventually, picking up her phone and wiping her cheeks.

She looked so lost, and I wanted to be there to give her a hug. I'd only had half a glass of wine, but I never touched a drop if I was driving. I'd have to get a taxi. I stood up and went in search of some shoes and a jacket.

'I'm coming over. I'll be with you in an hour or so.'

'Don't you dare!'

'But you're upset.'

'So what? I wasn't expecting to cry about it and now I feel ridiculous, especially for worrying you. It's nothing and I don't want you to come over. I'm running a bath right now and then I've got lines to learn so you'd only have to turn round and go straight back home. Promise me you'll stay put.'

I sat on the sofa with a sigh. 'Okay, but you have to tell me what's going on.'

She wiped her eyes. 'There's this man on the crew. I don't know his name. Every time I look round, he's watching me.'

'Creepy watching?'

'No, not really.'

'Maybe he fancies you.'

'Ew, no, he's old enough to be my dad.'

'Just because you're not attracted to him doesn't mean he wouldn't be attracted to you. You're stunning, Soph.'

'You're very sweet,' she said, smiling at last, 'but it's not that sort of look.'

'Maybe he's seen one or more of your guest appearances and is trying to work out where he knows you from. Or he could have watched *Mercury's Rising* and be having a fan moment.'

She was quiet for a moment, then she slowly nodded. 'Either of those is possible. I should have thought about that. I'd convinced myself he recognised me from *The House*.'

'Oh, Soph, no wonder you were upset. I won't lie and say it's impossible, but it's highly unlikely. *The House* wasn't a ratings winner, it was on an obscure channel and it got pulled from air. If you're concerned about this guy looking at you, why don't you talk to him?'

'I couldn't do that.'

'Then maybe have a word with the director or another cast member who knows him.'

Sophie perked up at that suggestion. 'One of the cast – an older guy called Burt – is really sweet and he seems to know him. I'll talk to him about it. Thanks, Amber. I'm glad I called you.'

'I'm glad you did. Call me any time and, if you need me, I can come to you. Or, if it gets too much and you want a break, you can always come here.'

'You're the best.'

I was keen to make sure she really was okay before the conversation ended, so I questioned her further on the cast and whether she'd seen much of York. By the end of the call, I was confident that she'd offloaded all her worries and I'd arranged to visit her at the weekend. I genuinely didn't think that anyone would have seen her in *The House*, but what if this crew member had? She definitely wasn't ready to face her past and neither was I.

35

AMBER

Five years ago

Sophie's eighteenth birthday fell on a Thursday. The original plan had been a big party in a country hotel on the Saturday night, but the birthday girl couldn't make that date now after being selected as one of twenty contestants for a brand-new reality television show called *The House*. The contestants would be entering 'the house' on Saturday night so there'd been a hasty change of plan to the evening of Sophie's actual birthday and a meal rather than a party.

'How long do you think this thing will go on for?' Parker peered into the illuminated mirror in our hotel room, which I was using to apply my make-up, and adjusted his tie.

'Parker! It's not a *thing*. It's my sister's eighteenth birthday. Maybe two or three hours.' I'm not sure how I managed to keep my voice so jovial with the frustration bubbling inside me at his obvious disdain.

He was still looking in the mirror, tweaking his dark hair, so I didn't miss the curl of his lip. My jaw tightened as I applied my mascara, not trusting myself to speak in case I started an argument and he refused to come downstairs. I couldn't help wondering if that was his end goal. Parker hated family gatherings. Estranged from his parents and with no siblings, he seemed to struggle to understand why I liked to spend so much time with my family. It was the only thing about our relationship which caused me any concern, but I repeatedly batted it aside. After all, he did join me at family events, even though I knew it wasn't his thing, and he had conceded to a big wedding next year instead of a private ceremony abroad like he wanted.

'We won't be expected to go back to Green Acres afterwards?'

It was a question but it sounded more like a statement and I pushed down the bubble of anger once more.

'Nobody's mentioned it.'

They hadn't needed to. An assumption would have been made that the party would continue afterwards and that we'd be there because that's how things were done in my family. This was about celebrating a special occasion rather than practicality. We'd been offered my old room at Green Acres, so continuing after the meal wouldn't have been an issue if we'd stayed there, but Parker wasn't comfortable staying in other people's houses – even when those people were my family – so we'd booked a room at the country hotel, just as we'd done when he joined us for Christmas.

'If they do, you'll have to go on your own,' he said. 'I need to work.'

He was sitting on the edge of the bed now, putting his shoes on. I could see his reflection in the mirror and the anger ebbed away, replaced by empathy. Parker was absolutely shattered, evidenced by the tension in his jaw and the dark shadows beneath his eyes. He'd been drafted in as the director on *The House* at the eleventh hour after the previous director pulled out following a bereavement. In theory, it was a conflict of interests and the nature of reality TV meant it wasn't ideal, but it was just one of those changes in circumstances we had to go with. Sophie would never have applied if Parker had already signed up as director. He'd been working crazy hours to get on top of things and he'd have been fully justified in pulling out of tonight, but he'd made no attempts to do so and I loved him for that.

I placed my mascara wand back in the bottle and joined him on the bed.

'If you need to give tonight a miss, that's okay. Everyone will understand. *I'll* understand.'

His shoulders relaxed and I thought he was going to accept my offer. He smiled at me – that dazzling smile of his which oozed confidence and charm – and his dark blue eyes shone, making me go weak at the knees, just like they had the first time we'd met.

'I'll still come, but I'll not stick around when the meal's done.'

'That's fine.'

'Thanks for offering, though.'

He placed his hand under my chin, tilted my face towards his and gave me a slow, lingering kiss which sent my heart racing. We might have different opinions on the importance of family but everything else about our relationship gave me a thrill. I loved that man so much.

* * *

After our starters had been cleared away, Dad stood up and tapped his knife against his champagne flute. The chatter hushed and everyone looked at him expectantly.

'In the early hours of the morning, eighteen years ago, my beautiful wife Jules and I welcomed our third child into the world, and boy, did she make her presence known. The midwives all said they'd never heard such loud cries and joked that, with a pair of lungs like that, she was either going to be a singer or an actor. She became both. And somehow she added dancing into the mix, despite her mother and I both having two left feet.'

'Speak for yourself!' Mum called, making everyone laugh.

'That triple threat meant she was perfect for the part of Mercury Addison and it has been a pleasure to watch our baby girl grow and develop alongside her character on *Mercury's Rising* for seven incredible years. Sophie's now about to embark on an exciting new project and we can't wait to see what comes after that because we just know that, whatever it is, she'll excel. Happy birthday, Sophie!'

We all toasted Sophie and persuaded her to stand up and give her own speech.

'Thanks for the lovely toast, Dad,' she said. 'I don't want to say much except thank you for coming, especially when it's a last-minute change of plans. I know you're dying to know what's happening on Saturday, but I've been sworn to secrecy. You'll know soon enough. Drink lots and enjoy your evening!'

Over the main course, speculation was rife outside of the family as to what Sophie's new project might be, but nobody mentioned reality television. The general consensus was that she'd secured a film role and Sophie's boyfriend Devon – an extra on *Mercury's Rising* who she'd been seeing since they were fourteen – appeared to be having fun with that, winding the guests up as to who she could be starring alongside.

It was warm in the restaurant so, while the table was cleared after our main course, several of the guests stepped out onto the terrace for some fresh air. Parker and I did the same and found a table tucked round a corner out of earshot of everyone.

'You're sure this is a good move for Sophie?' I asked.

'Good move? Who knows with these things? Bad move? I don't see how. Bunch of attractive eighteen- to thirty-year-olds lazing around in a grand mansion for two months with a holiday of a lifetime up for grabs? I'd have loved to do something like that at her age. What could go wrong?'

I pushed aside the niggle in my gut. Parker made it sound like a fun holiday when he put it like that, although I wasn't naïve enough to think there wouldn't be more to it than that.

He couldn't share any details and I respected that. I'd never have let anything slip to my sister, but I understood his need to protect his own back. I'd decided not to think about it and just go with the flow like Sophie was.

'Everyone's going back in,' Parker said, setting off towards the doors.

I grabbed his hand and tugged him back. 'You will look out for her, won't you? Make sure nothing bad happens to her?'

'Stop worrying. She's eighteen years old and she wants to do this, so you need to let her embrace the experience.'

It was only later when it all kicked off that I realised that Parker had never answered my question. While he could never have predicted the event which led to *The House* being taken off air, he'd known what Sophie was walking into. He'd known the risks. And he'd let his future sister-in-law, only just eighteen years old, walk into it. Bad move? Yes, the worst ever.

36

BARNEY

Present day

'Did you get it that time?' I asked Amber on Friday morning.

She looked at the cameraman who she'd introduced as Will, and he gave a thumbs up.

'Yes, we did,' Amber said. 'Thanks for indulging us. We'll try not to interrupt you very often as we want it to be natural, but there are certain key shots we want to get.'

Me emerging from the farmhouse in the darkness was one of them and it had taken four attempts to catch the right angle and lighting. Bear and Harley must have been curious as to what game we were playing.

Amber and Will followed me and the dogs over to the barn.

'Do you want me to talk to the camera and explain what I'm doing?' I asked.

'No. We just want footage of you out and about doing your normal morning routine. There'll be a narrator for any voiceover bits. We'll probably only use a small fraction of the footage, but this is a chance to showcase the beautiful countryside and your gorgeous farm, which is why we're here from sunrise – well, just after sunrise – to sunset.'

'There've been some impressive sunsets recently so let's hope you're in luck.' I stopped by the quad bike. 'The dogs will get on the back and we'll head up to check on the sheep. You're best off following me in your car and leaving it by the gate.'

They filmed the dogs and me getting onto the quad bike and pulling out of the barn from the side, the back, and the front and a couple of different angles of us going up the track.

'The rest of the crew will be here later,' Amber said, her expression apologetic. 'We won't need all the repetition at that point. I promise.'

'It's fine but, as it'll put me behind schedule, you're more than welcome to pull on a boilersuit and give me a hand.'

I was half-joking and had assumed she'd object, telling me that she was the producer, not a farmhand, but she surprised me by smiling widely. 'I'd love to. I've got some overalls in the boot. See you up there.'

I rode up to Top Field, where I kept the Swaledale sheep, and went straight over to the water trough and filled it. Amber's 4x4 stopped by the gate as I finished and I rode back across the field.

'Will's going to get some shots of the sheep,' Amber said, approaching me in a boilersuit and wellies, looking like she'd been doing this all her life. 'What do you need me to do?'

'It's all about checks. I need to go round the perimeter and check no escape routes have suddenly appeared like gaps in the hedge or holes in the wire fencing. It's much easier at this time of year, when the sun rises before I'm up. It'll be even lighter by the time we've done that, so we'll give the flock a once-over. Then we repeat the same thing in the other fields. Do you want to hop on while we do the perimeter?'

'I love quad bikes so I want to say yes, but Will's going to want to do some filming and I can't be in the shot riding pillion.'

'How about we ride to the gate then I can head south and you can go north and we'll meet somewhere along the way?'

'You're on!'

I shuffled forward and Amber jumped on behind me. I was about to point out where the handholds were but she threaded her arms round my waist.

'Is this okay?' she asked when I didn't turn the throttle.

'Yes. Good. Fine. Let's go.'

Milo had been on the bike with me and so had Fizz, but the last time someone had held me round the waist had been Elle – none of my exes had been interested in getting on the quad bike – and I couldn't remember how that felt anymore.

Amber's hold was strong, her body was warm against mine, and I felt an unexpected twinge of disappointment when we reached the gate and she dismounted.

The sunrise was gentle rather than dramatic. A band of pale lemon faded into baby blue as the sun continued its ascent. Moving round the perimeter, I stopped to remove a piece of plastic sheeting attached to the hedge, meaning Amber had made it further round on foot than I might have expected. As I rode across the top edge to meet her, she bent down to pick up a piece of litter. A branch sticking out from the hedge knocked her baseball cap off her head. The force must have taken her hair bobble with it as the hair I'd only ever seen tied up was now free and hanging in waves. The rising sun caught the side of her face and hair, bathing her in golden light. She was breathtakingly beautiful.

'Hat and hair disaster,' she called to me, retrieving her cap from the grass. 'I can't find my bobble, but I don't want one of your sheep to swallow it.'

I grabbed a torch from beneath the quad bike's seat and we soon spotted the bobble in the torch's beam. She passed me her cap so she could scrape her hair back into another ponytail.

'You've got gorgeous hair,' I blurted out.

She looked surprised as she released the tresses in her hands, and I kicked myself for speaking before thinking. It was probably really inappropriate to compliment the female TV producer of a show focused on finding me love. I wondered whether I should apologise but she smiled as she pulled the bobble onto her wrist.

'Thank you. I used to hate the colour – easy target for the school bullies – but my mum's a redhead and she always rocked it, so I learned to embrace it. My sister's a redhead too. Mum's is darker than mine and Sophie's is lighter.' She paused and laughed. 'That was a lot of information about my family and our hair which I'm sure you have no interest in whatsoever.'

We'd spent so much time talking about me that it was good to get a brief insight into Amber's life.

'Is your sister older or younger?' I asked her.

'Eleven years younger and I have a brother too, Brad, who's two years older and, as I can't keep you hanging with half a riveting story, Brad has dark hair like my dad.'

We smiled at each other.

'So what's next?' she asked. 'You said something about giving the flock a once-over. Tell me what I'm looking for and I'll move out of your way so Will can film you.'

'You're comfortable around sheep?'

'Yeah, I've produced *Countryside Calendar* for the past five years and, even though I have a behind-camera role, there've still been plenty of hands-on moments.'

'Favourite farm animal?' I asked as we headed towards the flock.

'You can't ask me that! It's an impossible choice. They all have something endearing about them, although I do have a fondness for sheep, particularly herdies. They have such beautiful faces.'

'They're my mum's favourite too and we have a field full of them.'

Herdies was a shortened name for the Herdwick breed. Both the Swaledales and Herdwicks were more typically found in the Dales and Cumbria as they were extremely hardy and good with hills. At Bumblebee Barn, our hills were gentle, but Granddad had introduced a few from both breeds before my time and they'd thrived so they were now all we had.

'Aw, I can't wait to see them. I'd assumed you only had Swaledales.'

'If I'd known you were such an expert, I'd have shown you the herdies on our tour too.' I hadn't mentioned the name of the breed grazing in Top Field and was impressed that she knew, although five years on *Countryside Calendar* should have given her a good basic knowledge of all things farm related.

I ran through some of the checks on the flock. Amber was really knowledgeable on some aspects and keen to learn on others. She seemed so relaxed out and about on the farm – more than when she was behind the camera.

'That's Will signalling,' she said. 'I'll get out of shot and re-join you when he's got what he needs.'

That twinge of disappointment was there again when she walked away. It had been a long time since anyone had shown a genuine interest in the farm, and I'd wanted our conversation to continue. I hadn't been sure about Amber from our first meeting. Nothing against her as such but more of a vibe that she didn't particularly like me, but I'd watched her chatting with my family in the kitchen on Monday morning and had really appreciated the interest she'd shown in them. And now, seeing her out in her boilersuit with her hair hanging loose talking about her love for sheep, I saw another, different side to her – a side I wanted to get to know better. Which wasn't ideal given the reason for her being here.

37

AMBER

The flock of Herdwicks in Double Top Field were gorgeous, especially the lambs, although, at two months old, they were getting big. The breed was distinctive, with white faces and a grey fleece. I'd seen herdies before with brown or black fleeces, but all Barney's were grey.

'That's Dora,' Barney said, pointing to a large ewe munching near the top hedge. 'Named after Dora the Explorer because of her penchant for escaping and exploring the farm. Don't let her size deceive you. That little lady can get through the smallest of gaps.'

'Do you name them all?'

'No. Just a few of the characters. Fizz started it when we were kids and we used to out-compete each other for the best names. It kind of stuck.'

'Any others with names?'

Barney looked round and pointed. 'You see the one near the water trough. That's...' He started laughing. 'I'm a bit embarrassed about this one 'cos it's really cheesy.'

His laugh was infectious, and I couldn't help laughing along with him. 'Go on.'

'Her name's Sandra as in Sandra Bullock because there used to be a bull in the field next door and she befriended it. I told you it was bad.'

He could barely say the words for laughing and soon we were both in fits of giggles.

'That's awful,' I said when I managed to compose myself, 'but also a little bit genius.'

'We named the bull Keanu Reeves because he was friends with Sandra Bullock and could move at speed.'

That set us both off again. My dad had a fondness for eighties and nineties action films, so *Speed* had been regular family viewing growing up.

Will was ready to film again so I had to move away from Barney, which was a shame as I was dying to hear more of his brilliant names. He'd joked before about the field names lacking creativity, but there was definitely imagination in the animal names.

* * *

'Breakfast time,' Barney said when we'd finished with the sheep. 'Can I interest you in a bacon butty?'

'I don't want to put you to any trouble.'

'It's no trouble.'

Will was invited to join us, but he declined, saying he had a few phone calls to make.

'Did you ever consider anything other than farming?' I asked Barney while we waited for the bacon to grill.

'Never. Growing up, I knew the farm would pass down to my uncle and, if he had kids, it would pass down to them, so I'd always work here rather than own it, but I was fine with that. When he cleared off and I had the chance to take over, it felt right – like this was what I was destined to do. Mum and Dad were brilliant. They told me there was no pressure on me, they'd understand if I wanted to go in another direction, and that I wasn't to worry about Granddad's reaction if I did something different, but it was what I wanted and it still is.'

'Ever had any regrets?'

'Once.' He looked wistful for a moment, then shook his head, smiling. 'But it was a long time ago and I made the right decision.'

I wondered whether it was connected to the broken heart I was sure he was nursing, but I wasn't going to intrude and risk putting a dampener on our lovely morning.

'What about you?' he asked, flipping the bacon on the grill. 'Always wanted to be a TV producer?'

'Yes and, like you, it's in my blood too or, rather, television is. I'm the only one behind the camera...'

It turned out that *Darrington Detects* was his mum's favourite TV programme, the whole family loved Mum's cooking and gardening shows, and Fizz used to be obsessed with *Mercury's Rising*. Barney admitted to 'pretending not to watch it but it was really a guilty pleasure, although don't tell Fizz that or I'll never hear the end of it!' None of his family watched *Londoners* but he was familiar enough with the soap to know who Brad and Tabs were.

'So you know all of my family but haven't met any of them.' I winked at him. 'Probably best that way. They're really horrible in real life.'

'You must miss them when you're filming.'

'I do, but it makes time together even more special. Sophie's filming a new series in York and I'm going to see her this weekend and then, when we're finished filming, my parents will be visiting her and I'll join them, so we try to make it work. It's harder coordinating a full family meet-up.'

'I can imagine. So, with such a famous family, was there never any pressure on you to act or present?'

'My parents had the same outlook as yours – they'd have supported me if that was what I wanted but were equally encouraging of something different. I'm the introvert of the family, or I was until...' I faltered, stopping myself from saying something about Sophie. Barney was so easy to open up to and I'd been completely off-guard for a moment.

'Until...?' he prompted.

'Nothing. Not sure where I was going with that. And I hear voices outside, but it's a bit early for the crew.'

Barney went to the door and called back, 'It's just Will on speakerphone.'

'We should probably get back to work,' I said, clearing the plates off the table. Probably just as well we'd been interrupted, as I was in danger of giving Barney my entire life story and there were certain chapters that needed to stay closed.

For the next hour or so, it was just Barney, me and the animals while Will went off on his own to film some general shots of the farm. Barney's passion for farming and his love for Bumblebee Barn emanated from him. As we worked, he spoke of a pilot his mum had been running to host children's parties at the farm with animal feeding and petting experiences, and about a longer-term project to open a farm shop. I was fascinated by his plans and also his devotion to his animals and could have happily talked to him all day, but Zara, Matt and the rest of the crew arrived, and I needed to revert to the role of producer.

Will left around mid-afternoon to spend the weekend with his family and Matt was ready to head off not long after. He said his goodbyes to Zara and the crew, and I walked him to his car so we could have a final moment on our own.

'I hope we get to work together again,' he said, hugging me goodbye. 'I'm so sorry for abandoning you.'

'Don't be, Matt. Like I said before, I'd have gone too if I could.'

'Have they told you who's replacing me yet?'

'I picked up an email earlier. Giles Snyder?' I shrugged. 'I don't know him, but I don't care. I'm just grateful it's not my ex-fiancé. That would have been hell on earth.'

'I worked with your ex before I went to the States. Not my favourite person.'

'Not mine either. You think Grant and Liza Lennon are vile? They're like pussycats compared to Parker.'

We smiled at each other.

'Don't be a stranger,' he said, giving me another hug.

'Same to you. If I hear of any directing jobs, I'll let you know.'

I felt tearful as Matt drove away, even though I was certain our paths would cross again at some point, and was dabbing my eyes with a tissue as I walked back across the farmyard and straight into Barney.

'I'm so sorry,' I said, backing away and sniffing. 'First rule of farm safety – look where you're going!'

'Are you okay?' he asked, looking at me with concern.

'Yeah, I'm fine. I'm not good at goodbyes.'

'Your boyfriend?'

'Matt? No. He's been a great director, so I'm sad that we won't be working together anymore.'

'He's not back next week?'

'No, there's a director change from Monday, but I'll still be here for continuity, and Zara and the rest of the crew. Aren't you the lucky one?'

He cocked his head to one side, a ghost of a smile playing on his lips. 'Very lucky.'

A sudden gust of wind blew some seed heads from a dandelion clock past us and Barney ducked backwards to avoid one landing on his face.

'Fizz used to call them fairies,' he said. 'You've got one in your hair. Do you want me to...?'

'Please.'

I held my breath as he reached forward to extract it, his fingers gently tugging at my hair.

'Make a wish and blow it away,' he said, resting it in his palm. 'Quick, before it blows away on its own.'

I closed my eyes for a moment and wished the first thing that came into my head before I blew it away.

'I hope it was a good one,' he said gently.

'It was.'

I'd wished for Barney to find love on the farm. If anyone deserved it, he did.

We turned at the sound of a car and I was surprised to see Matt pulling back into the farmyard.

'He must have forgotten something,' I said.

'I'll be in the garage if you need me for anything.'

Barney headed off and I wandered over to Matt's car.

'Missing us already?' I joked, smiling at him as he got out.

'Angelique sent me back. She says I have to tell you something.'

'Okay. Sounds intriguing.'

He ran his hands through his hair, evidently feeling uncomfortable.

'How long have you and Dan been together?'

'This time round, since New Year. We were together for eighteen months, eight years back. Why?'

'Remember when we first met? I thought I recognised Dan and we concluded I'd probably seen him on TV.'

'Yes.' I had a bad feeling in my gut about where this might be heading.

'I didn't think that would be the case, as I don't actually watch much TV and I'd been living in the States. Angelique got me to watch a drama with her last night. I can't even tell you what the programme was, but Dan was in it – just a small part – and I pointed out that he was your boyfriend and that I thought I'd recognised him from somewhere. She's brilliant with faces and she knew exactly where I'd seen him because she saw him there too.'

'Go on,' I said when he fell silent, biting his lip.

'I was working on a three-part thriller earlier this year – *The Dove That Cried* – and Dan was on set.'

'Are you sure? I've never heard him mention it.'

'He wasn't acting in it. He was... erm... he was the guest of the female lead, Fliss Edwards.'

My stomach plummeted to the ground. I knew that name. She was Dan's ex and one of the hottest actors of the moment. They'd had an on-off relationship which had been off for several months when we reconnected at New Year.

'I'm really sorry, Amber,' he said, lightly placing his hand on my arm.

'When was this?' My voice sounded higher than usual.

'March.'

'And what were they doing?'

'You really want to know?'

Not really, but I had to know how badly the one man I'd trusted above anyone else had betrayed me. If indeed he had.

'I want to know.'

'I saw them kissing once, but Angelique walked in on them in the toilets. Please don't make me spell it out.'

I closed my eyes and inhaled deeply. Not Dan. He wasn't like that.

'I'm so sorry, Amber. Should I have kept quiet?'

I opened my eyes and looked up at him. 'You're absolutely sure it was him?'

He scrolled for something on his phone.

'One of the crew took a couple of photos of Angelique and me at the wrap party. I won't show you them if you don't want to see them, but Dan and Fliss are in the background.'

I needed to see it to believe it and held my hand out for the phone. In the foreground was a photo of Matt with his wife and, exactly as he'd said, Fliss Edwards was behind, standing very close to my boyfriend.

'Scroll forward,' Matt said softly.

In the next photo, Fliss and Dan were kissing. I enlarged it, just in case it could be an innocent peck, but it was obvious it was so much more. They had their eyes closed, their bodies pressed together, her hands were in his hair and his were on her bottom.

I returned Matt's phone, my mind racing. Had he lied about it being off with Fliss when we met up at New Year, or had he picked up with her again later? Were they still together now? All those late nights, the cancelled trip to Wales, the uncle's eightieth birthday, had any of them been genuine or had they just been excuses to spend time with her?

'I'm sorry,' Matt repeated, bringing my attention back to him. 'Will you be all right?'

'I'll survive. I really thought... Never mind. Best I know now. You'd better hit the road. Thank you for everything.'

'Take care.' He gave me a weak smile before getting back in his car and setting off for the second time.

I stood in the middle of the farmyard, watching Matt travelling along the track and out of sight, fighting back the tears, biting back the urge to scream. I'd trusted Dan. I'd believed he was one of the good ones and, just like Parker, he'd let me down. Silent tears tracked down my cheeks and dripped onto my shirt.

38

BARNEY

I'd really enjoyed Amber's company today and was looking forward to spending more time with her this evening. Amber had said that one of the camera crew would return to film the sunset and had asked if it was okay for her to stick around on the farm rather than drive back to Hedgehog Hollow only to return an hour or so later.

When Matt pulled out of the farmyard for the second time, I leaned against the quad bike in the garage, intending to call Amber over as she passed and ask if she wanted to help me with the pigs before joining me for tea.

But she didn't walk past. She stood in the middle of the farmyard, motionless, staring down the track. Whatever it was he'd said to her and shown her on his phone had clearly affected her. I took a couple of steps closer to the barn entrance and watched her raise her hand and wipe both cheeks.

I was torn between running up to her and giving her a comforting hug and slipping back into the shadows to give her some peace. My natural instinct was the hug, but we'd only just started to get to know each other, and I had no idea how she'd feel if she knew I'd seen her at a vulnerable moment. But I hated the thought of her being upset.

Approaching voices made the decision for me.

'There you are!' Zara called, striding towards her with an armful of bags and folders, followed by the remaining crew members.

Amber waved at her and placed her producer's cap back on her head. I wondered if she'd done that so Zara couldn't see she'd been crying. Zara loaded some of the items into the boot of Amber's 4x4 and others into her own car while Amber spoke to the crew and then they all left. Amber sat in her car for a couple of minutes, tapping something into her phone, and then she pulled away. At that moment, my phone beeped with a text.

FROM AMBER

> Something's come up and I need to leave. I'll be back by 6.30 with Hazel to film the sunset

TO AMBER

> Hope everything's OK. Looking forward to seeing you later

I looked at what I'd just typed and changed the second sentence to a simpler 'see you later' and sent it. Maybe it was just as well she'd left, as I sensed things could become complicated between us if we spent much more time alone.

39

AMBER

I felt bad texting Barney rather than saying goodbye in person, but I couldn't let him see me like this. I wasn't much of a crier, but I couldn't seem to stop the tears from falling as I drove back to Hedgehog Hollow. I could barely see through them and had to pull into the entrance to a field to compose myself.

I knew it wasn't just Dan. It was a combination of everything that had been building and Dan's betrayal had been the straw that broke the camel's back. It felt like everything was falling apart right now – worrying about Sophie, working on a show I no longer believed in, frustration at letting Barney down, sadness at Matt leaving, and now this.

By the time I pulled up outside Meadow View, my eyes were stinging, I'd gone through an entire packet of tissues and still the tears tumbled. Just as well I hadn't stayed at the farm. Barney hadn't signed up to *Love on the Farm* to deal with the producer having an emotional meltdown.

Zara was in the shower, so I dipped into the en suite in my bedroom, blew my nose, splashed some cold water on my face and held a cool flannel against my eyes to reduce the redness and swelling. I wanted to speak to Dan now. I needed to hear his side of the story. And I needed to end it.

'I was just thinking about you,' he said, accepting my FaceTime request and giving me a warm smile. 'How was the sunrise this morning?'

'Sunrise was lovely and I'm heading back to the farm shortly to catch the sunset, but there's something I need to ask you first.' There was no point in beating about the bush. 'When we got together at New Year, you told me that you and Fliss Edwards had broken up. Was that the truth?'

I didn't miss the flinch at her name, but he managed to keep smiling.

'Yes. Why would I lie?'

'I don't know, Dan. Why would you?' I stared at his face on the screen, my eyebrows raised in question and finally his smile faltered.

'What's going on?'

'I don't know, Dan,' I repeated. 'Why don't you tell me?'

'Tell you what?'

I felt angry now. How long was he going to play this game?

'You and Fliss Edwards. I know you were together in March on the set of *The Dove That Cried*. Are you still seeing her?'

His smile had completely vanished. 'It's complicated with Fliss and me.'

'Answer the question. Are you still seeing her?'

Silence, but he did at least have the decency to bow his head.

'I'll take that as a yes. Were you seeing her at New Year?'

His head shot up. 'No! I swear, we'd broken up and I thought it was over for good that time.'

'But it wasn't. So when did it start again?'

'She messaged me saying she'd made a mistake and she asked

me to meet her on set. I went to tell her it was over once and for all.'

'Clearly that conversation went well. A little too well.'

'I'm sorry. I kept trying to end it.'

I shook my head. 'Don't insult me. If you'd really wanted to end it, you would have. How many of those late nights and weekends working were genuine?'

No response.

'I'll take that as *none of them*. What about the weekend when you didn't come to Wales?'

There was a pause before he said, 'Fliss,' the name coming out strangled.

'The friend in Windsor?'

'Also Fliss.'

'Rushing off to your uncle's eightieth?'

'That was real.'

'Why, Dan? You said you hated infidelity after what your ex-wife did, and you swore you'd never do that to anyone.'

He winced and my stomach sank. 'Oh, my God, Dan! It was you who had the affair!'

He nodded slowly. 'With Fliss.'

'Bloody hell! What is it with you two? Was she worth the end of your marriage? The end of us? Does she know about me?' My voice was way too high and loud for my liking, but I couldn't quite believe all these revelations. Who was Dan Mercer? Certainly not the man I thought I knew.

'Yes.'

'And it didn't bother her?'

'She only wants me when she can't have me.'

'That's twisted. I hope you realise that. I don't know what hold she has over you but, if I were you, I'd end it. A relationship like that is going nowhere fast.'

'I'm sorry I hurt you. I never meant to.'

I didn't have the patience for it anymore. 'Good luck, Dan,' I said, and ended the call.

My eyes were still stinging but from earlier rather than any fresh tears. He wasn't worth it. He'd lied to me from the start about why his marriage ended and the lies had kept on coming. Someone like that didn't deserve my tears.

A feeling of weariness overcame me. The temptation to crawl into bed was strong. I longed to close my eyes and block out the day. Although it hadn't all been bad. The start of the day seeing the sunrise at Bumblebee Barn had been pretty special. Ending it with a stunning sunset would be too. It was just all the crap in the middle that I wanted to forget.

40

BARNEY

I was used to being on my own on the farm and, after a busy day with someone from Amber's crew everywhere I turned, I'd have expected to appreciate the solace. Instead, I found it oppressive.

I heated up one of the batch meals Mum had prepared to keep me going across filming when I'd have no time to cook, but only ate a few forkfuls before shoving it aside and downing a glass of water instead. Amber was on my mind. I felt her arms round me on the quad bike. I pictured her in Top Field with her hair loose, her beautiful smile as she met the herdies, the tears in her eyes when she'd said goodbye to Matt, and the effort it had taken to focus on removing that 'fairy' when, for reasons I couldn't explain, I'd really wanted to entwine my fingers in her hair and draw her into a kiss. I pictured her wiping tears away after Matt returned and wished I could have comforted her and helped ease the pain.

Shortly before six, I heard a vehicle pulling into the farm-yard and my heart leapt, thinking it might be Amber back early, but it was Dad. I opened the kitchen door and Bear and Harley ran out to greet him, but he barely acknowledged them, his expression sombre as he strode towards me. Goosebumps prickled my arms and I had a horrible feeling he was the bearer of the news I'd been dreading ever since Granddad's first mini-stroke.

'Everything okay?' I asked, knowing full well it wasn't.

'I've got some sad news about your granddad.'

My stomach lurched as I stepped back to let him in. If he'd said 'bad' news, it might have meant a further stroke, but he'd said 'sad', and that could only mean one thing. Tears burned my eyes and my throat felt tight as we sat down at the table.

'I'm so sorry, son. He died this afternoon.'

I bit hard on my lip as I lowered my head, trying to absorb the words, desperately wanting to have misheard them. He couldn't be gone. Not Granddad. He was meant to go on forever. All those years of working alongside each other at the farm when he'd demonstrated boundless strength and energy didn't tally with the frailty of the past eighteen months.

'How?' I whispered.

'We don't know yet. The paramedics reckoned a heart attack, but they can't say for sure. There'll be checks.'

'Where was he?'

'On his favourite bench in the back garden. Your grandma found him about an hour ago. She thought he was asleep until she noticed he hadn't touched the brew she'd given him an hour earlier.'

I imagined Grandma approaching him, giving him a gentle nudge, softly saying his name, panic building when she couldn't arouse him, and the tears broke free.

'Is she...' My throat was so blocked with emotion, I couldn't form the rest of the words.

'Your grandma's devastated, naturally, but she's relieved he went peacefully. Your mum's with her now. She's okay too. Trying to stay strong for your grandma.'

Dad's voice was hoarse with emotion, and I could tell he was struggling too.

I hated that there'd been tension between Granddad and me recently. At least I knew why, and our last conversation had been a good one. I'm not sure I could have handled it if he'd never returned after lunch to talk about the farm.

'Water?' Dad asked.

I nodded, appreciative of being given a moment to try to take it in. I'd been expecting it at some point – especially after what Grandma said about Granddad's fears for his mortality – but it didn't make it any easier. This was the man who I'd worked alongside since childhood, who'd taught me everything I knew, who'd shaped and influenced my life more than anyone else. And now he was gone.

My heart broke for Grandma. They'd been together for fifty-seven years. Granddad could be set in his ways and they'd had the occasional niggle over the years, but Grandma always said they'd had a wonderful marriage and I'd seen that first-hand. If only the last eighteen months hadn't been so tough. Bloody Melvin.

Dad returned with a couple of glasses of water, and I wiped my cheeks on my sleeve.

'Does Fizz know?' I asked, finally finding my voice.

'Not yet. I wanted to break the news in person. I'm heading to Bayberry Cottage next. I wanted to tell you first because I thought she might need a bit more support.'

'You think she'll blame herself?'

'I hope not, but it's possible and I want to nip that in the bud.'

I sniffed and wiped at my eyes once more. 'You should go to her.'

'I can stay a bit longer.'

'No, I'm okay. Amber's coming back with one of the crew to film the sunset, so they'll be here soon anyway.'

'Would you not be best to cancel?'

'It's a bit late and the distraction will be good. Give my love to Fizz, Mum and Grandma.'

The tears were pooling once more. Dad rose and gave me a tight hug, patted me on the back, then left.

The air in the kitchen felt sticky, so I left the door open and sank back onto the bench with my head in my hands. Harley jumped up beside me and I didn't shoo her down like I normally would. She lay across the bench with her head on my knee and Bear rested his head on the other one. I imagined Raven doing the same thing to Grandma right now. Dogs were invaluable during difficult times and I was so glad Grandma had Raven to bring her some comfort.

'Granddad's dead,' I whispered, lightly stroking each of their heads before resting my elbows back on the table and sinking my head back into my hands. Tears splashed onto the battered wooden table and I didn't make any attempt to stop them or wipe them away. A very special man had left us and there'd be a big hole in all our lives.

I knew I'd need to move from my position at the kitchen table at some point, but I couldn't muster any energy. I'd lost all sense of time and a gentle knock on the door surprised me. I looked up to see Amber in the doorway, her hair down, a pale blue shirt unfastened over a white vest top.

Her mouth fell open and I hastily wiped at my cheeks.

'What's happened?'

'My granddad's died.'

'Oh, no! I'm so sorry.' She slipped into the chair Dad had vacated earlier and took one of my hands in both of hers. 'Are you okay? Obviously not. Stupid question.'

I gave her a weak smile. 'It's fine. Expected, but still a big shock if that makes sense.'

'It does. Is there anything I can do for you? Call someone?'

'No. My dad's just been – that's how I found out – and he'll be with Fizz now. My mum's with my grandma.' Tears pooled in my eyes, thinking about Grandma again and how lost she'd be without Granddad.

'We can forget about filming tonight,' Amber said, her voice soft. 'It's not a problem. You should be with your family.' She squeezed my hand then released it.

'Thanks, but Dad said Grandma just wants to be with Mum tonight to give her time to process it. I'll see her tomorrow or Sunday, depending on when she's ready.'

'We can still leave the filming till another time. Give you some space. I know how much losing a grandparent hurts.'

She twiddled with her locket once more. Her eyes were full of compassion, and I wondered if it had been a gift from a grandparent.

'Thanks, but I'd rather do it. It'll be good to have something different to focus on and I'd appreciate the company.'

'Okay. But if you want to stop at any point, please just say.'

The camera operator, Hazel, arrived and I ran upstairs to splash some cold water on my face and change my damp shirt.

I took Harley and Bear up to Double Top Field on the quad bike and Amber drove up with Hazel. I knew it was for practical reasons – they needed to discuss their plans for the evening's filming – but I wished she'd ridden with me.

Hazel filmed me sitting on the gate, capturing the early stages of sunset. It was shaping up to be a spectacular one. The low clouds were illuminated with gold, and swathes of orange and yellow were deepening with each minute.

When Hazel moved away to film the Herdwicks against the sunset, Amber clambered onto the gate beside me.

'How are you feeling?'

'He's the first family member I've lost, so it all feels a bit weird. It's like I'm in a dream and he hasn't really gone. I keep expecting to wake up any minute and see him among the sheep.'

'I felt the same when my grandparents died.' Her hand reached for the locket once more. 'They were my first losses too.'

'What happened to them?'

'Car crash.'

I twisted on the gate to face her, but she was staring into the distance. 'Both together?'

'Yeah.'

'I'm so sorry. That must have been horrendous. How long ago?'

'February four years ago.' She inhaled deeply then turned to me, tears glistening in her eyes. 'It was two weeks after I turned thirty. Granddad had been battling cancer and they'd been to hospital first thing to get some test results. It was a freezing cold day and Nanna was driving them home when a van hit some black ice on a bend and ploughed into them. Their car flipped. Nanna was killed instantly and Granddad died in the air ambulance.'

'Oh, Amber. I'm so sorry.'

'It was a hell of a shock. We found out later that Granddad had got the all-clear at hospital that morning. Cancer-free.' Her voice cracked and a couple of tears trickled down her cheeks. 'They should have had years more together.'

She swiped at her cheeks. 'Sorry, Barney, we were meant to be talking about your granddad.'

'We can talk about both. What were your grandparents like?'

She smiled through her tears. 'They were the best...'

As the oranges and yellows in the sky became steadily more vibrant before giving way to shades of pink and purple, we talked about our grandparents. Amber's were also from her mum's side and they'd been really close, just like mine.

Hazel returned to film me against the changed sky. Amber moved out of shot and, as soon as she left my side, I missed her.

'I'm finished with you, Barney,' Hazel said eventually. 'I'm going for a final shot of the farmhouse with the setting sun, so I'll see you on Monday. Amber, do you want a lift back down?'

'I can take you down on the quad bike later,' I said, hoping she'd stay longer.

'Sorry, Hazel,' Amber said, 'but the quad bike wins every time. Thanks for today. Have a great weekend.'

Hazel drove off and Amber clambered back onto the gate.

'Where were we?' she asked.

'You'd started to tell me about your locket.'

As I suspected, the locket was connected to her grandparents. They'd bought if for her thirtieth birthday and, with the accident being only a fortnight later, it had been the last gift she'd received from them, making it extra-special.

'There are tiny photos inside of me as a baby and Nanna and Granddad on their wedding day.'

She opened the locket and I shuffled closer to her on the gate so I could see the pictures. My leg touched hers for a moment and my pulse raced as electricity surged through me. Had she felt it too?

When she closed the locket, I didn't want to move away, but I didn't want her to feel like I was invading her personal space either. Just because I was drawn to her, it didn't mean she felt the same. I adjusted position to give her some space – but not too much – and placed my hand on the metal bar between us.

'Thanks for telling me about your grandparents,' I said. 'And for listening to me talk about mine. It's helped.'

'It's helped me as well, so thank you too.'

The sun slipped lower on the horizon and the colours paled.

'What a beautiful sunset,' Amber whispered. 'So dramatic.'

'Granddad's parting gift.'

She interlaced her fingers with mine and we sat there, hand in hand, watching nature's changing artwork as I silently said goodbye to Granddad.

42

AMBER

I'd enjoyed thousands of sunrises and sunsets over the years, but tonight's was up there with the most spectacular. It had also been one of the most special, supporting Barney as he grieved for the loss of his grandfather and thinking about my own grandparents. But as the sun slipped below the horizon and the sky darkened, that magical moment drew to an end.

'I hate to say it...' Barney started after I shivered in the cool night air.

'Me too, but it's cold and dark, so it's time.'

Riding back down to the barn on his quad bike, I held on tightly. I felt an urge to close my eyes and rest my head against his back, but fought against it. It felt like I'd already crossed over from professional to personal this evening and I needed to regain focus on why I was here.

'Do you want to come in for a cuppa?' Barney asked once we'd parked back in the barn.

I hesitated as I removed my helmet. I wanted to, but I probably shouldn't. We'd been caught up in a moment earlier and I needed to get that professional distance back.

'And to warm up,' he added as a gust of wind blew round us and I shivered once more.

There was nothing untoward about getting warm and having a drink, was there? I followed him and the dogs inside.

'I can't believe I didn't bring a hoodie,' I said, rubbing my hands over my goosebump-covered arms. 'I'm normally much better prepared.'

'I'll grab you one of mine.'

Barney directed me into the lounge. I hadn't been in there before, but it was a gorgeous room with a real fire, a huge corner sofa and a couple of snuggle chairs. I sank onto the sofa, still rubbing my arms. Barney appeared and tossed me a grey fleecy hoodie which I pulled on gratefully. It was so soft and warmed me instantly. The dogs stayed with me while he went to make drinks, Harley cosied up to my side, Bear leaning against my legs.

'I realised I didn't ask you what you wanted,' he said, returning with a tray. 'I made hot chocolate but I can make coffee or tea if you prefer.'

'Hot chocolate's perfect.' I helped myself to one of the mugs.

'Marshmallows?'

He tipped the packet over my drink and asked me to tell him when to stop. I didn't stop him, resulting in a marshmallow mountain.

'One of those days?' he asked.

'Definitely.'

'Me too.' He added what was left of the packet to his mug and sat down on the other side of Harley.

'You're a big hit with my dogs,' he said.

'They're a big hit with me.' I stroked Harley's ears. 'How are you holding up?'

'Still feeling like I'm in a dream. What about you, and I don't mean about your grandparents? I was in the garage when Matt came back earlier, and it looked like you were crying.'

The concerned expression on his face was touching and, while telling him about Dan kept things personal rather than professional, what harm was there while we were still in that zone? He was so easy to talk to.

'At New Year, I got back together with my ex, Dan. We were apart a lot because of our jobs – he's an actor – so it wasn't without its challenges, but I thought we were strong. It turns out that Dan's also been seeing his ex-girlfriend. Matt had seen them together.'

Barney grimaced. 'Why do people do that?'

'I've no idea. I certainly couldn't.'

'Me neither. It's so disrespectful.'

'Sorry about leaving earlier. I needed some space to clear my head and confront him.'

I told Barney about the conversation with Dan and what seemed to me like an unhealthy obsession with a woman who was going to break his heart over and over.

'It's all the lies I can't stand,' I said. 'He'd go on about how hurt he was by his ex-wife's infidelity and how he'd never put anyone through the hell he'd been through. Now I'm wondering if that was a deliberate ploy to get me to trust him because if I knew it was really him who'd had the affair, I might have run a mile.'

'It sounds like you could be right, but it's so calculated.'

'Isn't it? But maybe getting back with me was calculated too. He said Fliss was only interested in him when he wasn't available. How easy did it make things by getting back with me? We had a past history, I trusted him, I was away nearly all the time – absolutely perfect. For him, anyway.'

Somewhere in the room, a clock chimed. I glanced at my watch.

'I can't believe it's eleven already. I'd better head off.' I stood up and placed the empty mug I'd been cradling on the tray. 'Thanks for listening.'

'Right back at you.'

The dogs joined us as I followed Barney through the kitchen and outside. A light on the side of the house gently illuminated the farmyard and I felt unexpectedly nervous as we walked towards my car.

'Your hoodie!' I said, tugging on the sleeve.

'Keep it on or you'll be cold again by the time you get back.'

I smiled gratefully. 'It's very cosy.'

'Then you need to keep it. It looks way better on you than it ever did on me.'

'Really? Aw, that's so lovely. Thank you, Barney.'

The kind gesture and the compliment brought tears to my eyes, and I instinctively reached out to hug him. His arms were strong and comforting as he held me close. My body fit perfectly against his and my heart started racing as I breathed in a mixture of straw, soap and the sweetness of hot chocolate.

I didn't want to let go, but I had to. We'd already held on too long for a friendly thank you hug and that thought made my heart race even faster as it meant Barney didn't want to let go either.

We both let go at the same time, laughing.

'Good hug,' he said. 'I needed that.'

'Me too. Right, I really must go.'

I crouched down and gave Bear and Harley a head scratch before getting into the car. I turned the ignition and lowered the window.

'I'm really sorry about your granddad. Will you be all right tonight?'

'Yeah. It helped having you here. And I'm sorry about your grandparents and your ex. For what it's worth, the man's an idiot and he didn't deserve you. Have a great time with your sister this weekend and I'll see you on Monday.'

My heart was still pounding as I pulled away. In the rear-view mirror, I saw Barney in the middle of the yard, a dog either side of him, watching me drive away. I took a few steadying breaths. So much for avoiding the personal and staying professional. Something had shifted between us tonight and I was sure it wasn't just me who felt that way. Just as well we were about to have two days apart. We could both regain some perspective.

43

AMBER

I woke up at six on Saturday morning, feeling refreshed after a really deep sleep. I lay on my back for a few minutes, reflecting on yesterday. I'd have expected to feel upset or angry about Dan, but it was Barney who occupied my thoughts. Butterflies stirred as I thought about us sitting on the gate, our hands joined as we watched that spectacular sunset, how good it felt to be held by him, and how reluctant I'd felt to drive away.

My fingers brushed against something soft, and I glanced over at his fleecy hoodie on the bed beside me. I picked it up and held it against my face, breathing in the scent.

Feeling like I was in danger of drifting off to sleep once more, I pulled the hoodie on and wandered into the kitchen to make a coffee, which I took over to the wedding gazebo.

The morning air was cool and fresh, the sky pale with wispy cirrus clouds. Looking out over the meadow, breathing in the smell of fresh coffee, my body tingled with the excitement of a fresh start. I felt betrayed by Dan and humiliated by his lies, but was I devastated it was over? Not really. There'd been question marks around whether we could have a long-term future even if we did manage to survive through so much time apart – his love for the city versus mine for the country – and whether he really was the sort to settle down and have a family. I hated how it had happened, but it was probably best it had ended now before I'd had a chance to fall any deeper.

When I returned to Meadow View a little later, there was a text from Dan.

FROM DAN

Just checking you're OK this morning. I'm really sorry. I know I'm probably asking the impossible, but I'd love it if we can stay friends

I swore at my phone and angrily tapped in a response.

TO DAN

I'm good and, yes, you're asking the impossible

Why would he want to remain friends? And what would that look like to him? He'd barely made time to see me when we'd been a couple, so there was no way he'd make the effort to meet up when we weren't and he knew I barely looked at social media so virtual friends was pointless.

I stared at my phone, daring him to reply, but a text appeared from Barney instead.

FROM BARNEY

Tough day for us both yesterday. Thanks for helping me through mine. Bear and Harley hope they helped you through yours

I immediately went from being irritated by Dan's message to feeling lifted by Barney's.

TO BARNEY

> They did. And so did you. And your hoodie.
> Take care

It was hard not to add a kiss on the end instead of the smiley.

* * *

I knocked on Sophie's hotel room door in York city centre later that morning. I'd told her I was keen to see where she was staying and check out the fabulous view she'd described, but I really wanted to seek some reassurance that things weren't slipping. Her usually tidy bedroom at home had become as messy as her mind and her emotions after *The House*, and I needed to be sure she wasn't unravelling again.

When we hugged, she clung on a little longer than usual, giving me nervous butterflies. And when I commented on it being a lovely room, feeling relieved to see it was tidy, they fluttered even more with her response.

'Thanks. I've just spent the last half an hour tidying it. It was a right mess.'

We could have sat on the bed and talked, but I didn't want her to get into a pattern of staying in her room, so I suggested a walk round the city walls.

After making it some way round, we arrived at one of the battlements just as an elderly couple vacated a lone bench and I saw the opportunity to sit down and talk.

'How did it go with that cameraman who you thought was looking at you?' I asked. 'Did you ask someone to speak to him?'

'Yeah, Burt had a word. Turned out I look a lot like his daughter. She's working abroad and he hasn't seen her for six months, so he'd found it disorientating seeing me. He was mortified he'd worried me, but it's all good now.'

'And everything else is going well?'

'Erm... yeah. It's going to be such a good series. Becca Scarsdale's such a talented writer.'

Neither the hesitation nor the deflection were lost on me.

'You know that's not what I'm asking. How are you? Big part, big move...'

She looked away, but I'd already spotted the tears in her eyes.

'It's different. I'd got used to turning up, doing my thing, going home, coming back the next day... Sometimes I made friends and sometimes I didn't, but it didn't matter as I wasn't there for long, but here...'

Her voice cracked and I shuffled closer, putting my arm round her shoulders and cuddling her to my side.

'Did I ever tell you about my first producing gig away from home? I cried myself to sleep for the first three nights...'

As I shared my story of feeling alone and completely out of my depth, Sophie seemed to perk up.

'What did you do?'

'I forced myself to make friends. You know me – Mrs Introvert – so it wasn't easy, but I started with the crew who looked the friendliest and would make a beeline for them during breaks, opening up conversations about the coffee, the pastries, the weather, just to get a dialogue going and then asked them about their role and how long they'd been doing it. Friendships built from there. People love talking about themselves and the great thing is that you may be a bunch of strangers, but you have something in common with them all – the programme you're making – so there's always something to talk about.'

Sophie said she'd make more of an effort from tomorrow, but I was still worried that this was too much for her.

Her emotions were up and down across the day, and I didn't want to leave her, but I accepted that Dan had been right about one thing – she was nearly twenty-four and she had to stand on her own two feet at one point – so all I could do was keep encouraging her and stay in touch.

We stopped for a late lunch at a café by the river. After we'd eaten, I checked the time on my mobile.

'How's it half two already?' I asked Sophie, rolling my eyes. 'I'd better head back. I've got some prep to do for tomorrow and you must have lines to run. Will you guard my phone and bag while I nip to the ladies?'

When I returned, she was frowning at my phone. 'Have you and Dan split up? A notification came up and I tried not to read it. Sorry.'

I took the phone from her and read the text.

FROM DAN

> I'm so sorry I messed up and hurt you. Please reconsider being friends x

'Yes, we've split up,' I told her. 'He was—'

But I didn't get to finish the sentence as another text from him flashed up.

FROM DAN

> Just remembered you're seeing Sophie today. Say hi from me. I'm so impressed with her for securing a Becca Scarsdale lead. Remind her to put in a good word for me! x

Wow! Had he really just had the audacity to do that? I put my phone on silent and tossed it into my bag, disgusted with him. Barney had used the word 'calculated' and he'd called it. How had I not spotted this about Dan before? I'd got hooked into the romantic idea of finding our way back to each other when the truth was the time apart had changed us and made us incompatible. Dan, once a genuinely lovely person, was now a user and a cheat and he deserved nothing from me – not even a reply.

44

BARNEY

Mid-morning on Saturday, Dad joined me on the farm to help get on top of everything so I could join him, Mum and Fizz at Grandma's for tea. The help was much appreciated, giving me one less thing to worry about.

Dad was more valuable to me if we worked separately, like Milo and I did, so we spent most of the day apart, keeping in touch via the walkie-talkie. My mind didn't slow down for one minute. Memories of working alongside Granddad mingled with fresh memories of Amber. I already missed him, but I missed her too. How was that possible when I barely knew her?

Over breakfast this morning, I'd looked up Fliss Edwards and Dan Mercer online. I recognised her but not him. She was attractive but not a patch on Amber. He looked a bit suave for my liking. I searched on Dan's name with Amber's but didn't find any photos of them together. There were several of Amber with her family and crew at awards ceremonies and also with the same dark-haired man. A little more research revealed him to be a director called Parker Knowles who'd been engaged to Amber five years ago.

Feeling like I was going down an intrusive rabbit hole, I closed down my search and finished my food. I knew nothing about Parker, but I couldn't help thinking that both him and Dan were a little too groomed and television-perfect for her. She seemed like a country lass, happier caked in mud with the wind in her hair. But then I realised I didn't know much about Amber either. Those photos online could be her real world and what I'd thought I'd seen was wishful thinking.

* * *

'Are you okay?' Dad asked as we pulled onto the drive outside Grandma and Granddad's bungalow late that afternoon. Fizz's Mini was already on the drive.

I shrugged. 'Feels weird knowing Granddad's not going to be there.'

'Yeah, I felt that way last night and still do now. Probably will for quite some time.'

I'd have left Bear and Harley at the farm, but Grandma had wanted them to come. They usually raced each other into the house, seeking out Granddad who always had treats ready in his shirt pockets. Today they trotted alongside me, heads down, as though they knew something was wrong.

Fizz and Grandma were standing in the lounge, hugging each other. Fizz was crying and Grandma looked pale and exhausted. She glanced up and beckoned me to join them in a group hug.

'I'm so sorry,' I said, my voice catching in my throat.

She nodded and patted my back.

The French doors opened and Mum stepped inside with Raven. Bear and Harley went over to their mum and nudged their noses against her face instead of clambering over her like they usually did.

Grandma looked down at my dogs and her face crumpled. 'I haven't got any treats out. That's your granddad's job... *was* his job.'

Fizz sobbed loudly as tears spilled down Grandma's cheeks and I fought to stay strong. I had no words. All I could do was hug her again.

45

AMBER

I was up with the sunrise on Monday morning, watching it from the wedding gazebo by Hedgehog Hollow's meadow – my new happy place. I hadn't intended to rise quite so early but, when I'd woken up at 3.30 a.m. feeling thirsty, I'd had too much circling round my mind to settle back to sleep.

I was dreading working with the new director Giles Snyder this week – not because he was somebody new but because I knew what his brief would be. I'd investigated him online and his directing credits included several manipulated, scandalous, car-crash reality TV shows with Clementine Creates, so Grant and Liza knew he was capable of turning our lovely family-friendly show into a carbon copy of their other delights.

Then there was Barney. I was looking forward to seeing him again way more than I should be and way more than was appropriate for my role. *Love on the Farm* was meant to be about him finding love with one of the 'carefully' selected matches; not one of the production team!

Nothing untoward had happened between us, but I wasn't stupid. *Something* had happened and he'd felt it too, otherwise he wouldn't have held my hand as the sun set, he wouldn't have felt so relaxed in my arms as he rode the quad bike back, and he wouldn't have hugged me for so long in the farmyard afterwards. That hadn't just been a comforting thank you hug. That had been a hug which meant something.

And now I was going to have to spend the next six days watching him with three other women, all of whom were completely unsuitable for him. I didn't think Tayla would have flirted with him even if she was single, but I was sure that Rayn would be all over him. She'd quite literally act the part of the perfect girlfriend and it was going to be uncomfortable to watch. Marley with her pig phobia was an unknown. If she saw his pigs, she might turn damsel in distress and there'd be lots of excuses for touching. That would be hard too.

The format for the week was that each match would spend a full day – lunchtime to lunchtime – working with Barney on the farm. In reality, it wasn't close to a full day because they were staying overnight in a local B&B rather than the farmhouse. Tayla was first and Rayn would be last, leaving at Thursday lunchtime. Friday would see all three women back to work together with Barney, after which he'd make a decision on which one to take to the final stage – the big date – on Monday. If I didn't get a hold on my feelings, that was going to be a nightmare to watch too.

* * *

Giles Snyder was already in the farmyard when Zara and I arrived and, despite us being half an hour earlier than the agreed meeting time, he tapped his watch impatiently as we pulled up.

'How to make a cracking first impression,' Zara muttered while giving him a sweet smile and a wave. 'Dickhead.'

Giles sauntered over to us, lip curled up, looking me up and down with clear disdain. I knew from his online profile that he was fifty-eight, but he wasn't ageing with dignity. His jeans were way too tight and his shirt buttons were close to bursting over his stomach. His shirt was fastened too low at the top, revealing a mass of grey curly hair and three gold medallions. A greying comb-over, burst blood vessels in his shiny nose and unruly eyebrows completed the vision before us.

'I've seen the Wales footage,' he said. 'What a snooze-fest.' He followed that up with the most enormous fake snore accompanied by an eyes-closed head loll.

He opened his eyes and looked Zara up and down this time, his gaze lingering too long on her breasts. 'I've been summoned to sort out your shit and save your sorry arses. Just as well one of us knows what they're doing.'

Even though I hated confrontation, there was no way I was standing for that. Nobody spoke to me or my crew in such a disrespectful manner or looked at Zara or me in such a disgusting, misogynistic way.

'We appear to have skipped the introductions, Giles,' I said, adopting my strongest no-nonsense tone. 'I'm Amber Crawford, producer, and this is my assistant, Zara Timmins. We have no "shit" to sort out and there are no "sorry arses" to save. If you've been properly brought up to speed, you'll know that the episode in Wales was filmed *exactly* to the original brief, but Grant and Liza have since decided that some changes in direction would work better for the Clementine Creates brand. Our highly experienced and exceptionally talented crew have been working to that new brief. Should I show you where we're filming today and run through the schedule, or would you like to hurl a few more insults first?'

I wish I could have captured his shocked expression on film. A flush of red spread up his neck and coloured his cheeks and I tensed myself, waiting for the explosion, but it didn't come.

'Glad we've got that clear,' he said, as though he was the one who'd set the record straight. His face returned to a normal colour, if you could call fake tan normal. 'Let's run through the plan.'

'If you'd like to make your way over there…' I pointed to the field beyond the original Bumblebee Barn, '…you'll find the marquee. We'll join you there in two minutes.'

I exhaled slowly as he left. This project had just taken another massive downturn.

'Wow! That man is vile,' Zara said, 'but you were awesome.'

'I had to say something, although, for a minute, I thought he was going to sack me on the spot.'

'Would that have been such a bad thing?'

It was a rhetorical question, which was just as well, because I was conflicted. No, it wouldn't be a bad thing to be rid of this horrendous show, but it would be bad never to see Barney again. As I reached for my satchel from behind the driver's seat, I glanced up at the farmhouse but there was no sign of Barney. Maybe just as well, as I needed to keep my wits about me to deal with Giles Snyder.

* * *

The first glimpse of Barney half an hour later set my pulse racing. I introduced him to Giles, praying Giles wouldn't make any inappropriate comments, but he was surprisingly professional and I wondered if we'd caught him at a bad moment this morning, tired, anxious or perhaps attempting to make a joke that translated as several insults. I'd give him the benefit of the doubt for now.

'How are you holding up?' I asked Barney when Giles left us.

'It's been a tough weekend, but I'm okay. We all gathered at

Grandma's on Saturday night and it was really sad at first, but we shared some stories and memories and it was uplifting. Mum's staying with her for a few days. They're hoping to sort out a funeral date today. They reckon it'll be the end of next week, so there shouldn't be any clashes with filming.'

'If it does clash, I'm sure we can sort something out.'

'Thank you. I appreciate that.'

He looked tired and I longed to hug him again, but I was aware of Giles and Zara watching me, and the last thing I wanted to do was give them an inkling that I was attracted to our farmer. Zara would be discreet, but I didn't trust Giles one iota.

'I haven't told anyone about your granddad. I wasn't sure if you'd want it to be public.'

'Probably not for the moment, if that's okay.'

'Of course. So how are you feeling about match number one?'

He grimaced. 'Would it sound bad if I said I hadn't given it much thought?'

'You've had other more important things on your mind so I completely understand. Do you have any questions?'

'I don't think so.'

'In that case, I'll let you get on with the rest of your morning. Can you be back in the farmyard for half twelve and we'll get you wired up ready for match one arriving at one? We'll tell you her name just before you meet her but that's all the information I can give. See you later.'

I'd walked a few paces when Barney called my name. I turned to face him, butterflies fluttering inside me as he joined me.

'I just wanted to say thank you again for Friday and I don't just mean the evening. From sunrise to sunset, it was a special day for me. I'm hoping it was for you too.'

I hesitated, knowing I should give a professional response, but my heart wouldn't let me.

'It was. Which isn't ideal, given the reason I'm here.'

He smiled ruefully. 'Yeah. Not the best.'

'Is Giles still watching us?'

'That new director bloke? Yes.'

'I'll have to go. Can I give you some advice? Throw yourself into this week, enjoy your time with each of your matches, and forget about me.'

'The first part I can do and the second part I'll try. As for the third, you're asking the impossible.'

His eyes searched mine and I felt a longing for him that I'd never felt towards Parker or Dan. I yearned to touch him, to kiss him, to hold him tight. But I'd only just come out of a relationship and Barney had experienced a bereavement. We both needed time to heal. Whatever this was sizzling between us might be our heightened emotions at a difficult time, confusing friendship and empathy for something more. I needed to put a stop to it before one or both of us got hurt.

'Nothing can happen between us, Barney. I'm so sorry. I've got to go.'

My legs felt like liquid and I honestly don't know how they managed to carry me back to the crew. It took all my strength not to turn back around and look at Barney, especially when I could feel him watching me.

'Everything all right?' Zara asked, eyeing me suspiciously.

'Yes. Barney had a few questions, so I've set him straight.' It wasn't a lie.

'Is he nervous?'

'We both are.' I pulled my producer cap on. 'Let's get cracking.'

Just three matches and the big date to get through and then I'd be leaving and Barney and I could forget about Friday night and any feelings stirred up by a stunning sunset on an emotional day. I could do that. I was a professional. It would be fine.

* * *

Even though I knew Tayla had a boyfriend and wasn't interested in Barney, I couldn't stop my stomach churning when I heard through my earpiece that her driver had just pulled onto the farm track.

I stopped the car before it pulled into the farmyard so I could say hello to Tayla and check for any final questions. Each of the matches had been given a different coloured boilersuit to wear with the branding for *Love on the Farm* and their name printed across the back and on the front pocket. The outfit was partly to create the illusion that the two half-days of filming were shot in one day and partly to make it easy to distinguish the three women from each other on Friday when they all worked together. Tayla's boilersuit was burgundy and the colour was extremely flattering on her, bringing out the grey in her eyes. She was pretty in an understated way, an air of sweet innocence making her even more endearing.

'Any change of circumstances since last week?' I asked, taking care to keep my voice low.

'No.'

'Okay. Keep that to yourself and do your best to act natural.'

'I will.'

I raised my voice again. 'Your farmer is called Barney and I hope you enjoy your time together.'

I walked back up to the farmyard to prepare for the first meeting. There was one camera on Tayla and another on Barney the whole time to catch their genuine first reactions. I didn't want to watch Barney, but I couldn't help it. Would he like the look of Tayla? Would he regret what he'd said to me?

Barney smiled when Tayla stepped out of the car, shook her hand, and welcomed her to Bumblebee Barn. She smiled shyly back at him and told him she was looking forward to their day together.

Giles called cut and that was the first scene done. I released the breath I'd been holding.

* * *

For their individual 'day' on the farm, each match had been assigned one animal and one general farm task to work on alongside Barney. I'd allocated the horses to Tayla, the pigs to Rayn and the sheep to Marley. It hadn't seemed fair to give Marley the horses when she was already an expert, and there was no way I could allocate her the pigs when she had a phobia. Giles had immediately swapped Rayn and Marley's animals round. I'd known he would – someone with a pig phobia having to deal with pigs would make for 'hilarious' viewing – and the disregard he and the Lennons had for people made me feel sick. We'd had several heated exchanges, but he refused to budge.

Tayla had never ridden before and was initially a little apprehensive around the six horses in the stables but, with Barney's calm guidance and reassurance, it didn't take long for her to find her confidence. Barney's groom had already done his work in the stables first thing, but Tayla's task was to help muck out the stables again, feed and water the horses, groom them and trim their manes and tails.

The idea was that, as they worked, they'd talk and get to know each other and viewers would learn about farm life while watching their relationship develop. When filming in Wales, we'd let everything play out naturally and, in my opinion, we'd captured some lovely, genuine moments. But that was too 'tediously boring' for Giles. He constantly cut filming to bark instructions at the pair. His first order was for Tayla to act as though she was disgusted by the sight and smell of the horse manure. When she said it didn't bother her, he snapped, 'Well, pretend it does!'

I personally saw some lovely moments for Barney and Tayla, where common interests emerged along with the potential for friendship. I could imagine viewers finding them a sweet pairing and rooting for them to move beyond the friendzone. Sadly, I was fairly certain none of those moments would make it to the episode which, instead, would be full of the scenes contrived by Giles.

While they were mucking out, Giles stopped filming and declared he wanted a straw fight. Bit cheesy, but fair enough. Except he wanted them to do it with the soiled straw. Barney point blank refused which, from the colour rising up Giles's neck, didn't go down well. Although Giles conceded to them having the fight using the replacement fresh straw instead, I suspected Barney's card was marked.

To give Barney and Tayla their dues, they went along with the increasingly ridiculous orders from Giles. I suspected they'd both realised where this was going and couldn't be bothered to fight it. Tayla would be conveyed as sweet but squeamish and wholly unsuitable to life on a farm – despite having been raised on one – and Barney would be shown as patient and understanding to get the viewers onside. For now. Giles would likely rip him to shreds by the end of the week.

Giles kept feeding them conversation topics and, if they shared the same viewpoint, he stopped filming and insisted on some conflict. I could imagine Rayn thriving on that, but Barney and Tayla weren't actors and trying to force clashes between two thoughtful, kind individuals didn't work.

As the afternoon drew to a close, Giles wanted the pair of them to ride the horses across the farmyard. I suspected he was hoping that Tayla's initial nervousness around the horses would translate into her not wanting to ride one, but Barney had done such a great job of making her comfortable that she was excited to give it a try and impressed us all with a dignified mount into the saddle on her first attempt.

'Cut!' Giles called. 'What the hell was that?'

Barney and Tayla exchanged confused looks, as did Zara and I.

'You think that makes good television?' Giles demanded. 'Do it again except, this time, you slip and he catches you.'

'You're saying you want her to fall off the horse?' Barney asked, his eyebrows raised.

'Yes, but you'll catch her. Romantic moment.'

'And what if she falls and I don't manage to catch her? She could hurt herself.'

'I don't want to get hurt,' Tayla said, her expression fearful.

'And I'm not willing to spook my horse for no reason,' Barney added.

I'd had enough of this nonsense.

'Can I have a quick word, Giles?' I smiled sweetly at him as I led him away from the stables. 'I like your idea of creating a romantic moment, but I'm concerned about a court case if Tayla gets hurt or something happens to the horse. What if Barney helps her down from the saddle at the end of their ride instead? They can hold onto each other, gazing into each other's eyes, leaving the viewer wondering if there's something between them.'

We returned to the stables and Giles announced his (my) great idea to Barney and Tayla, who were happy to go along with it. I think Tayla would have done pretty much anything to avoid the risk of falling, and who could blame her?

* * *

Shortly after Tayla left for an evening at the B&B, Giles left too. I rolled my shoulders, trying to alleviate some of the tension.

'I'll repeat my verdict from earlier,' Zara said. 'That man is vile.'

'He certainly is. And so's what they're doing to this show. Can you give me five minutes?'

'Sure. Are you off to find a remote field to scream in?'

I gave her a weak smile. 'Something like that.'

When we'd been filming in the stables earlier, I'd seen a footpath leading to a meadow. I hadn't noticed it before, and it wasn't somewhere we were using for filming, so I'd hopefully get a moment's peace there to try and get my head together.

The meadow didn't have as many flowers as the one at Hedgehog Hollow, or as much variety, but it was still beautiful. There was a stile into it and a public footpath up one side. I sat on the top of the stile, breathing in the stunning view.

What a day! Giles Snyder couldn't have had a more perfect surname. When he wasn't barking ridiculous orders, he was making snide remarks to anyone, about anyone. He fake snored, pointed two fingers to his temple and made explosive sounds, pretended he had a noose round his neck, and made a stack of other offensive, inappropriate and completely unprofessional gestures. I was fairly sure Barney and Tayla had clocked him doing them too. What must they think?

A twig cracked and I turned to see Barney approaching.

'I saw you come down here and wanted to check you were okay, but I can go if you'd rather be alone.'

'The only place I want to be is a million miles from Giles Snyder.'

Barney came closer. 'Yeah, I can relate to that. Today was interesting.'

'That's one word for it.'

'What are the others?'

I smiled. 'This place is too beautiful to sour with a pile of expletives.'

He clambered onto the fence beside the stile. 'I know you've got a job to do and part of that is keeping schtum about the behind-the-scenes stuff. I'm not going to pressure you to tell me anything, but if I took a guess and you indicated whether I was on the right lines, you wouldn't have broken any television vows or contracts or whatever it is you're bound by, would you?'

'What's your guess?'

'Something's changed and this isn't the same show originally planned.'

I stared straight ahead at the meadow and slowly nodded.

'It's not about being "passionate about our countryside and the vital role farmers play" anymore.'

I recognised the quote from the participant call and nodded again.

'The matches have a different purpose now. The aim isn't to find love. It's to entertain.'

A bumblebee buzzed round a clover near the stile, and I kept my focus on it, unable to look Barney in the eye for fear of seeing any judgement in his eyes – even though I couldn't hear any in his voice – as I nodded for a third time.

'You hate the changes, but you have no power to do anything about it.'

I nodded once more.

'Final guess,' he said, his voice soft and gentle. 'Matt hated the changes too and that's why he left.'

Another nod.

'So why are you still here?'

The question I asked myself every single hour of every single day.

'It's complicated. I don't—'

'Amber! Barney!'

We both turned in the direction of Zara running along the track.

'Sorry for interrupting,' she said, planting her hands on her thighs as she caught her breath. 'Amber, the crew are getting twitchy and want to head off and Barney, your friend Joel's here to see you.'

'We'll catch up later,' I said, clambering back over the stile. 'I'm so sorry about it all, Barney. It's... there aren't really words for it. Well, not clean ones.'

'You have nothing to be sorry for.'

Maybe not directly, but it didn't stop me feeling sorry.

46

BARNEY

'Just stopped by to see how filming was going,' Joel said when we returned to the farmyard.

'It's going,' I said, catching Amber's eye and giving her what I hoped was an understanding smile.

She disappeared with Zara.

'I really called round to say how gutted I am about Frank,' Joel said. 'I wasn't sure if you'd have told the TV people.'

'Amber knows. She came up to do some filming just after I'd found out, but I've asked her to keep it quiet. You got time for a beer?'

'Just the one.'

I grabbed a couple of cold lagers from the fridge and we went into the garden with the dogs. I'd texted Joel to let him know the news about Granddad, but I filled him in on the details and how it had been seeing Grandma on Saturday.

'He was a good bloke,' Joel said, clinking his bottle against mine. 'I'm sorry.'

We sat in silence for a few moments, sipping on our drinks.

'You said filming was going,' Joel prompted. 'That doesn't sound very positive.'

'It's not what I expected, but it's not what Amber expected either. I managed to get out of her that the show's changed, but we didn't get a chance to go into any detail.'

'Changed in what way?'

'There's this new director and you won't believe some of the stuff he wanted us to do...'

* * *

When Joel left an hour later, I hoped Amber would still be around, but she'd gone. Whatever was going on with the show clearly didn't sit comfortably with her and I imagined she'd been told to put up and shut up. I pictured her hunched up on that stile, eyes downcast, unable to look at me. Something was very wrong, but it wasn't right to chase her about it. She'd tell me if and when she was ready.

Much as I couldn't stand that Giles bloke, I had enjoyed most of today. Tayla had been easy company and, if we'd met under other circumstances, I could see us being friends. She was an attractive woman but there was no chemistry between us, and I was certain there wouldn't have been even if my thoughts hadn't been filled with Amber.

Tomorrow Tayla would help me with some repair works to a couple of our unused stable stalls and I imagined it would be a pleasant morning... or it would be when Giles wasn't interfering.

'Bear! Harley!' The dogs joined me over by the quad bike. 'Final checks for the day.'

They jumped up and we rode up to Double Top Field.

As the sun set later that evening – an explosion of pink, purple and violet – I wished Amber was here to see it with me. I wondered if she was watching it at Hedgehog Hollow and if she was thinking about me too, despite telling me we couldn't be together.

It was strange how I still barely knew her but I couldn't stop thinking about her. Was it because I'd finally laid Elle to rest and was ready to let someone in again, or was it Amber who'd helped me lay Elle to rest?

47

BARNEY

I didn't get any time alone with Amber on Tuesday morning before filming started. Giles seemed to be watching her like a hawk and I wasn't going to risk doing anything that might get her into trouble, so I kept my distance.

I'd been instructed to brief Tayla on what we were doing to the stables – two new doors to be made and installed – and we'd be filmed as we worked together. Granddad had taught me the DIY skills I'd need on the farm and I'd built up a good collection of power tools over the years. It transpired that Tayla's auntie and uncle ran a business making bespoke treehouses and playhouses and she often helped them when they had a heavy workload. Her expertise was therefore far superior to mine, and I had no qualms about admitting that, much to Giles's disgust.

'I need you to look like you don't know what you're doing,' he shouted at Tayla, cutting filming for the umpteenth time.

'But I *do* know what I'm doing,' she challenged back.

'The viewers won't know that.'

'But my friends and family who watch it will.'

'I don't care. Do as you're asked.'

The filming resumed but Tayla refused to play ball, suggesting to me an alternative – and superior – way of creating joints.

'Stop!' Giles cried. 'What part of *play dumb* don't you understand?'

'What part of *I'm not dumb* don't you understand?'

There were sniggers from the crew and I wanted to cheer and give her a high five.

'I've got no problem with Tayla sharing her expertise,' I said gently, hoping to diffuse things. 'She obviously knows way more than I do.'

'But you should know more. You're the farmer.'

'So I know more about crops and livestock than Tayla, but she knows more about wood than me. What's the problem in me learning from her?'

'Because... because...'

'Because I'm a woman?' Tayla suggested. 'I played along yesterday with the non-rider incompetent in the saddle stuff because that was fair enough. It's not a skill I have. But I will *not* go on national television making out I don't know the difference between a butt joint and a mitre joint, or a circular saw and a router.'

'How about we take a quick break?' Amber suggested. 'Grab a coffee in the marquee and be back here in ten minutes.'

With no cameras following us – the crew presumably eager to watch the spat between Giles and Amber – it was our first time alone.

'I'm sorry if I'm making a mess of things,' Tayla said when we left the stables and made our way towards the marquee.

'You're not. I thought what you said to him just now was brilliant.'

'You did? Thank you. And thanks for backing me up.'

'I meant every word. What century is he living in?'

'I'm so glad you said that. I think he wants to portray me as some sort of ditzy female who can't do anything for herself. I was so annoyed with him last night, but my boyfriend said...' She stopped, gasped and clapped her hand over her mouth.

'Your boyfriend?' I asked, stopping too and raising my eyebrows at her.

'I'm sorry. It's recent but...' She bit her lip, cringing.

'It's fine. Can you keep a secret? I've met someone recently too. Nothing's happened, but there's the possibility it might.'

She smiled at me. 'I hope it does. You're a nice guy. You deserve to find someone special. Amber's a good choice.'

I glanced round me to make sure nobody was in earshot and gently pulled her under the shade of a tree, just in case.

'How did you...?'

'My boyfriend, Aston, used to come into the farm shop where I worked, and I really liked him. I had no idea whether he liked me back or how to show him I was interested so I started looking into body language. I became a bit obsessed, watching a scary number of documentaries and reading stacks of books. Frustratingly, he stopped coming into the shop for a few months – he'd been doing it for his grandma while she was ill and she got better – but he came back recently and let's say the research paid off. As for you and Amber, I'm certain nobody else would notice it, so don't look so worried.'

'I'm glad it worked out for you and Aston. You have no idea how guilty I was feeling about not being interested.'

'Me too. But I think we both know that, if there wasn't an Aston or Amber in the picture, it'd just be friendship for us, wouldn't it?'

'Yep.'

'Maybe we can stay in touch and go on a double date.'

'I'd be up for that, but Amber says she and I can't get involved.'

'Because of the show?'

I shrugged. 'It's one of the reasons.'

'It's probably awkward because of the show, but after filming stops...' She lightly touched my arm. 'Don't give up hope. If it's meant to be, it'll happen.'

'Thanks. In the meantime, we have a pair of stable doors to build, or rather I do, and you need to watch and pass me things. Job for a man, you know. Step away from the power tools, young lady, and get back in the kitchen.'

Tayla giggled at the upper-class 'manly' tone I'd adopted. 'Scarily enough, I think that's exactly what was running through Giles's head.'

'Then let's have some fun with it and show him what you're capable of.'

When we returned after a coffee, Amber advised us that Tayla was very welcome to demonstrate her abilities with wood. Giles didn't say a thing. We spent the rest of the morning working on the stable doors with limited intervention from him. I suspect he'd already written us off as boring. It didn't take a body language expert to read him.

* * *

There was an hour's turnaround between saying goodbye to Tayla and filming the next arrival. As before, I was given her name – Marley – but knew nothing about her. I couldn't shake the feeling that I'd been lulled into a false sense of security with Tayla and that Marley would be a much stronger personality brought in to stir things up.

Amber was deep in conversation with Giles and a couple of crew members and there seemed to be people rushing around everywhere so there was no chance of getting any time alone with her. I headed into the kitchen for some lunch and had been in there about twenty minutes when my phone pinged.

> FROM AMBER
>
> I can't say much. I shouldn't even be saying this. Expect the unexpected & prepare for the worst. I'm so sorry

The text was accompanied by a pig emoji. As Marley's assigned animals were the pigs, that gave nothing away.

> TO AMBER
>
> Very cryptic! Thanks for the heads-up

'She says to expect the unexpected,' I said to the dogs. 'Nothing about this show so far has been expected, so bring it on.'

* * *

It could have been a coincidence but, as soon as Marley stepped out of the taxi in a turquoise boilersuit, I couldn't help wondering if she'd been specifically selected for her resemblance to my previous girlfriends. There was no denying that Marley was gorgeous and, if I'd met her before the show, I'd have been drawn to her, but things had changed. Was this another reason Amber said nothing could happen between us – because she thought I'd fall for Marley with her being my type? If only she knew.

'Great to meet you, Barney,' Marley said, kissing me on either cheek.

'And you. Ready for a day on the farm?'

'I can't wait to get stuck in.'

Giles stopped the filming and said he wanted Marley to wear a blindfold as we led her to her first task and told me I wasn't to speak to her until it had been lifted. They hadn't done the blindfold thing with Tayla, and I wondered if it had something to do with Amber's text earlier.

Despite Amber's warning to expect the unexpected, the blood-curdling scream Marley emitted when I removed her blindfold by the gate to Bottom Pig was a huge surprise. Marley running off and vomiting over the verge was even more unexpected. And the filthy look Amber directed at Giles before rushing over to Marley and ushering her away confirmed that none of this was her doing. He really was a piece of work.

'What am I expected to do now?' I asked Giles, hoping he could hear the disgust in my voice.

He didn't even have the decency to look at me.

Zara said something to him which elicited a non-committal shrug. She said something else, shook her head, and strode over to me.

'Sorry about this, Barney. Why don't you start doing what you were going to do with the pigs and I'll see what's going on?'

'Do you think she's all right?'

'If you mean Marley, probably not. If you mean Amber, definitely not. She begged him not to do this.'

'I'm guessing Marley's scared of pigs.'

'Worse than that. Marley has a pig phobia, but apparently that's great entertainment.' She sighed. 'Apologies for being so unprofessional, but he started it.'

'The pigs can wait. Why don't I go and see Marley instead? She'll probably want to freshen up and I've got a spare toothbrush in the house.'

She smiled at me. 'You're a good guy, Barney. I wish there were more like you.' She shot a filthy look in Giles's direction, but he was looking at his phone and missed it.

We found Marley and Amber on the bench beside the farmhouse. Marley's face was pale as she sipped from a bottle of water.

'Just wanted to check you're okay,' I said.

'I'm as well as a person who's just chucked their guts up while being filmed for a TV show can be.' She sounded more embarrassed than angry.

'The pigs send their apologies for scaring you.'

She smiled. 'I probably scared them more. I'm so sorry. I've never thrown up before. It was the surprise. I honestly didn't think that, after I'd shared my phobia, they'd get me to work with pigs. And now I realise how naïve that makes me sound. Of course I'd be given pigs.'

She turned to Amber. 'I'm sorry for letting you down, but I can't do it. If I was just a bit wary, I'd have given it my best shot, but I'm terrified. I'll have to pull out.'

'How are you with sheep?' I asked, feeling sorry for her. She'd been intentionally humiliated. There was no excuse for that.

'I'm good with all animals except pigs.'

'Amber, can we swap the animals round and do the sheep with Marley?'

'That's how Amber originally planned it,' Zara said.

'Would you stay if you worked with the sheep instead, Marley?' Amber asked.

'Yes, but...' She glanced down at her boilersuit and grimaced. 'I've got some sick on my clothes and in my hair. I stink.'

'We've got another boilersuit ready for Friday so you can use that one and we'll get this one washed,' Amber said, 'and I'm sure Barney won't mind you using his bathroom to give your hair a rinse.'

'I can give you a spare toothbrush too,' I said.

Marley looked up at me and gave me a grateful smile. 'That'd be great, thanks.'

Zara ran off to get the replacement boilersuit and Marley's bag.

'I'm so embarrassed,' Marley said. 'What a first impression.'

'Forget it happened,' I said.

Amber nodded. 'Definitely. You shouldn't have been put in that situation and I can't apologise enough. We'll get you sorted and start over, yeah?'

Amber and Marley followed me into the farmhouse and upstairs to the main bathroom.

'There's spare toiletries in the cabinet and clean towels on the shelves,' I told her.

'Take your time,' Amber said. 'I'll knock when your bag and clothes arrive.'

We left her in peace and went downstairs into the hall.

'I'm so sorry, Barney.' Amber looked and sounded on the verge of tears. I didn't care if Zara walked in on us as I wrapped my arms round her. My instinct was to kiss the top of her head, but I didn't want to overstep the mark. I felt her shaking and hated that she was clearly being made to be part of something with which she wasn't comfortable.

At the sound of the kitchen door opening and Zara calling out, 'Only me!' I lowered my arms.

'In here!' Amber called.

'One puke-free boilersuit and one handbag,' Zara said, holding up both items.

I directed her up to the bathroom. I couldn't risk hugging Amber again in case Zara came straight back down. They seemed to have a great relationship and, from Zara's reaction to the situation so far, she was firmly on Amber's side, but I couldn't risk adding to Amber's problems if I'd read things wrong. However, I did want her to know that I didn't hold her in any way responsible for what had just happened.

There was an old church pew in the hall, so I steered her towards it and sat down beside her. She placed her hand on the pew between us and I interlinked my fingers with hers, just as we'd done when we watched the sunset on Friday. I'd needed her then and she needed me now.

48

AMBER

The gentle touch of Barney's fingers against mine meant everything to me. He understood, he didn't judge, and I had an ally. I knew none of this was my fault and I couldn't have fought any harder than I had to avoid Marley having a pig encounter, but that didn't make me feel any better. That poor woman!

It was a testament to her intelligence and strength of character that she was willing to stick around and try again. Giles had called me in my earpiece several times, but I'd removed it. He might officially be in charge but he had no right to call the shots round here after the stunt he'd pulled.

'She'll be about ten minutes,' Zara said, coming down the stairs.

I reluctantly released Barney's hand and stood up. 'I need to brief the crew on what's happening. Zara, can you bring Barney and Marley over when Marley's ready?'

'I'll see you to the door,' Barney said. 'You can steal my seat, Zara.'

Zara swapped places – great tactic from Barney in ensuring she didn't follow us through the kitchen.

'Give him hell,' Barney said as I paused by the kitchen door. 'You're right and he's wrong.'

Encouraged by his words, I strode across the yard towards the marquee. I had some serious arse-kicking to do.

* * *

Giles wasn't impressed but that seemed to be his default mode and, frankly, I couldn't care less how he felt. I got a mouthful first about disappearing and not responding to his demands that I return, then there was a rant about how 'pathetic' it was for a grown woman to vomit at the sight of a pig. Clearly he had no understanding or experience of phobias and no empathy with anyone who had one. He lacked empathy full stop, although that was likely a positive for the type of show in which he specialised – no guilt or remorse for the ritual humiliation he caused. Just like Parker all those years ago.

A few choice phrases like 'blatant disregard for mental health' and 'seeking legal advice' finally calmed him down and he accepted that, if we didn't want Marley to walk out, the pigs would need to wait for Rayn.

When Marley appeared in the marquee a little later with Barney and Zara, Giles rushed up to her.

'Are you all right?' he gushed. 'I'm so sorry. Communications breakdown on my part, I'm afraid. I was told about your feelings towards certain animals and I didn't understand the severity of it, so my profuse apologies for any distress and embarrassment caused.'

He'd underestimated her if he thought she'd believe for one moment that he was being sincere, but Marley accepted his apology gracefully and the afternoon progressed without further hitches.

I was initially shocked he'd apologised and even more stunned that he'd accepted the blame himself, but then I realised he was just protecting the production company from a backlash by playing the 'misunderstanding' card. I suspected this wasn't the first time he'd made such a speech when things had been pushed way too far.

* * *

Zara headed back to Hedgehog Hollow before we finished filming for the day as she had some work to do on the *Countryside Calendar* production schedule.

As soon as we were done filming, I took Marley aside and apologised once more.

'Honestly, don't worry about it. I've had a great afternoon with the sheep instead. There's no harm done and I promise I *will* return tomorrow.'

'Thanks for your understanding.'

When she'd gone, I hesitated in the farmyard, wondering whether I should try to catch Barney. I thought about his fingers entwined with mine earlier, how it felt to have his arms around me, comforting me and conveying that he didn't hold me responsible for what had happened. The butterflies soared and I knew I couldn't stay. I needed to give him space to finish this. I needed space too.

I drove back to Hedgehog Hollow, craving a hot shower to remove the grubbiness of today's experience.

'Any more drama?' Zara asked, looking up from the table when I arrived back at Meadow View.

'No. I think we had our fair share earlier.'

'That was horrible to see.'

'Too right.'

'I hope you're not blaming yourself because you fought him all the way on that.'

'No, I'm not, but I still feel bad about it. Marley's been great, though. I caught her before she went back to her B&B to apologise again, and she was so gracious about it. She loved the sheep so she left on a high and promised to return tomorrow. What are your plans for tonight?'

'Long hot soak in the bath and an early night for me. I feel shattered. What about you?'

'Shower, catch up with Sophie, and probably an early night too.'

* * *

I emerged from the shower a little later to three messages.

FROM SOPHIE

> Feeling much more settled this week. Starting to make friends. A few of us are going out for a meal tonight. Thanks again for Saturday. You're the best xxxxxxxx

I felt so comforted reading that and sent her three blowing kisses emojis in response.

FROM BARNEY

> Sorry I didn't catch you before you left. I wanted to check you're OK after the pigcident. That Giles is a prize [insert insult of choice here] & you weren't to blame

His text made me laugh out loud and I was grinning as I replied.

TO BARNEY

> Apologies for heading straight off – bit drained after the drama. I promise there's nothing like that coming up tomorrow. Thanks for your understanding about Marley. Really appreciate it. Pigcident – hilarious!

I added three crying with laughter emojis before sending it but the lightness I felt from the exchange with Barney left me when I opened the third message.

FROM DAN

> Hope you've had a good week. Just checking you got my last text xx

I shook my head in disbelief as I re-read his previous text, which I'd ignored – the one about Sophie putting in a good word for him with Becca Scarsdale. He had a nerve chasing me.

TO DAN

> Yes I did and I don't think it takes a genius to work out why I didn't respond. Good luck and goodbye

As soon as it sent, I blocked his number then deleted him from my contacts. I didn't need or want someone like Dan Mercer in my life, just like I didn't want Parker Knowles. I wasn't sure what I wanted anymore.

I'd keep telling myself that lie.

49

BARNEY

Rayn Masterson arrived at Bumblebee Barn yesterday afternoon an hour after Marley left. Dressed in a lilac boilersuit and with an uncanny resemblance to my recent exes, she rushed over to me with an excitable squeal, planted a kiss on each cheek, and gushed about how thrilled she was to meet me.

She was exceptionally confident and very comfortable in front of the camera, so it was no surprise to hear she had a drama degree. It didn't take me long to suss her out. From the over-the-top enthusiasm accompanying each activity, I was certain she was acting a part.

Whether I saw the real Rayn on our first day was debatable, but she was good comedy value and, as a result, the atmosphere felt lighter than it had for the past couple of days. It was refreshing to hear laughter from the crew instead of grumbles from Giles.

Rayn burst into song at every opportunity. While mucking out the pig sties, she sang chart music and, while feeding them, it was songs from musicals, as though demonstrating her versatility. Her voice was fantastic, although I'm not sure the pigs were too enamoured, which was just as well because I couldn't imagine Milo singing to them on his return.

She regaled me with happy childhood memories of visiting her grandparents and helping out on their smallholding, which didn't convince me either. The stories sounded rehearsed but, heeding Amber's advice, I played along.

By the time she left, I felt exhausted, desperate for a break from her constant high energy.

This morning had been more of the same. She even repeated some of her smallholding stories as though she'd forgotten which ones she'd shared yesterday but hadn't prepared enough of them to fill today too.

I'd laughed a lot, but my ears were ringing by the time she waved goodbye just before lunchtime and I was grateful for half an hour on my own in the kitchen in welcome silence.

After lunch, I was filmed summarising my thoughts on my day with Rayn, how I felt about all three of the matches, and who I thought might be the current frontrunner for Monday's big date.

I guessed Giles would want me to say something unkind or controversial, but I wasn't going to play that game. They were nice women – if a bit loud and irritating in Rayn's case – and I wasn't prepared to say anything nasty which might humiliate them on national television. I picked out one thing I liked about the personality of each of them and something I'd admired about them in the tasks, but kept it fairly non-committal otherwise.

'Is that it?' Giles challenged, hands on his hip, lip curled up in disgust.

'I was asked to keep it short.'

'Yes, but surely you can't have liked all three of them that much. What about the disaster with Marley and the pigs?'

'I thought you weren't using that footage.'

His cheeks flushed. 'We're not. But I refuse to believe you didn't find anything negative about any of them.'

'You want me to say something nasty?'

'Yes.'

'Which they'll get to see when it airs?'

'Yes. You have a problem with that?'

'Actually, I do. I was raised on the idea that, if you can't say something nice, you don't say anything at all.'

Beside him, Amber was smiling, and I could see Zara in the background waving both hands in the air, clapping inaudibly.

'That's very honourable of you, but how does that make for great viewing?'

'I think that might be your problem, not mine. Are we done because this is a working farm and I have a job to do?' I'd long since exhausted my patience with him.

He flung his arms in the air, muttered a few expletives and stormed off.

'That's a wrap,' Amber confirmed, the relief clear on her face. 'Thanks, Barney. Zara and I need to discuss the plans for tomorrow with you, but I need to go through some details with the crew first. Are you okay to meet us back here in a couple of hours? It can be a bit later if that works better round you.'

I glanced at my watch. 'Four's fine. See you then.'

I called for Bear and Harley and took the quad bike up to Double Top Field to find Mum.

A storm was forecast for this evening, which would hopefully break the recent mugginess. Tomorrow's activities with all three matches had originally been planned for outside but we were expecting rain all day. Even though that was realistic of life on a farm and working in torrential rain would be a good challenge for the matches, it wouldn't translate well onto television, so I'd had to come up with a back-up plan, which presumably Amber was discussing with the crew right now.

Mum had just exited the Herdwick field. 'All finished for today?' she asked as she closed the gate.

'Filming is but I'm running through the plans for tomorrow with Amber and Zara at four.'

'So how was your second day with Queen Elsa?' Mum asked, smiling at me. 'More singing?'

I rested my arms on the gate, looking out over the herdies, and Mum did the same.

'I didn't think it was possible to top yesterday, but she managed.'

'I'm guessing you won't be choosing her for Monday's big date?'

'My ears won't take it.'

'Tayla and Marley both seemed nice.' Mum had spent a few hours at the farm each day, so she'd caught some of the filming.

'They were, but who do I choose for Monday? The one with the boyfriend or the one with the pig phobia?'

Mum's mouth dropped open. 'You're not winding me up, are you?'

I shook my head. 'It's been an interesting week...'

We rode down to Top Field to check on the Swaledales and I filled Mum in on what I knew from Amber and what I'd observed myself. The more I spoke, the more incensed I felt on Amber's behalf for having to work with changes that didn't sit comfortably with her and for having to put up with that medallioned idiot of a director.

'Are you disappointed that, after all this effort, you haven't found someone?' Mum asked after we'd discussed the events of the week.

'Who says I haven't?'

She frowned. 'Oh! So you do like Marley or Tayla.'

I shook my head.

'Then I don't under... Oh! It's not one of the matches. It's one of the production team. Beautiful smile? Gorgeous red hair?'

I'd already tied the arms of my boilersuit round my waist due to the heat, but I wafted my T-shirt, feeling even hotter all of a sudden.

'Does she know?'

'Yes.'

'And how does she feel?'

'The same, I think, but she's got her job to do. I doubt dating the farmer is part of the job description.'

'What about when the film crew have gone and the noise has died down?'

I shrugged. I really wanted to believe that was possible but, conflict of interests aside, Amber was fresh out of a relationship and I was grieving for Granddad.

Time wasn't on our side, though. It was now or never because, when filming finished on Monday, they'd head to the next farm to start the process all over again and I wouldn't see Amber until the follow-up in three months' time and it might be too late by then.

'I'm no good at this stuff,' I muttered.

'Are any of us?' Mum asked, giving me a gentle nudge. 'If you think Amber could be the one, you need to fight for her. Don't let her walk away next week not knowing that you love her.'

I stepped back, shaking my head. 'I never said I loved her.'

'Maybe not in words, but your eyes did and your voice did. Fight for her, Barney. Give it all you've got. I need to head over to your grandma's, but you know where I am if you want to talk.'

'Thanks, Mum.'

She set off down the track but turned round after a few paces and made me smile with a few boxing moves. Fight for her? Easier said than done. I'd tried to fight for Elle, but all I'd done was get her up against the ropes from where she'd dealt me a sucker punch.

* * *

I rode back down to find Amber and Zara as agreed. The sky had darkened and there'd been a clear drop in temperature, with a light wind carrying a few droplets of rain. That storm could be on its way sooner than predicted.

The crew were packing away the final pieces of equipment but there was no sign of Amber. There was no sign of Giles either and I hoped something hadn't kicked off between them.

Zara strode across the farmyard, scrolling on her tablet. She looked up as she approached me and smiled. 'Perfect timing. Amber's with Giles, but I have a list and we can get started if that's okay with you.'

I'd clearly failed to hide my disappointment as she lightly tapped me on the arm with her tablet. 'Don't look so sad. She'll be with us shortly.'

I wasn't sure how to respond to that, so I followed her to Events Barn. Formerly the milking barn from the days of being a dairy farm, it was now where Mum stored all the equipment for her business. Tomorrow's task was working on something for her. She had a cart which she hired out for weddings with a pair of my horses, but she'd acquired another cart which she wanted turning into a festive one to hire out at Christmas. It had already been stripped back and repaired, so it just needed painting.

The brief was for me to work with all three matches together, seeing how they interacted with me and each other, but I suspected there'd be a revised plan to play them off against each other, instigate conflict and cause some embarrassment. I was dreading it.

'Wow! This place is amazing,' Zara said, turning in a circle.

Everything was divided into bays depending on the occasion such as wedding, children's party, Halloween. Some bays were full of racking and plastic crates labelled with the contents. Others had larger pieces of equipment like a wedding pergola, a couple of candy carts, and giant inflatables.

'I could spend hours in here looking at everything,' Zara said, 'but we'd better crack on. Show me to the Santa cart.'

An hour later, we'd been through everything and there was still no sign of Amber. The rain hadn't arrived, but the sky was a dark inky blue and I could smell the ozone which accompanied an approaching storm.

'Giles's car's gone.' Zara picked up her radio and called for Amber, but there was no response. She tried her mobile too. 'Voicemail. That's weird.'

'Do you think she's all right?' I asked.

'Not sure. It's not like her to go silent. I'm not sure where she'd have gone. She's not in her car.'

I had a sickening sensation in my gut that something was wrong. I called the dogs over. 'Where's Amber?' I asked them. 'Go and find Amber.'

They both shot off towards the garage. Harley went inside and Bear stayed by the entrance, looking at me as he wagged his tail. Zara and I ran over to them. *Please let Amber be okay.*

50

AMBER

When Giles asked me to accompany him to the original Bumblebee Barn to discuss something in private, I anticipated more bad news about changes to the show's format. I hadn't expected good news.

'It was my last day today,' he said.

'You're leaving?'

'That's right. I'm not going to lie and say it's been a pleasure to work with you.' He narrowed his eyes at me. 'Quite frankly, I hope our paths never cross again.'

I wasn't going to even try to disguise my delight at that news. While the lack of continuity wasn't ideal, the thought of not working with him again was the best news I'd heard all week.

'I believe that, if you can't say anything nice, you don't say anything at all – so I'll just say goodbye.'

'Clever,' he said. 'You won't look so smug when you discover who's replacing me from tomorrow.'

I had no enemies in the industry so that could only mean one thing. My heart started thumping and I felt sick.

'I believe you two were engaged at one point. I'm almost sorry I won't be here to see the fireworks.' With a raise of his eyebrows, he turned and left.

Parker Knowles? They wouldn't do that to me. Every time Esther negotiated a contract, she made it clear that a condition of the job was that I wouldn't work with Parker.

'Amber, darling, how's it going?' Esther asked, answering the phone within two rings.

'Did you know Parker's the new director on *Love on the Farm*?'

'What are you talking about? Giles Snyder's the director.'

'Not anymore. He's just told me that Parker's taking over tomorrow. You didn't know?'

'Of course I didn't. Are you sure?'

'Why would he lie?'

'There must be a misunderstanding. Leave it with me. I'll make a call and come straight back to you.'

'You did tell Grant and Liza I won't work with Parker?'

'Of course! I *always* do that.' She sounded hurt. 'I'd *never* have pitched it to you if I thought he was even in sniffing distance of it.'

'Okay. Sorry. I had to ask.'

Her voice softened. 'I understand. I'll call you back shortly. Bye for now.'

She hung up and all I could do was sit there, trying to push down the ball of panic rising inside me.

Five agonising minutes passed. Six. Seven. And then my phone rang.

'I'm so sorry, darling,' Esther said. 'There's no mistake. I wish there was. Apparently they appointed Parker after Matt resigned but he wasn't free immediately so Giles was brought in to cover.'

'Did you remind them of my refusal to work with him?'

'Several times. Vehemently. But they said it's not in your contract, so they're not committed to anything.'

'A verbal agreement counts for nothing?' My voice was getting steadily louder and higher.

'Not to them. I'm so sorry. They won't budge. Parker Knowles has signed up to the rest of the series.'

'Does he know I'm the producer?'

There was a pause before she answered, 'Yes.'

I closed my eyes for a moment and took a few gulps of air.

'What do you want to do, darling?' Esther asked, her voice gentle.

A wave of anger swept through me. 'Find out what the hell he's playing at. I've deleted his number. Do you have it?'

'I'll send it over. Let me know what you want to do next. I know I pushed you into this, but I hope you know I'd never have done that if I'd had the slightest inkling he'd be involved.'

I could tell from her tone that she was as shaken by this as I was, and I didn't want her to feel guilty.

'I know, and I don't blame you. I'm annoyed with myself more than anything. You play with the dragons, you're going to get burnt. Clementine Creates represent everything I hate about this industry and I don't know why I'm even surprised that Parker's in bed with them.'

'Whatever you decide to do, you have my support.'

'I'll let you know. It might not be today.'

'That's fine. I'm here if you want to talk. I really am sorry.'

'Thanks, Esther. I'll speak to you soon.'

Moments after disconnecting, Parker's phone number pinged through. Better call him immediately before I talked myself out of it. I was actually shaking. I hated that he still had this effect on me. Each ring filled me with dread. On the sixth, confidence fading, I was about to hang up, but he answered.

'I take it someone's spilled the beans and ruined my fun,' he said.

Fear turned to anger. Fun? He'd been planning to rock up tomorrow with no word of warning and he actually thought that would be funny? Could he be any more unprofessional or insensitive? Not that I should be surprised. Humiliation was his speciality.

'Why did you sign up to this when you knew I was the producer?' I demanded, my voice stronger than I felt.

'Because they showed me the tedium of episode one and asked me if I'd be up for the challenge.'

'You haven't answered my question.'

'You're not still whining on about your sister?'

'Whining? Did you really just say that?'

'It's been five years. Get over it!'

'Get over it? Seriously? Have you any idea what you did to Sophie and to our family?'

'Bloody hell, Amber, I'm not raking over all of this again.'

'Again? We never *raked* over it at the time. You ghosted me. No explanation, no apology, no remorse, no...'

I removed my phone from my ear and stared at it in disbelief. He'd hung up on me.

My heart was still pounding and now my head was. The urge to scream lodged itself in my throat as my emotions swirled between anger, fear and the desire to burst into tears.

I paced up and down, my hands clenching and unclenching, debating what to do. Ring Esther and ask her to tell the Lennons I quit with immediate effect? Ring Grant or Liza directly and tell them what I thought of them – likely to result in them sacking me? Finish at Bumblebee Barn but refuse to film any other episodes unless they replaced Parker? I shook my head and tutted at that one. The Lennons wouldn't dismiss Parker. He was exactly what they needed to turn this into the worst kind of reality TV – their specialism – and they'd probably be glad to see the back of me so they could bring in a producer who was on board with their vision.

The only certainty for me was that I could not and would not work with Parker Knowles, so continuing into the Dales for our second Yorkshire-based farmer was out of the question.

I'd feel so much better about myself if I walked away from a show I now hated. I didn't need the money and I didn't need the show. I'd only agreed to it to be near Sophie, but it turned out that Dan had been right about us being overprotective. She'd only had one hiccup and it hadn't been a biggie, so she'd have been fine having us all at the end of the phone.

What if I ditched the show and took some long overdue holiday time? I could stay at Hedgehog Hollow or close by if they were fully booked, work on my rescue centre proposal and spend some quality time with my sister when she wasn't filming.

Barney's face drifted into my mind. I could spend time with him too. I'd tried to fight it, but my feelings for him had grown stronger every day. After the big date on Monday, with Barney's episode a wrap, we could get together guilt-free and explore whether there really was something there.

I *would* quit. Life was too short to spend it with a man I couldn't abide, working for a production company I didn't respect, selling my soul to the devil. The only decision was whether to pull out right now or whether I could cast all my personal feelings aside and finish what I'd started at Bumblebee Barn. It would be a nightmare sticking around, but I couldn't help feeling I owed it to Barney, Tayla, Marley and Rayn to see this through. And the crew too. They'd already had masses of upheaval.

I glanced up at the original Bumblebee Barn sign on the pillar beside me, and the photograph of Jennifer with the lavender and bee. I ran my fingers down the glass. That little girl had faced way more adversity than me. If she could find the strength to remain positive, so could I. It was only a couple more days. I'd put my big girl's pants on and show Parker that he hadn't broken me.

Feeling much calmer, I was about to head off in search of Zara and Barney when my phone rang with an unknown number.

'Is that Amber Crawford?' The woman on the end of the phone had a Liverpudlian accent.

'Speaking.'

'Hi, my name's Jessie Lyon. I'm on the production team of *The Book Sleuths* and I don't want you to panic...'

Why did people use that phrase? The one thing it was guaranteed to do was make a person panic.

'...but there's been an incident on set. She's gonna be fine – it's nothing serious – but Sophie's been taken to hospital.'

I felt sick. 'What happened?'

'We were working on a scene where another character yells at Sophie then throws a punch. It should have been straightforward with Sophie ducking before the punch, but it was really weird. It was like she froze when she was getting yelled at and, when the punch came, she never ducked. She's got one heck of a shiner. She said she's been hit in that eye before so the hospital want to do some checks, just to be on the safe side.'

I could barely form any words. 'Which hospital?'

'York. It's on Wigginton Road in Clifton.'

I had no idea where that was, but I could soon find out. 'I'll be there as soon as I can.'

Call ended, I pressed a shaking hand to my mouth. What was that I'd just been telling myself about there only being one hiccup with Sophie and it not being a biggie? I replayed Jessie's words: *It was like she froze when she was getting yelled at and, when the punch came, she never ducked. It was like she froze.* That reaction might have seemed strange to Jessie, but it made perfect sense to me. She'd been back *there*. She'd regressed five years to her time in *The*

House with Alisha in her face, yelling and hurling accusations. It seemed like she hadn't dealt with it after all, just as we'd feared.

Tears pooled in my eyes, but I didn't have time for that now – I needed to get to the hospital to be with my sister – so I tried to blink them back, but they broke free and streaked down my cheeks. Sniffing, I spotted a roll of blue tissue paper on a nearby work bench and tore off a piece. With each wipe, more tears flowed. I'd just about managed to compose myself when Harley appeared and nudged against my leg. I crouched down to stroke her ears. She placed her front paws on my legs as though trying to give me a hug. The loving gesture set me off again.

'What's happened?' Zara asked, running over. 'Has Giles had a go at you?'

'Giles has gone,' I said, simultaneously shaking my head and wiping my cheeks.

'I know. His car's not there.'

'No! He's gone gone. As in off the project.'

'Really? Then isn't that cause for celebration?' she asked, giving me a bewildered look. 'Unless... Oh, my God! Who's replacing him?'

'Parker.'

'They can't do that.'

'They just have.'

'Didn't Esther tell them you can't work with him?'

'She's already given them hell, but they don't care and neither does he.'

'You've spoken to him?'

I wiped my eyes and sniffed once more. 'It wasn't pretty. I can't believe I wanted to marry that man.'

Zara squeezed my shoulders. 'He fooled us all because he was a charmer. You had a lucky escape.'

'The thought of seeing him tomorrow...'

'You won't be alone. You've got me and Barney and the crew.'

At the mention of his name, I looked up and realised Barney was with her. I gave him a weak smile. 'I bet you wish you'd never signed up to this.'

'Best decision I ever made.'

His expression in his eyes was so tender and I knew I had to see this week out and give this thing between us a chance. But I had something else I had to do right now.

'It's not just Parker,' I told them. 'Sophie's had an incident on set and she's been taken to hospital.'

'Is she all right?' Zara asked.

'I'm not sure. Physically, she will be. It's another black eye and hopefully nothing serious. Mentally, I'm not so sure.' I turned to Barney. 'Which side of York is the hospital?'

'This side. I'll take you.'

'You don't have to do that.'

'But I want to. I know where I'm going so it'll be quicker.'

'Thank you.'

Barney took the dogs inside while I went to the marquee with Zara to retrieve my jacket and handbag.

'I'm so pissed off about Parker,' she said. 'You must be fuming.'

'I am. I can't work with him. How would you feel if I quit the show after we wrap on Monday?'

She linked her arm through mine and gave it a squeeze. 'I'd say yes, please. Every change they've made has made me squirm a bit more and this latest stunt is taking the piss.'

Barney was waiting for us by his jeep.

'Are you okay packing the rest of the stuff away?' I asked Zara.

'No problem. Send Sophie my love and I'll see you later.'

She hugged me then I climbed into the jeep beside Barney, waving to Zara as we pulled away.

'I've put a bottle of water and a box of paracetamol in the

glovebox,' Barney said. 'Fizz always gets a headache when she cries.'

'That's so thoughtful. Thank you.'

My head was pounding so I gratefully swallowed a couple of tablets with water as we drove down the track.

'It'll take about forty minutes to get to the hospital,' Barney said. 'I can put music on, sit in silence, you can make phone calls, or we can talk about Parker or Sophie. Whatever you need.'

He glanced across and gave me a reassuring smile. I thought about the call I'd had with Zara on this very road after I first met Barney. I'd told her I thought he might have depths. He did. And he had emotional intelligence – something both Parker and Dan had massively lacked.

'Parker was my fiancé,' I said. 'He's a director and we met on set six years ago before I started on *Countryside Calendar*. I thought things were good but, looking back, there were red flags and I only noticed them after Sophie appeared on a new reality TV show called *The House*. Parker was drafted in last minute as the director and it all went horribly wrong...'

51

AMBER

Five years ago

Mum, Dad, Brad, Tabs and I gathered round the TV at Green Acres that first Saturday evening to watch the contestants enter *The House*.

'Welcome to *The House*, where inhibitions need to be left at the door,' the voiceover actor – a woman with a deep, seductive voice – announced to the viewers. 'This is a *very* special mansion house. She has many identities and surprises which the contestants will discover over the next two months as they move within her sub-houses. The first sub-house is the Gingerbread House. Our twenty contestants haven't eaten since breakfast. They've been told that dinner will be served once everyone has arrived, but they must resist any of the sweet treats in the meantime. After all, they wouldn't want to spoil their dinner...'

The Gingerbread House was like something out of *Charlie and the Chocolate Factory*. Absolutely everything in there – furniture, soft furnishings and décor – had a sweet theme. We gasped alongside the contestants as they entered the room one at a time, marvelling at the creativity of the set designers and drooling at the candy cart, chocolate fountain and various jars laden with every type of sweet you could possibly imagine.

Sophie was the eighth contestant to be admitted and we cheered as she entered the room, accompanied by a quick bio.

As the episode went on, it was revealed that one of *The House*'s many secrets was that, as the twenty contestants – ten male, ten female – moved round the sub-houses, they'd have no idea that they were participating in social experiments connected to the theme of that sub-house. Some would be inspired by major psychological experiments and others would be just for a bit of fun, like the first one which was seeing whether contestants could resist helping themselves to the sweet treats even though they'd been told not to. For those who could resist, could they still do so after a little goading from other contestants?

It was fun to watch, especially seeing Sophie's cheeks bulging with marshmallows after one of the contestants sneaked a couple in and encouraged her to do the same.

'What did you think?' Mum asked when the first episode ended.

The general consensus was that the first episode had been fun if predictable. It was obvious that all the contestants would slip at least one sweet into their mouth, especially when they saw others doing it. We concluded we wouldn't have enjoyed it nearly as much if we hadn't known one of the contestants.

The viewing figures hadn't been anywhere near what they'd predicted and Parker, as director, blamed the marketing team. In an effort not to reveal the secrets around sub-houses and social experiments, the pre-launch adverts had been a little too cryptic and hadn't generated a buzz.

The response from the media was bad. *Boring, dull, House of Yawn, monotonous, aimed at kids, not worth your time...*

'*Tropical Heat* wasn't an instant ratings success,' Parker said defensively when, halfway through the first week, the comments were still derogatory. 'And now it's one of the biggest reality shows around.'

I felt bad for him and tried my best to placate him while thinking that the press and public were right. The premise of *The House* was clever but perhaps a little too clever for mainstream television. If you stripped it down to the basic premise, twenty strangers participating in social experiments was never going to be a ratings winner.

I watched as many episodes as I was able to around work commitments, but it was background viewing rather than active watching and I really only focused on it when Sophie was on screen.

Some sub-houses were more memorable than others such as the Ghost House which included an actual ghost train on tracks to move between the rooms. The set was phenomenal, with cobwebs, eerie green glows, and flickering candles everywhere. The contestants had to sleep in coffins which generated a fair bit of hysteria and it was interesting seeing how easily contestants could be freaked out after others claimed to have heard a sound or felt something.

During the second week, I became aware of certain contestants having way more screen time than others and some of the individuals coming across negatively.

'Are you deliberately favouring certain contestants?' I asked Parker over the phone one evening.

'You know I can't talk about the show, especially when your sister's a contestant.'

'Yes, but you promised me you'd look out for her.'

'I'm not her dad. Sophie chose to go into *The House*. She knows how these things work.'

A couple of days later, I was in no doubt that they were trying to influence public opinion negatively and, for some reason, my sister seemed to be their target. She came across as obsessed with her hair, constantly brushing and flicking it, and it appeared as though she had her eye on several male contestants with long, lingering glances when I knew she was besotted with Devon and would never do anything to jeopardise what they had.

I didn't want to say anything to my parents in case it was just me, but Zara watched an episode with me and agreed with my verdict. For reasons I couldn't fathom – especially when she was the youngest contestant – they'd placed a label on Sophie as a self-obsessed flirt.

A couple of the contestants – Max and Alisha – had got together but it looked as though Sophie was after Max too. They were frequently shown whispering and giggling together.

The contestants moved into a new sub-house – the House of Cards – where the contestants were divided into hearts or spades and given a card to represent the role they'd play in the house. Sophie was given the queen of spades to Max's king and Alisha was the queen of hearts and there was no way it wasn't going to end badly.

The alleged love triangle became a huge focus, with Sophie shown confiding in her jack that she really liked Max while Alisha was shown in tears, devastated that Sophie was after her boyfriend. I kept telling myself it had to be manipulated – Sophie loved Devon and would never do anything to hurt him – but it was so convincingly done that even I began to wonder if it was real.

Parker and I argued constantly about it. His stock phrase was, 'If you don't like watching her, switch the bloody TV off.' Not helpful at all.

The last day in the House of Cards was going to be a banquet for the royal cards served by the lower numbers followed by a private ball for the kings and queens. They were given dance lessons the day before but, while Sophie and Max were having their lesson, Alisha was in the interview room being told that Sophie was planning to kiss Max during the dance. The footage kept cutting between Sophie and Max looking very close as they practised their dance and Alisha in floods of tears. A heated next episode was promised.

* * *

Present day

'You don't have to continue if it's too hard,' Barney said when I tailed off and stared out of the window.

'No, it's all right. I want you to know.' I took a deep breath. 'The launch night had been broadcast a few hours after the live event with some speedy editing, but the rest of the episodes were put out a day late to allow them time to do a heavy edit and manipulate the footage. So while viewers were watching the build-up to the banquet and ball, the actual banquet and ball was happening and it all kicked off.

'They'd all been drinking – very heavily in Alisha's case – and they hadn't even finished the first dance before she stormed across the dance floor to Sophie and Max, shouting, swearing, and calling Sophie names. Next minute, she thumped her. Sophie fell and hit her head and, even though she was knocked unconscious, Alisha went for her again. Max tried to stop her and it was only security rushing in at that point that prevented her from beating up Sophie. Shortly after the previous episode aired, we were called to say she was in hospital. She had a swollen black eye, a bust cheek, she'd split the back of her head open and had fractured her arm when she fell. All because they'd fed a pack of lies to Alisha.'

'That's horrendous. Why would they do that?'

'Good TV allegedly.' I struggled to keep my voice steady. 'The physical damage was pretty bad, but those wounds healed in time. The emotional damage from the whole experience – not just the assault – was far worse and we nearly lost her.'

Feeling tears burning in my eyes, I opened the glovebox and took a couple of swigs of my water.

Barney continued driving in silence – another example of his emotional intelligence in giving me the space I needed.

'Alisha was arrested,' I said when I felt in control of my emotions once more. 'The show was pulled off air and it didn't return. There were too many question marks over the ethics and validity of what they were doing. Viewers never saw any footage from the night of the assault. I've often wondered if it would have been better for Sophie if they had shown it because she might at least have had some sympathy. Instead, all the viewers had seen was the alleged bad stuff.

'She spent three days in hospital and she was okay at that point, confused about what had happened and why, embarrassed, humiliated, but it was after she was discharged that it all fell apart. I was between filming so I moved back home and was there when Devon brought her back from hospital. She was meant to be getting some bed rest with a film on. Devon was downstairs with me when we heard her screaming. Curiosity had got the better of her and she'd started watching *The House* on catch-up. We'd stupidly assumed pulling the plug meant it disappeared completely, but all it meant was no more new episodes were made and everyone was sent home. She hadn't just raced through the clips. She'd also gone down the rabbit hole and found all the stuff in the tabloids including kiss-and-tell stories from men she didn't even know.'

I closed my eyes, feeling drained. I could still see her pale face, her haunted eyes, the tears streaking down her cheeks as she pointed to her TV. *That's not what I said! They've strung two sentences together. That's out of context. That's me repeating something the director said.* Then she picked up her iPad, scrolling frantically through various articles. *Lies! I don't even know these people. Why would they say that?*

'She was distraught,' I told Barney. 'She got herself so upset that she couldn't catch her breath. She said she had chest pains and I thought she was having a heart attack, but it turned out to be a massive panic attack.

'We had to remove her TV, phone and tablet because she couldn't seem to stop scrolling. Devon was an absolute rock. He pulled out of his next acting role to be with her, which was huge because it would have been a springboard for his career but, as far as he was concerned, no part was more important than Sophie.'

I shook my head, my heart breaking for the damage inflicted on that relationship too.

'A few weeks passed and we all thought it was time for Sophie to get out and about so she agreed to go into Maidstone with Devon. I needed to do some shopping so I went in with them, intending to go off and do my own thing. As we walked from the car park, I was aware of us being stared at, but I thought nothing of it at first. Sophie and Devon were an attractive couple and often drew appreciative glances. But I realised the stares were directed only at Sophie and they weren't appreciative. She picked up on it too and wanted to go back, but Devon and I convinced her to keep going. I decided not to leave them just yet and we went into Sophie's favourite clothes shop. The whispers started and then the louder-than-whispering nasty comments. I felt scared, so Sophie had to have been terrified. We decided to leave and we were heading down the main street when this random woman came up to her, called her a bitch, and spat on her.'

Barney gasped and his head shot round, his eyes wide. 'What is wrong with people?'

'I know! I can't even...' I shook my head. 'Sophie ran back to the car in tears and she lost it after that. She didn't feel safe leaving the house, scared it would happen again. She stopped singing and dancing, lost her confidence, lost her sparkle. On the occasions she absolutely had to leave the house for a medical appointment, she went in disguise with her hair pulled back under a hoodie and dark glasses. Even so, she was convinced everyone knew it was her and was talking about her.

'She had regular migraines and, before long, she was hooked on prescription painkillers. Devon did his best but he became her emotional punchbag and she drove him away, saying she was holding him back and he needed to find someone who wasn't. Bless that boy, he fought against it as much as he could for a year, maybe more, but she wouldn't let him back in. And that broke her too.'

'I'm so sorry. She must have gone through hell. You said she's acting in York now, so I'm assuming she's in a different place mentally now.'

'We had two and a half years where we wondered if she'd ever come back to us, then, on New Year's Day two years ago, she announced that enough was enough and she was reclaiming her life. I don't know where it came from – she'd refused any form of counselling – but she stuck to it. It was baby steps. She did some local theatre and then she started going to auditions for adverts and guest appearances on shows – one-episode parts – and she was brilliant at securing them. Most were emotional roles playing women who'd been assaulted and she joked it didn't take much effort to act them.'

I told him about her surprise audition for the Becca Scarsdale drama, the relief when she didn't get it, and the panic when that changed.

'I'm guessing you agreed to produce *Love on the Farm* so you'd be near Sophie?' Barney said.

'Spot on. For obvious reasons, I hate reality TV, but *Love on the Farm* wasn't meant to be anything like *The House* or programmes like it. They'd specifically wanted me as producer because the plan was to appeal to the *Countryside Calendar* demographic and challenge the idea that reality TV is fake and manipulated. And then they changed their mind – and kept doing that – and it became all the things it wasn't meant to be. I'm so sorry you were caught in the middle of it.'

'I'm sorry you were too. And you were trapped. Couldn't walk away like Matt did because you needed to be here for Sophie.'

'Exactly.' I bit my lip. It would be a logical moment to tell him that Sophie hadn't been the only one keeping me here, but I still couldn't do it. I knew there was no future for him with Tayla, Marley or Rayn, but I felt I'd already challenged my morals way more than was comfortable so far. Barney was driving, I was worried about Sophie and stressed about Parker. If and when I told Barney I had feelings for him, I wanted to be able to look him in the eye and, if he still felt the same way, kiss him for the first time. Telling him during an emergency hospital dash wasn't the moment.

My eyes were drawn to his lips and I had to turn away and look out of the window at the passing countryside, pushing all romantic thoughts from my mind. For now.

52

BARNEY

'Can I ask you a question?' I glanced across at Amber and she nodded. 'What happened with Parker? I presume he apologised.'

Amber snorted. 'Sorry doesn't feature in Parker's vocabulary. I got sick of having conversations with his voicemail. Even if we had spoken, there'd have been no way back from it, so I texted him with a date I wanted to collect my stuff from the house and asked him to stay away. He confirmed he would, but there was no apology, no regrets, no attempts to talk me out of it. I hired a van, and my brother and his girlfriend helped me clear my stuff, and that was that. I left my engagement ring on his bedside drawers, posted the keys back through the letterbox, and we never spoke again until I rang him earlier to ask him what the hell he was playing at.'

'I hate him already. Who doesn't apologise after something like that?'

'Someone with a stone-cold heart. After that, I started thinking about all the things that were wrong with our relationship – the sort of stuff you don't realise until you take a step back. I wish Soph hadn't gone through any of that, but the silver lining was waking up to who Parker really was and getting out of there.'

'How do you think he'll be with you tomorrow?'

'It's an unknown. Professional, I hope. He *is* brilliant at his job, even if he has no scruples. I'm telling myself it's only two days.'

We continued in companionable silence for a while, and I turned the music on low.

'I'll drop you off at the main entrance then find somewhere to park,' I said but, as I drove towards the drop-off point, Amber gasped.

'That's Sophie outside!'

There were several people gathered outside and leaning against a wall was a redhead who was presumably Amber's sister.

'Are you okay to hang on for a minute?' Amber asked as she pushed the door open.

'There's a few cars behind me so I'll do a lap.'

She got out and I drove away. In the rear-view mirror, I saw her rushing up to her sister and the two women embraced. I had no idea what their plan would be – whether Amber would want to stay over in York or whether she'd take Sophie back to Hedgehog Hollow – but I'd help however I could.

53

AMBER

'Amber! What are you doing here?' Sophie asked as I ran towards her outside York Hospital.

'Jessie called me.' I took care not to knock her face as I hugged her.

'She shouldn't have. I didn't want anyone worrying.'

I stepped back and studied her face. Her eye was bruised and swollen, only open to a slit.

'That looks painful.'

'It is, but it's superficial. I can't believe Jessie called you when I specifically said not to.'

'But you're hurt.'

'Yeah, but it's not serious. And it's my fault for being a numpty and not ducking when I was meant to. Epic fail!'

I was thrown by how blasé she sounded about the whole thing. I'd rushed over here fearing she'd had some sort of regressive episode and here she was, laughing about it and calling herself names.

'Are you okay?' she asked. 'You're very pale. Have you been crying?'

'I thought something really bad had happened to you.'

'Ooh! This is why I didn't want you to know.'

A pretty brunette who looked to be about Sophie's age joined us, pulling on a denim jacket. 'That's better. You all set, Soph?'

'Cora, this is my sister Amber,' Sophie said. 'Amber, this is my co-star Cora Drew, also known as Right Hook.'

The two of them giggled.

'It's so lovely to meet you,' Cora said, moving forward to kiss me on either cheek. 'Sorry about decking your sister.'

The pair of them giggled again.

'So what actually happened?' I asked, confused by how lightly they both seemed to be taking it.

'Cora plays my housemate, Fi, and there's this scene where she thinks Amelie's spent their rent money so she confronts her, gives her a mouthful of abuse and throws a punch.'

'Only Soph didn't duck,' Cora finished, rolling her eyes.

'Jessie said you froze. I thought maybe, with the shouting and everything, you'd...' I glanced at Cora as I tailed off, not wanting to say anything about *The House* in front of her when Sophie kept the whole experience such a closely guarded secret.

'Oh, my God' Sophie cried, launching herself at me for another hug. 'You thought I'd had some sort of episode.'

She stepped back, shaking her head. 'No wonder you look so upset.'

A nearby bench had just been vacated, so Sophie pulled me over to it and we sat down while Cora stood nearby.

'Truth is, I *was* back there,' Sophie admitted, 'but not in the way you're thinking. I was struggling with the scene, not feeling I had the emotions quite right, when I had a lightbulb moment. I could channel my experience from *The House* to make a really impactful scene, only I had that lightbulb moment at completely the wrong point and got so absorbed in my train of thought that I missed my cue to duck, and this is the result.' She pointed to her eye and shrugged.

'And it's okay, Cora knows. I had another lightbulb moment after I spoke to Mick, the cameraman. I've spent too many years hiding from what happened, as though it's a dirty secret and all my fault. I've spent too much time worrying about what people think of me, but what happened in *The House* is yesterday's news and if I come across anyone who remembers it and thinks I'm the person they made me out to be, I can either put them straight or I can walk away.'

'Too right,' Cora said. 'We all know you're fabulous.'

They smiled at each other, and it warmed my heart to see that my sister had made a friend.

'You have no idea how relieved I am to hear you say that,' I said, taking her hand in mine. 'So you're really okay?'

'I'm really okay. Other than the swollen eye and the pounding head.'

'There's our taxi,' Cora said. 'I'll ask him to give us two minutes.'

As Cora walked over to the stopped car, I noticed Barney driving past to do another lap.

'I'm so sorry they called you,' Sophie said, squeezing my hand. 'Five minutes later and you'd have missed us and you couldn't have called me 'cos I stupidly left my bag on set. One of the others is taking it back to the hotel for me.'

'It's fine. I got to see you and that's the main thing. I was going to ask if you wanted to come back to Hedgehog Hollow for a few days. I'm assuming they won't be able to film with you like this.'

'That's so sweet, but we're still filming tomorrow. I've got a real black eye, so we might as well take advantage of it.'

She released my hand and stood up. 'I'm sorry you've had a

wasted trip. I don't have any plans for Sunday. I could come and visit then.'

'That'd be lovely. And Cora's welcome too, or any other friends.'

Sophie hugged me and confirmed she'd be in touch and then they left, waving at me from the back of the taxi.

I felt weak and tired as I waited for Barney to complete his lap and pick me up, all the adrenaline from the emergency hospital dash now gone. I also felt guilty for dragging Barney away from the farm when I knew how tough a week he'd had trying to keep on top of the work around filming. I should have trusted Sophie more. There might be eleven years between us, but she wasn't my baby sister anymore. She was a grown woman who knew her own mind and didn't need my protection. I shouldn't have panicked about her getting the part and rushed into producing *Love on the Farm* thinking she hadn't dealt with what happened on *The House* and she needed me. The truth was that it was me who hadn't dealt with it. It was me who was carrying round the demons of what happened with Parker. It was me who was struggling.

54

BARNEY

Amber looked drained as she clambered back into the jeep, apologising profusely for dragging me to York only to turn round and drive straight home again.

'It really wasn't a problem bringing you,' I assured her after she'd told me about her fears behind why Sophie had frozen versus what had really happened. 'I'm glad your sister's okay.'

'Me too, but I'm annoyed with myself. I panicked and over-reacted.'

'It wasn't an over-reaction. You got a phone call saying your sister was in hospital and the circumstances set off alarm bells. I'd have done exactly the same in your position. You needed peace of mind.'

I hoped my words were going in. She seemed distracted, fiddling with her locket one minute and her hair the next, tugging at the cuffs of her jacket and chewing on her lip.

'Are you okay?' I asked.

'Just tired.'

She sank back into her seat, looking out of the side window, and I turned up the music a notch. While she'd been at the hospital, I'd pulled over, plugged my phone in and found a relaxing playlist. It worked its magic on Amber as she nodded off, only stirring when I pulled onto the track at Hedgehog Hollow.

'Great company I am,' she said, yawning and brushing her hair back from her face. 'Sorry, Barney.'

'Don't be. You obviously needed the sleep.'

Fizz's Mini was in the farmyard, so she was either working or seeing Phoebe. I parked beside Amber's 4x4 and opened my door.

'I'll say hello to Fizz while I'm here.'

I really needed to get back to the farm, but she'd give me grief if she discovered I'd been here and not stopped by. Ten minutes more wouldn't make any difference, especially when I'd anticipated being out a lot longer with Amber.

'Thanks again for tonight,' Amber said as we stood together by the boot of my jeep.

'Any time. I'll walk you to your door – make sure you get home safe. Lots of dangerous wildlife round here, you know.'

She smiled and I thought she'd object, but she let me accompany her. I knew better than to read anything into it.

'Will you be able to catch up with everything at the farm?' she asked.

'Yeah, it'll be fine. My dad'll be there now and he's like a machine, so he'll have done loads.'

'How are you feeling about the group task tomorrow?'

'I'm not sure. With another director change, I can't help thinking there's going to be a curveball tomorrow.'

Amber stopped walking and looked at me, wide-eyed. 'It never occurred to me, but I bet you're right. Urgh! I haven't been told anything, but I wouldn't put it past Parker to have something up his sleeve.'

'I'll expect the unexpected again.'

'Definitely. And me too.'

We set off walking once more.

'Do you know who you're going to pick for the big date?' Amber asked.

'Definitely not Rayn. I don't think I can cope with any more of her singing.'

Amber laughed. 'She's certainly a character.'

'Yeah, and acting like one too. I don't think I know who Rayn is.'

'I don't think any of us do. I'm not sure even Rayn does!'

We'd reached Amber's holiday cottage and paused outside.

'Tayla's got a boyfriend, so...'

I paused as Amber's eyebrows shot up. 'You know that?'

'She let it slip when we had to take a time-out on Tuesday. I don't think she'd appreciate being picked and it wouldn't be fair on her or her boyfriend.'

'We only found out about the boyfriend after we'd filmed all of Tayla's interviews. It was too late to do anything about it by then.'

'It's fine. It would only ever have been friendship for us even if he hadn't been on the scene.'

'Which just leaves Marley.'

I nodded. 'I kind of feel I owe her to have a fun day out after the pig incident so, unless something kicks off with her tomorrow, I'm thinking I'll pick Marley. Unless you've got a different idea.'

'No. You should choose who you want to be with.'

I couldn't help myself. I fixed my eyes on hers. 'Then I choose you.'

She held my gaze, but I couldn't read her expression and had no idea what she was thinking. She hadn't gone inside and slammed the door in my face, so that was something to hang onto.

'Say something,' I whispered.

'I can't. Not yet. After the big date, though. I promise we'll talk then.'

Her voice sounded thick with emotion, and I wondered what she was grappling with. I'd just told her that I wasn't interested in any of the matches – the reason she'd stepped back in the first place – and reiterated that I was interested in her. Was it Parker? Was it possible that, despite the protestations, she still had feelings for him and needed to see how that played out tomorrow? I knew it was possible to love and hate someone at the same time.

She placed her hands on the tops of my arms, stood on her tiptoes, and kissed me on my right cheek. Her lips were soft and warm against my skin.

'Good night, Barney,' she said, opening the door and stepping inside. 'After filming's over. I promise.'

She closed the door behind her and I stood there for a moment, my fingertips brushing down where she'd just kissed. I could wait until the madness had ended, the crew was gone, and we'd had some breathing space. Amber was worth it.

55

How I stopped myself from kissing Barney on the lips, I'll never know. Him saying he'd choose me was such a special moment which sent butterflies soaring in my stomach, but I'd had to stay strong and not give anything away for now. It wouldn't be fair on him to start anything until I'd properly finished things with Parker.

'Is that you, Amber?' Zara called from inside.

'Yeah, it's me!'

'Is Sophie okay?'

I kicked off my trainers and went to join her. She was sitting at the dining table with her laptop open, surrounded by paperwork.

'She's fine. False alarm.'

I sat down opposite her and filled her in on what had happened.

'She sounds on top of things,' Zara said when I'd finished. 'I thought I'd tidy everything up ready for a handover, assuming we're still leaving.'

'We're definitely leaving, but I'd rather wait till we wrap the big date before I announce it. Everyone's had enough disruption.'

'I'm fine with that. No one will hear it from me.' She removed a piece of paper from Tayla's profile. 'I was looking down your checklist earlier.'

I glanced at the one I'd done for Tayla and shook my head. 'None of them scored very high. If I'd had to do that for Rayn and Marley, I think Rayn would have scored lower than all three originals. Marley might have done okay, though.'

'Yeah, but remove twenty points for pig phobia.'

I picked up Tayla's profile and slotted the checklist back inside.

Zara passed me a piece of paper. 'I took the liberty of doing another one while you were out.'

I scanned down it, noting the fives in nearly all the boxes.

'Near perfect match,' I said, handing it back. 'Whose is it?'

'Yours.'

I scanned down the document again and looked up at Zara, frowning. 'What made you do mine?'

'Oh, come on, Amber. I've worked for you for five years now and we've spent a ridiculous amount of that time holed up in hotels and holiday cottages together. Never, in the whole of that time, have I seen you light up when you talk about a man – not even Dan – and I've seen how Barney looks at you too. I told you he couldn't take his eyes off you last week.'

The butterflies swarmed again and my cheeks burned. Her sixth sense had been right after all.

'You're perfect for each other,' she continued. 'So has anything happened between you?'

'No.'

'Why not?'

'Why do you think? I'm meant to be finding him the woman of his dreams.'

'Mission accomplished.'

'And that woman wasn't meant to be me!'

'Why the hell not? Thanks to the muppets at HQ and their minion, Gold Medallion Twat, there was no chance of it happening with one of the participants, so why not with one of the production team?'

I couldn't help laughing. 'You have a wonderful way with words.'

'And you love me for it.'

'I do.'

'Go get him, tiger.' She released a little growl, making me laugh again. 'Seriously, though, you really should go for it, Amber.'

'I want to, but knowing Parker's here tomorrow, I can't. It's too messy.'

'Why? Because he might notice something?'

'That's one of the reasons. I don't need the grief and Barney certainly doesn't.'

'And the other reasons are...?'

My shoulders sagged just thinking about it.

Zara raised her eyebrows. 'Please say you don't still have feelings for him. You can't have! Not after what he did.'

'I don't know! I've spent the last five years hating him because of what happened to Sophie, but I only ever focused on that and never dealt with us. I know we had our differences, but I did love him.'

'And you're worried there might still be something there when you see him tomorrow?'

I nodded. 'What we had was passionate and intense and then it was gone just like that.' I clicked my fingers. 'I'd *never* have him back, but I can't start something with Barney until I've dealt with my past baggage. That wouldn't be fair on either of us.'

Zara came round the table, wrapped her arms round me from behind, and pressed her head against mine.

'I get it, and I'm here for you.'

'Thank you. I'm not sure what I'd do without you.'

'You'll never find out. You're stuck with me. Even if you changed your job and didn't need me anymore, I'd still be your friend for life.'

She kissed the top of my head and released me. 'I'm starving. I picked up some stuff to make fajitas on the way home. Can I convince you?'

'Did you get salsa, sour cream and guacamole?'

'Of course. Illegal not to have all the extras.'

I smiled gratefully. 'I'm in. Thanks for listening and thanks for not judging.'

'I think you're judging yourself enough. You don't need me to add to it.'

She was right.

56

AMBER

I slept surprisingly well, but woke up with my stomach churning at the prospect of seeing Parker again.

A message arrived from Sophie while I was in the shower.

FROM SOPHIE

3 things...

1. Thought I'd pre-empt you getting in touch and tell you I'm fine – just a bit embarrassed about missing my cue!

2. Cora and I would love to visit on Sunday

3. Are you OK? You didn't look so good yesterday, no insult intended xx

TO SOPHIE

In response to your 3 things...

1. Yes, you beat me to it. Glad you're OK. Don't be embarrassed. These things happen xx

2. Yay. Will be great to see you both

> 3. Not really. Long story but they keep changing the brief on the show and I hate it. Director keeps changing. Third one starts today. It's Parker. You can probably imagine how much I'm looking forward to that.

> Hugs to you xx

FROM SOPHIE

> Shiiiiiiiiiiiiit!!!!!!!!!! But remember this – he can't hurt you unless you let him. So don't let him. Hugs back to you xx

'*He can't hurt you unless you let him. So don't let him,*' I whispered. It was good advice and, as I drove Zara to Bumblebee Barn a little later, those words remained in my head. He couldn't do anything to me anymore unless I allowed it and I wasn't going to allow it. This would end today.

For years, I'd feared crossing paths once more with Parker Knowles. The world of television wasn't really large enough to avoid each other, even though our projects were vastly different, but I'd done everything I could to avoid him. I'd even 'done an Amber' several times, leaving early from events where he might show up.

Yesterday, I'd been floored by the idea of seeing him and, first thing this morning, I'd felt sick. But driving into the farmyard at Bumblebee Barn and seeing Barney smiling and waving at me, I felt powerful. All the people I cared about – Barney included – had given me strength and confidence not to let this pathetic excuse for a human being have any further hold over my life. He could only control me if I let him. And I wasn't going to let him. Today, I'd get my closure.

Parker was just the sort to turn up on set early to get the upper hand, so Zara and I had arrived at Bumblebee Barn stupidly early. *I* was the one in charge here.

'How are you feeling today?' Barney asked.

'A bit sick first thing, but surprisingly positive now.'

'You look gorgeous, by the way.'

Zara had offered to curl my hair so I could look my absolute best and I nearly accepted, but I thought about how Parker's mind worked. If I did something special with my hair, he'd think it was for his benefit. I left it loose but with the sides gathered into a fish-tail plait down the back as I didn't like my hair falling into my eyes when I was at work. Parker would hate it. He preferred short on women. I'd had my hair cut to shoulder-length shortly after we met – another example of Parker controlling me without me real-ising it. I'd only ever had it trimmed since then.

The farm looked lush and the air was fresh. Last night's storm had thankfully broken the recent mugginess. Today it was dry and pleasantly warm but, when a top-of-the-range Audi pulled into the farmyard, I felt a distinct drop in temperature.

'Is that him?' Barney muttered, looking up from the schedule for today.

I gave an involuntary shudder. 'That's him.'

'Shame about all the muddy puddles mucking up his paintwork.'

I couldn't help smiling at that. Parker hated it when his car was dirty and I couldn't imagine he'd have thought to bring wellies with him. I doubted he even owned a pair. This set-up really wasn't his thing.

Parker opened the car door but didn't seem to notice me nearby, too busy searching for somewhere to put his feet down. I'd toyed with asking Barney whether he had a scabby old pair of wellies he could lend to Parker, but why should I be helpful? He knew he was coming to a farm. If he hadn't brought the appropriate clothing or footwear, that was his problem.

He gingerly lowered his expensive Italian leather shoes onto the ground to one side of a puddle, his lip curled in disgust. As he straightened up, I noticed he'd put on a little weight round his middle and his hair was greying at the temples. Otherwise, he hadn't changed.

'He can't hurt you,' Zara whispered, and I straightened my shoulders. On the way here, I'd told her what Sophie wrote in her message and she thought it should be my mantra for the day.

'You're in control,' she added. 'You're the professional.'

It was exactly the encouragement I needed to spur me forward. We were at work, we were colleagues, and it was only for two days.

'Welcome to Bumblebee Barn, Parker,' I declared, my voice strong and confident. 'I hope you had a good journey.'

He did a double-take. 'What have you done with your hair?'

'Grown it how I want it. What do you want to do first? Farm tour, run through the schedule, or meet Barney?'

'I'd rather have a coffee.' He'd have been racking his brain to think of an alternative option, just to be awkward, and it amused me that this was the best he could come up with. He was in for a shock.

'It's a small set on a farm so it's a case of make your own in the marquee. You can do that while I run through the schedule.'

My first small win and confirmation that he had no control over me anymore. That revelation gave me so much strength and I could feel it building across the morning. Every snide comment, I met with a look. Every criticism, I met with praise for the participants or crew. Every dig at me, I just laughed and walked away – far more powerful than stooping to his level. It worked. He became more subdued as the morning wore on and perhaps a little less self-confident.

The group task was fun, at first. The three matches made a surprisingly strong team. Rayn was the creative one – no surprise there, Tayla had small, steady hands making her brilliant with the fiddly work and Marley was exceptionally quick at painting the larger blocks of colour on the Christmas carriage. Barney moved round all the tasks, and, as none of the matches were interested in him romantically, there was no tension. Marley shared a love for musical theatre which made her Rayn's instant best friend and Tayla turned out to have a sweet singing voice – she was in the church choir – which harmonised well with Rayn's.

Did a bit of painting, chatter and singing make great television? Not if the whole thing was viewed, but there were enough paint spillage incidents and other humorous moments to use in whatever narrative we wanted.

We took a break from filming around eleven and went to the marquee for a drinks break. Joel was in there grabbing a coffee and Barney introduced him to Tayla, Marley and Rayn while I went to one side with Zara to check over the schedule. I noticed Parker joined the group and say something to Rayn, who followed him out of the marquee.

'What does he want with her?' Zara murmured as we watched them go outside.

'I've no idea and I dread to think.'

Break over, we returned to Events Barn and filming resumed. Tayla asked Barney how long he'd been running the farm and I felt a lump in my throat when he told her that he'd worked alongside his granddad since he was small boy but he'd passed away last week.

It was quiet for a few minutes after that while everyone focused on their painting, and I glanced across at Parker, expecting to see a bored expression on his face, but he had a smile playing on his lips, as though he was pleased with himself. I noticed Rayn looking over at him and him nodding at her, giving me a sinking feeling in my stomach.

'So, Barney,' Rayn said, 'tell us about your relationship history.'

Barney froze for a moment before shrugging. 'Nothing much to tell.'

'There must be! When was your last long-term relationship?'

'I've never had a long-term relationship.'

Rayn put her paintbrush down and planted her hands on her hips. 'I don't believe that for a minute. Come on, let us in. I bet there's been someone special in your past.'

The other two had stopped what they were doing and were watching the exchange with interest.

'There hasn't,' Barney insisted. 'I've been unlucky in love, which is why I'm here.'

'Still not buying it,' Rayn said. 'I reckon you had a childhood sweetheart. Girl next door type who broke your heart.'

'You reckon wrong.' Barney's voice wasn't so confident this time.

Rayn narrowed her eyes at him. 'I've hit the nail on the head, haven't I?'

Barney sighed as he put his paintbrush down. 'Okay, yes. I had a girlfriend through school and college, but it couldn't be serious because she wanted to travel the world when she left college and I wanted to run the farm. Satisfied?'

Even if I hadn't already picked up on this after challenging him about it in his first interview, his expression and tone just now confirmed that it might not have been serious for her, but it had been for him.

'What was her name?'

'Does it matter?'

'No. Just making conversation. So what was it?'

'I'm not saying.'

'If it meant nothing, why not just say it?'

'I don't want to.'

I glanced towards Parker again and he was clearly loving this. He'd given Rayn her part and she was playing it to perfection.

'Go on,' she persisted. 'What harm can it do?'

'I'm not doing this, Rayn.'

I admired how Barney managed to remain calm when he had to be rattled.

'Please. It's just a name. You don't even have to give her surname.'

Barney stared at her, shaking his head. 'If I say her name, will you drop it?'

'Of course.'

'Elle.'

'Elle? Aw, that's a pretty name. Bit like Elsa. And you know what that means.'

She broke into another *Frozen* song. It lightened the mood, but Barney's expression remained dark. I hoped this was the end of the games, but I feared I'd been right all along – when they'd finished humiliating the matches, they'd move onto vilifying Barney. What else was Parker scheming?

* * *

'What was all that stuff about the ex-girlfriend?' I challenged Parker when we broke for lunch. The others had gone to the marquee and we were in Events Barn on our own.

'No idea. Rayn asked the questions.'

'Because you told her to.'

'Nothing to do with me. It was a perfectly reasonable question for a match to ask on a dating show. Barney knew what the show was about. If he wasn't comfortable with questions about his dating past, he shouldn't have applied.'

It echoed his reaction to me asking him to tone down what they were doing to Sophie: *I'm not her dad. Sophie chose to go into The House. She knows how these things work.*

I wanted to tell him he was pathetic but managed to bite my tongue. With a shake of my head, I left the barn.

I wanted to check Barney was all right, but I heard the sound of quad bikes and stepped back as he passed by on his with the dogs, with Joel following behind on the second bike. Either he needed to work, or he needed some space but, if he wanted to talk, his best mate was on hand. It was good timing that Joel was on the rota today to help in Milo's absence.

* * *

Barney was back by the time we were ready to resume filming for the afternoon. Zara went to mic him up, but I lightly touched her hand.

'Pretend you've just had a phone call,' I whispered, 'and pass me the mic pack.'

Without missing a beat, Zara picked up her phone.

'Hello? Oh, hi! Thanks for getting back to me. Hang on one second.' She passed me the mic pack. 'Can you sort Barney out while I get this?' Then she walked away with her phone pressed to her ear.

I steered Barney away from the group and deliberately placed him with his back to them so he'd block me from Parker but I'd still be able to see over his shoulder if Parker approached us.

'I'm so sorry about Rayn's questions,' I said as I attached the pack to his jeans and passed him the mic to thread up inside his T-shirt. 'I had no idea that was coming. It was all Parker.'

'I figured as much, but I don't get what the point of it was.'

'Me neither. Matt and I deleted the footage about Elmira from your mum's interview and yours, but I'm thinking one of the camera crew must have told him and he'd decided it would be fun to make you uncomfortable.'

'If that was it, it worked.'

'Hopefully he's done playing games and that's the end of it.' I fastened the mic to his collar.

'You were right about Elle,' he said, his voice low. 'It *was* serious and she broke my heart, but it was a very long time ago. When this is all over, I'll tell you about her.'

'Amber!' Parker shouted. 'What's taking so long?'

I sighed. 'I've got to go. Hang on in there. Only a few more hours to go today.'

* * *

There was a lot of laughter across the afternoon. The task was to move the Herdwicks to another field and seeing the three women trying to do the work normally done by highly trained Bear and Harley had my sides aching. Even Parker laughed.

We couldn't have scripted the disastrous attempts with the flock going anywhere but where intended. Barney was on hand to make sure none of the sheep were put in danger and, in the end, had to step in with the dogs and finish the task.

The four of them were filmed making their way back down to the farmyard, laughing as they reviewed the task. They'd have a break before we captured some final soundbites from all four of them individually and Barney announced his final decision about who'd be joining him on the big date.

I'd expected the filming to stop when we reached the marquee, but the cameras kept rolling. I looked to Parker, who smiled and pressed his fingers to his lips to silence any questions.

And then I saw her – a stunning brunette sitting at one of the tables. Her legs were crossed but a long split in her floaty summer dress revealed tanned legs. My stomach sank. Now the questions made sense. She had to be...

Barney stopped dead. 'Elle!'

57

BARNEY

'Hello, Barney,' Elle said, standing up and sashaying towards me.

She air kissed me on either side, and I gulped. She still used the same perfume and it instantly transported me back to all those times in our shelter.

'It's been a long time.' She had an accent – not immediately placeable to any particular country, probably a blend of all those she'd visited.

My heart was pounding and I felt lightheaded. What was she doing here? How was she here? This wasn't meant to be part of the show.

I couldn't tear my eyes away. She looked just like the Elle I'd known as a teenager, but more sophisticated, more confident.

'Lost for words?' she asked, her voice teasing. 'You remind me of that eleven-year-old boy I first met in French class – like a deer in the headlights.'

All I could do was stare.

'I'm sorry,' she said, directing her gaze to the others, 'I'd better introduce myself since Barney's forgotten his manners. I'm Elmira, but you can call me Elle. You are?'

Each of the matches gave their names, and I heard the confusion in their voices. Why wasn't anyone asking what she was doing here? And why was Elle treating her presence as though it was nothing out of the ordinary?

'Does nobody have anything to say?' she asked.

Tayla shrugged, her cheeks pink. Rayn was frowning, as though confused as to what part she was meant to be playing now, but Marley thankfully found the words that I couldn't seem to.

'I do! Who are you and what's going on?'

'I'm Barney's ex-girlfriend. How long was it, Barney? Seven years? All the way through school and college. You know what? Being back here brings back so many memories. Is our shelter still there?'

Her eyes gleamed and her voice was full of energy, as though this was some exciting happy reunion. It wasn't exciting for me, and it was anything but happy. I finally found my voice, although the words sounded squeaky and distant.

'Why are you here?'

'Why do you think I'm here?'

I had absolutely no idea. The only response I could think of was: *to mess with my head.* She'd done that for the whole time we were together and I'd allowed her to continue doing it for far too long afterwards.

'You've barely changed at all,' she said, looking up at me through her long lashes. 'I've missed you.'

I gulped again, my head spinning. She hadn't answered my question. Why was she here? I glanced at the cameraman moving closer and it all fell into place. Another unexpected change – bring back the ex to cause friction. In the background, Parker was watching us intently and contempt for him and all of this flowed through me.

I marched up to him.

'Whatever it is you think you've masterminded here, you can forget about it.' I pulled out the mic pack and thrust it at him. 'I'm not having any part of it. Show's over. I quit.'

Amber was standing between Parker and Elle, her fingers clutching her locket. It was clear from her shocked expression that she was as blindsided as me, not that I'd have doubted it for a minute. There was no way she wouldn't have warned me if she'd known this was what was planned.

I had no idea how they'd tracked Elle down, what they were hoping to achieve by bringing her here today, or why she'd agreed to come, and I wasn't sticking around to find out. It was over.

I grabbed my helmet, jumped on the quad bike and raced up to The Quad.

58

AMBER

I couldn't blame Barney for rushing off. I didn't know the details of what had happened between him and Elle, but she'd broken his heart just like Parker had broken mine and I could imagine the emotions whirring inside him at their unexpected reunion.

'Can you make sure the matches are okay?' I asked Zara. 'And Elle, I guess. Goodness knows what she's been told. I'm going to speak with our esteemed director.'

'Give him hell,' she said.

That was certainly my intention. 'I need a word, Parker.'

'You're not in charge.'

I narrowed my eyes at him and gave him the best *don't mess with me* look I could muster.

He sighed and rolled his eyes. 'Cut!'

The crew looked relieved to put their cameras down.

I strode out of the marquee and over to the original Bumblebee Barn.

'What was that?' I demanded as soon as Parker joined me.

'It should have been TV gold, but the stupid farmer buggered off without a word.'

'TV gold? You really think that? Why does she think she's here?'

'To be on television.'

'Yes, but what's her brief? What does she think she's here to do? You might as well tell me.'

'I don't have to tell you anything.'

'Of course you do. How am I supposed to produce a show when I'm kept out of the loop?'

'How am I supposed to direct a show when you keep information to yourself?'

'Like what?'

'Like the farmer's mother telling you about his long-term girlfriend and you deciding to delete the footage when he was uncomfortable being questioned about her.'

That confirmed my suspicions that one of the crew had spilled the beans. I couldn't blame them. They'd probably been interrogated and felt like they had to share.

'Matt was the director at the time and we made that decision together. You were nothing to do with the show.'

I stared at him defiantly, but there was no response he could give to that.

'So what are we supposed to do now?' I asked. 'You've made Barney quit.'

'You need to get him to come back.'

'Why me? I'm not the one who dragged his ex into this. You messed this up so you should be the one to sort it out.'

When he defiantly glared at me, his dark eyes flashing angrily, I couldn't hold back any longer.

'But, of course, you won't do that, will you, because that's not the way you do things? Your way is to light the fire and wait for someone else to put out the flames. I don't know how you saw this playing out, but I think it's safe to say that Barney doesn't want to see Elle and, even if he was willing to talk to her, there's no way he'd do it on camera. You surely can't be shocked that your surprise reunion has made him quit.'

'He can't quit. He's under contract and he needs to get his sorry arse back down here. He knew what he was signing up to.'

'No, he didn't. This was *never* what the show was about. Have the show's psychologists interviewed Barney and given their written consent for Elle to be here? No? Then we're the ones in breach of contract and you know it. I might be able to talk him into coming back and finishing the planned show, but there's no guarantees. If I was him, I'm not sure I'd be compliant.'

'Just get him back down here.'

'Not until you confirm that we return to the planned format, which means no Elle.'

If he wanted a staring match, he could have one, but he broke first.

'Okay. You win. Get him back. You have thirty minutes.'

'It's not about winning,' I called as I left the barn. 'It's about what's right.'

59

BARNEY

I thought that soaring over ramps and tearing through the swamp on the quad bike would help clear my mind, but I didn't make it as far as The Quad. I slowed down as I approached Spring Field, my eyes drawn to the stone shelter in the distance, and I stopped altogether by the entrance. That's where she found me, my arms resting on the gate.

'I thought I might find you here,' she said. 'Looking at our place.'

'Watching the dogs,' I corrected, nodding towards Bear and Harley, who were chasing each other round the field.

I turned my head towards her, feeling weary. 'Why are you here, Elle?'

She left a gap between us – enough space for another person – and rested her arms on the gate too.

'You want the truth?'

'Are you capable of telling it?'

She sighed. 'As I told you at the time, I've always been honest with you.'

'Our ideas of honesty are very different.'

She slid the bolt and pushed open the gate. 'I want to see our shelter again. Are you coming?'

'No.'

'Suit yourself.'

As she crossed the field, I noticed she was wearing wellies and recognised the daisies on them. She must have borrowed Zara's. I felt numb watching her, feeling like this was some strange dream instead of the real Elmira De Luca back on my farm after thirteen years.

She made it halfway across the field before curiosity got the better of me and I followed her. I didn't call her or try to catch up. I needed the headspace.

When she stepped into the shelter, I had a strong feeling of déjà vu. She emerged again as I reached it.

'It's in ruins,' she said.

'It was always destined to be.'

She smiled ruefully. 'A fitting metaphor for our relationship, yes?'

'If you say so.'

She steepled her hands against her lips and looked at me from beneath her lashes. 'This is harder than I thought it would be.'

'Being back here?'

'Being here, seeing you... I made a mistake.'

'Coming to the farm?'

'No. Back then.' She wrapped her arms round her waist, and I couldn't help noticing that she'd lost weight over the years. I hadn't noticed at first because of the loose dress.

'I was selfish and impulsive and I let you down,' she continued. 'I let me down too.'

I hadn't expected an apology. The earlier confidence seemed to have gone, replaced by a vulnerability, reminding me of the scared young girl who'd tearfully told me she was pregnant.

'Is that why you're here? To apologise?'

'Yes.'

'Why now? Why rake it all up again after thirteen years and why do it when I'm in the middle of recording a television show?'

Bear and Harley must have had enough exercise as they both flopped by my feet, panting.

Elle stepped out of the shelter and sat down on the boulder. 'I did what I dreamed of. I've travelled the world, several times over. I'm a travel influencer.'

I wasn't going to share that I already knew that. I didn't want her to read anything into it.

'It's been incredible,' she continued. 'But I'm taking some time out. I've been in the UK for a few months now, trying to psyche myself up to coming to the farm.'

My stomach did a backflip. Surely she wasn't here to tell me she'd finally got the travel bug out of her system and was ready to settle down with me.

'The TV programme gave me the perfect excuse. It was the strangest thing. This researcher got in touch and said you were on a dating show, and they were hoping to speak to me as an ex. Agreeing to take part meant I couldn't talk myself out of seeing you.'

She ran her fingers through her hair. 'I don't know why I'm finding it so hard to say this.'

Say what? She'd already said she'd made a mistake. That had to mean she was wanting me back. It was completely out of the question and I didn't want to have that discussion.

'I don't know if you were expecting the red carpet treatment, but you hurt me and it took me a long time to get past that. It was a long time ago and I don't think it's going to help either of us to rake over painful memories. I appreciate your apology, but I'd really like it if you left. Okay?'

Tears pooled in her eyes, but I had to harden myself to it. I hadn't asked her to come here. I didn't want this.

'Come on,' I said to the dogs. With an apologetic smile, I took a few strides towards the gate.

'Please come back,' she called.

I shook my head and continued walking.

'I've got cancer.'

I stopped rigid, letting those three words sink in. I felt as though a cold hand had wrapped itself around me and squeezed. I turned slowly. Elle was standing up now. She looked so small, nibbling on her thumbnail.

'It's stage one ovarian cancer.' She took a couple of steps closer to me. 'You know I told you I wasn't sure I even wanted children? I do now, but I can't have them. My ovaries, tubes and womb have gone.'

'I'm sorry.'

'Me too. Apparently it's rare for someone my age. Trust me to be the special case. I've got one more round of chemo to face and I have to hope they get it all and it doesn't return. I'm scared, Barney.'

Suddenly none of it mattered. As she broke down in tears, I wrapped my arms round her and held her tightly.

60

AMBER

I spotted Barney's quad bike parked next to Spring Field and leaned against the gate, squinting in the sunlight. Was that Barney near the shelter? I put my hands over my eyes to shield them from the sun and my stomach plummeted. Barney wasn't alone. He was with Elle and they were holding each other. They might even be kissing – I wasn't close enough to tell.

I had no right to feel disappointed or let down when we weren't even together, but I couldn't help it. With a heavy heart, I traipsed back down to the marquee. I'd tell Parker I couldn't find him.

As I was passing Middle Pig, my mobile started ringing. Even though I didn't feel like speaking to anyone right now, I was still at work, and it could be Zara needing some support with the matches, who were likely feeling very confused and frustrated by now. Welcome to the club!

It wasn't Zara, though. It was Esther's name flashing up on the screen.

'Amber, darling, I'm so sorry.'

'About what?'

'Clementine Creates pulling the plug, of course.'

I stopped, my heart thumping. 'They've done what?'

It was Esther's turn to sound shocked. 'They haven't told you yet? That treacherous snake Parker Knowles has reported back to them that *Love on the Farm* is still dull as ditch water, despite their changes, not salvageable at all, and they'd be better to cut their losses, so they have.'

'Just like that? Without even seeing the footage?'

'Just like that. They trust his judgement, especially when it echoes the feedback from Giles Snyder.'

'What about Monday's big date?'

'Not happening.'

'That's ridiculous!'

'Believe me, darling, you're preaching to the converted. I told them what I think, but they're not budging.'

'So what happens now?'

'They're going to contact everyone involved in the future shows to let them know it's been axed, but they want you to let the Bumblebee Barn farmer and the matches know.'

'Why me? That's such a cop-out.'

'They say you have a relationship with them all and can smooth it over. I told them it was a cheek.'

'Yeah, but they know I'll do it.'

'I'll rue the day I told you about this,' Esther said. 'In all my years as an agent, I've never come across so much unprofessionalism in such a short space of time. I'm so sorry that you've been messed about so much.'

'You weren't to know this would happen.' I didn't want Esther feeling any guiltier than she already did. I knew she'd only pushed for my involvement because she'd believed the hype. So had I.

'I know you're not motivated by money, darling, but the silver lining is they called time before you could quit so you'll get paid in full without the show ever being aired. Please tell me that's a win for you.'

I smiled at that. 'Yes, it's a win. For us both. I'd better go and break the news.'

'Let me know how it goes.'

'I will, but promise me one thing – you'll never put me forward for another reality TV show unless it's docu-style.'

'Cross my heart and hope to die.'

We said our goodbyes and I paused for a moment, looking at the pigs, taking some deep calming breaths. Parker wouldn't have told them to axe it just to spite me but pulling the plug like this would have given him pleasure. Passing the buck to me to give the 'good news' would have pleased him too. Did that man ever take responsibility for the dirty work?

Deep down, I wasn't surprised at the decision and should have seen it coming. The premise wasn't right for them, and it wasn't a setting or format which could be massively spiced up. Parker had even admitted that bringing in Elle hadn't had the desired effect and that had likely been the trigger to call it a day. I bet he'd been on the phone to the Lennons the second he sent me in search of Barney, knowing it was dead in the water. The crazy thing is, if they'd stuck with the original brief, they'd have had a lovely family-friendly show, but that wasn't their brand.

My phone rang again – Zara this time.

'Where are you?' she asked, panic in her voice.

'Next to Middle Pig.'

'Can you come back? Parker's gone and the crew are packing up. Hazel says they've cancelled the show.'

I set off walking. 'They have. I've literally just put the phone down to Esther. Keep the matches there. I'm on my way.'

'Barney's not here.'

'I know. He's with Elle. I'll be with you in five minutes.'

* * *

Zara must have been watching for me as she came running out of the marquee as I approached.

'Is it really over? Surely they can't do that.'

'They can and they have. Are they all still in there?'

'Yeah. Joel's in there too. He came in to grab a coffee and they swamped him with questions about Elle.'

I could see the questions in her eyes about Barney and Elle, especially after last night's conversation, but they'd have to wait for now. I had some news to deliver.

Inside the marquee, Tayla and Marley were making drinks, deep in conversation, and Rayn appeared to be interrogating Joel.

'Can I have your attention?' I called, putting an immediate stop to the chatter. 'Please all grab a seat.'

'Should I go?' Joel asked.

'No, you can stay. This affects you too.'

'My apologies for the unexpected disruption this afternoon,' I said when they'd all settled. 'I know you'll all have questions, but can I ask for you to hold off for the moment while I go through what I know?'

Tayla and Marley were shocked and frustrated by the news, but Rayn was really angry.

'Right bloody waste of time this turned out to be,' she shouted.

'I understand you feeling like that, but this does happen from time to time.'

'I bet you've known all week.'

'You want to know when I found out, Rayn? Ten minutes before you. Believe me, I'm as shocked and disappointed as all of you.'

'Where's Barney?' Rayn demanded. 'Off snogging his ex?'

My stomach churned as I pictured them by the ruined shelter

and I fought to keep my voice steady.

'Barney's with Elle. He had no idea she was coming and neither did Zara or I. At this point in time, Barney doesn't know the programme's been cancelled either.'

'Could they not have finished the episode before they called time?' Marley asked.

I shrugged. 'My guess is the decision had already been made and time is money. I know that's frustrating.'

'This whole thing has been a joke!' Rayn snapped, banging her fist on the table. 'Anyone else feel like they've been free labour on the farm all week?'

They all started talking at once. Joel had his piece to say too, defending Barney and pointing out that they'd been a hindrance rather than a help and Barney had needed his family and Joel all week to help catch up.

I felt defensive towards Barney too and tried to get their attention, but nobody was listening. Zara put her fingers in her mouth and released the loudest whistle I'd ever heard. That soon shut them up and I mouthed 'thank you' to her.

'I understand the frustrations,' I said. 'I'm not happy about what's happened either, but let's not turn on Barney. You all saw what happened with Elle earlier. You know he's been dealt a low blow here. Barney was genuinely looking for love and I know that any suggestion otherwise is only because you're shocked and disappointed, but let's talk reality here for a moment. Hand on heart, who has fallen for our farmer and sees a future with him?'

My fingers twitched with the temptation to raise my hand in the air and declare, 'Me!'

Rayn stared at me defiantly, but the other two looked uncomfortable.

'Didn't think so,' I said. 'I've been watching carefully and, while I saw the potential for friendship in a couple of cases, there was no chemistry. Yes, it's frustrating not getting to the end and knowing everything you've done so far will never be aired, but please don't act like you're gutted about not going on the big date when you know it was never going to go beyond that for any of you.'

It was more transparent than I'd have liked it to be, but at least it shut down any further gripes. I took the opportunity to remind them of the NDA (non-disclosure agreement) in their contracts and spell out that this meant no taking their story to the press.

'On a positive note, there'll be a small compensation payment for the inconvenience, which the central team will contact you about and, even more exciting, you get to keep the boilersuits and wellies.'

That drew another glower from Rayn, but Marley and Tayla both laughed.

'The final thing to say is thank you. I've enjoyed the week and you've all laughed a lot so, despite it ending differently to how we expected, do try to focus on the positives. You've all done things this week you've never done before and should be proud of yourselves. Your cars will be here in ten minutes, so if you have any further questions, please grab Zara or me before you go. Good luck for the future.'

Rayn was still sulking, arms crossed, lips pouting, but the other two thanked us and confirmed they'd enjoyed the week. Tayla expressed gratitude for helping her address a long-held wariness around horses, which led to Marley telling her about her auntie and uncle's equestrian centre and inviting Tayla for a lesson.

I needed a coffee. Joel joined me.

'Thanks for defending Barney,' he said.

'Of course. He didn't deserve that, but they were hurt and lashing out. They won't have meant it.'

'I appreciate it and he will too. I'd better go and find him. You said he was with Elle?'

'Yeah, they were in Spring Field.'

Joel winced. 'Not good. See you later.'

I had no idea what 'not good' meant, but I couldn't give any more headspace to Barney right now. I knew nothing about his history with Elle and speculation was dangerous.

I'd finished making my coffee when Tayla joined me.

'I'm sorry you've been messed around,' she said. 'Can't be easy but I wanted to say thank you. I've really enjoyed this week and it's been great working with you and Zara and the crew. Everyone's been so friendly. Well, not Giles and not Parker, but everyone else. And Barney's lovely too. I'm hoping we'll stay in touch as friends. Can you give him my contact details?' She handed me a piece of paper with her email and phone number on it.

'I'll pass these on. You seemed to really hit it off, so I'm sure you'll meet up again.'

'In which case, I'll probably see you again too.'

'What do you mean?'

'The psychologists might not have got it right with any of us, but I think Barney still found his perfect match. And I don't mean Elle.'

Zara announced that the cars had arrived, which was just as well as I had no response to that.

'Don't let a ghost from the past stop you having a future together,' Tayla said as she hugged me goodbye.

Marley hugged me and thanked me for everything, but Rayn left without saying goodbye.

'And the real Rayn exits stage left,' Zara muttered. 'Didn't think she was going to let it go earlier.'

She burst into song, making me smile, but Tayla's words were still ringing in my ears. Dan had been a ghost from the past who I should never have let back into my life. Would it be the same for Barney's?

61

BARNEY

I rode back down to the garage with Elle riding pillion, her arms round my waist. I'd felt so relaxed riding with Amber holding onto me. I felt tense with Elle.

We'd sat side by side in the shelter doorway while she talked about being plagued by stomach pains, feeling bloated and a loss of appetite which she'd put down to a combination of too much rich food and fatigue after a particularly gruelling travel schedule.

Returning to the Wolds to visit her parents for Christmas, she'd been persuaded to get checked out, and her scans had shown the cancer, so she'd been through the operation and five rounds of chemo so far.

She wanted to talk about what had happened between us and properly apologise, but today wasn't the right time. I was in shock and she'd found it more emotional than she'd expected seeing me again, so we agreed to meet on Tuesday evening once the filming of *Love on the Farm* was complete. I could give her my undivided attention then. I felt a bit hot-headed for storming off and quitting, but I was prepared to see the show to the end as long as they were prepared to forget about the stuff with Elle.

I dropped her by her car and waved her off and it was only then that I registered how empty the farmyard was. Joel's car was there but where was everyone else's?

Bear and Harley followed me into the marquee. Not only was it empty of people, but there weren't any bags, coats or equipment – just the drinks facilities and the chairs and tables. Had they abandoned the shoot for the day because I'd stormed off or had they accepted me saying I quit and it was over?

I checked my phone and there were several missed calls from Joel but nothing from Amber or Zara.

Joel answered on the third ring.

'I'm in the marquee,' I said. 'It's like a ghost town. Where is everyone?'

'Gone. I'm in Top Pig. Come and find me.'

* * *

My heart pounded as I drove from the farm to Hedgehog Hollow, praying I wasn't too late to catch Amber. I couldn't believe they'd cancelled the show and Parker had abandoned ship, leaving Amber to give everyone the news. That couldn't have been easy. I'd been certain Amber would have had nothing to do with Elle's appearance and Joel had confirmed that and told me about her springing to my defence, which had given me some reassurance that she wasn't angry with me for walking out.

As I neared the end of the track, my eyes scanned for Amber's 4x4 in the farmyard and I felt weak with relief when I spotted it. She hadn't gone, then. Although that didn't mean she wasn't packing to leave right now.

I dumped my jeep at a dodgy angle beside her car, ran across the farmyard and banged on the knocker of Meadow View. Zara answered the door, and did a double-take.

'I need to speak to Amber.'

'She's over there.'

She pointed towards the wedding gazebo in the distance and I squinted in the sun, just making out a figure. Thanking Zara, I ran over to the gazebo.

Amber was leaning on the back railings with her back towards me, but she turned round as I approached.

'Barney! I wasn't expecting to see you.'

'Can we talk?' I asked, trying to catch my breath.

She indicated the wide steps and I joined her on them.

'Joel told me what happened. I was worried you'd have gone.'

'Not yet. The show might be over, but we've got the cottage until a week on Sunday and plenty of work to get on with.' She fixed her eyes on mine. 'So, how are you after the surprise reunion?'

A straightforward question, but without a straightforward answer.

'Right now, I'm really not sure.'

Amber looked away and busied herself brushing a couple of leaves off the steps. 'Old feelings resurfacing?'

'When you asked me about her on camera, it really threw me. You were there, you saw it, and you were right about her. She *was* the one who got away, she *did* break my heart, and I *did* go for women who looked the opposite of her because I didn't want any reminders.'

'I'm sorry,' she said, finally looking up at me. 'I didn't want to be right.'

'It's okay. I hated the questions, but they were exactly what I needed. They helped me get some focus and finally realise that I was over Elle and I needed to stop using her as an excuse for choosing girlfriends I knew there was no future with just to avoid getting hurt again.'

'But now she's back and she's stirred up those feelings again?'

'Different feelings. She's got ovarian cancer.'

'Oh no! Is she going to be okay?'

'She doesn't know yet. She's still going through chemo.' I forced down the lump in my throat as I pictured the fear in her eyes, heard the tremble in her voice. 'What are you supposed to say when the person you've convinced yourself you hate turns up out of the blue and drops that on you?'

'I don't think there's anything you can say.'

We sat in silence for a few minutes.

'Oh, my God! Is that why she turned up today?' Amber asked, sounding shocked. 'Were they planning to film her telling you she has cancer?'

'No. She didn't tell them, although, if she had, I wouldn't put it past them to have tried to film it. We didn't talk much about the show – the cancer news took over – so I'm not really sure what the plan was. I guess it doesn't matter now. I'm sorry for walking out.'

'Don't be. I'd have done the same in your shoes.'

'I did come back to finish the planned show, but I was too late. I can't believe how quickly they canned it and left.'

'Me neither.' Amber sighed. 'I can't help thinking Parker came here looking for a reason to end it. I'm just so sorry you've all been messed around. In all my years in television, I've never experienced anything like it.'

'It's not like that on the set of *Countryside Calendar*?' I asked, playfully nudging her.

'Gosh, no! I think I'd be a gibbering wreck by now if it was. So what happens now? Will you see Elle again?'

I still hated that Elle had made the decision to end her pregnancy without discussing it with me, and the cold uncaring way she'd called time on our relationship, but we'd had seven years of amazing friendship before that point and those positive memories felt the most alive in my mind. My friend had told me she was scared. I was scared too, but I could and would find a way of being strong for her.

'I want to tell you what happened with us,' I said, evading the question for now. I wanted Amber to have the context first.

'You don't have to. Not if it's too raw.'

'If you're okay to listen, I need you to know.'

Amber nodded. 'I'm here for you.'

I really hoped she meant that.

62

AMBER

Barney suggested we go for a walk, so we set off down the track towards Wildflower Byre while he shared the story of how he and Elle got together and how it was never meant to be serious because of their future careers pulling them in different directions. My heart broke for both of them when he told me about the baby and what happened next.

We'd walked past Crafty Hollow and found ourselves in a clearing with a magnificent view across the fields, so we paused by the fence to look at it.

'You asked if I'll see her again,' he said. 'We're meeting on Tuesday night to talk.'

My heart sank. That was when I'd been hoping that Barney and I could talk - after the big date, after the crew had gone, after the craziness was over. Not that the big date was happening now.

'I can't help thinking it's better to let sleeping dogs lie,' he continued, 'but, if she wants to make her peace, I can hardly refuse her in the circumstances.'

'Maybe not, but it's okay to draw the line with where that

conversation goes. It's your granddad's funeral next week too, so you've already got an emotional week ahead of you.'

'We need to talk too.'

I lowered my eyes, my heart heavy. 'We don't.'

'You've changed your mind?'

'No, but...'

'You're worried about Elle being back?'

'It's more than that.'

I looked up at him, my heart racing. We were standing so close together and all I wanted to do was kiss him, but it wasn't fair on him when he had so much to deal with right now.

'I'd be lying if I said I didn't have feelings for you, but I'd also be lying if I said I wasn't worried about Elle being back. When an ex comes back into your life, things get complicated and feelings get stirred up, even if you think you've got a hold on them. Add in emotional circumstances like Elle's and it's even more inevitable.'

'I'm *not* going to fall for Elle again.'

'You say that now, but you don't know.'

'I *do* know.'

'You don't.' I didn't mean to shout, but I couldn't help myself.

He raised his voice too. 'Yes, I do!'

'How? How can you possibly know you're not going to fall for Elle again?'

'Because I've already fallen for you.'

We stared at each other, electricity crackling between us. Next moment, our bodies collided as we kissed each other with a passion and urgency I'd never experienced before. His hands were in my hair as mine ran down his back. We stumbled on the uneven ground, but our lips never parted.

I was completely lost to him, surrendering to the feelings I'd been trying to squash all week. Everything about this man was what I'd always dreamed of. He was caring, compassionate, empathetic, wore his heart on his sleeve...

Reality hit me. Yes, he was all of those things and that was why I needed to end this right now. Elle needed him, his family needed him, and he needed space to grieve without me being a distraction. If he really had fallen for me, he'd come back to me when he was emotionally stronger. In the meantime, I couldn't risk him breaking my already fragile heart.

'I can't do this,' I said, my voice full of regret as I pulled away. 'I'm so sorry.'

'Don't say that.'

'I have to. You need to take care of Elle, your family and you, and I need to take care of me.'

'We can take care of each other.'

'It's too much at once. You can't be there for everyone.'

With another 'sorry', I ran back to Meadow View, ignoring him calling my name. Perhaps my explanation didn't make sense to him, but I was speaking from experience. This time four years ago with my grandparents gone, Sophie a mess, and my parents at breaking point, I'd been the strong one, keeping the family together, and it broke me. There was nobody there for me and, much as I wanted to be the strong one for Barney, my heart had only just healed and I couldn't let it be broken again when he couldn't be there for me in return.

63

AMBER

Zara had gone back home to Lincolnshire for the weekend and I was at the dining table the following morning studying the production schedule for *Countryside Calendar* when a FaceTime request came through from Mum.

'How's your week been?' she asked, smiling warmly.

I sighed. 'You really want to know?'

So it all tumbled out about the unmitigated disaster that *Love on the Farm* had been and the situation with Barney.

'Barney sounds wonderful,' she said. 'You're not walking away completely, are you?'

'No. I'm just giving him time and space.'

'Is that what he wants?'

'It's what he needs.'

'It's what you need, you mean.'

'Maybe.'

'Aw, sweetheart, I'll give you lots of hugs when we're up next weekend, but I wish I could give you one right now.'

'I wish you could too.'

'If filming is finished and you're avoiding Barney, are you going to do some more work on that rescue centre proposal?'

I hadn't considered it, but it was the perfect opportunity to devote some quality time to it. 'I might just do that.'

'Good, because I might have mentioned it to Róisín and she's all over it. And before you get het up about nepotism, we were having coffee and she's the one who told me she's on the lookout for a new docu-series. I know she loves wildlife, so I told her what you were thinking and she's keen to see your proposal.'

'Oh, my gosh! That's amazing! Thanks, Mum.' Róisín Brennan headed up the production company who made Mum's programmes and they'd be the perfect fit – completely different to Clementine Creates.

Feeling more positive after offloading to Mum and hearing the news about Róisín, I spent the rest of the morning pulling together some thoughts, had some lunch, then went over to the rescue centre to sound out Samantha and Fizz.

'We'd need to run it by Josh and my dad,' Samantha said after I'd outlined my proposal to her and Fizz, 'but I can't see why they'd have any objections. It's a chance to raise awareness, dispel a few myths and hopefully raise some funds.'

'It'd be awesome,' Fizz said, 'if it gets made.'

She smiled and winked at me, so I knew she was only teasing.

'You've spoken to Barney?'

'I haven't, but Mum has and she told me. Sounds like you've had a nightmare.'

'Most challenging programme I've ever worked on and I'm sorry your brother got caught up in the mess.'

'He'll be fine. He was never convinced about being on telly anyway.'

Her smile was reassuring and I hoped she was right. I couldn't bear the thought of Barney being hurt by all of this on top of what he was already going through.

64

BARNEY

I wasn't in the mood for company, but I needed to see Grandma. I hated that I'd barely seen her this week, but Mum had assured me she understood.

Mum's car was on the drive when I pulled up outside Grandma's bungalow on Saturday evening.

'Barney! What a lovely surprise!' Grandma hugged me tightly then fussed around Bear and Harley.

Mum was in the kitchen making a pot of tea, so I'd timed that well.

'How are you doing?' I asked Grandma once we were settled in the lounge with our drinks while Bear and Harley chased Raven round the back garden.

'It still doesn't feel real, love. I keep expecting him to walk through the door. I'm surprised each morning I wake up and he's not beside me.'

Tears welled in her eyes and I had to swallow down the lump in my throat.

'It's only been a week,' I said, gently. It was all I could offer. I had no words of wisdom because I couldn't imagine going through what she was going through – and I wasn't sure they'd help even if I had.

'Show Barney the video,' Mum prompted.

'Oh, yes!' Grandma lifted her iPad off a side table. 'Your granddad felt bad about his reaction to your TV programme and about saying no to being filmed. I said we should record our own video and, if the TV people wanted to use it, they could. I know they're not making the programme anymore, but I think you'll still want to see this.'

She passed me the iPad and I pressed play. Granddad was seated on his bench in the garden surrounded by tubs of flowers. The video zoned in, and Granddad smiled at the camera.

'I'm Frank Dodds, Barney's granddad. Ey, he's a good kid is our Barney. I used to run Bumblebee Barn – me and his grandma – and he was always up there as a little 'un. Him and his sister, Fizz, loved the animals and vehicles and we always knew he'd make a right good farmer.'

He paused and frowned as he looked up from the camera. 'Am I doing this right, Mary? Should I be talking about him or to him? What? It doesn't matter. Oh, okay.'

I looked up and smiled at them. 'That's very Granddad.'

'Where was I?' he said, looking back at the camera. 'Oh, yeah. So we were right and our Barney is an exceptional farmer. Barney, son, we could have had some right barneys over the years – excuse the pun – 'cos I can be a stubborn bug... erm, man, but it never came to that because you always understood that it wasn't that I didn't like your ideas – it was just that I sometimes struggled with the pace of change. You were so patient. Thanks for humouring me. I'm so very proud of you. I hope you win *Love on the Farm*. What's that, Mary? He doesn't win anything? What's the point then? He gets a girlfriend? I didn't think he had any trouble doing that.'

He shrugged at the camera. 'I'm not sure what this thing is you're doing but I hope you enjoy it and I'm sorry I weren't too enthusiastic at first. I don't get modern dating stuff.' He shrugged once more. 'I know I'm not good with emotional stuff, but I love you, son. Take care.'

He kissed two fingers and pointed them to the camera.

I looked up at Mum and Grandma, tears rolling down my cheeks. Mum rushed over and perched on the chair arm, hugging me to her side as I pressed play again.

'I'm so glad you did that,' I managed when I'd watched it for a third time. 'Whatever you do, don't delete it by mistake.'

'I've already emailed it to my account,' Mum said. 'I'll forward it to you.'

'Thank you for that, Grandma. That's really special. Just like Granddad.'

65

AMBER

Cora and Sophie arrived at Hedgehog Hollow just before noon on Sunday. They'd told me they'd sort lunch out and handed me a bag full of treats from a delicatessen they'd found. We filled the fridge then went for a walk round the farm to build up our appetites.

'How's the eye?' I asked Sophie. The swelling had gone and the bruising had faded.

'Getting better. But never get into a fight with Right Hook here. She doesn't know her own strength.'

They giggled together and my heart warmed at the friendship that had developed.

We had a delicious lunch on the patio out the back of Meadow View and Cora insisted Sophie and I relax and catch up while she cleared everything away.

'This place really suits you,' Sophie said, smiling at me.

'In what way?'

'You seem more relaxed here, more you.'

'I feel more me. It's beautiful here and at Bumblebee Barn. I could stay here forever.'

'So why don't you? Sell the flat in London and buy a place here. It's not like you're ever there and I know you hate it when you are.'

'I can't do that.'

'Why not?'

'Because...' But I didn't have a good reason. I didn't need it as a base. Realistically, it was a very expensive storage facility.

'I bet you could get a mansion round here for what your flat would sell for.'

'Probably not a mansion, but I could afford something bigger and be mortgage-free.'

'Then you should do that! It's a good central base for *Country-side Calendar*.'

'It is.'

'But you'd rather be at Bumblebee Barn, wouldn't you?'

I rolled my eyes at her. 'I only spoke to Mum yesterday.'

'Mum hasn't told me anything. But you just have.'

I sighed. 'It's bad timing.'

'That's an excuse and a crap one at that. What's really going on?'

66

BARNEY

I was in the garage before sunrise on Wednesday morning. Later today, we'd say a final goodbye to Granddad at his funeral and I had a feeling he'd send a spectacular farewell sunrise over his beloved Bumblebee Barn.

The dogs had jumped on the back and I was about to pull out when the yard was illuminated by headlights. My heart leapt. Amber? I scrambled off the bike, but it was a taxi. Elle exited the car and waved.

'What are you doing here?' I asked, joining her.

'You told me you wanted to catch the sunrise and I thought you might appreciate some company. I can go if you prefer.'

'No, it's fine. Company would be good.'

She paid the taxi driver and followed me over to the bike.

'I promise to be quiet,' she said. 'You can lose yourself in your thoughts. Sorry about cancelling last night. I had a bad day so it wouldn't have been a good talk.'

'Are you sure you're feeling okay now?'

'Yes. I've been awake for a while anyway and I can always rest later.'

* * *

Elle was true to her promise. We sat on the gate to Top Field in silence and watched. The sunrise was gentle at first with yellow and pale gold seeping into the inky blue but, as the sun steadily rose in the sky, it brought the most vivid oranges, golds and magentas, as though the sky was on fire. *Red sky in the morning, shepherd's warning.* This former shepherd was going out with a bang.

Elle slipped her arm through mine. 'Goodbye, Frank,' she whispered.

I nodded, but I couldn't speak. I was battling the emotions from two losses this morning. The farm was quiet without the camera crew, but empty without Amber. I'd applied to *Love on the Farm* to find love and take away the loneliness. I'd found love, and I'd never felt more lonely than I had this week.

Beside me, Elle shivered. She was wearing a coat and was wrapped in a blanket, but the cold could soon find a way in when sat still.

'We'll go back down,' I said, taking her hand to help her down from the gate. The old Elle would have accepted the chivalry, then run off laughing, her sprinter's legs crossing Spring Field well ahead of me. The Elle with me now barely had the strength to clamber back onto the quad bike.

'I'll take you home,' I said when we returned to the garage.

'You've got stuff to do before the funeral.'

'I can do it after. No arguments. I bet your parents don't even know you're here.'

'Throwback to how it used to be,' she said, smiling weakly.

The early start had clearly taken it out of her. We weren't even halfway down the track before she'd dozed off.

She woke up when I pulled up outside her parents' house and switched off the ignition.

'Sorry for nodding off,' she said, giving me a weak smile as she stretched out her back.

'You've been through a lot. It's bound to take it out of you.'

'I want to apologise,' she said, her words laboured with fatigue.

'Get inside and get some sleep. We can talk another time.'

'No, I need to say it now.' She fixed her dark eyes on mine. 'I don't regret the decision I made back then, but I do regret the way I went about it. You were right. I should have involved you and it was selfish of me not to. I'm so sorry for how badly I hurt you.'

I wasn't going to say it was okay because it really wasn't, but I appreciated the apology. It was all I'd ever really wanted to hear. As I'd said to her at the time, it was ultimately her body and what hurt the most was that she'd gone ahead with it with no warning, no discussion and no support.

'Thank you,' I whispered.

'I thought about you a lot over the years. Travelling the world has been incredible, but I had a lot of downtime in airports and train stations and in those quieter moments, you'd always pop into my head. Sometimes I'd replay our final months together. Sometimes I'd imagine I stayed and picture us running through Spring Field chasing a little boy.'

She smiled wistfully then looked down at her hands. 'I don't know why, but it's always a boy, never a girl. And sometimes I'd imagine that same scene but without me in it. You'd found someone new and you were happily married with lots of children.'

Her eyes met mine once more. 'I'm sorry that hasn't happened for you. Was that my fault? Be honest.'

'It was a combination of things, but what happened with us didn't help.'

'Do you think it's too late for us now?'

How many years had I longed to hear her say something like that?

'Elle, I'm not—'

She pushed the door open, silencing me.

'I shouldn't have asked that, especially not today of all days. Can we pretend I didn't say it out loud? I hope all goes well at the funeral. Look after yourself.'

And then she was gone.

I sank back into the seat and closed my eyes. *Do you think it's too late for us now?* Right now, I couldn't think straight. I needed to get back to the farm and do my rounds before getting ready for Granddad's funeral.

* * *

The funeral was heart-breaking but heart-warming. None of the immediate family wanted to give a eulogy – far too emotional – but a friend of Dad's who'd known Granddad well read out something to which we'd all contributed, and it worked brilliantly. Grandma had asked whether we could show the video Granddad had made for *Love on the Farm* as it was so typically him. It drew smiles and tears from all the attendees, and it was especially fitting that the film ended on him blowing a kiss out and smiling. It was like he was saying goodbye to us all. They kept that image on the screen as we all moved out.

The wake was held in The Silver Birch, a smart pub and restaurant on the way to Reddfield. There was a great turnout. Granddad had been well known and highly respected in the farming community and he'd have been touched to see how many people wanted to say goodbye and share their fond memories.

Across the afternoon, I learned so much about Granddad that I didn't already know. There were some familiar anecdotes, but most were new and all carried a strong theme: a man who loved his family and his farm in equal measure, who could be stubborn and set in his ways but who wasn't afraid to admit when he was in the wrong (eventually) and someone who everyone loved.

'How are you holding up?' I asked, sitting beside Fizz while Phoebe went to the bar to get them another drink.

'Constantly on the edge of tears,' she said, her lip wobbling as tears pooled in her eyes. 'It breaks my heart that we fell out and, even though we got through it, things were never quite the same again.'

I put my arm round her and hugged her to my side. 'I know. He needed more time and he didn't have it. He still loved you, though.'

'I hope so.'

'Of course he did and, if he's up there, he'll be looking down and feeling sad that he never got to tell you.'

Her face crumpled and she turned her head onto my chest, her tears soaking into my shirt.

Phoebe returned from the bar with a couple of glasses of wine and looked like she might cry herself when she saw how upset Fizz was.

'Would you like to head home?' she asked gently.

Fizz sniffed and wiped at her tears. 'No, I'll only kick myself if I do. I'll be fine in a minute. Just having a moment but nothing that a Barney bear hug won't sort out.'

I tightened my hold on my sister. Sometimes words weren't needed.

67

AMBER

I rose super early on Wednesday morning and drove to Bumblebee Barn. For the past few days, I'd been battling with how I'd left things with Barney. I thought about Sophie's accusation that bad timing was a crap excuse, and about what Mum had said about making sure Barney was clear that it was a no for now, not forever. And I thought about that kiss. Constantly.

Crap excuse or not, timing *was* an issue. I needed to let him have his conversation with Elle. He needed closure on the past and there wasn't much time for him to get it. I'd been so restless last night, knowing they were going to be meeting, but I'd made a decision. I didn't want him to be by himself this morning. On the morning of my grandparents' funeral, I'd felt so lost and alone. Today, he'd need to be strong for his family and I could be the one who was strong for him.

As I drove up the track towards Bumblebee Barn, convinced he'd be up to catch the sunrise, a taxi passed me in the other direction. I parked in the farmyard and switched off the ignition. I could hear the revving of the quad bike and ran towards the barn, hoping to catch him, but I was too late. The bike shot out of the garage with two dogs and two people on board. The taxi I'd passed must have been dropping Elle off.

With a sinking heart, I returned to Hedgehog Hollow. Would Elle be going to the funeral too? It wasn't illogical. She'd have known Barney's granddad. He'd owned the farm for the whole of the time Barney and her were together.

Back in my room at Meadow View, I sat down on the edge of my bed, staring into space. I was still there when Zara rose an hour or so later.

She knocked lightly on my door and pushed it open. 'Are you ready for another coffee?'

'Yes, and I'm ready for something else too.'

'What's that?'

'I'm ready to leave.'

She sat beside me. 'I had a feeling you'd say that.'

'It's too hard knowing he's so close and needing to keep that distance.'

'Will it feel better if you're an hour away? Two hours? Five? Ten?'

I exhaled deeply. 'Probably not, but I have to give it a try.'

68

BARNEY

It was summer solstice – the longest day of the year – two days after Granddad's funeral and I woke up feeling lighter than I had in a long time now that I was no longer keeping a secret from my family.

Dad had taken a couple of days off work – for the funeral on Wednesday and to help me on the farm yesterday. Last night, Mum joined us for tea and I told them both everything. Elle had told her parents after she'd had her diagnosis and it didn't feel right to keep mine in the dark.

Mum had been upset that I hadn't felt I was able to tell them, and I knew where that thought process was going as Fizz hadn't told them about Uncle Melvin either. I emphasised how approachable they both were and it was about me not wanting to share what happened rather than feeling unable to. To prove that, I updated her on the situation with Amber too.

Mum had said she'd drop by around mid-morning today to help on the farm, but I hadn't expected her to bring Grandma with her.

'I'm going stir crazy indoors,' Grandma said as she helped me feed the pigs in Lower Pig. 'I keep thinking that I need to sort through your granddad's belongings and I can't face it.'

'There's no rush.'

'I know there isn't, but he's not coming back so I'm only delaying the inevitable. Speaking of people coming back...'

I should have known there was more to her visit than wanting to get out of the house.

'...what's this your mum tells me about Elle being back?'

'I'm guessing you already know the full story.'

'We have no secrets in this family. Not anymore.'

'It's not about shutting people out. Sometimes things are too painful to talk about.'

I finished scattering the pellets across the ground in Lower Pig while Grandma distributed some carrots.

'It's summer solstice today,' she said as I pushed the barrow up to Middle Pig.

'I know.'

'Spiritually, it's when we yearn to be out and about, moving about, feeling alive, celebrating. That's probably why I couldn't bear to stay in the house today.'

I smiled at her. 'Is that so?' That and being desperate to share her thoughts about Amber and Elle which I could guarantee were coming my way any minute.

'Yes. It's an important day for setting intentions to nurture ourselves across the summer. So what are your intentions with Elle?'

'To be a friend.'

'And with Amber?'

'It's difficult. She doesn't want to get in the way. She thinks it's too much for me to have lost Granddad, be there for Elle, and start a new relationship with her, so she's stepped back.'

Grandma walked beside me in silence, dropping the carrots on the ground, and I could almost hear the cogs whirring.

'It's no good,' she said eventually. 'I can't find a tactful way of saying this. Elle walked out of your life thirteen years ago, leaving a mess behind. She gallivanted all over the world, just like she wanted, and didn't spare you a second thought. I'm sorry she's got cancer. That's horrible, but why is it your problem? She has her parents and sister to be there for her and it's selfish of her to expect you to be her crutch too. She took away your future back then and now, when you have a chance of exploring a different future with Amber, she's taking that away too. I'm sorry if that sounds harsh, but that's how I feel.'

Her speech was delivered with rousing passion and, while the message was blunt, she spoke sense. And then she added the final equally valid point.

'If she'd been back from her travels a picture of good health, would you have given her the time of day?'

* * *

Mum left after lunch to drop Grandma back home and I was about to go back to work when the post arrived – a single pale blue handwritten envelope. I ripped it open and removed the sheet of paper, my stomach sinking as I scanned down the letter.

Dear Barney,

I'm sorry to go without saying goodbye in person but I think it's for the best for both of us.

Your granddad sent a spectacular sunrise over Bumblebee Barn on Wednesday. I hope it brought you some light on a dark day.

There are two types of second chance – those which should ·

never have been reignited – like mine with Dan – and those which were always meant to be. I can't stick around while you explore which type of second chance you and Elle have.

Love on the Farm will never appear on my CV – a job best forgotten – but my time at Bumblebee Barn will remain forever in my heart.

Take care of you and take time to heal. I'll do the same and, once we manage that, perhaps we'll have our own second chance one day. Unless yours with Elle was meant to be, in which case I wish you every happiness for the future.

Amber x

I sank onto the bench by the kitchen table, re-reading Amber's words. She'd specifically mentioned a spectacular sunrise over Bumblebee Barn. Had she been here and seen me with Elle? If she had, that had to hurt when sunrises and sunsets carried special meaning for Amber and me. She probably thought I'd invited Elle to share one with me, and on an emotional day too. No wonder she'd gone.

Grandma had been right to challenge me about spending time with Elle instead of Amber. Elle wasn't my responsibility, but that didn't mean I should push her away.

I picked up my phone and looked at the text she'd sent me yesterday.

FROM ELLE

> Hope yesterday wasn't too hard for you all. Please, please, please ignore what I asked when you brought me home. It's my final round of chemo next week and my head's a mess. I only ever wanted to say sorry – not to mess up your life again x

I returned to Amber's letter. Which type of second chance did I have with Elle? Grandma's question this morning was pertinent to that: *If she'd been back from her travels a picture of good health, would you have given her the time of day?*

I opened up my texts to Amber, then closed them again. A text was inadequate. She'd written me a letter and I owed her the same. She hadn't put an address on it, but she'd have given Samantha her address for her stay at Hedgehog Hollow. Samantha would pass the letter on for me and I'd have to hope I could find the right words because this could be the most important letter I'd ever written.

69

AMBER

Three weeks later

'I haven't been here for weeks, so I apologise for the dust,' I said to Meera, the estate agent who'd arrived to value my flat. I'd pulled into the car park at the same time as her, thanks to an accident on the M25 delaying my return from Green Acres. With the axing of *Love on the Farm* leaving a gap in my diary, I'd decided to spend it with my parents rather than all alone in the flat and I'd come to some big decisions – one of those being to sell my expensive 'storage unit'.

'It's lovely,' Meera said, wandering over to the window to look out at the view. 'We won't have any problem selling this quickly.'

I followed her round as she checked the room dimensions using a laser measure and scribbled notes in her portfolio.

'Can I ask the reason for selling?' she said when she'd finished.

'I'm hardly ever here. I travel with my job, and my heart's in the countryside, not the city.' Specifically in East Yorkshire with

Barney, but I needed to stop dreaming about a happy ever after for us. Three weeks had passed since I left Hedgehog Hollow and posted my letter and I hadn't heard from him. Either he had found his meant-to-be second chance with Elle or he was still hoping to find it.

'Are you buying in the country?' Meera asked.

'Not yet, but hopefully one day.'

Bumblebee Barn came to mind, and I pushed the image aside. It wasn't going to happen. Maybe I'd been wrong to take myself out of the game, but I'd had no strength left to stay and fight for him. I did want to start over in the countryside, though, and selling the flat was the first step towards that. There was no need to rush into any decisions on where to settle. I'd continue my life on the road for now and stay at Green Acres in any downtime.

Meera and I agreed on an asking price and I handed her a spare set of keys and the entry code.

When she'd gone, I grabbed a suitcase from under the bed and packed more summer clothes. As I left the building, I emptied my post locker and shoved the large bundle into my case. It would mainly be junk but I didn't have time to sort it now as I needed to hit the road again to meet Róisín Brennan for afternoon tea in Cambridge. She'd had my rescue centre docu-series proposal for a fortnight and wanted to discuss it in person.

* * *

It was after 8 p.m. when I pulled up outside the Airbnb in the Peak District National Park where Zara and I were staying for the next few weeks to film the summer season of *Countryside Calendar*.

My meeting with Róisín had me on a high and I couldn't wait to share the news with Zara. Róisín had given me the go-ahead to make Hedgehog Hollow the main focus for an eight-part docu-series spanning a year in the life of the rescue centre, with additional footage from another four rescue centres around the country to show different sizes and approaches.

The next step was getting the final approval from the team at Hedgehog Hollow. I really wanted to do that in person, which meant being near Bumblebee Barn. Would I be brave enough to visit?

Even though I regretted leaving like I did, I knew I couldn't have stayed. It was all too emotional and messy. I'd needed some space to separate all the negative emotions and see whether there was anything left or whether my feelings for Barney had been about grasping at something positive amid the confusion. There were so many negatives from breaking up with Dan, seeing Parker again, the challenges of working on *Love on the Farm*, and the worries about Sophie, but they'd all come to a head now. The remaining strong emotion was a longing for a future with Barney. Even though we'd only kissed once and hadn't even dated, there was a connection with him that I'd never felt with anyone else. I could imagine a future for us. I frequently drifted off into daydreams of living on the farm with the dogs, the cat I'd always longed for, and children. I still believed in second chances. Would Barney's be with me? Or with Elle?

I dumped my cases in my bedroom at the Airbnb and gratefully accepted a mug of tea from Zara.

'How did it go with Róisín?' she asked as we each settled in a high-backed armchair.

'She loved it and we've got approval to start filming next year.'

'Oh, my God! That's fantastic!'

I told her all about the meeting and the format we'd agreed and I loved that she was as excited as I was about it.

'How do you feel about going back to East Yorkshire?' she asked.

'I can't wait. Hedgehog Hollow's amazing. I'll ring Samantha tomorrow and see whether she's free next weekend to discuss it all.'

'You know I don't mean the rescue centre. Have you heard from him?'

My shoulders sagged. 'No. Nothing.'

'Will you see him when you're there?'

'I don't know. I want to, but if he's with Elle...' I winced. 'I might have to interrogate Fizz first.'

'He won't be with Elle.'

'He might be.'

'He *won't* be.'

I wish I shared her optimism. As a television producer, it was my job to anticipate all potential problems so we were still ready and prepared to film to schedule and budget if they arose. The downside was how that translated into everyday life with me anticipating – and potentially catastrophising – all sorts of things that could go wrong. And Barney choosing Elle was one of those things.

* * *

The following morning, I was up later than usual – tired from the travel and meetings yesterday – so Zara was already up scrolling through her phone when I padded through to the lounge in my PJs with my pile of post.

'What's all that?' Zara asked.

'Post from the flat. I didn't have time to look at it earlier, so I shoved it in my case.'

I plonked myself down on the sofa and created a pile on the floor for takeaway menus and circulars and one on the sofa for anything that looked important. My stomach lurched as I came to a handwritten envelope. I stared at it for a few moments, my heart pounding, before ripping open the envelope.

Dear Amber,

I got your letter today and was going to text but it feels too impersonal, so it's a letter from me too and a hope that Samantha doesn't mind sending it on.

There is a second chance for Elle and me, but I'd like to throw in a third type – a second chance at friendship. That's how Elle and I started and it's all I feel towards her now.

After our first sunrise and sunset, you asked me to forget about you and I told you that was asking the impossible. I still mean that.

On the morning of Granddad's funeral, a car pulled into the farmyard and my heart leapt because I thought it might be you. It was Elle, but I think you already know that. I didn't have the heart to send her away but, when Granddad sent us that final spectacular sunrise, you were the one I wanted by my side.

The only person I want to watch the sun rise and set with each day is you. I knew you were the one for me when you held my hand as the sun went down the day Granddad died. If you feel the same and you're ready to try for our second chance, come and find me at sunrise. It'll be a new dawn and a new day. Could it be the start of a new life together?

I'll be waiting for you.

Barney x

'Amber? Are you okay?' Zara rushed to my side.

I handed her the letter as I wiped my tears.

'Aw, that's adorable.' She grabbed her phone and tapped something into it. 'Sunrise is just before five tomorrow.'

'I can't drop everything and drive up there today.'

She grinned at me. 'You can and you will.'

'We've got work to do.'

'Then why don't I come with you? We can work in the car on the way, see Samantha this afternoon if she's free, and stay over tonight. You'll catch the Sunday sunrise and can start your new life with Farmer Hottie.'

She stood up and pointed for me to leave the room. 'Go on! Get yourself showered and sorted. This is happening.'

My heart thumped with excitement as I scrambled off the sofa, sending the rest of the post scattering. Yes, it was happening. *Second chance, here I come!*

70

BARNEY

I pushed open the boot room door early on Sunday morning and Harley and Bear scampered out into the farmyard, tails wagging. The outside light illuminated the farmyard and I felt that familiar sinking feeling at the empty space. No Amber.

There was still hope. If she wanted to surprise me, she wouldn't leave her car in the farmyard. She'd park where Elle used to and cut across Spring Field.

I'd wondered whether the letter had been a mistake and I'd have been better off texting Amber, but Fizz and Phoebe insisted it was romantic and that a follow-up text would negate the message that I was waiting for her when she was ready.

Elle had been for her final round of chemo and I'd seen her a few times since then. She'd been really down the first time, questioning whether the cancer was her punishment for ending her pregnancy and being unable to have children now being karma. I'd repeatedly reassured her that wasn't how it worked, but she was full of guilt, self-blame and regret. The next time I saw her, she seemed stronger, but she asked again whether it was too late for us.

'It's not too late to be friends,' I said gently, 'but nothing more.'

She hung her head. 'Is there someone else?'

'I'm hoping so. But even if it doesn't happen with her, we had our time, Elle, and I'm fairly certain that, deep down, you feel the same.'

A few days ago, we met up once more and had a really long talk about everything – past, present and future. She admitted I was right about her feelings. She was scared and wanted to feel safe. I'd always been her safety net, so it was easy to cling onto nostalgia and build a fantasy of us recapturing that in the future, when the truth was too much had happened and we were too different to make it work now. I felt so much lighter after that conversation.

'Up you get,' I instructed the dogs. They jumped onto the back of the quad bike and we set off up to Top Field with the sky starting to lighten.

Bear and Harley both barked as we approached Top Field and my pulse quickened as I spotted the silhouette of someone sitting on the gate.

The moment I stopped the bike and cut the engine, the dogs were down and racing up to her. She slipped down from the gate and stroked them.

'Hi, you two, I've missed you loads.'

She straightened up and looked at me.

'I've missed you loads too. I liked your letter, but I only got it yesterday.'

I took a couple of steps closer. 'And you came for the first sunrise?'

'I did.'

She climbed up the gate, sat on the top and patted the space beside her. I climbed up to join her. The sun had already peeped over the horizon with a golden band of light beneath a deep violet sky.

I placed my hand on the gate between us and Amber placed her hand over mine. My heart thumped as my fingers entwined with hers. Our eyes met and, moments later, our lips did too. Our second kiss was slower than our first and so tender and meaningful. We'd had the time and space we needed to both heal our broken hearts and we were now ready to embrace our second chance, which I was certain was the meant-to-be type.

'There was a question at the end of your letter,' Amber said as we cuddled together, watching the sunrise, with Bear and Harley lying on the grass beneath us. '*Could it be the start of a new life together?*'

'That's right. What do you say?'

'I say yes.'

'Me too.'

We kissed again beneath another spectacular sunrise over Bumblebee Barn. It had been a strange couple of months, full of the unexpected, but the biggest surprise had been that *Love on the Farm* had worked. The programme itself might have been a disaster but, thanks to it, I'd found exactly what I'd always longed for. With Amber by my side, I didn't feel alone anymore, and that dream of a family of my own wasn't quite so blurred. I could imagine Granddad looking down on me and saying, 'That's more like it. You didn't need some stupid dating show after all, son.' Without *Love on the Farm*, I'd never have met Amber, but I wouldn't point that out. I'd let him have his win because now I wasn't only winning at farming. I finally felt like I was winning at life.

ACKNOWLEDGMENTS

Some books are a dream, pretty much writing themselves, and others feel like wading backwards through treacle. This was one of the latter!

As soon as Fizz appeared in the Hedgehog Hollow series of books and mentioned her brother Barney, who repeatedly chose unsuitable girlfriends, I wanted to write his story. I knew it would feature a reality TV show and that he'd ultimately find love with the producer rather than one of the contestants. While that's still the premise for *Healing Hearts at Bumblebee Barn*, the way I'd planned for it to unfold was completely different. They were going to start off as enemies and I imagined all the clashes they'd have before admitting their attraction. But Barney and Amber had other ideas. As soon as he arrived on the page, I knew he had depths and was hiding a broken heart. He had emotional intelligence and wasn't the sort who'd clash with anyone. When Amber appeared, I knew she'd be too professional to clash, would also have been hurt, and the pair would recognise that in each other. So I had to go in a completely different direction.

On top of that, I felt the pressure of how disappointed readers were that I'd ended the Hedgehog Hollow series and I wanted to give them the gift of a glimpse into life at the rescue centre through this book. However, this is *not* a Hedgehog Hollow story, and it was a tricky balance making sure that any glimpses I gave were relevant, moved the Bumblebee Barn story forward, and didn't alienate readers who hadn't read that series.

Although a challenge to write, the result is actually one of my favourite stories so far and I hope readers love Barney and Amber's story as much as I do.

Thank you to Tricia Thorne from my Facebook group, Redland's Readers, for helping me come up with Barney's Barbies. Thanks to another member, Em Morgan, for some amazing legal advice. Em – I didn't use the storyline I explored with you, but I really appreciated your time and guidance on this which helped me conclude it was too big, important and too much of a minefield to do justice to in this particular book.

Thank you to fellow Boldwood author Leonie Mack for some help with my German section and a friend of hers for the French. My apologies for any errors in tense or gender of any of the other languages and translations but, as Barney himself says, he's no expert and had to rely on Google Translate. I trust you'll forgive him!

A huge team at the amazing Boldwood Books work behind the scenes to help my books get to readers and listeners. Thank you to everyone involved in this one including copy-editor Cecily Blench, proofreader Clare Black, Debbie Clement for another divine cover (my new favourite!), Megan Townsend for the technical stuff, Claire Fenby for the marketing, Rachel Gilbey and all the bloggers on the tour, and my fantastic editor, Nia Beynon, who helped me wade through that treacle and knock this sticky story into shape.

For the audio, thanks to Gareth Bennett-Ryan and Rebecca Norfolk for lending their voice-acting talents, and to ISIS Audio and Ulverscroft for the recording and distribution.

As always, an enormous thank you to my amazing husband Mark, our daughter Ashleigh, my proud mum Joyce, my bestie (and super talented author) Sharon Booth, the Write Romanics and the other Boldwood authors for their support and encouragement. Thanks also to all the wonderful library staff who promote and support my work – so very much appreciated – and the fabulous Facebook book groups that champion my writing. A particular shout out and big hug to Adrienne, Hazel, Louise, Marie and Sarah at The Friendly Book Community and to Sue, Fiona and Heidi on Heidi Swain and Friends - A Facebook Book Club. I'm so grateful for your time, enthusiasm and generosity.

And thank you to you. Without your enthusiasm, kind reviews, and recommendations to others, I wouldn't be able to keep writing. If you haven't already taken a trip to Hedgehog Hollow, you might like to do so. A full six-book series awaits you. If you haven't been to Whitsborough Bay, there are lots of stories to enjoy by the sea. And if you haven't already done so, please feel welcome to join Redland's Readers on Facebook.

Big hugs
Jessica xx

MORE FROM JESSICA REDLAND

We hope you enjoyed reading *Healing Hearts at Bumblebee Barn*. If you did, please leave a review.

If you'd like to gift a copy, this book is also available as an ebook, digital audio download and audiobook CD.

Sign up to Jessica Redland's mailing list for news, competitions and updates on future books.

http://bit.ly/JessicaRedlandNewsletter

Finding Love at Hedgehog Hollow, the first in Jessica Redland's heartwarming Hedgehog Hollow Series, is available to buy now:

ABOUT THE AUTHOR

Jessica Redland writes uplifting stories of love, friendship, family and community set in Yorkshire where she lives. Her Whitsborough Bay books transport readers to the stunning North Yorkshire Coast and her Hedgehog Hollow series takes them into beautiful countryside of the Yorkshire Wolds.

Visit Jessica's website: https://www.jessicaredland.com/

Follow Jessica on social media:

facebook.com/JessicaRedlandAuthor

twitter.com/JessicaRedland

instagram.com/JessicaRedlandAuthor

bookbub.com/authors/jessica-redland

ALSO BY JESSICA REDLAND

Welcome to Whitsborough Bay Series

Making Wishes at Bay View

New Beginnings at Seaside Blooms

Finding Hope at Lighthouse Cove

Coming Home to Seashell Cottage

Other Whitsborough Bay Books

All You Need is Love

The Secret to Happiness

Christmas on Castle Street

Christmas Wishes at the Chocolate Shop

Christmas at Carly's Cupcakes

Starry Skies Over The Chocolate Pot Café

The Starfish Café Series

Snowflakes Over The Starfish Café

Spring Tides at The Starfish Café

Hedgehog Hollow Series

Finding Love at Hedgehog Hollow

New Arrivals at Hedgehog Hollow

Family Secrets at Hedgehog Hollow

A Wedding at Hedgehog Hollow

Boldw∞d

Boldwood Books is an award-winning fiction publishing company seeking out the best stories from around the world.

Find out more at www.boldwoodbooks.com

Join our reader community for brilliant books, competitions and offers!

Follow us
@BoldwoodBooks
@BookandTonic

Sign up to our weekly deals newsletter

https://bit.ly/BoldwoodBNewsletter

Printed in Great Britain
by Amazon